HIS EY
ON

As the train pulled away from Luton station, Kitteridge spoke again. "I suppose we should introduce ourselves. I'm Wesley Carlyle."

"How do you do?" the other man said pleasantly. Kitteridge felt the man's genuine warmth. "I'm...Omega."

A small hole appeared in Omega's newspaper. The muffled, thumping noise sounded simultaneously. Kitteridge's head jerked back violently. His body lurched, then gently slumped onto the seat. Blood trickled from his nose and mouth. The blank eyes did not move.

Omega stood and walked calmly from the death that lay behind him. "Communist bastard," he hissed.

ALPHA
AND
OMEGA

BERT WHITTIER

ALPHA AND OMEGA

A GOLD EAGLE BOOK

London · Toronto · New York · Sydney

First published in Great Britain 1988 by Gold Eagle

© Bert Whittier 1988

*Australian copyright 1988
Philippine copyright 1988
This edition 1988*

ISBN 0 373 97057 9

20/8812

Printed and bound in Great Britain by Cox & Wyman Ltd, Reading

ALPHA
AND
OMEGA

PROLOGUE

Letchworth, England, 1953

THE SUN DID NOT BELONG here in this place, and it was properly hidden in the damp mists of early morning. The persistent fog made the man irritable. If he let his imagination have rein, he would have begun to believe it was smothering him. He didn't like it, but then, there was little about this assignment he did like. In the first place, it was 7:45. Too early. It was too damp. The phone box was too cramped. And, since he was complaining, he'd been waiting too long. Damn it to hell, he thought, this is the last goddamn time I'll let *them* call the shots.

He had gotten a cable just two days earlier. "Party in question would appreciate visit in Letchworth, Wednesday a.m."

"The last goddamn time," he murmured. Usually he'd get the necessary information, develop his own operation and execute it—his way. It was efficient, certain—*and* enjoyable. "Damn it to hell," he breathed, "no enjoyment here."

And then, there was the weather. "Godda..." But now the door—or more precisely, the misty ghost of the door—was finally opening. The "party in question" stepped out of the cottage into the quiet alley. He paused, looked around and stepped back into the doorway. Was there a problem? The man who waited in the phone booth at the corner wondered. He settled, allowing his instincts to take control. All the vague irritations were purged from his consciousness. He could feel the change in himself. He sought the ritual memory of the tiger. It was in the foothills of Balaspur in western India. The vivid image surged over him, and he savored it.

The tiger was stalking him. He watched, learning from the animal as it half crouched, half sat. Poised. Ready. Anticipating. When the animal sprang, he fired his modified Colt .45-caliber handgun. Before the tiger's hind legs left the ground, two shots had rung out, one tearing up through the beast's white neck, through its throat and into its brain. The other exploded deep in its heart. He always went for the head first—regardless of his prey. Now the animal half roared, half whined, and fell onto him. Lying under the weight of the beast, the man could feel his clothes becoming warm and wet from the animal's life. The smell mixed with his own. Damn it to hell, he thought. I should have read him better. I should have fired sooner. The beast twitched. The man reached around the massive head and fired into its ear. "Bastard," he rasped at the corpse.

The memory had accomplished its purpose. It had wrought the changes so essential, so elemental, so necessary. The memory—and the changes—now dominated the man's consciousness. His eyes again focused on his prey, as it once more appeared at the doorway. An energy flowed through him. He knew he could not fail. He was certain about everything. He knew, for example, that he appeared as casual as the man now approaching him.

The party in question was Wilson W. Kitteridge, an apparent nobody. The man who stared unblinking at Kitteridge now allowed a thin smile to form. He knew why Kitteridge had stepped back into the house. He had forgotten his umbrella. Or was there another reason? The waiting man's expression did not change.

When he judged Kitteridge to be a comfortable distance—about seventy-five feet—from the phone box, the man stepped out and started walking ahead of him. He walked in the same direction.

Kitteridge noticed the man now, and studied him with a kind of casual intensity. The man walked with a slight limp, or rather, a stiffness. Wilson Kitteridge surmised the walker up ahead had suffered an injury. In the war, he told himself. It was to be his only correct guess on this day blurred by mists and uncertainty. It was not a bad injury. The dampness of the English morning made it just stiff enough to notice.

After two blocks the men were about forty feet apart. Kitteridge continued to watch the other man, as he slowly gained on him. Turning the moment into a sort of game, he began to build a hypothetical dossier. He practiced stalking the man with the limp as though he were an assignment. He tried to imagine who he was, what he did, where he was going. The man came to a halt at the bus stop. After a few moments, Kitteridge stepped up next to him.

"Morning." Kitteridge spoke. The man nodded and smiled pleasantly; he smiled because he had read Kitteridge correctly. He opened a newspaper and began to skim its pages.

"Bloody cold for this time of year," Kitteridge interrupted.

"Yes," replied the man, noncommittally.

"Showers in order, I expect."

The conversation continued—a few words at a time—as they boarded the bus.

"Going to Luton?" Kitteridge asked.

"Just to the station. Going to London, actually," the man said.

Kitteridge took the station to be the train station. "You don't say. I'm going to London myself." Again the other nodded.

At the train station, they waited just five minutes. Kitteridge continued talking. "What part of America are you from—Midwest?" He watched the man closely, expecting some note of surprise. He was disappointed when none came.

"New Haven, Connecticut, actually," the man replied.

"You sound as though you're Midwestern," Kitteridge said uneasily.

"Sorry." He smiled at Kitteridge's disappointment.

The "party in question" was disheartened. "Actually, I consider myself something of a student of language," Kitteridge enunciated.

I bet you do, thought the man. I consider you something of a fool. He looked at Kitteridge. You've let your guard down. Not only are you the enemy, you're stupid and insipid as well. He wondered whether Kitteridge was able to read the contempt in his gaze. Then he turned his attention once more to the newspaper's headlines: America's Joseph McCarthy Cries Foul. Why can't they just leave him alone? he thought.

He thinks I'm a bore. The notion haunted Kitteridge. Inside he fumed. In the midst of his uneasiness, a thought came creeping into his awareness that brought him a sense of satisfaction. If he only knew, thought Kitteridge. If he only knew who I really am—about my work. Then he wouldn't be so bored with me. The thought comforted him only slightly; a touch of the uneasiness remained, a fear that just maybe the elusive person sitting across from him would still think him boring.

As the train pulled away from Luton station, Kitteridge spoke again. "I suppose we should introduce ourselves. I'm Wesley Carlyle."

You lie well, the man reflected. What else had been a lie today? What if it were all a lie? What if Kitteridge were on to him? The man lowered the paper and focused his full attention on Kitteridge. He could see his sudden interest had similarly focused the prey. His hand caressed his weapon. This was the moment he had been waiting for. He leaned forward, half crouching, half sitting.

Well, thought Kitteridge, suddenly he can tear himself away from that paper.

"How do you do," the man said pleasantly. Kitteridge felt the man's genuine warmth, then heard him go on, "I'm . . . Omega."

A flash of—of what? Fear? No, not really. Just surprise. Kitteridge covered it quickly. Then he was rising, reaching for his coat pocket. A small hole appeared in Omega's newspaper. The muffled, thumping noise sounded simultaneously. Kitteridge's head jerked back violently. His hand started to move upward. His eyes bulged out, staring as if in disbelief. His body lurched backward, then gently slumped onto the seat. His eyes stared unblinking at the light above Omega's head. Blood trickled from his nose and mouth. The blank eyes did not move.

Well placed, thought the man who was Omega. He smiled. Damn well placed. His heart raced. The moment of death was an excitement no one could take away from him. He longed to know what the body across from him had felt in its last instant of life.

The bullet had entered through the roof of the mouth. Not even a tooth chipped. Damn, I'm good, he thought. He lifted the shade on the compartment door and glanced down the aisle. All clear. He sat back, and again aimed his gun.

He studied the trajectory. Anyone else would have been satisfied with a hit anywhere on the head, or worse, in the chest. "But not Omega," he told the corpse.

He tore pieces of Kitteridge's handkerchief and stuffed them up into the bleeding nostrils. He pulled the lids over the eyes and wiped the blood from the face. Finally, he tilted the head back into the corner of the compartment, so that the blood would flow down the throat. Omega looked down at his handiwork. The party in question had become as pale as the gray-white sky. But aside from that, he appeared to be dozing. Without a care in the world, thought Omega. He smiled at the strange truth of that statement. Omega took Kitteridge's ticket and stepped outside the compartment. The man who was Omega slipped the ticket between the door and the jamb and walked calmly from the death that lay behind him. "Communist bastard," he hissed.

1

Craig's Harbor, Maine, 1987

JASON THAYER WINSLOW groped for his alarm clock. Keeping his eyes closed to block out the sunlight that probed his bedroom, he turned off the alarm, rolled over on his back, stretched and started to sleep again. Then, as was the routine, Dog came to him and lapped his face.

"Blah," the man spit. "Okay, I'm up." The golden retriever barked once, headed for the door, stopped, looked back and returned to his master. He barked again. "Okay, okay." Jason sat on the edge of the bed for just a moment, rose and pulled on his running shorts and sweatshirt. He tried to pull on his socks while standing, but fell back onto the bed. "Damn," he muttered. He put on his running shoes. "Okay, Dog, let's go." Dog was way ahead of him.

Jason Winslow loved this time of day, this time of year. Six-thirty on a crisp morning in early October on the Maine coast. "Finest kind," the local folks said, and it was. It was spiritual.

He smiled and thought about the people, who seemed to use their homes almost as hiding places—as fortifications. He liked them, and he thought they liked him, but at times they were distant. He could see it in their faces; they almost seemed embarrassed about it. There was no apparent reason for this distance—except that he was an "outsider." He saw it often in times of trouble. And yet, it was precisely for those times that he was there. He was their pastor.

It was weird, and it was confusing. It felt as though they were too good for him. Yet, at the same time, it seemed as if they felt ashamed. "Of what?" he breathed aloud. There were no big moral torments in Craig's Harbor—not like in the cities, anyway. Of course there were troubles here—there were everywhere. But here life was simpler. That was what attracted him to the Maine coast in the first place. He could have stayed in Boston—or even gone back home to the Midwest. But he wanted to work in Maine. He was in love with the place—the land and sea—but he was also in love with these distant people he longed to be a part of. They appeared as strong and rugged as the coast itself. But they did have weaknesses; he had gotten glimpses of the weaknesses, almost always by accident. But, he told himself, if I'm going to accomplish anything here, I've got to break through their granite armor. These thoughts prodded at Jason, as he rounded the point at the mouth of the harbor. They were in no way idle thoughts. They were part of his job.

It was Sunday morning, and as he did on every Sunday morning workout, he was now putting the finishing touches on his sermon. Today he would preach on "Living with Your Conscience." Rather presumptuous, he reflected. A twenty-seven-year-old kid talking to a congregation whose average age was twice that. He shook his head once. Perhaps, after all, it was really as it appeared: maybe there were no moral torments in Craig's Harbor. He smiled. "What do you think?" he asked Dog. Running along beside him, the animal responded with a half-swallowed bark. "That so," answered Jason.

As he and Dog ran along the streets of the town—there were only half a dozen or so—he allowed his mind to drift.

He surveyed his parish. The Donaldsons have a new car. Old Mrs. Sherman's got her storm windows on already. I should be doing that myself, he thought. Lights are on in the Bailey house. Oh, right. They're going out to North Island for a picnic today. With all the Bailey kids out of Sunday school, the place will be deserted. He shook off the thought, shrugged and ran on, thinking again about his sermon.

"Hey, Reverend Winslow!" The voice of Jimmy Sampson broke through.

"What's happening, Jimmy?"

"Bad accident in Kennebunk, last night. The President wants more military spending. Unemployment's up by two-tenths of a percent. And Boston's out of the play-offs... again."

The minister waved to the newsboy and then he and Dog were alone again. The kid's going to be a newscaster someday, Jason thought. Hell, he already is. "Isn't that right, Dog?" But Jason knew that Jimmy would probably end up living his entire life right here in the Harbor. Spend some time with him, Jason told himself. Maybe I can stretch his mind a little, give him a glimpse of another world.

The paperboy's recap had been correct. As Jason worked on his cantaloupe, he scanned the *Press-Herald*. Six Teens Hospitalized Following Crash. He'd stop in to see them tomorrow. God, he thought, there's so much damn pain in the world. More Weapons, Stronger Peace, Says President. Jason sighed. He knew these were really the words of the President's national security adviser, Alex Delacourte. He was great for the media. He provided plenty of colorful, outrageous copy. But God, thought the pastor, if he really means it, we're on the brink of nuclear disaster every minute of the day. "Strength ensures peace." That was Delacourte's favorite saying. Ass, Jason thought. He smiled as he pictured himself delivering that pronouncement from the pulpit. "Brothers and sisters, Alex Delacourte is an ass." Poor old Mrs. Sherman would faint. Either that or throw her hymnal at him. And those lobstermen, the same ones who swore like pirates on their boats, wouldn't tolerate a good "damn it all" from the pastor. "Shit," he said. Dog raised his eyes and looked disapprovingly at Jason. The minister smiled.

Enough of that, Jason decided, and turned the page. Nothing there. Next. Nothing. Wait. British Protest Alpha and Omega. What's this? Something religious? In with the hard news? He read. Not even close. Seemed as though some British reporter had found a bit of evidence suggesting that the United States had had a British agent assassinated in the early fifties. The article provided a few tantalizing details, the name of the operation, for example. Alpha/Omega. It also reported that the rumored evidence named the agent code-named Alpha. No one, the article went on, knew the identity of Omega, the actual assassin, except Alpha. The British government, the story concluded, was expected to seek a response from the Americans. And, of course, the British, honorable gentlemen and ladies that they were, were refusing to identify the source of this seemingly ancient history.

There was something that attracted Jason to the story. There was mystery, adventure—a kind of romance—all the elements of the James Bond novels he liked to read. The stories provided some excitement in his mostly humdrum life. But the news article was troubling; it wasn't fiction. The article confirmed something he had, of course, known for years: that spies—agents, he corrected himself—were real, that they were the tools of the violence one nation perpetrates on another, that hatred and fear seemed to form the base for much of the world's international relations. This was reality, not fiction. But despite his disapproval of this reality, there was something in the article that fascinated him. It was exciting. Primitive. Essential. He knew the realities, and he still found it fascinating. Perhaps this was most troubling of all. He forced himself to look away from the article.

"Let's see what Eleanor MacMillan's into today," he said to Dog. He turned to the Living section to his favorite syndicated column. He always read it; first, because it was generally funny; and second, because Jennifer Seidkamp was one of MacMillan's writers.

Jason hadn't seen Jennifer since high school. In certain moments he deeply regretted the distance between them. He had had a few dates with her in high school. Dates? He reddened now when he thought of those times. They were disasters. But after all these years, there was something about Jennifer that remained exciting, compelling. His parents kept him informed of her career in their frequent phone calls and letters. He was pleased to know she was successful. But she'd have to be, he told himself. She was that kind of person. At times he wondered if she ever thought of him—and if she did, what exactly she thought. He sighed, and stirred his tea and honey and settled down to read Eleanor MacMillan's epistle for the day.

2

IT WAS, IN EVERY WAY, a typical Sunday morning. Following the service there were the predictable, polite handshakes and fractured conversations. "How's your Aunt Bessie doing? Good, good. I'll get up to see her tomorrow." "Fishing any better this week, Ralph?" Out of the corner of his eye, Jason caught Mrs. O'Brien lurking at the end of the line. What was she up to now? Oh yes, tonight's "hot date."

"Yes, Mrs. O'Brien, I'll be there at six-thirty sharp." Jason smiled to cover his irritation. Who's she trying to fix me up with this time? The matchmakers. They were a problem in a parish like this. It wasn't anything disastrous; it was simply bothersome. He knew they were simply trying to be helpful. They would never understand if he tried to explain how he felt about their efforts. He just wished they'd stop. Someone was always arranging for him to meet some decent girl, some lovely girl, some girl who's just like so-and-so's cousin. Just once, he'd like to be introduced to a *woman*—a woman who was not afraid to think, who felt, who was alive. He smiled at the thought, still shaking Mrs. O'Brien's hand. She was pleased that he seemed happy. "I'll be there at six-thirty. Don't you worry."

He shut the door, stepped back inside the little church and walked back through the foyer, into the sanctuary. He shut off the lights and started for the back door.

"Mr. Winslow." The words startled him. He turned abruptly. "Didn't mean to shake you."

Old Mr. Sullivan was standing in front of a window. The harsh glare of the sunshine silhouetted the figure. Jason squinted into the almost painful brightness. He smiled reassuringly at the man, but this act of invitation was met by a disquieting silence. What does he want? Jason wondered. Sullivan was a strange one. Jason guessed he was about seventy-two or -three. Though he had moved to Craig's Harbor about twenty-five years ago, folks in town still called him a newcomer. He had been a career man in the Navy, retiring early. Sullivan spent his days alone now. In fact he'd always been alone according to the natives. "'Cept for his flowers," they'd add. "Spends a lot of time in the garden, he does." He rarely came to church. Today was a "treat."

"Mr. Sullivan?" Has he forgotten what he wanted? No, Jason could see it was something else. Why that old bastard, he's waiting for me to pay attention. Jason looked into his eyes and got the impression that Sullivan knew exactly what he was thinking. He shifted uneasily under the old man's gaze. When Jason had properly focused his attention, Sullivan spoke.

"I'd like to talk to you."

"Sure, Mr. Sullivan. When would be convenient?" Jason was almost in shock. Had he said something that had upset the man? Or could he want some counseling? That was the last thing Jason would have expected.

"Soon. Today, maybe tomorrow." There was just a note of irritation in Sullivan's voice. "You'll be around all day, today?" Maybe he'd like a written schedule, Jason told himself.

"Yes, except for the youth group meeting this afternoon."

"Okay, I'll be in touch." Then the old man was on his way out. Just like that. Strange, thought the pastor. A real weird one. If he doesn't get in touch with me in a day or two, maybe I should drop by.

THE MAN SIGHED. It was finally beginning, he thought. He stared at the story an instant longer, then slowly folded the newspaper that the maid had brought him just a few moments earlier. He let it slide off the side of his bed onto the floor. His wife, in the bed next to him, rolled over.

"Something wrong, dear?"

"Nothing." It was one of those obvious lies she had learned to live with, one that meant don't ask.

Omega leaned back against the headboard to think. In a way, he'd been waiting for this moment. He'd always known it would come someday. Lately, in fact, he'd been thinking a lot about the past and in particular about the man with whom he had created an effective and ruthless counterforce. He smiled quietly as those distant places and times flooded back upon him. For years most of the memories had lain dormant, but for the past few months, they had been increasingly in his thoughts.

Even though this moment was expected, the matter still required some thinking. There was a lot to do if he were to survive. "Damn," he breathed. Then, after a moment, he flung back the covers and stepped onto the floor. "I've got to make a phone call," he said, and left the room.

THE DAY HAD BEEN UNEVENTFUL. Jason Winslow had spent an hour or so with a half dozen kids. They'd watched a film about peer pressure and then discussed it. Peer pressure. It was a damnable thing, he reflected. As he drove toward Mrs. O'Brien's "dating service," he remembered his own teenage years.

There was always a lot of pressure to conform. He remembered feeling a little left out of things most of the time.

It hadn't bothered him much—not enough to change at any rate. He'd decided he didn't want to drink, for example. It wasn't some big momentous decision for him; drinking simply didn't make a lot of sense. Because of his decision, he had taken a lot of grief from his friends. Now, in more cynical moments, he wondered if they'd really been his friends anyway. Hell, all he had been to them was a cabdriver. When they were too drunk to drive, he'd give them a ride home. But he really didn't mind. How many lives had he saved? Maybe dozens. He laughed out loud now. "Maybe none, asshole," he muttered as he pulled into Mrs. O'Brien's driveway.

Mrs. O'Brien's dinner was tasty as usual. A bowl of fresh, rich seafood chowder—chunks of haddock, crabmeat, scallops and clams—and the best homemade oatmeal bread, still warm from the oven. Nothing fancy but full of flavor. Mrs. O'Brien's recipes were her own Down East basics. She didn't own a cookbook. She was to church suppers what Julia Child was to French cuisine.

And the company? Well, Jason guessed the meal made up for it. Everything Mrs. O'Brien said about Sally Staples was true. She was sweet, attractive, quiet, pleasant and so on. And she was trying to be attentive. Very attentive. Too attentive. As he ate his strawberry shortcake, he imagined leaping across the table, tearing off Sally's clothes and transporting her to heights of wild ecstasy. All this, right in front of Mrs. O'Brien. He smiled at his whipped cream and flushed with embarrassment. He readily admitted to himself that thoughts like that embarrassed him. He glanced up at the others, wondering if they had noticed his unexplained amusement. He found himself almost opening his mouth to explain what he'd just been thinking. He came so close. My God, you're crazy! The thought of the description, however, brought a smile to his face once more.

"Enjoying yourself, Reverend Winslow?" Mrs. O'Brien brought him out of his fantasy. She waited for his answer. It was important to her.

"As always, Ellie," he lied. In a town that stood on formality, he had learned that using someone's given name at just the right moment made a big impact. Mrs. O'Brien beamed. So, obligingly, did Sally.

Jason predicted Mrs. O'Brien's next line. "Why don't you young people go on into the front room while I do the dishes." Sally shifted slightly. She wouldn't like that any more than I would, he thought. Jason rose and picked up his dishes as if on cue. "Oh, we couldn't do that, Mrs. O'Brien. Here..." He reached out and cleared more dishes. "It will just take a few minutes, if we all help."

He left at eight-thirty after playing two games of Scrabble. "I'm so sorry, Mrs. O'Brien, but I really do need to do some reading tonight," he said at the door.

"Of course, Reverend Winslow."

"Sometimes I just feel like letting the reading slide."

"Now, now, Mr. Winslow. You can't do that. Goodness knows a pastor has to do his reading!"

He smiled weakly and stepped into the cold, damp darkness. Should he tell her that his assignment for the evening was a rereading of *Doctor No*? "It was nice meeting you...Sally." Christ, he thought, I almost forgot her damn name. "See you at the board meeting, Mrs. O'Brien."

"Of course. Of course," Mrs. O'Brien called after him. "My, there's going to be frost on the pumpkin tonight."

"There'll be frost on *this* pumpkin if I don't get moving," he said, gesturing at himself. More predictable and polite laughter. "Bye now." He walked to his car. "Thanks again." He waved and drove away through the fog, which was once again returning to the land.

The phone was ringing when he got home. He could hear it as he got out of his car. Dog was barking at the door. That's strange, Jason thought. He hurried inside and picked up the phone, took a breath and spoke calmly. "Jason Winslow."

"I thought you were going to be home all day."

Jason was puzzled. "Who is this?"

"Sullivan."

"Oh, Mr. Sullivan. I'm sorry. I guess I forgot. I had a dinner engagement." There was a silence filled with disdain. Then Sullivan spoke again.

"I'll be there in a few minutes." There was a click and he was gone.

Jason stared at Dog, then back to the phone. "Sure, fine, Mr. Sullivan. No inconvenience at all. Come right over," he said to no one. "The man just hung up. What do you think of that—huh, ol' Dog?" Dog looked up, blinked, yawned and dropped his head onto his paws. "Well, don't make such a big deal of it." This time Dog simply rolled his eyes up at him without moving his head at all. Jason laughed, knelt down on the floor and butted Dog with his head. Dog growled. Jason laughed. "You're a killer!"

3

JASON WAS STILL on the floor with Dog when Sullivan knocked.

"Door's open. Come on in," Jason called.

Sullivan looked down with disapproval as Jason got up off the floor. "Sorry about this afternoon, Mr. Sullivan." Jason offered his hand, but Sullivan simply stared coldly at him. Lowering his hand, Jason tried to drive out the heaviness of the moment. "How's the fog out there?"

"Thick," Sullivan finally breathed. After another moment of awkward silence, they sat. The quiet that seemed to surround Sullivan wherever he went pressed Jason into his chair. Then, abruptly, as he relentlessly studied Jason, Sullivan slashed through the silence.

"What do you think of killing, Reverend Winslow?"

The question stunned—rocked—the minister. Whatever he'd been expecting, it was not this.

"It's wrong." Jason stared at the man. Did he expect him to say something different?

Sullivan sort of nodded his head, appearing for just an instant somewhat defeated. He was a troubled man. Jason knew that the townspeople thought Sullivan was strange, but this was more than strange. It was frightening.

"Ministers are supposed to have certain . . . professional privileges—confidentiality, and so on." Sullivan waved his hand to give form to the "and so on."

"Mr. Sullivan, I . . ." Jason never finished.

"I'm asking you if I can trust you." Sullivan's tone slashed through Jason. The comment demanded a response.

"Yes, of course." Jason spoke too quickly. Even as he said the words, he realized how empty his assurance sounded. He wondered what the old man had really meant and what he had inferred from the answer.

"I'm not sure about that." Sullivan's statement hung in the air. It was a challenge.

Jason studied the man sitting across from him. He wondered what was going on in his head. Thirty seconds passed. Then forty. Almost a minute. They studied each other. Jason felt as though he were being probed by some sort of invisible ray. He tried to ignore the feeling. He focused on the man sitting across from him. Finally Sullivan broke the impasse, speaking in an almost sinister tone.

"I'm going to ask you to do something for me."

This guy's right on the edge, thought Jason. A real bizarro. Ready to flip out. It was unnerving. He felt his body tensing. His heart was pumping harder. His palms were getting moist.

"I'm not sure I can promise to do anything until I know what it is."

Sullivan smiled. "I don't like you." Forthright, anyway, Jason reflected. "But," continued Sullivan, "it's too late to do anything different." He repeated "too late," again in that quiet tone of defeat, then recovered, and spoke more strongly. "And you're moral." His tone was anything but complimentary.

Still, Jason forced himself to appear as though he had been praised. "In my business," said Sullivan, "that was a fault." Jason worked to keep his ministerial smile from dissolving.

"I'm going to tell you a story. And when I'm finished, either you'll promise to do what I ask or you'll promise to do nothing. Nothing—at all. No matter what," he continued, "you'll promise not to say anything to anyone else. Now."

Jason stared, amazed, and was even more amazed when he found himself agreeing with the bizarre old man's request.

Sullivan then began in earnest. "Do you know who Joseph McCarthy was?"

Jason nodded again. "He led the witch-hunts of the fifties—harassing supposed Communists."

Sullivan glared in contempt. "He was a senator—a United States senator—who saw Communism for what it was: a threat." Sullivan paused. He pulled a newspaper clipping from his pocket and thrust it out toward Jason. "You see this?" It was the story headlined British Protest Alpha and Omega.

"I skimmed it."

"Read it again."

Jason did. At the height of the McCarthy era, two United States CIA operatives apparently had set up a network for killing their Communist counterparts. The one code-named Alpha was the government link to the actual assassin, code-named Omega. There was a great mystery about Omega. Apparently only Alpha knew Omega's identity. The British had just found out that one of their agents was assassinated by the United States under that operation. Now, the British wanted to know just what the truth was. They also apparently knew who Alpha was. Jason's apprehension grew as he wondered where the conversation was headed. Why was the old man suddenly interested in spies? He looked up.

Sullivan probed Jason with his eyes, with his very presence. His stare had almost a physical reality. It reminded

Jason of the seminary professors who had questioned him during his orals. Imperious, sanctimonious, innately better. But Sullivan wasn't better. Was he? Jason felt a cold bead of sweat start to trail down the middle of his back. He leaned back against his chair to stop it.

"So what does all this mean?" Sullivan asked the obvious question. His voice was quiet, barely audible.

Jason stared at him, and in that moment, permitted the barely believable to become the obvious. "You're one of them," he said simply. "Alpha or Omega."

Sullivan snickered. "Only one man in the world knows who Omega is. If I was Omega, why would I be talking to you?"

The sharp logic of the response caught Jason off balance, but then, everything about this meeting had. His face colored slightly with embarrassment. Obvious, he thought. I should have figured that out.

"You're Alpha. I can ask the same question. Why are you telling me?" He studied Sullivan, then continued. "It still doesn't make any sense. Why talk to me?"

Something far beyond Jason's sense of reality was unfolding here. The immensity of the moment was slowly settling in, and as it became clear, he felt any sort of control beginning to slip away from him. "What can *I* do for you? I mean, what can a small-town preacher possibly do for a goddamn secret agent?" Warning signals rang in his brain. Don't lose it. Hold on to the control. Hold on to it.

During his teens, Jason's emotions had caused trouble for him. Even before that, when he was a child, Jason's temper had been fierce. His fits of fury frightened his parents, and even frightened him. He would flail about wildly. He was small enough, however, that any such outburst usually ended with him being the worse for it. He never remembered winning a fight. But he did remember the fury. By the

time he got into high school, he'd given up on fighting—
with his hands. Instead, he had discovered the power of
words. His mouth had become his weapon. He could be
brutal. He had an ability to use language like a sword. It was
in those years that Jason drew into himself, and learned an
almost terrible self-control. It gave him a quiet, but very real
power.

Once Jason had gotten the class bully so upset that the kid
had begun to cry. The boy wanted to fight, but Jason refused. He simply talked to him. Baiting him, drawing him
out, slicing, until he reduced the poor bastard to tears in
front of everybody. The kid was no match for Jason. Jason
had savored the victory, but it was precisely that sense of
triumph that bothered him the most. He felt that a terrible
violence seethed just beneath his usually amiable exterior.
It frightened him.

There was a lot of talk in church about changing one's
life. Rebirth. He believed he could change. If he were truly
in control of his life, then he would abdicate his own inner
violence. He would not, could not, abdicate control in his
own life. But he would let go of the bitterness and hate that
he knew were a part of him. Years later he would realize that
this desire to control was still in conflict with much of what
the Christian life was about, but regardless, it provided the
motivation for the change he desperately sought. In the end,
he simply decided to command his seething, buried fury. To
subdue it. To force it to cease. Since then he had largely
succeeded. His life's vocation fostered a nonviolent posture. The seminary psychologist had described him as
"being in control." "Even tempered" was the term his parishioners frequently applied to him. They knew nothing of
that shadowy monster that lurked somewhere in his past,
and that was the way he wanted it. Now, facing Sullivan, he

realized that his fear was entwined with this hidden fury and he forced himself to relax, to regain that cherished control.

Sullivan watched the minister go to the brink, then pull back. It surprised him. Maybe there was more to the man than he thought. He hadn't thought Jason had that much willpower. This understanding gave Sullivan permission to open himself—to risk—just a little.

In the instant after he recovered, Jason glimpsed something new in Sullivan's face. Was it sorrow? Remorse? Guilt? Guilt, Jason thought. No, that seemed out of character. And when he next spoke, Sullivan crumbled Jason's holier-than-thou indignation like castles of drying sand.

"What can you do for me, Pastor?" Sullivan calmly repeated Jason's question. He frowned, paused and then sighed. "I came to ask you to pray for me."

Jason felt his shallow righteousness rip through his soul. It left him empty and weak. He sat silently, listening. He was caught up in the details of the story, but more than that, he was caught up in the storyteller. Sullivan had come to him seeking something—what exactly, Jason didn't know, but whatever it was, in these moments he had almost denied Sullivan any chance to find it. He would not make that mistake again.

"I was with the Agency from the beginning," Sullivan began, and Jason understood the Agency to be the Central Intelligence Agency. "And before that, the OSS."

"OSS?" Jason interrupted.

"Office of Strategic Services," Sullivan replied, with annoyance. He continued without a break. "I was not a *spy*." He spit out the word with scorn. "Officially, I was a librarian." He smiled. "More like a file clerk. I kept lists. Lists of good people. Lists of bad people. I studied them. Collected data on them. Developed dossiers for each of them." Sullivan paused, recalling—reliving—the events. "I was good at what I did," he added.

"Then one day my superior dropped by. It was spring. 1953. One of the first warm days. Cherry blossoms and all. Well, seemed as though we had a problem. One of our allies had a Communist agent in their ranks. For some reason we couldn't go through normal channels. We had infiltrated their operation clandestinely; we'd broken a treaty or some such bullshit."

His sudden outburst focused Jason. Sullivan sneered. "There was always bullshit." He paused for a moment, lost in thought. "So my boss informed me that the Agency had decided to eliminate the man. Permanently, swiftly and with as little risk to our international relations as possible. Then the clincher. He told me that I'd been doing a good job with the dossiers. 'No, Morrison—'" Sullivan stopped suddenly. His words appeared to startle him. Then his eyes seemed to focus on something far, far in the distance.

"My...other name is Sam...Samuel Morrison." He spoke haltingly as if he were trying to put a name with some faded picture in a class yearbook. His strange and distant look lasted only an instant. Then he became the same intense narrator driven to relate an unbelievable story. "'No,' my boss said, 'not a good job—a great job. You're a hell of a credit to the Agency. And the ol' man knows it.' I was hooked. And I hadn't even been handed the bait yet. 'We want you to sift through your files. Find someone who can do the job. And Sam: we need to be clean on this one—real clean. He's got to be from the outside, with no strings.' He patted me on the back as he walked to the door. 'Get back to me. Let me know how you make out. Remember, they really want this to work. They'll appreciate anything you can do.' *They.*" Sullivan laughed once, then continued. "I remember it like it was yesterday. I thought he was leaving, so

I started to turn away. 'One more thing.' He stepped back into my office and shut the door. 'This has got to be top secret. Top secret. We want only one person to know this guy's name. You. You'll be the contact. We'll give you the instructions. You'll relay them to him. It'll mean absolute security. I'm sure you realize how much we need it on this one.' He was no fool. He knew I was a company man through and through.''

Sullivan—Morrison—stared at Jason. There was a glazed, crazed sort of look in his eyes. ''Top secret,'' Sullivan sneered. ''Hell, we never used words like that.'' He slumped back into his chair and stared at Jason as he summoned his strength to go on. ''I did such a damn good job that we kept the operation going for more than thirty months. They tried—all of them—to figure out who Omega was. But they couldn't. It was like Omega was schizophrenic.'' Sullivan smiled as if proud of his accomplishment, then continued. ''He operated unpredictably. . . with devastating effectiveness.''

His eyes now focused on Jason's, and suddenly the pastor was aware that the old man's eyes were those of a young man. They gave verve and intensity to his entire being.

''I personally ordered the elimination of seventeen people.'' He paused. ''What the hell. They were Communists. Threats to the free world. All of them had done worse than kill people.'' He looked away, past Jason, through the window, into the thickening gray mists. When he spoke again, it was with a true sense of impending doom. ''I killed them as certainly as if I pulled the trigger myself.'' A tortured prayer followed in a rasping whisper. ''God help me.''

Again the silence that had punctuated their meeting settled thickly upon them. Then, slowly, Sullivan turned to Jason.

"Those people, the victims—they're all I've got. I know them all . . . like family you'd like to forget, but can't. I live with them every damn day." Sullivan laughed—heaved—once, empty and tired. "Now *I* could preach a sermon on Living with Your Conscience." Jason's mind flashed to his suddenly shallow and inconsequential meditation earlier in the day. Sullivan continued quietly. "You can't murder seventeen people and . . ." Sullivan did not finish the sentence. There was no need.

Jason sat quietly. He said nothing; there was nothing to say. All he could do was hope that the silence was understood.

The hollow laugh came again from deep inside Sullivan, growing into an agonizing, cancerous cough. And the man who had been Alpha made his confession. "I believe what you believe, Pastor. For all these years, I've believed."

The words brought Jason to consciousness. He looked up not comprehending the older man's words.

"I believe that killing . . . that murder," Sullivan corrected himself, "is a sin, and I am damned."

"I believe . . ." Jason began, then paused, searching the old man's eyes, "that a sinner can seek forgiveness and be redeemed." Jason reflected on the words he had just spoken. They surprised him. They were words he rarely used. They sounded strange coming from his mouth, but he felt compelled to say them. There was no need for subtle psychological counseling here. No, what Sullivan desperately needed was a sense that in the universal order of things, he still had a place. Jason could have said a thousand things, but these words now seemed exactly right.

"Do you believe that? Really?" Sullivan's eyes could cut through everything. They'd probe any weakness. His question alone indicated that.

Jason was silent. Sullivan waited. The answer that the pastor was seeking was not for the man sitting across from him. It was for that part within himself that found glib answers intolerable. Jason realized his breaths were short and sharp. He forced himself to breathe more slowly. When at last he was ready, Jason spoke. "Yes, Mr. Sullivan, I believe that."

"Will you pray for me?"

Jason was used to praying. He prayed at weddings, at funerals, in church, at meetings, at community dinners, even at parades. He was the professional Christian. Praying was in the job description.

Tonight, however, his prayer was different. Alone in the presence of this strange old man, he allowed himself to struggle with the secrets that he shared with the other. Later he would try to recall the words; he would not be able to. But when the prayer had been completed, the room seemed lighter. Not as though some heavenly fluorescent light had been turned on, but as if thirty tons of crap had been gently lifted from both of them. In moments like this, Jason was less skeptical of mysticism. He was certain that in this communion experience, their souls had touched, merged. If Sullivan had been a different person, Jason would simply have reached out and held him. Instead, the two men just sat and waited—for nothing, for everything. It was Sullivan who first broke the silence.

"I'm not afraid of death."

Jason nodded.

"A lot of people wanted to know who we were—Omega and I. Most of them are dead now—those from the old days." He smiled. "Or retired." Sullivan changed his tone.

"You have contact with him?"

"Who?"

"Omega." Jason said the name and almost felt embarrassed. Code names didn't fit into his world.

Now Sullivan smiled. "No, but you hear things," he said, "the way you always hear things. You know?"

No, Jason thought, I don't know.

"No," continued Sullivan, "I haven't had anything to do with him since . . . then."

"What will he do if the British push this thing?" Jason asked. Days later, as he reflected on this evening, he would realize exactly how stupid the question was. Even his tone would bother him. It sounded as if he were merely making conversation at the Sunday morning coffee hour.

"Whether they do or don't doesn't matter now. He's already decided what must be done. He'll kill me." The matter-of-fact, sublimely logical response fell heavily upon Jason. It sounded distant and muffled, and it was followed by another agonizing silence. "Because I know who he is," Sullivan responded to Jason's unasked question. "Because I could ruin him. Because I'm not worth the risk."

"But that would be murd . . ." Jason caught himself and tried to recover. "I mean outright, illegal, cold-blooded murder."

Sullivan smiled. "You really can't understand, can you?" He reflected for a moment. "The man was an assassin. He went to work, killed someone and got a paycheck. Assassins think differently." He paused again. A sour look crossed his face. "Omega's favorite story was about allowing himself to be stalked by a tiger. He waited until it sprang at him. Only then did he kill it.

"Omega would kill anyone. Me. You." Sullivan paused for effect, then continued. "Anyone, if it was . . . expedient. He was totally without conscience." He formed a strange half smile. "I have enough conscience for both of us." Sullivan sat thinking, studying the pastor. "I'll tell you something I've never told anyone. One of the reasons I picked him for the job was because he enjoyed killing. The planning, the waiting, the execution. It was all . . . all a sort of ultimate recreation for him." Sullivan slowly looked down, with just the slightest shake of his head.

"How will he find you?" Jason finally asked.

"He already has. I'm sure of it." Sullivan shrugged.

"Maybe you can hide or . . ."

Sullivan closed his eyes and, almost imperceptibly, shook his head. Now when he looked up, he was spent, with the soft, misty eyes of a man who has grown weary of seeing so much of the world. "I'll just wait."

Jason struggled with that finality. "I . . ." He looked up at the older man with a childlike perplexity. "I . . . don't understand. . . ." Jason felt stupid. What the man standing before him had just said was torturously clear. Omega was going to kill him. But why? Why was it so inevitable? Why was this outcome so apparent to Sullivan but so shapeless for him? He wanted to shake his head violently, as if to drive some drunken fog from his mind, but he was stone-cold sober.

Sullivan smiled as a grandfather might smile at a grandchild who was trying to be particularly grown-up. He shrugged and stood up.

"I've done something terrible, Mr. Winslow, but I'd do it again. Yes, the Agency used me. But it was for the good of the nation. And so I let myself be used. I'd do it again," he repeated. "Who of us wouldn't?" He paused here, almost as an invitation for Jason to respond, but Jason was silent.

"Omega knows me. He has known all along that the secret has been safe. But *I* also know Omega," Sullivan continued. "The tiny buffer of security between the world and him was me...and suddenly I'm no longer any kind of buffer at all.''

"But—" Jason began.

"Would I reveal the Omega identity?" Again he smiled that impenetrable smile. "Depends who asks, I guess. But, no. We had an agreement. No, I wouldn't identify Omega. I've never breathed a word." He could see the questioning in Jason's eyes. "No, Reverend, I haven't even told you—not really, not half of it. I took a vow, Mr. Winslow. 'On my honor...'" His voice trailed off, and his face darkened. "But...perhaps..." He shrugged, and seemed for a moment to tremble.

"Why now—after all these years?" The older man's voice was filled with pain. "After all these years?" He shook his head slowly. "It makes no sense." Suddenly Sullivan stiffened with anger. "It was my secret! *I* was the custodian! I'm the one whose life has been walled up for all these years. Not theirs. I've held their goddamned dear secret. I've kept them safe. And now. And now..." He looked up at Jason, through him. "I've turned the thing that kept me imprisoned into my reason for living. Every day, Mr. Winslow, every day, I look out at my neighbors, and I tell myself that keeping the secret is keeping them safe...keeping America safe. That's the myth I've chosen to live by. It worked. Until now..." he repeated slowly. Again, he shook his head defeatedly.

Slowly Jason began to understand what Sullivan himself seemed only now to be realizing. They'd betrayed him. "I've taken a vow," he had said. It was not some casual arrangement of convenience. It was a profound commitment. And the betrayal was no less profound. It was the sudden, heart-rending forsaking of a lover. Sullivan desperately needed to stay in love despite his partner's abandonment.

"No," Sullivan murmured easily. "I'll keep their precious secret." But he convinced neither of them. "But why should I? If *they* don't care, why should *I*?" he asked again, expecting no answer. A long silence followed. "Omega is wondering the same thing. Omega knows me well. Better—perhaps—than I know myself." Sullivan's stare cut like pure light into Jason's consciousness. "I'm an old man whose conviction is suddenly suspect. He will kill me...soon... hopefully swiftly—" his voice had become a haunting whisper, and he leaned in to Jason that he might share a terrible truth "—to keep the secret safe."

The fog had grown denser. It overpowered the night and was waiting for them at the door. When Sullivan stepped off the porch, his reality seemed to fade as he moved into the mists. Jason lifted his head and peered out after the old man. He called out to him.

"Good night, Mr...Morrison."

Sullivan kept walking, unfalteringly, as if he hadn't heard a thing. In the distance, the sea rumbled rhythmically, a welcome signal of some sort of constancy. Sullivan walked a few more paces, almost into oblivion, then stopped. He turned, and like the mist itself, drifted back in on Jason. And when he had become real again, his words came in hushed waves.

"My name is Richard Sullivan. Mr. Morrison is dead. He died a long time ago. In another place." Sullivan's tone was one of disquieting confidentiality. "I'll tell you something, Reverend Winslow. Something absolutely true. I buried Morrison, buried him and everything about him. Buried him under the ashes of time, in an airtight casket so that nothing would ever leak out." He paused now and nodded in agreement with his own statement. "The man built himself a marker. The last act of a dying man." He saw that the pastor was confused. He smiled pleasantly at Jason, turned and stepped away. "Forget it, Reverend Winslow." Once more he stopped. He stood with his back to Jason for a long moment, then turned to face the minister once more.

"I think I'll go home and listen to some music." He thought about this for a moment, then continued. "I have a record of an English boys' choir. I've almost worn it out. The voices...there's a purity...it gives me..." His words trailed off, and he simply shook his head. "It gives me peace. Peace, Reverend. What more can I ask for?"

Jason nodded, in awe of the old man, who was once more merely a shadow. "Good night, Mr. Sullivan." Jason's words became visible and mingled with fog.

"Goodbye." Sullivan's words drifted toward him through the emptiness.

Now the cold wetness reached through Jason's shirt, tightening his body. It made him alert. It sharpened his movements and heightened his senses. He did not want to stand out there any longer. He didn't feel comfortable. Slowly he realized that comfortable was the wrong word. Safe, he thought. I don't feel safe.

Back inside, Jason thought that he was becoming paranoid. "A secret agent behind every tree, huh, Dog?" He glanced down at the animal and was surprised. Dog's fur had lifted up on his shoulders. He half crouched, half sat, waiting. His low growl was hardly audible. He stared toward the door.

"Hey, Dog. Dog! It's okay! Come on. Let's go to bed." The animal remained at the door. "Dog," Jason said sharply. "Come here. It's all right." Reluctantly, Dog moved to his master's side.

Jason lay in his bed, carefully reviewing the events of the evening. They were barely believable. Some things still didn't make sense to him. "What should I do?" he asked. Then he realized that he was talking out loud, to no one. He was exhausted. He forced himself to stop thinking. He closed his eyes, allowing the distant sounds of the sea to lull him. In a misty half dream, he reasoned that people like Sullivan tended to be a little dramatic.

That night the James Bond novel on the bedside table remained untouched, and when the Reverend Jason Winslow's easy and regular breathing indicated he was finally asleep, the dog moved back to the parsonage door. He settled down, half crouching, half sitting, waiting for the fog to stalk its prey.

4

THE MORNING WAS COLD and wet. The fog, though not as thick as it had been during the night, continued to drift in off the water. Jason shivered as he stepped out of the parsonage for his ritual run. The clanging of the harbor's bell buoy gave him his tempo. He planned his day as he jogged along the streets of Craig's Harbor. Although it was his day off, he planned to go over to the hospital to see the kids who'd been in the accident. He didn't have to go, but they were friends of some of his own kids, and besides, the hospital liked to have him stop in. He understood kids; he spoke their language. The nurses often told him his visits really seemed to help.

And then there was Mr. Sullivan. There must be something he could do, some way to help. As he ran, he began to grow upset with himself. He hadn't even offered the man help. Now he told himself that it would be enough to let Sullivan know someone cared. After all, he had made that clear last night, hadn't he? And there were those mysterious statements Sullivan made as he was leaving. The way he said them, they almost sounded like codes. Just forget it, Jason told himself. You're being overly dramatic. But still...

As he was waking up, Jason had thought for a moment that he had dreamed Sullivan's visit, but his first vague awareness of the previous evening's events brought him sharply to full consciousness. He knew he had imagined nothing.

As he ran, he worked to put the visit into some logical order. He realized that he'd been so unprepared to deal with Sullivan that he'd forgotten how to minister to the man, who obviously had some real needs. Jason wondered, did Sullivan need to be ministered to? He shrugged. The man seemed to have it together pretty well. There didn't seem to be any of the emotions one might expect: denial, anger, whatever. Still, the man must need some sort of support.

Then Jason realized something that shamed and frightened him. It became clear as he considered how calmly he was dealing with Sullivan's unbelievable story. It was, in fact, just that. Unbelievable. Deep down, he really didn't believe Sullivan. His story was just too bizarre. It sounded more like the novels Jason liked to read. Fiction. My God, he told himself, if I really thought every detail of his tale was true would I have let him go home? I mean, he sat right in my living room and told me that this Omega character was going to kill him. And all I did was sit there and nod as if he were telling me about some TV show he'd just seen. Jason was sweating now—more than his jogging justified. He came to a large elm tree and leaned back against it. Dog stood impatiently at his feet. The pastor looked out into the fog. He squinted to see something—anything—through the waves of mist.

While he leaned there panting, the obvious broke through his clouded thoughts. It suddenly seemed as clear as the bell buoy he heard ringing through the fog. The idea caught in his consciousness and screamed at him. What if everything Sullivan had said was the absolute truth! "God help me," he whispered. He looked toward Sullivan's house. I should go there now, he thought. He started toward the house, then slowed. It's only seven in the morning. What if I wake him up? He'll think I'm a fool. *What if it was the truth.* The words screamed in his mind. I don't care what he thinks.

Jason ran toward the house. He was breathing hard now, in short breaths. He couldn't believe he'd been so . . . so stupid . . . so unprofessional. Now he could see a huge dark shape forming dimly in the fog. As he ran on, the dark presence became a house. In one stride, Jason stepped up onto the porch.

He pounded on the door. "Mr. Sullivan!" There was no answer, no sound inside. "Mr. Sullivan!" He pounded again. "Open the door!" He waited. He heard another door open. He peered across the yard to the next house.

Henry DiLuca stepped out of his house and yelled through the waves of fog. "Hey—what's going on over there?"

Jason couldn't think of a thing to say. He felt foolish. Now, as DiLuca marched toward him, the neighbor recognized Jason. "Oh, Reverend Winslow. Anything wrong?"

Jason swallowed. How do I explain this? he thought. "I don't know." God, he's coming over here. Do something. Jason glanced in front of him and found his hand on the doorknob. He turned it and stepped inside.

The minister realized that he had never been inside Sullivan's house. It was fastidious. Neat. Simple. Clean. "Mr. Sullivan," he shouted. Still no answer. He looked in the other rooms on the first floor. DiLuca joined him. He could see from Jason's face something *was* wrong. He asked no questions. The upstairs was empty. The one bed in the house was neatly made.

"He wasn't going anywhere, was he?" Jason asked.

DiLuca shrugged. "Wouldn't tell us even if he planned to. Besides, far as we knew, he didn't have a soul to visit." He paused, then added, "'Course we did notice he'd gone somewhere last night. We went to bed 'fore he got back."

DiLuca said it with a sort of ominous quality to his voice. Jason simply nodded.

Then the two men heard something unnerving. It was an awful foreign-sounding yowl—like that of a wild animal in pain. "Dog!" Jason moved instantly toward the sound, nearly stumbling down the stairs. He stepped out the door and jumped over the porch rail, almost tripping again. As he straightened, he saw Dog sitting in front of Sullivan's garage door. The animal continued his unnatural wailing. Jason spoke firmly. "Okay. It's okay, Dog." Dog turned toward him, seemingly comforted to hear the assurance. Jason stepped to the garage door, twisted the handle and swung one of the two doors open.

The warm smell of exhaust washed around him. He moved to the car. Sullivan was slumped over in the driver's seat. Jason pulled out the body. He and DiLuca carried it out into the misty fresh air.

"I'll call for an ambulance," DiLuca said, and was gone. Jason searched for vital signs. There were none. The joints were already stiffening and the skin was cold and empty. He pushed a finger against Sullivan's neck. The tissue had lost its resilience. He searched in vain for some sign of life.

Jason's mind was filled with oddly shaped thoughts—like a puzzle box full of unassembled pieces. The strangest of these thoughts, given the circumstances, was nonetheless the clearest. Over and over again, it came to him. Who's going to take care of the man's garden?

A siren intruded irreverently upon the silence, calling the volunteer ambulance squad. It startled Jason, and brought him back to the present. It was shrill, long and melancholy. In the fog, it seemed to come from everywhere. It was still sounding when DiLuca returned. "I called the sheriff's patrol, too."

The ambulance crew was there in five minutes. There was not much for them to do. They covered Sullivan with a blanket and waited.

DiLuca talked to the ambulance crew. "Poor ol' bastard—sorry, Reverend—he must'a just decided to end it all." Jason wanted to shout, No! Omega did this! but he knew he couldn't say that. Instead, he simply stared at the pale blue blanket that covered the equally blue body. I had a part in this, he thought. Dear God in heaven, I killed him. Jason crouched next to Dog and patted him. He was glad the animal was there.

As he knelt there in the midst of that misty scene, Jason longed for someone to lash out at. Those around him had no idea of the fury that raged within him. It was a fury born of lies, of his silence, of the changes that he felt happening to him—changes that were beyond his control. The fury was an emotion buried so deep in his past that it confused him. But there was no way to let it go. It would be more confusing to the men gathered at a respectful distance from the body. And so, in his silence, he knelt there and let the rage sear a hatred of an unknown enemy deep into his soul.

His life was changing. He understood why—at least to a degree. Out of necessity. He was reacting to events, events he could not control. He knew, for example, that when the sheriff's patrol arrived he would tell them only that Sullivan had visited him last night. That they had talked. That Sullivan had seemed despondent, but not severely so. He would relate none of the details of the conversation. He would say that the dead man had seemed in good spirits when he left. That he left a little after 11:15 p.m. He would report only facts and only those requested.

DiLuca's words intruded upon his thoughts. He realized that the man was asking him something about Sullivan's "suicide."

"Yeah," said the minister, "I wish I had realized. I could have done something to help." Jason's comment was absolutely true, but he knew it meant something very different from what Henry DiLuca understood it to mean. His duplicity tore at him. Then, slowly, he realized something else. He was afraid. He was afraid, almost beyond control. Come on, he told himself, calm down. The attack of anxiety—and anxiety was exactly what it was—frightened him as much as or more than anything else in these ten hours had. It was one more sign of the cherished control he felt slipping away.

When the sheriff arrived, Jason related the whole morning's happenings. He told him about last night in the way he had rehearsed. The sheriff, Harold Bates from over in Willisville, listened intently. As the minister talked, the officer chewed nervously on the stub of an unlit cigar. Jason found himself staring at the man's brown-stained teeth. He had to force himself to look away from Harold's busy mouth into his eyes.

The sheriff asked Jason to go through Sullivan's house with him while he looked for personal effects, records of next of kin and so on. They searched slowly and carefully.

It was during the search process that Jason began to notice something. For such an apparently neat man, Sullivan had left little things that did not quite fit the overall picture. The books in the bookcase, for example, were not lined up evenly across the shelves. The drawer of a filing cabinet was not fully closed. Small stacks of paper were haphazardly piled up. Someone as fastidious as Sullivan seemed to be would have clipped the loose papers or at least straightened them up so their edges were even. He leaned over Sullivan's writing desk, and began to align the piles of papers, then stopped abruptly.

Damn it, you're doing it again, he told himself. You're letting your imagination run wild. You don't know how Sullivan lived. He probably did commit suicide. It's more

likely than the other possibility. And besides, if it is true—
the other possibility—you should be telling the police.

"Find anything?" The sheriff's voice startled him. He
pulled his hand from the pile of papers and turned. His face
flushed.

"No!" Jason said, then added more quietly, "Ahh,
no...no, I didn't. I didn't find a thing."

"This is the damnedest..." Bates chewed on his cigar.
"This guy didn't even have a Christmas card list. No phone
book. Nothing! How the hell—'scuse me, Reverend—how
the heck d'you suppose he survived without a past?" Jason
gazed beyond the sheriff as he thought about the irony of his
words. How do you suppose he could have survived *with* a
past? Jason thought.

"Hey, look at this." The sheriff's voice intruded upon
Jason's temporary escape. Jason looked back up. Harold's
mushy-tipped cigar was aimed toward a stereo system. A
light indicated that it was on. "Must have been listening to
a record when he decided to do it." He looked at Jason for
approval of the theory.

Jason stepped to the record player and placed the needle
on the record. A choir of boys sang a gentle but somber and
haunting requiem. Peace, thought Jason, it brought him
peace.

"Damn," Harold Bates intoned. "I do believe that would
drive me to end it all, too." Crass laughter punctuated his
thoughts. "Know what I mean, Reverend?" Jason looked
up and saw—for an instant—the hollow caricature of a fool.
In that moment, the minister's anger sought to be directed.
But even as it was focusing on this buffoon of a policeman,
Jason half nodded and deliberately turned away. He looked
out into the white mist beyond the window. He looked away
from the despised sheriff to keep from becoming sick. The

unease passed quickly, and when he looked back the sheriff had turned and was walking out the door.

"Now the damn county's gonna have t' bury him," Harold pronounced.

"Sheriff," Jason called. The officer turned. Jason felt as though he were about to erupt. When he finally spoke, what he intended to say, his confession, was smothered. Instead, he simply said, "I'll take care of the funeral arrangements."

"Gee, Reverend," the officer said, beaming, "that's really nice of you."

"It kind of goes with the territory." Jason smiled his best pastoral smile. He turned to the stereo, listened to the music for a moment longer, then solemnly lifted the tone arm and turned off the power.

Outside, the fog had begun to lift. The sun's rays stretched through the mist. The brightness caused the men to squint as they watched the body being loaded into the ambulance.

"Sheriff?"

"Yes, Reverend."

"You going to have an autopsy done?" Jason spoke as casually as possible, but his heart pounded. The sheriff looked up and studied him intently. The man's mouth worked rapidly on the soggy cigar. His squinting eyes narrowed even more.

"What for?" he asked.

Jason shrugged. "Just in case there was anything..."

"Unusual?" The sheriff finished the sentence for him. Jason regretted even mentioning the thought. Now he forced a laugh and spoke.

"Yeah, I guess so."

The officer's expression darkened and he leaned toward Jason. He took the mushy stump of his cigar out of his mouth. Pieces of the thing stuck to his lower lip. "You think he was murdered?" The ominous tone had a greater effect than the words. In the instant following the sheriff's inquiry, Jason felt the blood flow into his face. But in the next instant, shoving the cigar back into his mouth, the sheriff burst into laughter.

"Sorry, Reverend. You ought to see the expression on your face! I'll tell you what. I think you've been watching too many of them TV shows." He walked to his cruiser, still laughing. Jason turned away, unsure of himself.

"I'll have the papers ready for you this afternoon," the sheriff offered.

"Thanks," Jason responded weakly.

"Thank *you*, Reverend." He glanced over at the covered body in the ambulance. He took the cigar out of his mouth and spit. "Poor ol' bastard. Sure give folks in Craig's Harbor something to talk about."

Jason nodded. That much, he knew, was the truth.

5

THE FOG HAD LIFTED by the time Jason got home. He stepped into his front hall, shut the door and leaned back against it. He felt weak and sick and chilled. He unconsciously rubbed his arms to rid himself of the chilling wetness. He shivered uncontrollably.

"What the hell am I going to do?" Asking the question didn't help. He was part of the reason Sullivan was now dead. He tried to tell himself that just wasn't true. He tried to think coolly about the situation. He told himself that Sullivan had chosen the way he wanted to live, and that he had chosen the way he would die. All Jason might have been able to do was delay the inevitable. Or worse, thought Jason, if he had gotten Sullivan to stay with him last night, maybe they'd both be dead now. He shivered again. He did not feel any better.

The cold seemed to emanate from somewhere deep inside him. He had been only dimly aware of it before, but now it flowed into his consciousness. It moved him out of his thoughts. He climbed the stairs, grabbed a towel, stripped and stepped into the shower. He turned the faucet to as hot as he could stand it. The streams of steaming water slashed across his body. It almost hurt. He forced himself to concentrate on the water. Its effect was powerful. He felt himself being cleansed. He thought of the ocean's waves pounding against Maine's granite coastline. And then he toyed with the symbolism of baptism. He began to consider what sort of baptism he was undergoing now, but forced the idea out of his mind. It was senseless. He allowed himself to drift into oblivion. He was only conscious of the stinging, pulsing water, beating against his body, and then of not even that.

Dog's bark intruded on his thoughts. Only then did he hear the phone ringing. He stepped out of the shower, slipping—almost falling—on the linoleum. "Damn," he breathed, as he wrapped the towel around himself.

"Hello!" He realized he had spoken with more intensity than he had intended. He recovered, speaking more calmly. "Hello." He listened. There was no response. "Hello?" More silence. I must have missed it, he thought, and started to hang up.

"Jason Winslow?" The voice sounded distant. Jason moved the receiver back to his ear.

"Yes. Hello?"

The voice on the other end was cold and deep. It seemed to have a familiar quality, but not really. "Winslow."

"Yes."

"I have decided you are a dangerous man."

Jason's mind raced. What was happening to him?

"Who is this?"

"You know more than you should. You are privy to secrets—dangerous secrets."

"Who is this!" Jason demanded.

"Morrison was a risk." The voice paused. "And now he's dead." There was a longer pause. "As it should be."

Jason could feel the fear well up within him. He was certain that the man on the phone must sense it also. Stop it! Think! Get a hold on things, his mind screamed.

"Reverend Winslow." The voice on the other end spoke with studied condescension.

"I don't know who you are, or what you think you're doing," Jason interrupted, "but I'll tell you this. You're terribly mistaken." He waited for a response.

After a moment, when it finally came, it was not what Jason expected. "You're going to die before you get—"

"Who is this?" demanded Jason.

There was a short derisive laugh; it was almost a sneer, and then the studied, condescending tone again. "Who the hell do you think it is, Pastor?"

Jason's mind worked furiously. He considered the options, and decided to hang up. But as he began to put the phone down, he paused. He saw one glimpse of hope to end this whole thing. It must work. It's only logical, he told himself. It had to work.

"Look," Jason spoke desperately, "Sullivan's dead. You've killed the only person who could identify you. You're safe." Jason listened. The response was chilling.

"But he could have told you, and now you have become a risk. A risk that must be eliminated."

The voice was quieter now. The man sounded more determined, more certain. Jason desperately wished he was hearing some kind of sick joke, but he knew it was not. It was far from that.

"For God's sake," Jason said, "why the hell should he have told me? If you want to know the truth, I didn't believe half of what he did tell me." Jason paused, before completing his argument. "And besides, if he had told me, I'd have already gone to the police." Jason scanned the tapes of the past few minutes. He reviewed the conversation. He tried to analyze the person he was talking to.

The man showed no fear, no impatience. Whoever he was, he was methodical, calculating, complex. There was something else. What was it Sullivan had said? Omega *enjoyed* his work. A notion—barely believable—slowly crystallized in Jason's mind. The man was savoring the minister's fear. And so Jason began to change. He paused, forcing himself to grow calmer. When he spoke again, his words—now as calculating as the caller's—cut away at the killer's strength.

"Either way," Jason said into the mouthpiece, "killing me would accomplish nothing." There was silence. Then the voice spoke again.

"Killing you would give me a moment of supreme pleasure."

The words and the voice had their desired effect. Jason again felt a stinging, inescapable fear flow through him. He had been sure he had stymied his adversary. God, he thought, I'm standing here playing mind games with someone who's telling me he's going to kill me. Now he heard himself laughing. Not insanely, not desperately, but almost compassionately. Even as he spoke the words, Jason wondered at their source, for they were strange and uncalculated.

"You forget who you're talking to, Omega." He said the name for the first time. "I am part of the Body of Christ, who promises eternal life to all who believe in him." He paused and, when he spoke again, sounded as chilling as Omega. "I have no fear of death. I put my trust in the Giver of Life."

There was silence, then, abruptly, a click. Omega had hung up. Jason placed the receiver on the phone. He stood in his bedroom and his eyes focused on his reflection in the mirror. He still dripped from the shower. His skin was drained white. His mouth was dry. His breath was quick and shallow. Then the fear returned in a ball of burning pain in his stomach. He moved back to the bathroom and vomited. He rested his head in his arms and breathed out an impassioned prayer. "Oh God, help me!"

OMEGA SAT, STARING at the phone he'd just hung up. Had he gone too far? Maybe the despised clergyman was telling the truth. He suddenly straightened and swung around in his high-backed leather chair. His fingers pressed into its padded arms. Damn it, he thought, that son of a bitch has gotten to me. He's going to be dangerous. "Maybe he's telling the truth," he said aloud. The words troubled him. Since when had he made any decision based on "maybe"? No, thought Omega, the good reverend will have a chance to test his faith. Now he sneered at the pastor's words as he had been unable to do only moments before. A smile formed on Omega's face. He reached for his phone and pushed a button.

"Yes, sir," an electronic voice responded.

"Check my schedule for the next few days. See what appointments can be canceled or postponed."

"Yes, sir."

"Has Mr. Harrington called back?"

"He called about twenty minutes ago."

"Good. Good," replied Omega. "Is our dinner appointment all set?"

"Yes, sir. He said he's anxious to see you. He'll be arriving at National late this afternoon. He'll call from the airport."

"Tell him I'll send a car out to pick him up." He paused for a moment and then continued. "And get me Donlevy over in McLean."

"Yes, sir."

Omega reviewed once more his plan for killing the man he would be meeting for dinner. He had already played the events over in his mind a dozen times. The repetition indicated indecision. He understood why, but still, it bothered him. Years, more than twenty-five of them, had passed since he had last killed someone by his own hand. Now that he had ordered one death and was about to carry out another, his old senses were beginning to sharpen. His whole being was affected. It was...uplifting. Hadn't his secretary told him he seemed—what was it she had said—"bright-eyed and bushy-tailed"? He chuckled to himself. He could feel the energy returning. He was nearing the prey. Tonight would be the first killing. It would not be the last. The risk would be real, but it was necessary. Now he settled back and pondered the event. In his mind he caressed the trigger of his gun. The fantasy set a whole series of memories stirring. He was anxious for the night to come.

The light on the phone glowed, but before it could buzz, Omega had the phone at his ear. "Yes?" He spoke with an intensity his secretary did not fail to notice.

"Mr. Donlevy on two, sir."

He punched the flashing button. "Chris, how are you?"

There was a pause. Christopher Donlevy was already on his guard. "Everything's just fine, sir."

"Good, good. Listen Chris, you know about this Alpha/Omega business?"

Now the pause was longer, the answer more tentative. "What I've seen in the media."

"Well, one of my sources called just now and said that Alpha—Morrison or whatever the hell name he's using—died last night." The pause grew into a long silence.

"Jesus," whispered Donlevy. "How?"

"Damned if I know. It was sudden, though. What with all the press on the British business, thought you might want to check it out—pass it along. Feather in your cap."

"Thanks for thinking of me," Donlevy said coolly. "Anything else?" He waited. He knew there was often something else. This time he hoped against hope there would not be.

"No. Just thought you'd want to know about it. Tell the old man about it—at the right time. It'll please him, the way you're on top of things."

"I appreciate the intelligence."

"Good, good . . . Oh, Chris, you still there?"

Of course I am, Donlevy thought. You don't think I'd hang up on you. "Yes, sir," he replied.

"If the British do press the issue, it might be a good idea to stall any response till we know just what happened to Morrison. Suggest that to the director. I'm sure he'll agree."

"Good idea." So, thought Donlevy, there is something else, after all.

"And one more thing." Omega paused for a moment. "Maybe you should set up an outpost office and safe phone. Talbot, down at the Bureau, should be handling this, but it seems as though it belongs to you. Keep it in the family, you know? Keep it quiet and routine."

"I understand, sir."

"Listen, this has sort of got my curiosity up. Sort of a final chapter. Let me know what happens, huh?"

"Yes . . ." Donlevy started to speak, but the man on the line had already hung up. Donlevy set down the receiver, then pulled out a handkerchief and wiped his sweaty palms. When he realized he was muttering out loud, the thought was complete. The words were not unfamiliar. "What a way to screw up a Monday."

6

JASON'S STRENGTH RETURNED slowly. When he felt strong enough to stand, he went to the telephone and dialed the sheriff's office. He explained that it was imperative that he see the sheriff immediately. He called the state police and made the same request. Then he dressed and made one more call.

"Bishop Merrill's office."

"Is he in? This is Jason Winslow calling."

"Who?" The coolness of the secretary's voice both amused and irritated him. In an institution whose commission is to be caring, the aloofness of so many of the participants presented an irony that Jason noted often. He smiled. He always introduced himself as Jason Winslow. He avoided using "Reverend" whenever possible. Clearly, he thought, the system was geared to just the opposite. Putting a title in front of your name—or letters behind it—was often the best way to produce results.

"*Reverend* Jason Winslow from Craig's Harbor."

"Oh, of course. I'm sorry, Reverend Winslow. The bishop is in a meeting right now." Jason was aware of the secretary's change in tone.

"I'd really like to have a word with him, if I can," Jason urged.

"I'm sorry, Reverend," she responded, her condescending tone returning, "but as I explained, he's in a meeting."

Jason was quiet for a moment. Usually he'd simply, politely, call back later, but now his fear and anger and frustration surged over him.

"I know what you explained," Jason pressed, "but I really need to speak to him—*now*."

"Well," began the secretary, "perhaps if you'll tell me what you think is so important—"

"Damn it," Jason seethed, "I want to talk to him now!"

The startled and suddenly indignant voice mumbled something and there was a click. Did she hang up or put me on hold? Jason wondered. Almost instantly he heard the bishop's voice. He'd heard it only five or six times before. It was always the same, the epitome of the soothing, pastoral voice.

"Yes?"

"Bishop Merrill, I apologize for interrupting."

"I think your apology belongs to my secretary." There was the clear note of disapproval in the bishop's tone.

"Yes, Bishop." Jason breathed deeply, then began his story. "Bishop, something has come up." Jason waited.

"Yes?"

"My life was threatened today."

The comment was met by a momentary silence, then a gasped, "What!"

Jason smiled. Well, that apparently cut to the meat of it, he thought. "Last night a member of the parish came to me..." he continued, replaying some of the events of the past twelve hours.

The bishop listened without interrupting. When Jason finished, he finally spoke. "I will make arrangements to have your parish covered. Feel free to do whatever you need to do—whatever the police recommend. Call me and let me know what you decide."

Jason was relieved. "Thank you, Bishop."

"And Jason..."

"Yes?"

"I'll smooth things over with my secretary. Don't worry." There was a hint of humor in his voice.

"Thank you, Bishop."

There was a silence, and when the bishop spoke again, he sounded self-conscious, almost awkward. "Peace be with you, Jason."

Jason paused momentarily. Over the years, he had developed a pretty good sense about the expressions of concern that often rolled too easily off the tongues of clergy types. However, the bishop's benediction carried a clear note of integrity. Jason answered softly, "And with you."

After he had hung up, he sat quietly, staring into nothingness. Slowly he got up and walked downstairs. He sat in the living room where he and Sullivan had sat only a dozen hours earlier. Dog came and sat in front of him, demanding some attention. As Jason patted him, he found himself thinking an almost incomprehensible thought: what did he own that he could use for a weapon, a deadly weapon?

He ran a film through his mind. Each time it was the same—with one exception. He was being stalked in his own home. The faceless assailant would raise his weapon, aim and, in the split second before he fired—this was the part that changed—Jason would disarm the enemy by throwing a knife, a rolling pin, a dictionary, a fireplace poker or a chair. "You're an idiot." His words dissolved the image. "You won't disarm him. If he has a gun, he'll kill you."

Jason became aware of his body. His breathing was quick, his muscles taut; he felt as though he were pulling in, contracting, tightening up. He spoke aloud, telling himself, "Relax. Relax." He consciously tried to follow his own direction. Jason rose and walked to the window. No police yet. "Where the hell are they?" Despite his self-instruction, relaxation did not come.

He thought about the violence that had suddenly thrust itself upon him. Violence evoked a strong response in Jason. He hated it, from its glorification on television to its ugly reality in the streets of American cities and towns. He recalled an earlier brush with violence while he had been attending the seminary in Boston. One night, as he was walking along Back Street, from Boston University to his apartment, he heard a noise. Peering into the shadows, he saw a Dumpster. As he watched, a hand reached up out of the container. Cautiously in the dimness, he stepped nearer. What he saw made him turn away. It was a bloody, filthy body, barely alive. "I'll get help," he shouted, but he was already running desperately back toward the school—propelled not so much by the urgency, but by the fear and horror of the violence he had happened on.

He did get help, and he returned with the police, though only long enough to show them the container. For a kid from a small Midwestern town, the violence of the city was frightening. Yet his reaction to the incident of that night was frightening, also. As a result, during his seminary training, he did volunteer work in the emergency ward of Boston City Hospital. He learned to deal with the results of violence, but in doing so, he found its reality became even more abhorrent to him.

The violence of the city was one reason why he chose to serve a rural pastorate. He was appalled at the constant potential for brutality in the city. He remembered Tuesday mornings in Kenmore Square with a special clarity. As he walked down Commonwealth Avenue, a Brink's truck would pull up in front of Riverside Bank and Trust. Usually it would be about eight-thirty. A guard would step out of the truck, carrying a drawn revolver, his finger on the trigger. Another guard carried two bags of money. In the truck, the driver held a shotgun. The entire scene bothered Jason. The apparent indifference of the people in the street was troubling. The drawn gun bothered him. The casual matter-of-factness of the guards also bothered him, as did the realization that it was necessary. Violence in the city—or the potential for it—was accepted. He hated it.

Now, as he considered what he might use as a suitable weapon, he felt the hatred welling up inside him again. It was a hatred of violence, a hatred of these events that were seemingly beyond his control—it was all of this, and a hatred of this man who had placed him in the situation.

"No!" Jason's abrupt protest caused him to jump. Dog looked sharply up at him. No, he repeated to himself. I will not let this change me—this . . . this . . . presence.

This should not be happening to me. This should not be happening to Jason Winslow of Craig's Harbor. This kind of violence is out of place here, he argued silently. It wasn't that rural communities didn't experience violence. They did. But it was different there. Maybe it had to do with the support of the community. Merely the *awareness* of the community made a difference. Jason had seen an unchecked outpouring of concern on more than one occasion. Once a young lobsterman had drowned. Another time, a high school boy had been killed in an automobile accident. And once, in a nearby town, a man had killed another man who was having an affair with his wife. In all instances, violence thundered into the minds of the townspeople. The inhabitants of Craig's Harbor were outraged. It was this sense of violation that was different. Jason wasn't sure similar incidents in urban areas were met with the same outrage and indignation. They were, in those places, inevitable.

As he sat, Jason also struggled with something else. I am a man of peace, he told himself. I am now considering a cold, calculated act of violence. But it would be self-defense, he told himself. That's irrelevant, he argued back. You're still letting him control you. Resist him. You control your own destiny.

This last awareness drew the noose that Jason had carefully created in his imagination tightly around his neck. "Destiny," he sneered out loud. The debate raged within. At one point, the words of Jennifer Seidkamp came ringing into his head. They were words from long ago, from his high school days, but they had lost none of their pointedness in the past eight years. He had spent days working himself up to ask her for a date. They went to a movie, then afterward, to a quiet place in the corner of his father's farm.

In his active adolescent imagination, he had created some fantasy expectation of the moment, but that night it became clear it would remain only an unfulfilled dream. Sitting in the car among the rows of corn, Jennifer Seidkamp turned to him and said, "Jason, you think too much." He was never quite certain what she had meant, but he found himself recalling the words every once in a while. He did tend to work out a scene in his mind; it was part of his desire to be in control. He wanted things planned out. Jennifer, he reflected, was one who could simply—gloriously— react to the moment. He admired her, he admired anyone, who could live that way.

"You think too much." The statement crept up from his memory now as he imagined a plan for dealing with these events before him. He must have muttered the statement aloud, because Dog lifted his head and issued a quiet half-swallowed bark. Jason smiled, leaned over and scratched the animal's ear. "And you're agreeing with me, hmm?" he said.

The state police arrived just after ten o'clock. Jason knew the trooper. Sheriff Bates pulled up moments later. When they had seated themselves in the living room, Jason went through the entire, implausible story. The officers listened carefully. They watched him as if he were a cornered animal. Occasionally one would glance at the other. Jason knew they were finding it a hard story to believe. Sheriff Bates, particularly, seemed almost intimidated by this clearly unfamiliar territory. In fact Bates was surprisingly uncertain. His usual brash demeanor, so much in evidence earlier in the morning, faded almost from Jason's first sentences. He sat unmoving, with his trademark cigar held still in hand.

When Jason had finished, they asked him to repeat the whole thing. Then they asked him questions, most of which he had to answer, "I don't know."

This process went on until noon. Jason's frustration was mounting. "What the hell are you going to do?" He stared at the men and waited for a reply.

The two officers looked again at each other. Finally the state policeman spoke. "Frankly, Reverend Winslow, I'm not sure. We really can't do much."

"What!" Jason was incredulous. "I've just spent the past two hours describing a situation in which one man's been killed—"

"We don't know that for sure, Reverend," interrupted the sheriff.

Jason was as much thrown by the interruption as by the fact that the man was openly questioning his story. "Well—" Jason regrouped his thoughts and continued "—I *am* certain that my life has been threatened by some lunatic killer. And you're telling me there's not much you can do!" He rose and walked to the window, fuming. He held open the curtains and looked out across the tranquil scene of "downtown" Craig's Harbor. He searched for peace and composure. It did not come.

"You understand," the trooper said quietly, breaking into Jason's thoughts, "that if someone is trying to kill you, he could have done it just now when you lifted that curtain." Jason stiffened slightly, stepped back and let the curtain drift back in front of the pane. "That's one reason why we can't really do too much. We simply can't cover every possibility. We're not the Secret Service."

"And you're not the President," Sheriff Bates added for emphasis.

The trooper glanced up at Jason. He looked uncomfortable, almost embarrassed. "The other reason," the trooper began, "is that technically this is not in our jurisdiction." A look of puzzlement swept across Jason's face and the officer continued. "Technically, this is the FBI's case."

"Or maybe the CIA," interrupted the sheriff. Jason noted a trace of mystery in the man's tone. The comment set off a discussion between the two officers about which agency has authority to do what. Finally they agreed that the FBI should be notified. The trooper called his superior, explained the situation briefly, then hung up. "They'll call back," he announced.

The sheriff looked awkwardly at his watch and stood. "I think I better get going," he said uneasily. When he got to the door, he turned. "Wish there was more I could do." He seemed to mean it. Jason felt sorry for the man. He was obviously feeling as helpless as Jason. Now the sheriff looked down at the floor and spoke quietly. "I'm sure everything will turn out okay." He smiled uncomfortably, unable to look into Jason's eyes. He knew he was not at all convincing.

Jason nodded. The sheriff looked quickly up at Jason, aware he had fulfilled some sort of obligation that suddenly made no sense. The man glanced at the trooper, turned and left.

When the sheriff had gone, the trooper spoke again. "I'll stay until we hear something definite." Jason appreciated his attempt to be comforting.

"Thanks," Jason said. "Would you like a sandwich or something?"

They ate in silence. Finally, the trooper cleared his throat and spoke. "You know, a lot can happen in twenty-five or thirty years. The FBI might know exactly who this Omega guy is. They might be able to take care of the whole business with one phone call." He sipped from his cup, occasionally moving it in small circles, so the coffee swirled inside it. As he stared at the centrifuge he was creating, he spoke again. "I'll tell you something else. I've only been involved in one other case anywhere near like this one. It was a drug case. There was this witness—a woman—who'd had her life threatened. So one morning at five-thirty we just swooped into her home and took her to the barracks. From there we put her in a disguise and took her to a motel in Waterville. For three weeks she never left that place. We checked everything: food, laundry, books, papers, even her damn Kotex. *For three weeks* this went on. Finally, one day, she just up and says, 'Okay, I've had it. I quit. I want to go outside. I want to see my friends. I want to go home.' So she did."

"What happened to her?" Jason asked.

"Nothing...not one damn thing. But you want to hear the clincher? A month or so after the whole thing was over a reporter from the *Press-Herald* comes up to me and says, 'How'd you like the Tiltin' Hilton?' 'The what?' I said. 'You know, that dump over in Waterville...where you were keeping that witness.' I couldn't believe my ears. 'How'd you know about that?' I says and he just smiles. 'Connections,' he says, and all the time he's just smiling. That bastard knew all along."

The trooper put his coffee cup on the table and looked up at Jason. "I'm just telling you this so you'll know what you're getting into." Jason managed a feeble smile. The trooper continued. "I'll tell you one thing. If I was in your position, I'd just pick up and hotfoot it out of town. I wouldn't tell a soul, not one damn person, where I was going. No one. Maybe once I was on my way, I'd give someone a call just to let them know everything was okay, but I'd do it all on my own. Then there's no one to blame but yourself."

Jason was thinking now. He listened to the trooper's words carefully. "Where would you go?"

The trooper shrugged. "Dunno. A big city, probably Boston. Maybe New York. Best place, I'd say, is somewhere where you know the place, but nobody knows you."

Jason thought about these newest options. The advice made a lot of sense to him. A phone call interrupted him. It was for the officer. After a few minutes, the trooper hung up.

"FBI's on their way, Reverend Winslow." The trooper paused for a moment, then continued. "D'you want me to stay?"

"No," answered Jason. "I guess that won't be necessary."

7

THE PEOPLE FROM THE FBI didn't show up until two-thirty. When Jason opened the door, he saw two men in their early thirties.

"FBI, Reverend Winslow," said the taller of the two. They both held out their ID.

"Come in, please," Jason said, examining the cards carefully. He suppressed a smile, a smile stemming partly from relief and partly from the fact that they held their identification cards up for an eternity. None of that movie stuff—a quick flash of the card and then it disappears. So this is the way it's really done, thought Jason.

"I'm Agent Foley and this is Agent MacDougall." Again, it was the taller one who spoke. He was evidently in charge.

"Sit down," Jason offered. They did. Jason watched them. They seemed as ill at ease as he was.

Finally Foley spoke again. "Before we forget, in case we miss something today, here's our card. Give us a call—*anytime*—day or night."

The second member of the duo pressed a card into Jason's hand. "Someone's always there," he added.

"Call collect, of course," said Foley. "It's our D.C. office."

Jason glanced at the card. "William MacDougall. Federal Bureau of Investigation. Department of Justice. Pennsylvania Avenue. Washington, D.C. 20015 (703) 555-2770." Washington, D.C.! If he needed them, what the hell good would it be for them to be in Washington? The two agents had not failed to notice his irritation. Jason shrugged and put the card in his shirt pocket.

"We're here to investigate the Sullivan incident," Foley began. "We understand you were the last person to speak to him."

Even that irritated Jason. Hell of a strange way to get at the reason for their visit, he thought, but they're the professionals. They probably have this kind of thing down to a routine. And they've certainly done their homework.

"We know this may be a little rough—" both men smiled ingratiatingly "—but we're here to make things easier." Then, still smiling, MacDougall went on. "Just start at the beginning. Tell us everything you can think of...."

"And if we have any questions, we'll just jump in," Foley finished. Both men now pulled out notebooks, and as Jason began they made notations.

Jason resolved to try to state only the facts. "Just the facts, ma'am." The words of Sergeant Joe Friday broke into his thoughts. You're crazy, he told himself, then focused once again on what he was going to say. He was determined to eliminate any hint of his overactive imagination. None of his amateur sleuthing, no deductions, no James Bond innuendos. The agents' way of listening and their questions helped him relax and feel confident. He felt that he was, at last, in capable hands. That awareness brought with it a sense of relief.

As Jason talked, he noticed that the two men occasionally glanced toward each other. He wondered if that was significant. One time he noted particularly. "And finally at around seven-thirty or so this morning, this Omega guy called and said he was going to kill me." The agents flashed a look of surprise and stopped writing. Odd, thought Jason. They seemed totally unaware, and yet that was why they were there in the first place.

Foley recovered and tried to smooth things out. "Sorry. It was just that you said that so matter-of-factly." He smiled. Jason reflected on his statement. He had in fact spoken as if he had been reciting a passage of biblical history. He shook his head, noting how quickly he had gotten used to saying that. After a moment, the agents probed him about the phone call.

"Well," concluded Foley, "if there's nothing else, we'll be on our way. And we'll be getting back to you soon, Reverend."

Jason could not believe what was happening. They were leaving, without doing anything, even after they had heard the business about Omega. "What about this threat on my life?" Jason pushed.

Foley glanced at MacDougall. "We'll make our report and alert the local authorities, Reverend Winslow."

"Report!" Jason snapped. "For God's sake, some lunatic is trying to kill me and you're going to file a report!"

Foley's pleasant demeanor diminished somewhat. "Reverend Winslow, this is a local police matter."

"There is no local police!"

"Then county or whatever."

Any sort of comfort that Jason had hoped would result from the agents' visit was now quickly replaced by the same feelings of uncertainty he had had all day. "They're the ones who contacted you!" Again there was a flash of surprise on Foley's face. It was just fleeting and almost instantly his pleasantness showed itself once again.

"It's hard to figure sometimes, Reverend. I know the strain you're under, believe me." Then MacDougall took over.

"I know all this bureaucratic garbage is frustrating, but Agent Foley's right. The local authorities are better equipped to handle your protection. And if it's any consolation, nine times out of ten, there are these kinds of mix-ups. We'll get it straightened out for you."

Jason's head was swirling. It isn't any consolation! he wanted to shout. He couldn't quite see the logic of all these comments, but they were being made with such logical intonations that he thought he must simply be too upset to understand them. Then Foley was pumping his hand.

"Thank you, Reverend Winslow. You've been very helpful."

The men moved quickly to their car. MacDougall, on the passenger side, waved as they drove off.

The ring of the telephone jolted him. He almost determined not to answer it. But then, he did. It was an impulse. Later he would reflect on the value of relying on impulses.

He drew a slow breath and spoke. "Hello, Jason Winslow."

"Reverend Winslow, this is Special Agent Harry Martin calling from the FBI office in Portland."

"Oh," replied Jason, "I'm sorry, but you just missed them."

There was a momentary silence at the other end. Then the man spoke again. "Them?" He paused then continued. "I'm not sure I..." He paused again. "Ah...I'm calling to apologize for the delay. We won't be able to get to Craig's Harbor for another hour."

"But your men just..." Jason didn't finish.

"Reverend Winslow? Reverend Winslow!" Jason barely heard the voice as he checked outside his house. The car was gone. No one was on the street except for little Timothy Bailey on his Big Wheel.

"Who is this!" Jason's tone was one of outrage and anger.

"Sir, this is Special Agent—"

"Look," interrupted Jason, "two men with full FBI credentials just left here. Now, I'd like to know what the hell's going on!"

Jason's outrage was met by silence. When the voice was heard again, it had changed. There was a tenseness to it. "Reverend Winslow, I'm going to record the rest of this conversation."

"No!" Jason heard himself saying. "No more talk. Somebody's trying to kill me. Maybe it's them…maybe it's you. But no more goddamn talk!" He slammed the handset into its cradle. The bell rang from the impact. He stood, his pulse rapid. "What the hell am I going to do?" When no answer came, he asked the question again with more intensity. The phone started to ring again. He pushed the sound into the back of his mind until it was a barely audible drone in the distance. Jason worked actively at his task. His mind raced over the events of the past few hours. It was too much to consider any greater period of time.

What did he know for certain? Whom could he trust? No one. Not true, he argued. There were people in his congregation. But it's not fair to tangle them up in this, he told himself. The local law enforcement people? But… Then he remembered the advice of the state trooper. He seemed to understand better than anyone else. "Don't tell a soul," he had said, "no one. Don't tell them where you're going or even that you are going."

Jason ran upstairs and threw some clothes into a backpack. When he came downstairs, Dog was waiting to go.

"No, Dog, you're going to have to stay here, this time." He'd get the Baileys to take care of Dog while he was gone. Gone, he thought. He didn't know how long he'd be gone or for that matter where he was even going. "Jesus Christ, what am I going to do?" This oath was wrenched from deep within him, and he realized that it was fundamentally, simply, a prayer of utter desperation. He sank to his knees and held Dog tightly. He spoke again, this time more quietly. "God, help me."

When Jason got to the Maine Turnpike he headed south. He stopped at the Howard Johnson's at the Kennebunk exit and called the Baileys to ask them to take care of Dog. "Unexpectedly called out of town," he told them. It was a lie, but he could easily live with it. As he got back into his car, he reflected on the past twenty-four hours. His entire life had become a lie.

Damn it, Jason thought. How come I've lost control? Things like this shouldn't happen to real people. On he drove, on toward Boston, playing all the while with notions of reality and unreality. His life had become a film—a spy thriller. Hell, he thought, this is the scene where the big black sedan is following the hero. "Sure, set yourself up, asshole. Hero? Easy for you to say." He spoke aloud as he glanced in the mirror—just in case. "Damn," he muttered. Not immediately behind him, but four cars back, there it was . . . not black, but the same car that had carried the FBI agents—real or fake—to his home. "Hell," he spoke aloud again. "What makes you think it's the exact same car?" There must be thousands like that one, he thought.

Jason pondered his options. I could just keep going and ignore the car, he thought. Or I could pull over and see what it does. And what if they stop, too, flea brain? I'll make a run for it. "You ass," he muttered.

As he drove along, Jason noticed his apprehension had given way to another kind of feeling. It was not fear; it was something else. It was a feeling he had had only a few times. It recalled to his memory an experience of his early teen years.

Jason's uncle had taken him hunting. He hadn't wanted to go, but his father had told him it would, "make his ol' Uncle Glenn proud." Reluctantly he agreed. He felt miserable the entire day. He didn't like the thought of killing anything. He did not enjoy carrying the rifle that his uncle had given him. The day was bleak. A cold wetness hung in the air. By late afternoon his feet were wet; his nose was running.

"Look there!" There was an urgency in his uncle's whispered words. When he followed the man's stare, he saw the tail of a deer. He stepped, and a twig broke. The deer vanished. He remembered clearly his uncle's look of disgust.

"I'm sorry," he whispered.

"It's okay, we'll get him, you'll see." There was a sense of conviction in the man's voice; he was being driven by a force totally unknown to Jason. Yet as they tracked the animal, Jason felt himself getting caught up in the quest. His heart beat faster. His body grew tense—no, not tense, not exactly; it seemed as though he was more alert. Everything seemed keener. And he realized it was the hunt—the anticipation of the kill. That was what his uncle must have felt. But even as he felt it more strongly, the exhilaration turned to lead. Its weight seemed unbearable. He feared the moment they might find the deer. As he watched his uncle ahead of him, he could tell that the man still felt the excitement. It made him slow his pace.

As they walked, Jason carefully lifted the safety, fingered the trigger and pointed the weapon off to the side. He slipped his right foot behind his left, intentionally tripping himself. As he fell, he pulled the trigger. The explosion echoed throughout the woods. And then all additional sound seemed muffled, except for the low, persistent ringing in his ears. Smoke hung around him and the acrid odor of the gunpowder stung his nostrils. Jason looked up as his uncle wheeled, his face drained and full of fear. And in the near bush, Jason heard their prey escaping.

"Damn it all, boy, what the hell are you doing!"

"I'm sorry." Jason settled himself down to the anger he knew would come.

"You're sorry. Damn! Now he's gone for good. Damn!" His uncle kicked the wet leaves that lay in front of Jason. It remained a vivid picture.

Now, as Jason came nearer and nearer to the New Hampshire border, he felt that anticipation returning. He was baiting a trap. He was planning a strategy and was going to find out whether or not he was being followed.

Jason imagined speeding up—seventy, eighty, ninety miles an hour—moving away from the traffic. Just the way they do it in the movies, and then, with the agents bearing down on him, he'd slam on the brakes, spin around and drive head-on at the villains, forcing them off the road. "Ass!" he shouted.

When he reached the last exit before the turnpike toll-booths, he put on his blinker, slowed and exited. Driving along the wide, arcing tree-lined exit ramp, he glanced in his mirror. No car. He snickered once and shook his head in disgust. Overactive imagination, once again. He was relieved that that was all it was.

As Jason approached the overpass that crossed the turn-pike, he looked down onto the highway. What he saw drew the blood from his face. The car that concerned him had slowed and pulled to a stop in the breakdown lane. It was now moving slowly up the exit ramp.

He fought the panic that was filling him. His mouth dried. "Normal," he shouted at himself. "Go step by step." As he approached the tollbooth, he thought through his next move. Be normal. Roll down the window, hand the card and a dollar to the toll taker. "Nice weatha'," the man was saying. Answer him, Jason's mind screamed. Smile.

"Hope it holds," Jason heard himself say, as he glanced into the mirror.

The car was closing in now. He couldn't really make out the driver's face. The other guy? Ha! He's covered himself with a map!

"Mista', your change. Mista'."

"Oh!" Jason was jolted back to the moment. "Yeah, thanks... There a diner around here?"

"Route 1, south, down a mile on the left."

"Thanks." Smile. Accelerate—slowly! Relax. Be normal.

Jason pulled into Trucker's Haven. Once he entered he moved to the far end of the counter and peered through a haze of cigarette smoke.

"What'll it be?"

Jason was surprised by the question. "Huh?"

"Your order."

"Oh, just a...a...hamburger." Jason's eyes focused now on the woman taking his order. She was young, but looked older than she should. The constant smoke seemed to have turned her skin a chalky gray.

"Anything to drink?" She seemed put out.

"Coke." Jason looked around. Damn, he thought, this is a movie. The diner was filled with truckers. A colorful lot to say the least. A dozen different conversations mixed up into one modern-day Tower of Babble. While Jason watched for what he dreaded, he listened to everything... and to nothing.

"You goin' down home or up ta Boston?"

"Up ta the city."

"Ooh yeah."

"Still drivin' for Stimpson, that ol' bastard?" Laughter.

"Hear 'bout the *Jeannie O*? She got a hell of a haul last night."

"Nice for the crew."

"Them damn pirates, I wouldn't wish anything good on 'em. 'Course, it's kinda nice for me. I'm haulin' some of their stock ta market." More laughter. And more laughter, still. And then the sounds faded. Jason focused again on the road, now strangely apart from the noise around him. The sedan he was waiting for pulled slowly into the dirt parking lot. It bounced roughly in great ruts formed by hundreds of trucks. Dust rose behind it, then swept in over the car.

When it had pulled to a stop, one of the men got out and went to a phone booth. The other stared intently into the diner. Jason wondered whether they could see him as well as he could see them.

"Your hamburger."

"Yeah, okay. Thanks."

"Ketchup?"

"No, no thanks."

A bang startled him, and he jumped. It was just his Coke being slammed onto the counter in front of him.

He stared at the two men—the two men who had questioned him in his home just hours ago. Damn it! he thought. What the hell am I going to do? He could feel the panic building again.

"Excuse me. Do you have a rest room?"

"Round the back, there."

Jason crossed, trying not to look outside at the car, but trying to see the men anyway. As he moved, Jason bumped into one driver who stood at the cash register.

"Je-sus Kee-rist! You got a problem?"

Jason excused himself and wondered how the driver would react if he took the time to answer the man's query.

Jason rounded the corner and stepped into the rest room. It was a misnomer. There was very little restful about it. It held the odors of all roadside rest rooms. Musty, rank, damp, with a stench of rotten disinfectant.

"Now what," Jason muttered. Think. Just relax and think for a minute. Open yourself up to the possibilities. That was how he often counseled people who came to him for advice. Sure, he thought, practice what you preach. He told himself that he was safe. What do you think is going to happen? You think they're going to come in here and "blow you away"? Maybe, he thought. "So, maybe we'll see ya' next trip!" Sounds from outside drew his attention for a moment.

"Don't count on nuthin' these days."

"Well, betta' get movin'. Fish won't keep foreva'."

"Take'er easy."

"A-yuh." Then the sound of one diesel engine winding up drowned out all other sounds.

Jason stood on the toilet seat and looked out the small screened-in window.

A driver—apparently one of the drivers who had just been talking—was checking the tie-downs on the tarp covering the truck. Jason made his decision quickly. He ripped out the screen and boosted himself up and through the narrow opening. Unseen, he dropped to his feet and approached the driver.

"You going to Boston?"

"Yeah." Jason realized now that it was the driver he had bumped into at the corner.

"Can I have a lift?"

"No." The driver started to walk off.

"I'll pay!" Jason was intent. The driver stopped and turned. He just stood.

What the hell is he waiting for? Jason wondered. Then he realized.

"Fifteen bucks—" then panicking "—twenty." Immediately he realized his error. "Twenty," he repeated firmly.

Reluctantly, the driver gestured to the cab, then moved around to the driver's side and climbed up. When Jason had climbed into the cab, the driver turned to him and spoke threateningly. "You get funny with me, and I'll break your goddamn skull." Jason felt a wave of anger flash across him. His eyes cut through the driver, who finally turned away from him.

Once the truck was moving, Jason felt calmer, but the relief was only fleeting. They might see me! He glanced quickly at the driver, then down at the floor. My shoes! Tie my shoes! He bent over—way over—and fumbled with his laces. He waited until the truck was fully on the highway before straightening up.

At 8:00 p.m., Jason stepped down off the truck onto the Boston Fish Pier. He walked around to the driver and handed him a ten and two fives.

"Thanks," Jason said. He meant it. He turned and walked toward Congress Street.

The driver watched his strange passenger. Whoever he was, the driver thought, he was out of place. The trucker frowned and called to the young man who was moving quickly away from him. "Hey!"

Jason stopped and turned. The driver beckoned to him. "Here," the man said, holding out a five dollar bill. "The deal was for fifteen."

"Thanks," Jason said again. He turned and started again for South Station.

DEEP WITHIN THE WALLS of the Pentagon, work continued without regard for the late hour. It was not at all unusual for the people who worked in that dim place. What a few of them did find unusual was the sudden emplacement of a new office. It bore no identifying marks—other than E-1329, a room number—but the people who noticed such things noticed that those who occupied the office were singularly unfriendly. On the rare occasions when someone would run into one of them in the cafeteria or the men's room, they responded coolly.

The other unusual fact was that the room had become the home—almost literally—of one Admiral Fritz Pederson. He had suddenly reappeared after three years of retirement. That was somewhat unusual. That and the fact that he happened to be the man the President trusted more than anyone when it came to military advice—a fact that irritated the joint chiefs no end. Those who noticed such things thought this unusual. Just how unusual, they had no idea, even the marine guards who stood just outside the doors.

"Yes, sir," Admiral Pederson said softly. "It does kind of put a bug in things. But our people are working on a solution."

"This thing is heating up," the man on the other end said. "I can't afford that, Fritz—not just now."

"I understand, sir."

"I know you do, and I appreciate that. But we're down to it now." The tired voice paused. "Do you agree?"

"I do, sir."

"Then I'm authorizing you to go ahead with whatever steps are necessary. Am I being clear?"

"Yes, sir."

"We must get him to show his hand—one way or another—and end it. End it swiftly—quietly. Professionally.

I know that's the only way it *will* be handled with you in charge.''

"Thank you, sir.''

"I mean it. You know I do.''

"Yes, sir.''

"Take care, Fritz. If I come out of this, I'll owe you one.''

"I think I'd just as soon put it to bed and forget it. Forever. If you don't mind.'' There was just the hint of a smile in Pederson's voice.

"God, Fritz, I don't know what I'd do without you. Thank you.''

"You're welcome, sir.''

"Good night.''

"Good night, Mr. President.'' Pederson paused for a moment and then called into the adjoining room. "McCann. Come on in here. We've got something hot.''

While he waited for his subordinate, Admiral Pederson hung up the phone and swung around in his chair. He did it just to feel some movement. He'd been sitting in that chair for hours. He tilted his head back and then rocked it from side to side. This was a tough one; it was messy. And now with the damned minister stepping into the middle of things, it had just become a lot messier.

8

THE MEETING WAS PLEASANT enough. There was a formality to it, though, and it certainly could not have been characterized as congenial. Neither of the men seemed to care about this apparent lack—or even to be aware of it. It did not matter. Mr. Harrington appreciated his employer's courtesy. He was always the gentleman, which was unique in these most ungentlemanly of business agreements.

The man sitting across from Mr. Harrington made stealing, blackmail, even murder seem honorable. The car at the airport, dinner at Le Lion d'Or and soon, the traditional celebrative glass of brandy at his home. An agreement truly among gentlemen. He is a good man to work for, thought Harrington. It was gratifying to have a working relationship with a man of his stature.

Omega touched the linen napkin to the corner of his mouth. "Anything else, Mr. Harrington?" He raised his eyebrows questioningly. Harrington smiled graciously and shook his head.

"No thank you, sir."

Omega raised his finger slightly and instantly one of the waiters was at his side.

"Sir?"

"Check please." The waiter departed and returned a moment later. Omega simply initialed the check, wrote in thirty-five dollars for the waiter and rose.

"Thank you, sir," the waiter was saying, but Omega was already moving away to the door. Just before he exited, he bowed—in deference—to a man sitting in a corner booth. The man was Hargrave Thompson, a recently appointed member of the Supreme Court. Thompson nodded back. In another glance, Omega picked up the location of his "keeper." That was the way he referred to his bodyguard. For an instant, he reflected on the Supreme Court. He was glad they were finally getting some good solid conservatives on the bench. Then his thoughts shifted again, focusing now on the imminent events of the evening. He was savoring them with anticipation.

The bodyguard had radioed the chauffeur when Omega got up from his table. As Omega and Mr. Harrington stepped out onto Connecticut Avenue, the car was pulling up to the curb. Immediately, the keeper opened the back door and the two men stepped in. Once the bodyguard had gotten into the front seat, Omega spoke.

"The shore house, please." The car moved off immediately. Mr. Harrington looked uncertain. "My wife is having some sort of party or something," Omega explained. "I thought the cottage would be more appropriate for our transaction." He smiled. Mr. Harrington nodded and returned his smile.

The air along the Potomac was heavy with mist. A fog was building. The water lapping against the shore was deceptively soothing. There was only one building with lights on along this stretch of the river. If there were others, they were hidden by the mists. The car moved toward the lights, which seemed to beckon them in from the cold.

The two men walked down a flight of stairs that led from the parking area to a deck. Crossing the deck, Omega opened the door and entered. He turned and, bowing slightly, said, "Welcome."

Inside, the chill of the evening seemed only an illusion. The yellow-white lamps illuminated the rich oak furnishings. The glasses on the bar sparkled with crystalline clarity. Oriental carpets cushioned Mr. Harrington's step. The bar was opposite the fireplace. The walls were covered with real wood; mere paneling just wasn't good enough. The space was warm and inviting.

"It's fabulous, sir," Harrington said with genuine awe. He marveled at the man next to him, a man who could call this place a cottage.

Omega cocked his head in acknowledgment.

"Brandy, Mr. Harrington?"

"Yes. Please."

Omega turned to the bar and began to pour some Cognac. It was a rare VSOP, thirty-year-old vintage, but this was, after all, a special occasion.

Harrington stepped closer to the walls. The wood was solid—nothing at all flimsy; some of the boards were twenty inches wide or more. The seams were barely visible. He reached out and touched the surface. It was as smooth as it looked. Each board was polished to a high sheen. It seemed as if a dim light glowed from within the wood, adding its own strange luminance to the room. "What kind of wood is this?" Harrington asked.

Omega looked up as if he had to be reminded himself. "Oh, that's African rosewood. I came across it years ago. When I built this place, I sent over for it. Took months to get it here. And then the workmen took another three months fitting it and polishing it. That's hand-rubbed, Mr. Harrington. Every piece." There was an obvious note of pride in Omega's words. "None of that polyurethane crap on my walls. But getting it through customs was particularly tiresome. My wife says it was worth it, though." Omega finished pouring the drinks, then casually reached into his suit coat's inner pocket. He turned slowly to Harrington.

"Your payment, Mr. Harrington." Harrington looked up and smiled. Omega withdrew an envelope and handed it to the man standing opposite him.

"Thank you, sir." Harrington took the envelope and placed it in his own pocket. He did not even think about looking at the $55,000 check he knew would be there. He had the utmost trust in his employer and he knew the balance on the job he had just completed would be just as he specified.

Omega offered Harrington his snifter.

"To success," Omega said. Both men drank to the sentiment. "Sit down." Omega gestured toward the chair opposite him. Harrington sat. He felt the soft red leather upholstery of the wing-backed chair. He gazed over at his host. As he waited for the man to get on with the debriefing—for that was what this really was—he idly fingered the brass fasteners that lined the outer edges of the chair's arm. Omega sat on a love seat opposite him, sipped his brandy and waited for the right moment.

"So, Mr. Harrington, how did the presentation go?"

"Very well, sir."

"What about this...this... Who is he?" Omega waved his glass to indicate insignificance and continued, "This minister?"

"Oh, him." Harrington shook his head indifferently. "All I know is that Sullivan visited him for a few hours last night. I left as soon as I completed the assignment. And I called you as soon as I could find a pay phone in that goddamn place." Omega looked at him. He clearly wanted to hear more. Harrington continued. "It's just that there's nothing there. A damn little hole carved out of the seacoast with a few houses built around it. It took me twenty minutes to find a telephone."

Omega smiled. "And you found nothing at Sullivan's?"

"Nothing unusual. Except the clippings I mentioned on the phone." Harrington reached into his coat pocket, withdrew a crumpled piece of newspaper, and handed it to Omega.

"You read it?"

"Yes, sir. Seems like ancient history to me. Only thing that made it significant was the fact that he had it."

Fool, thought Omega, as he nodded in response to Harrington's comment. You've just committed suicide.

"Anything else noteworthy?"

"No, sir. Exactly as planned." He paused for a moment, thinking.

"Mr. Harrington?"

"Well, actually, sir, there was one thing." Harrington looked up at Omega. "He seemed too submissive, so ready, almost as though he'd been expecting me."

Omega stared into Harrington's eyes and shook his head. "He must have realized it was his time," said Omega quietly. Harrington placed his glass on the table next to his chair and nodded.

Omega's right hand moved deliberately under a pillow next to him. His hand found the cold steel of his handgun. The warmth of the room had not reached through the pillow; it would be Omega's hand that would warm the weapon.

"What do you think, Harrington, about it being someone's time?"

"Sir?"

"Do you think there's some force in life that determines when it's *your time*?" Omega reveled in the knowledge that he could destroy the man across from him at any moment. Omega leaned forward, half sitting, half crouching, and smiled. In one sense he regretted what was about to happen, simply as a mechanic would regret the loss of a well-used tool. And Harrington was a valuable tool, indeed, but expendable. It would only be a matter of time before he figured out why he had been asked to kill a poor defenseless old man. He should know right now. Even as Omega watched him, his contempt for the man grew. Harrington trusted him too much—too much even to realize the obvious, that he was in the company of Omega and that Omega would kill him tonight in this serenity.

"I wouldn't think so, sir..." Harrington was responding to Omega's question about a life force. The question threw Harrington. It was strange. Harrington continued, trying to lighten the moment, "unless of course, it was you." He grimaced uncomfortably. He realized just how uncomfortable he suddenly felt. His little joke was at best strained. He also now realized that his employer's demeanor was very different from the usual. And slowly he realized that his hands were at rest, fingering the brass fasteners on the arms of the red leather chair. They were far from his own weapon, holstered under his left arm. All these things he realized too late.

"Yes," Omega was saying. He smiled now, relaxed, even congenial. He chuckled politely, though not enough to draw Harrington's attention from the movement of Omega's right hand.

In an instant, the pillow flipped downward. The gun in Omega's hand twisted forward. Harrington's hands moved with lightning quickness toward his own weapon.

The words that would echo throughout Mr. Harrington's journey into eternity would be the whispers of Omega. "...unless it's me, Mr. Harr..." The bullet entered Mr. Harrington's cranium immediately above his right eyebrow. A second bullet entered just to the right of his nose. His head jerked violently backward. His arms snapped straight out for a moment, then his body slumped, totally limp. Death was instantaneous.

Omega smiled. He sat staring at the body for a long time, fingering the weapon, which was now warm in his hand. He was visibly pleased with his performance. Finally he stood up and walked to his victim.

Omega removed a plastic bag from the drawer in the table next to Harrington's chair. He placed the bag over Harrington's head. Again he reached into the drawer and took out a roll of tape. Using the tape, he secured the bag around the man's neck. The removal would be neater this way. With practiced precision, he eliminated all traces of identification. Finally, he removed the envelope from Harrington's pocket, then grasping the body by the arms, he dragged it from the chair. He slowly moved the body outside the house to the dock that jutted out into the Potomac.

Omega checked to be sure the rubber raft he had put in the water earlier in the day was still there. It was, next to a skiff. He struggled briefly as he lowered Harrington's body into the raft. Except for the clank of a chain, there was only the quiet gurgling of water under the raft. Then he climbed down into the skiff. At one point he lost his balance and almost fell.

"Damn!" Omega muttered. Once in the boat, he leaned over the body. Lifting the heavy chains was a struggle, but he worked slowly and carefully, wrapping the body and wiring the chains securely. Then releasing the skiff and raft, he rowed some hundred yards toward the center of the river. As he moved into foggy oblivion, he raised his oars. The water dripped quickly at first, then slowed, leaving a series of rings expanding always into the preceding one. Lowering the oars back into the water, he slowed the skiff just enough to allow the raft to drift past the stern of the skiff.

He pulled the raft's plugs and watched it and its cargo as it sputtered gently into the cold darkness of the Potomac.

When it had completely submerged, Omega looked up. Instead of the satisfaction he expected, another feeling surged through his body. It was so alien that at first he didn't realize what it was. It pressed in on him as he snapped his head from side to side, staring out from the dinghy. It was panic that Omega felt.

With the task at hand successfully completed, the very thing that had aided Omega with his plan now became a fearsome enemy. The fog had surrounded him. He didn't know which way to go. He instantly started rowing, then logic prevailed and he stopped again, drifting. He forced his mind to think—to fight the urge to scream for help, to splash wildly with the oars. Instead, he worked himself into thinking about getting back to the shore. Look for the lights! He peered into the grayness, but saw nothing. Then, yes! There was a light—or did he just think it was a light? There it was again. He blinked; it was gone.

Obeying an impulse, he turned and stared out in the opposite direction. In his careless haste as he abruptly shifted position, the skiff rocked and almost tipped. Omega barely noticed. He was, instead, intent on finding something— anything—that would orient him. He stared straight ahead. But he saw nothing. Just a slight overall luminance, a vague gray . . .

Now Omega heard a sound. Traffic noises. But like the light, they too were dulled by the mist. He had no way of knowing whether they came from the Virginia shore or the D.C. side. Goddamn it, he thought. I'm drifting even farther away. Drifting. *Downstream!* That would put D.C. on the left. He felt more confident now. Once more he reviewed his logic. A hint of doubt crept into his mind. He could have sworn he had come from the opposite direction.

Damn it! "This has to be right," he breathed. He relaxed, dipped his oars into the water. His strokes were now slow, and steady, and firm.

The panic that had dominated him just moments ago now gave way to more familiar feelings of confidence, of being in control. And yet, after he had moved a short distance, the feelings began to creep insidiously back. He hadn't gone this far. He couldn't have. He should have been back by now. Something was wrong. He slowed his rowing once again. The miniature whirlpools created by the oars swirled past him. The sound of the water dripping off the oars into the water seemed magnified. It was more the sound of a stick on a tin drum. Keep going, his mind told him. Row. But his feelings balked.

If he gave in to his doubts, they would paralyze him. Once more he fought the panic and moved on. This time only moments had passed when, glancing over his shoulder, he saw a ghostly shape. It was so strange and ethereal that it startled him at first, but then rowing closer, he saw it was the house. Its presence brought a sigh of relief, and he rowed on toward the dock.

Omega climbed defiantly onto the dock. Before entering the home, he turned and stared out into the misty nothingness. He stared at—through—his enemy, for that was what the fog had become. He addressed it as he would any other enemy. It was real, and it would know he was not intimidated. "Damn you." His eyes narrowed. He spoke more forcefully through his clenched teeth. "Goddamn you." He pulled his collar up around him, for a chill had swept across his neck. "But I mastered you, you bastard. *I* mastered *you*." It was a foolish moment of empty bravado, for while his assault might have persuaded a more human enemy, it had no effect on the mists washing over the Potomac that night. And if nature were a consciousness surely this arrogance would have been seared into its memory.

Deep in his own thoughts, Omega knew, in truth, he had mastered nothing. He had, for the moment, merely escaped. He had been lucky. Perhaps it was that secret knowledge that forced him to turn and move back into the warmth of the house.

He was able to relax now, and in his calm, he replayed the scene that had unfolded just thirty-five minutes earlier. If any residual panic remained, this exercise washed it fully from his consciousness. He sat again in the love seat and evaluated his performance. His demeanor indicated approval. His eyes and the confident smile showed sublime contentment. Just one thing, he thought, he was on to you…just a bit too soon. Omega slapped his hands onto his knees in an extravagant and prideful manner. He rose and spoke aloud. "Not bad, not bad at all." Then his face darkened slightly. "I'll do better next time."

There would indeed be a next time. Two people had known of his involvement with the old man in Craig's Harbor, Maine. Now there was only one, but in some ways, he was the more dangerous. He was an unknown quantity. He was not "in the business," and therefore he could not be expected to react to circumstances in a predictable manner. Regardless, Omega thought, he's no match for me. He was certain of that just from the few minutes he had spent talking with him on the telephone. His thoughts focused again on the task at hand. He put the lights in the living room and in the guest room on a timer, then turned on the shower.

As he walked up to the car, he relished his newfound energy. He felt good. The events were unfolding just as he predicted. With Morrison dead, and now the man who had killed him, Omega was feeling that he was once again in control. It felt like…like what? he mused as he moved toward the car. The sense of power over life had intoxicated him throughout his career. Now he felt it again, as keenly as ever. "Like God," he murmured.

"Sir?" The sound of the bodyguard's voice startled him.

"Nothing," Omega responded in a more subdued tone. He stepped into the car and sank into the velvet cushions.

The chauffeur waited for a command. When none came, the driver spoke. "Are we waiting for the gentleman, sir?"

"Hmm?"

"The gentleman," the driver repeated.

"Sorry," replied Omega. "He's staying here tonight. He's got an early flight tomorrow, and he'll be much closer to the airport here."

"Where to, sir?"

"First, get Mr. Harrington's bags and take them down to him. I told him you'd bring them down."

When the chauffeur returned, Omega spoke again. "You give them to him?"

"He was in the shower, sir. I just left them in the guest room."

"Good." Omega studied the house a while longer. The driver followed his gaze. In a moment, the lights in the bedroom came on, followed a moment later by the lights in the living room going off. Omega was certain that the driver and the bodyguard both understood Mr. Harrington to be fully alive and active in the building below them. "Tell you what," said Omega. "It's early yet. Let's drive around the city once."

The driver crossed over to Constitution Avenue and moved eastward, past the White House, and on toward the Capitol. As they neared 4th Street, Omega spoke again. "Pull over." He got out of the car and walked toward Independence Avenue. A few people passed him and he noticed the momentary glimmer of recognition in their expressions. Some, he thought, would turn and watch him from behind. His bodyguard would be watching them closely. Omega smiled. He was contented; he had come home. Even the people who watched him now as he gazed up at the Capitol did not really know who they were looking at. He was someone altogether different. He was Omega.

A few long moments passed. His thoughts were pleasant, invigorating ones. He felt as though after a long illness he had miraculously been healed. But his exuberance was fleeting. The coolness of the autumn air suddenly bit savagely into his thoughts. The fog had, in fact, followed him up from the river. It seemed to tighten around him, almost choking him. A chill rushed across his body. He turned, looked once again at the gleaming white dome of the Capitol, now slowly fading in the clouds. He turned and strode back to the car. The warmth inside the car quickly drove out the cold. It was reassuring, and once again his sense of accomplishment returned.

He was whole again.

As the car moved back along the exclusive side roads of Washington, he contemplated the image of the only person who he believed could destroy him. The minister. He would take care of him himself. He would arrange for a few days off and kill him. His hand moved back and forth across the soft cushion of the seat, and his heart beat strongly as he planned his attack.

A buzz from the telephone ended his brooding. He reached out and picked up the receiver. "Yes."

"Donlevy here, sir."

"Yes."

"That Alpha/Omega thing?"

"Yes."

"Well, I sent two of my people up there with Bureau IDs to poke around. The local police weren't much help, but they came across this one guy..."

Omega tensed and straightened. "Who?"

"The local pastor," Donlevy replied.

"Damn it," whispered Omega.

"Sir."

"Nothing," rasped Omega. "What about him?"

"Well, he had quite a conversation with Morrison last night... and..." Donlevy was dreading what was to follow.

"Yes?"

"He's gone, sir." Donlevy waited for a barrage of abuse which he knew would come. He grew more uneasy.

"He's what!" The man worked to hide his irritation.

"He's gone, sir. My men had interviewed him and stopped once more at Morrison's place. They were getting nervous because the minister had called the local Bureau office."

"Jesus," interrupted Omega.

Donlevy continued. "They wanted out. You can imagine the embarrassment if the real Bureau people bumped into our people." There was silence at the other end. "Anyway," Donlevy went on, "they were just leaving town, when they saw the minister leaving, too. He was in such a goddamn tear, he never even saw them. Well, they were kind of curious, so they followed him."

"Where'd he go?"

There was silence. Omega waited. When Donlevy spoke again, he was even more subdued than before.

"They lost him."

"Jesus! How could two highly trained..." Omega realized it was pointless. "Damn it! Where's he come from?"

"We don't know," Donlevy responded. "Yet," he added quickly.

"Find out. Find him!"

"Yes, sir." Donlevy paused. "Sir, I really think the Bureau ought to be in on this one. It's in their purview."

"Damn it, Donlevy, I want you people to handle this . . . it's family!"

Donlevy knew he would suffer later for his perceived weakness. But he also knew what he was doing simply was not right. If his superiors or, God forbid, some congressional committee, got hold of this, he'd eat the biscuit for sure.

"One more thing, sir."

"Christ, what else?"

"The minister claimed that this Omega character called him and threatened to kill him. I figure he just got spooked and ran."

"Really? Well, I figure differently. I figure he killed Morrison himself and that the heat was getting too much for him. God only knows what he's really up to!"

Donlevy was puzzled now. What he was hearing seemed ridiculous. But, despite his brutal reputation, the man to whom he was speaking had a keen sense for locating and dealing with trouble. Maybe he should pursue the situation a little more vigorously.

"You still there, Donlevy?" The voice on the phone pulled him back to the more immediate reality.

"Yes, sir. I was just thinking about assignments."

"Do that on your own time."

"Yes, sir."

"And Donlevy."

"Sir?"

"Be discreet this time." Omega slammed down the phone. The bodyguard glanced up into the mirror on the visor and watched the man in the back seat. He leaned back, folded his arms and peered out at the walled homes along Foxhall Road. The bodyguard wondered what kind of phone call could change the man's mood so quickly. When Omega finally turned, their eyes met in the mirror's reflection. The bodyguard forced his gaze away. His eyes focused instead on the misty tunnel being formed by the car's headlights in the thickening fog.

9

HAD JASON KNOWN the success of his escape, he might have relaxed some. But he did not know, and he did not relax. As he walked from the fish pier toward downtown Boston, he considered his situation. "Damn," he murmured. He had no car, no clothes, no food, little money.

Stepping onto the Congress Street bridge, the memory of a cocktail party flooded his thoughts. One of the people there, a salesman—an inebriated salesman—had eyed Jason with suspicion. Then, suddenly, he had grabbed him by the arm, almost lifting him off the floor.

"You know something, Winslow?" the man breathed. "Your problem is that you're not aggressive enough! You know what I mean?" he slurred.

"Not really," replied Jason.

The inebriate nodded as if Jason's response had been particularly illuminating. "I'll tell you." He took a sip from his mostly Scotch and little soda. "Think of it this way. If you and I was both plunked—" a half belch gave emphasis to this word "—down in L.A., without a cent, who d'you think'd get back here first?"

Jason smiled. "Who?"

"You got that right!" asserted the salesman. "I would!" He spilled his drink for extra emphasis.

"And why would you get back first?"

"Because I'm aggressive!" Speaking louder now, the drunk continued. "I'd find a way to get the money for a ticket! I'm a salesman, remember. I can sell my way out of anything! But not you, brother!''

Jason chuckled as he remembered the scene. Anyway, he thought, here's a chance for me to prove the guy was wrong. Only I don't even know where I'm going. He stopped and leaned on the railing of the bridge and watched the reflection of the skyline in the still water. If they, whoever they were, found out about him—*when* they found out, he corrected himself—they'd know he had contacts in Boston and New York, family in Illinois. Where else? He weighed the possibilities. Illinois? No good. It was too far and besides, his only real contacts there were his parents. His parents. Their images triggered a thought that added to the clutter that filled his mind. Damn, he thought, it's their anniversary tomorrow. He was almost sorry he had remembered. No, Illinois is out, Boston is better, he thought. I know more people here. New York? He shrugged. Why bother? I've got better connections right here.

Jason slowly became aware that his teeth were clenched, almost to the point of pain. His jaw muscles ached. He drew in a deep breath and exhaled forcefully. What the hell am I going to get for their anniversary? he thought. He grew angry with himself, and he labored to force the intrusion out of his mind. He closed his eyes and his thoughts turned once again to his dilemma. Where would he stay in either place? A friend of his was the pastor at Old West Church in Boston. He'd be able to find a place for Jason to stay, and he could be trusted. And in New York, who? A few people in church bureaucracies.

Wait a minute. Jason caught himself. You're selecting people whom they could trace. They're all church contacts. He shook his head disgustedly. You need someone else, someone with no such associations. Damn, he thought, there isn't anyone. He considered how narrow his interests really were. All his close friends were religious types.

"Damn," he muttered, "there's got to be someplace." Then one possibility crashed into his consciousness. "I couldn't do that," he said aloud. Why the hell not, he mused. There was someone, without obvious links. She was in Washington, D.C., and he did know the city fairly well; he'd traveled there with groups of kids several times. He straightened and looked downward one last time at the rippling illusion of the skyline. Then he turned and started walking toward the city's reality. He suddenly felt better. He had a goal. He headed for South Station. He would go to Washington and, despite his misgivings, he would give Jennifer Seidkamp a call.

She'll think I'm crazy, he thought. Hell, she always thought that anyway. He remembered how she had reacted when he told her he was going to be a minister.

"You! For Chrissakes, Winslow, what the hell're you going to do that for!"

"Come on, Jenny. Give me a break, huh? Don't you think I'd make a good minister?"

"Sure, but jeez, I just never pictured you..." Jenny broke into laughter. "Christ, are you going to wear one of those collar things?" Her laughter communicated her disbelief better than her words. When she settled down a little, she uttered one more thought. "Shee-it," she pronounced. "Am I going to be able to swear when you're around anymore?" More laughter.

"Sit on it, Jenny." Jason was subdued.

Jenny pressed her hands together, and slowly, deliberately moved them to her breast. She watched Jason's eyes follow her hands and gaze upon her. When he finally glanced upward, to her eyes, she simply smiled that coy smile of hers and looked skyward. She then spoke with a sweetness that was pure mockery. "My goodness, Father Winslow, which chapter and verse is that?"

"God bless you, my child." Jason tried to sound as condescending as possible. He patted her on the head.

"You're one crazy bastard, you know that?" Jennifer spoke with fervor. Her tone had suddenly become more familiar. "Keerazy!" They ended by wiping the tears of laughter from each other's eyes. It could have become a sensuous moment had Jason allowed it, but he did not. He realized now that was the last time he had seen Jennifer. He smiled gently at the memory. He wondered what might have happened had he responded to Jennifer in the way she desired, he wondered how she might have changed in the years between then and now, and he wondered what she really thought of his vocation—and of him. What the hell, he thought. Whatever happens with Jenny, it will be good for a laugh.

God knows I need that, he thought.

Jason bought a ticket for a train leaving Boston at 10:14 p.m. to arrive at Union Station at 8:02 a.m.

The Amtrak agent smiled and handed Jason the ticket. "They call it 'the Senate Special,'" he said wryly.

Jason looked up at him. "The Senate Special, huh?"

The ticket agent smiled again and shrugged.

Jason had some time before the train was scheduled to leave. He went into a drugstore and bought a card for his parents. It irritated him that their anniversary had continually crept into his thinking since he had first remembered. You have more important things to think about, he told himself. And that made him more irritated. They're not more important, he argued, and again, he became aware of the hatred he was feeling toward the presence that was pursuing him.

The train was almost empty. There was a sense of finality as it jerked into its first tentative movement. The rhythm of the wheels on the tracks quickly dominated all that was happening in the car, and for that matter, all that was going on inside Jason's head.

There were only five other people in his car. His eyes scanned each one. His caution bothered him. He had always worked at accepting people unconditionally. As he studied first one, then another, he argued with himself. That's fine . . . except now there *are* conditions!

His gaze passed quickly from a young woman holding a baby to two college students. Then he focused on his last traveling companion. He was a lone male somewhat older than Jason. If there was one person in the car who might possibly be the one, it was he, Jason thought. It was a possibility.

Jason resolved to watch him. Yeah, right, he thought. Watch him. And if he pulls out his whatever and lets you have it, what'll you do then? There'll be little satisfaction in knowing you guessed the right one, that you were "watching him." Well, then, fool, what are you supposed to do? thought Jason. Go up to the man and strangle him? Go up to him and casually inquire if he's Omega? Go up to him and . . .

Jason abruptly snapped his head away from the man and peered out the window.

"Damn it," whispered Jason. "Stop it. No more!" His hot, angry breath formed a haze on the cool glass. The fog came and faded quickly with his short breaths. Don't make assumptions, he said to himself. Just let things be. Let things take their course. Relax. You've got to relax. You've got to get some rest. He reached up and pressed his fingers into the back of his neck. Probing deeply, he found a golf-ball-size knot of hard muscle. He realized that his entire body was similarly tense. His legs ached and his stomach was taut. It had been, for hours. It was as if for the past twenty-four hours he'd been expecting someone to turn around and suddenly punch him full force in the stomach.

As the train rumbled southward, Jason recalled a retreat that he had attended the preceding spring. A woman in the group was into massage. She had taught some of the participants a method for relaxation. Now he focused his full attention on the task. He started with his feet. "Allow the tension to flow away from your toes," she had said. He stretched and arched his feet and worked at relaxing. He felt his feet become heavier, then lighter and lighter, until they almost seemed to be floating in water. He worked methodically for as long as he could remember. At some point, he simply fell into an unexpected sleep.

Jason's rest was encouraged by the train's gentle, rhythmic motion. It was a deep sleep, free from troubling images. It was what he needed most of all. When the conductor passed by to collect Jason's ticket, he was struck by this traveler who seemed somehow apart from this world. He was envious of the sleeping figure. Somewhat in awe, he shook his head. He moved on down the aisle, thinking, here was a man truly at peace.

Jason awoke suddenly. One moment he was fully asleep, the next, fully awake. He glanced at the man whom he had labeled the killer. The man slept. The others did as well. The two college kids leaned against each other. The mother and baby huddled into the corner of the seat.

What had awakened him? He looked around. He saw nothing unusual. He heard nothing unusual. He shrugged and looked at his watch. 6:30. Maybe it was just his normal waking time. He absentmindedly reached down, expecting to pat Dog. He was instantly aware how much he missed his companion. He knew Dog was also missing him. Once he had been away on a month-long trip to Europe. When he returned, Dog would not leave his side for days. He would grasp Jason's hand in his mouth and take him for a walk. Unconditional love. That was the thing about Dog. The animal had no pretensions. He simply loved Jason, and he expected only a similar love in return. Jason stared out into the morning darkness, which was slowly giving way to a pinkish glow.

How come, he wondered, humans have such trouble loving each other? Too many people saw their so-called love as a bargain. I'll love you, but in exchange, you must give me something. Jason sadly shook his head. His eyes shifted focus from the distant horizon to the window just inches from his face. There he found his ghostly reflection staring intently back at him. The two studied each other.

In these moments, Jason considered the past two days. He reviewed the facts as best he could. Now, perhaps for the first time, he was able to think clearly about the events. It was as if the reflection were the person in trouble. Jason felt somehow detached from the reality.

Sullivan had been killed. By whom?

"Omega." He saw the dim reflection mouth the word.

Wrong, he told himself. You don't know that. It *could* have been Omega ... but it could have been someone else. Omega was not alone. Of course not. There were the two imposter FBI agents—Omega's flunkies. He caught himself again. You don't know they work for Omega. Who else would they work for? Someone who wanted to find out who Omega is. A foreign country. Reporters, maybe. Even an individual bent on revenge. Maybe even the U.S. government. Again Jason shook his head. No, he decided, it had to be Omega. And he realized that that was the way he wanted it to be. The prospect of someone else out to get him was something he couldn't even begin to think about.

Omega. The word had taken on a whole range of tones and feelings in the past thirty-six hours. Omega. For a moment, Jason felt as though his entire life was now being controlled by a word, a presence, a thing as fleeting as air, but nonetheless real.

"God," murmured the reflection. Omega took on greater dimensions. The word came to symbolize evil incarnate. The devil itself. Jason forced the thought to dissolve. It was merely an intellectual meandering, and it irritated him. It was simply an exercise, a diversion. Omega might be evil, but he was real, flesh and blood. Wicked, with a twisted mind and a terribly confused sense of justice, but he was human.

Jason snickered. Omega obviously thought his sense of justice was just fine, as long as he could be the judge. It was a flippant thought, but as the Senate Special droned toward Washington, Jason considered the thought's significance. Omega clearly liked the power to judge—to decide the fate of his victims.

Jason imagined Omega at work. Every one of his victims must at some point show some sort of fear or powerlessness. And that would be precisely what Omega would feed on. Jason paused for a moment, and considered his imagined opponent. What if that sense of power or judgment were denied him? How much would it throw him? Enough to cause him to make a mistake? Jason pondered for a while.

Power. Omega must be powerful. And what was the source of his power? His killing? Possibly, but there had to be something else—position, or wealth. He would have to have quite an organization in place for his lackeys to have been able to get to Jason's house so fast. And he would have to have money to pay for it. Correct? Yes, unless . . . Jason tensed. What if those men really were FBI agents? Well, maybe not FBI, but some supersecret group in the government? A part of the CIA. What if Omega were some government bigwig? You ass, thought Jason. You've been reading too many spy stories. Nobody like that would be in government. A murderer? Come on. And besides, what was it Sullivan had said? "My boss wanted someone outside the Agency." Jason rejected much of what he had been considering. Yes, he decided, Omega was powerful, but his strength came through money and the way he used it.

What else was there about the man? Jason's probing turned to Omega's intellect. It was well developed. He was certain about this. In his own warped way, Omega had to have a solid grasp of logic and reasoning. That was evident from the phone conversation. What were Omega's other strengths? What was it Sullivan had said? Omega enjoyed killing. Had Sullivan simply been overly dramatic? Jason decided no. Could this enjoyment also be a liability? Would it make Omega careless?

What *would* make him vulnerable? What did he fear? Was there anything? He had to have some point of weakness. Jason kept coming back to the fact that Omega enjoyed the killing. He enjoyed bringing death. Could it be that every time Omega killed, it allowed him to believe a little more that he could control his own mortality? Control. There it was again. Was it, Jason wondered, as much a driving force in Omega's life as it was in his own?

The changing speed of the train refocused his thinking. He looked at his watch. It was only 7:15. Maybe, he thought, we'll get in early. The slowing rhythm of the train was like a signal for the others in the car to awaken. As Jason watched them straighten up and look around, another question formed in his mind. What was he doing? Was he running away? Was this a defensive move? Or deep down, was this an offense? Was he contemplating his own hunt, was he preparing to go after Omega? Jason surveyed the activity in the car. He sighed, leaned his head back and closed his eyes. Questions flooded his mind, and the answers that were beginning to form were unexpected and troubling.

10

JASON MOVED FARTHER into the telephone booth and pressed the receiver against his ear. The phone rang once. Then again. Jason blocked his other ear to muffle the noise of Union Station. The phone rang a third time.

"At it again, you goddamn pervert?"

Jason was stunned. He paused, debating whether or not to hang up. Finally, timidly, he spoke again.

"Jenny?"

"Who is this!" It was more a command than a question.

"Jason." Now there was a pause at the other end.

"Who?"

"Jason." There was a longer pause.

"Winslow?" the voice said.

"Yeah, Jenny, it's me," Jason replied.

"Oh Christ." Another pause. "What the hell are you doing, calling me at—" there was a fumbling sound "—at . . . quarter to eight in the morning?"

"Sweet ol' Jenny," Jason murmured. "The kind of personality that could grow on you."

"Like a fungus, I know. Hey, Winslow, where the hell are you?"

"Union Station."

"Here!"

"Yep."

"Christ, I'll be right down. Look for an orange Rabbit." There was a pause. He started to hang up. "Hey, Jason . . . never mind."

There was a click. Somehow it was comforting to know Jennifer Seidkamp had not changed all that much.

Jason walked out onto the plaza adjoining Massachusetts Avenue and looked around. There were some new buildings and a different traffic pattern flowing around the station since he had last been in D.C. He shrugged and thought about the traffic in the city. It was crazy. He often understood the government's difficulty in making sound decisions when he saw some of the institution's most creative minds trying to drive their cars down Constitution Avenue. It was downright discouraging.

He smiled as his thoughts shifted to Jenny. He realized that he was anxious to see her again. Three times he started to the curb when he saw a small orange car approaching.

"Relax," Jason breathed aloud. You're like a damn schoolboy. Ease off. He leaned back against the huge stone entryway. He was determined to appear casual. He lifted his face to catch some of the sun that was just beginning to reach over the Capitol. It felt good. He glanced easily around at the morning activity—people on their way to work, a man hawking newspapers, a street sweeper passing by, a group of high school kids walking toward him. They were probably on the kind of tour he'd more than once chaperoned. The sounds of the morning mingled with the things that filled his consciousness.

"Goddamn it. Of all the times for Amtrak to be early." The voice of a man nearby wandered into Jason's thoughts. He absentmindedly listened to two men who had just exited the train station, and as he turned to survey the scene unfolding before him, he caught sight of them. Judging from their appearance, they were a pair of junior executives who had just missed meeting a colleague.

"Early!" the other mused. "I never even figure they'll be on time!"

"Damn it!" spit the first man. With one hand he pulled open his suit jacket and grabbed onto his belt. He raised his other hand to check his watch. Jason thought the man had been looking at too many ads for men's clothing. He smiled at the thought.

Then the second man spoke again. "What makes 'em think Winslow was coming here, anyway?"

Instantly Jason stiffened. He abruptly began to turn to run, but then froze. His mind was alert. Don't do anything to call attention to yourself, he thought. He scanned the scene before him. The group of high school kids was closer now. They might give him the chance he needed.

It was as if he had been jolted by an electrical charge. He could feel the change in him. His heart pounded. The group of students was passing between him and the two men. In his heightened sense, the footsteps of the kids seemed to echo in his ears. He felt the blood pounding through the arteries in his neck. He was alert; he was not panicking, not as he might have done yesterday. He was changing. He was becoming somehow like those who were pursuing him. He felt alive. He was conscious of a subtle fear, but it was the kind of fear a tightrope walker might feel every time he stepped onto the wire.

Now, as Jason prepared to move in among the students, the first man spoke again. "They got a positive on him in Boston."

"Christ," said the other. "What are we going to do now?"

"I don't want to be the one to tell Donlevy."

"Damn!" exclaimed the other.

Jason realized something that momentarily confounded him. As he watched the two men, it suddenly struck him that they were not the ones who had followed him in Maine. He had assumed that only they—and Omega—had been involved. Now there were more, at least two more. How big is this? he wondered. And then he became angry with himself. You can't answer that. Just focus on what you can answer. Concentrate on what's happening in front of you.

Now, as Jason prepared to join the student group, he glimpsed something else, a small orange car. It was Jenny. He could see her at the wheel and she had probably seen him. He knew instantly what was about to happen. She would get out of the car and call to him. The men in front of him would turn to find him standing just a few feet away, and then God knows what would happen.

Now, his mind momentarily blanked out virtually everything around him. Jenny, the car, even the men. Nothing intruded upon his thoughts. Instead, he simply acted—as a consummate performer might: decisively, with deliberate ease. As the crowd of students walked past the men, he fell in step with them. Most didn't even notice him. The few that did apparently thought he belonged with them. But he seemed aware of none of this. Once inside the station he moved out around the group, staying a few feet in front of them.

With the immediate risk past, a flood of questions returned. Who are the men? How did they find me? What's Jenny doing? How big is Omega? Do they know who he is? A shiver rippled through his body. Are there others inside the station? He almost physically shook those questions from his mind and instead focused on the one he had to answer. What am I going to do?

Jason scanned the station, searching for someplace where he would not be so conspicuous. His steps slowed and he realized the students had moved off in another direction. He headed for the men's room.

Across the station, James McCann sat in a chair against the far wall, high up on a riser. Occasionally, he glanced up from the folded *Washington Post* that he held in his lap. Another man stooped in front of him, working on his shoes. Jason was not even aware of McCann's existence, but the minister had caught McCann's attention almost immediately. He smiled and at the same time pressed an earphone into his ear. He glanced upward to the balcony and nodded once. The action was almost imperceptible. McCann then glanced back down to the floor and continued to watch as Jason moved across the rotunda.

"Hey buddy, got a quarter?"

Jason smelled the man before he heard him. When he turned, he saw a tired wreck of a man, who looked sixty, but who could have been much younger. He hadn't washed in days. His shoes were almost nonexistent. His long winter coat, his pants and a ragged ski cap were encrusted with layers of filth. Jason looked past him, through the doors, and saw the two men whom he had overheard, starting to turn toward him.

"Hey buddy," the drunk pressed. He was apparently not used to being ignored.

"Yeah? You want five bucks?" Jason dug desperately into his pockets and pulled out a bill. He flashed it in front of the man's eyes. The previously thin slits widened. "Come on," Jason urged. He took the man by the arm and headed toward the men's room. The man pulled away.

"Ohh, no-o-o, I ain't doin' nothin' weird, you goddamn pervert."

If Jason hadn't been so desperate he would have smiled. It was the second time in twenty minutes that someone had called him that.

"I won't ask you to, I promise." Jason spoke quietly. He used his best ministerial trust-me tones. "I promise," he repeated. "I just want to talk with you." If the trust-me tones didn't work, flapping the bill did. Together Jason and the drunk moved into the rest room.

Once inside, the derelict demanded his money.

"Just a minute," Jason said. "There's something I want in return."

Now the drunk grew more excited. "I knew it! I knew it! Pervert!"

A choked laugh emerged from one of the stalls. There followed a flush, and then the only other patron in the room exited quickly, stealing a furtive glance on the way.

"Look," said Jason. "I want your hat, your coat and your pants...and your shoes." I almost forgot the damn shoes, thought Jason. "In exchange, you get the five bucks, my shoes, pants and jacket."

The drunk looked suddenly sober. "Weirdo," he proclaimed. "Bona fide!" he added with an incredulous tone.

"Take it or leave it. I don't have much time." Jason waved the bill in front of the man's eyes. Again they widened. They were so bloodshot they looked sore. Jason hated himself for what he was doing. He was using the man who stood so hopelessly before him. He knew the drunk would go along with the bargain. Jason felt only empathy for him. He seemed so desperate.

If there were an irony to the moment, it was that the drunk, though living in the dulled stupor he sought in cheap booze, studied the young man across from him. From deep within that stupor, like an erupting, poisonous boil, came an emotion long dormant in the man. He felt sorrow, not for himself, but for this young one who stood, so desperate, across from him. The drunk abruptly turned away, and entered one of the stalls. Jason moved into the one next to his.

When they had exchanged their clothes and dressed again, they emerged and Jason handed the drunk the money.

"Now," said Jason, "go into one of the stalls and wait for fifteen minutes. When you come out, you'll find your shoes and coat—"

"How about the pants and hat?" interrupted the derelict.

"The hat, too," Jason added, "on the curb in front of the station."

"You're runnin' from somethin'." Jason looked at the drunk's suddenly penetrating stare. He didn't respond. The drunk started to turn, shaking his head sadly.

"Hey," called Jason. The man turned. Jason considered for a moment handing him a few more dollars. He'd tell him to buy some food with it. He gazed on the drunk, who now swayed expectantly before him. It all seemed so pointless.

"Thanks," Jason said simply, and he turned and started out.

"Buddy," called the drunk. Jason turned again. "Good luck." Jason nodded and stepped outside the rest room.

He surveyed the concourse. He stiffened. One of the men who had been outside was now practically on top of him. Jason looked down and rubbed his cheek. A day-old beard added to his character. He started to move, but realized he needed to shuffle rather than walk. His pace seemed painfully slow. The man he was trying to avoid walked right past him. Jason heard him mutter something under his breath about rotten drunks.

Across the way, McCann's shoes were being buffed to a high gloss. Although he appeared to be paying attention to nothing, he carefully cataloged the entire proceedings for the report he would write later on. McCann had noted the presence of the two men Jason was trying to avoid. They were only mildly interesting to him. The minister was the important one, and McCann studied him as a zoologist might observe a rare specimen in its natural habitat.

Jason slowly looked across the concourse. He had just avoided one of his foes. But now, where was his partner? With eyes squinted, he looked to the boarding area, then as he hitched himself along, he scanned the waiting area. Moving toward the center of the concourse, he was confronted with a new dilemma.

It was Jennifer. She was approaching the customer service counter. Jason knew he could not get to her in time, but just the same, he felt his gait quicken almost involuntarily. By now she was at the counter, speaking to a man in a maroon blazer. He smiled pleasantly at her. Jason wanted to shout to her, but knew that would be foolhardy. His eyes remained riveted on the scene as it was unfolding in front of him. Now the man was turning and reaching for something. It was too late.

Suddenly the insidious, all-pervasive background music common to all public places echoed to a halt. With that came a silence that, for Jason, canceled out all other sounds. He strained to get to Jennifer as fast as he could without moving too quickly. This apparent contradiction was lost on him in this moment of silence. Then the man with whom Jennifer had spoken pressed a tiny button on a microphone. A click echoed through the station. Jason was almost next to Jennifer now, but what he had feared was already happening. A voice, slow and deliberate, resonated everywhere.

"Jason Winslow, meet your party at the customer service counter."

The last words trailed off in an indistinct jumble. They were interrupted again by the voice as it repeated the message.

"Damn," muttered Jason. He was now at Jennifer's side. "Jenny."

She wheeled around, smiling, prepared to offer a big hello. Jason watched as she caught herself. Before she could offer any protest, he spoke.

"Come on, Jenny, fast." Though he spoke quietly, the desperation in his voice was undeniable. He took her by the arm and together they started moving toward the door. She opened her mouth as if to speak. He stopped her.

"Not now, Jenny."

The tenseness in his voice was easy to hear. She wondered what was happening. She wondered why she was not protesting.

Jason continued. "Walk to your car. I'll be right behind you." He let go of her arm.

She looked at him for just an instant longer, then complied. As she stepped away, she heard his whispered, "Thank you."

The man at the shoe-shine stand rose casually now, folded his newspaper and stepped down onto the concourse floor. He handed a bill to the man who had been working on his shoes. "Thanks," he murmured, as he strode off toward Jason.

Jason wondered how many in the station had seen the strange transaction between the drunk and the young woman. Had the wrong people seen it? He kept moving toward the door. By now Jennifer was a short distance ahead of him. He resisted the urge to turn to see what was happening behind him. He just kept moving. It seemed like one of those strange dreams where everything is in slow motion. Questions again assaulted his thoughts. Had one of the agents found the drunk in the rest room? Had the other one seen Jenny and him at the desk? What was going on behind him? He imagined the sound of footsteps rapidly approaching, then someone roughly grabbing at his arm. What would he do if that terrifying thought turned to reality?

In an effort to calm himself, he studied Jennifer's every move. Finally, she had reached the door. Now she was opening it and stepping through it. He breathed out, feeling as though some momentous milestone had been passed. Once outside, she moved quickly to the right and disappeared around the corner.

When he reached the same door, Jason felt a perceptible relief. He felt a sense of hope. As he exited, he glanced backward. In those few seconds, Jason saw enough to convince him to abandon his role as drunk and to move quickly. One of the men was already at the counter talking heatedly to the customer service agent. The man pointed back toward the trains. The agent shrugged. The other man was quickly approaching, but before he had even reached the counter, the first was moving off toward the trains. He gestured to the other to head out toward the front of the station.

Jason was still totally unaware of the third man, who was approaching from the opposite direction. His only concern was the two men he had first seen on the steps outside.

As Jason moved out past the door, his pace quickened. His legs felt as though he had been running with weights tied to them. He raced across the plaza. The drunk's shoes were cumbersome and he worried about slipping. As he hurried he tore off the coat, then the cap. He looked ahead. Jenny was in the car, and it was running. The passenger door was open. He dropped the coat and cap on the sidewalk and got in. Before he could get the door shut, Jenny had the car moving.

"Just like the movies," Jennifer was saying. Jason ignored her and turned to see what was happening behind him. Neither of the men appeared. In fact, the people out on the plaza seemed unaware that anything unusual had happened. He continued to watch. He thought he had escaped once. Now he barely dared to hope as much again.

When the car finally disappeared around the corner of the station, the man with the fresh shoe shine casually slipped his paper under his arm, pulled out a notebook and wrote Jenny's license plate number. One of the other men now stormed past him, toward the pile of filthy clothes. The man with the notebook turned and moved away from the other. The drunk was exiting the station now, and McCann resisted an urge to stay and hear the conversation that would ensue between the drunk and the man who had been so intent on catching the minister. As he moved up the street toward the senate office building, he smiled at the prospects of that conversation.

In the car, Jason's rapid breathing slowed to normal as Jenny announced, "Regular Bonnie an' Clyde, ain't we?"

"Faye Dunaway never looked better." Jason listened to himself speak. He had actually said that—out loud! He'd been with Jenny less than two minutes and already he'd embarrassed himself.

"You talking to me or the car?" Jenny's response eased Jason's discomfort. He turned to look at her now. It was the first time he had really done so. He smiled. It was good to see her.

She continued. "I'm glad you dumped the rags." She wrinkled her nose, as she stared at him from head to foot. "It would be an improvement if you tossed the pants, too." Again she eyed him coyly. "Know what I mean?" Her lecherous stare made it impossible to ignore her innuendo. She had always reveled in making him squirm. She hadn't lost her touch. He glanced down at his feet.

"Damn," he said disgustedly.

"What's the matter now?"

"I was supposed to leave the shoes."

"You want to go back?" She looked in deadly earnest.

"Right." Jason's exhaled word was filled with sarcasm.

They drove on, each wondering what the other was thinking. A minute passed, then two. Then without warning, Jenny swerved to the side of the road. She slammed on her brakes. Jason was totally unprepared. He lurched forward, almost hitting his head on the windshield. Had she seen something? What was going on? He turned quickly, looking out the back window, then back to her.

"Okay, Winslow, what the sweet Sally Shitski is going on!"

Jason grinned in spite of himself. One of Jenny's trademarks was her unusual constructions when it came to foul language.

"Sweet Sally Shitski?" Jason repeated.

"Winslow." Her tone was a foreboding don't-mess-with-me one. She sounded like a mother who was about to trap her child in a monstrous lie.

"First tell me why you called me a pervert," Jason baited her. She looked puzzled for a moment.

"Ohh," she said, rolling her eyes. "I've been getting obscene phone calls lately. Usually two or three in a row." She smiled, slightly embarrassed. "I got one this morning just before you called." Jason nodded with an exaggerated movement.

"Christ, it's the truth. First, he said—"

"That's all right! I believe you," Jason interrupted.

"Ah, that's better." She paused, then unable to wait any longer, she exploded. "Jeez, Winslow, get on with it!"

"Do you have a couple of hours?"

"That bad?" she asked.

Jason simply shrugged.

"What's the matter," she pushed. "You kill somebody?"

Jason shifted slightly. "Close." He glanced up at her, then, as if that were too painful, looked quickly away.

Jenny stared at him for a long while. This wasn't the Winslow she remembered. She had been aware of something new almost immediately. It was etched into his face. It almost seemed like—she searched for the right word—like fear. No, she thought, no, it was more than that. It bordered on utter desperation.

"You had breakfast?" she asked in casual defiance of the emotions flooding in upon her.

"No."

"Bacon and eggs okay?"

Jason nodded.

"My place?"

Jason looked up, smiled appreciatively and nodded again.

11

CHRISTOPHER DONLEVY SETTLED down behind his desk, picked up the secured folder and slipped his finger under the heavy paper band that sealed the package. When he lifted the seal, it split open with an audible snap. The rip slashed across the words: CLASSIFIED. KEEP SECURE. He removed the contents, then leaned back to read his installment of the Daily Intelligence Briefing.

Donlevy read through the first report synopsis. His assessment: more of the same crap about some hole in who-knows-where. He got through the first two paragraphs, then let the papers slide onto his desk. He looked away, lost in thought. Abruptly, as if to shake off the effects of some drug, he looked at his watch. He went back to the papers, realizing that he hadn't retained anything he had just read. His eyes moved across the first paragraph. Again he looked away.

"Damn it!" he cursed. He swung around in his chair and studied the Wyeth print that hung behind his desk. It was a serene scene, one that often calmed him. Its title was Perpetual Care. He sighed, rubbed his finger across his lips and continued to gaze at the picture of the country cemetery.

He despised what was happening. Through mere bureaucratic power-brokering, he was being asked to do something illegal, something expressly forbidden by law. And yet here he was, authorizing it to go on. It was not a case of simply allowing it to happen—that would be bad enough—no, this was worse. He was pushing his men to proceed.

Damn! he thought. What would the director say if he knew? Why in hell did I get fingered to do the damn job? He felt stuck in the middle. It was, he reasoned, really quite simple. He could refuse the man who had personally asked him to check this out. He could, but it would be out-and-out professional suicide. There were stories about what had happened to others who said no. On the other hand, he sure as hell couldn't tell his superiors. He was painfully aware of the truth. With something like this, they never wanted to know. Why would this time be any different? If they knew, they might feel forced to make a stink about it, and that would amount to one hell of a fight. No matter how he figured it, his ass would be the one in the trap. No, there were no options. Donlevy knew it had to go down the way it was.

"I hope to God nothing goes wrong." The words were quiet bursts of moist air hitting his hand. His eyes remained fixed on the painting.

A buzz, sounding strangely distant, brought him back from the country cemetery to reality. He pressed a button on his phone and spoke.

"Yes?"

"Mr. Cary on two, sir," said the electronic voice.

"Thank you, Helen." Donlevy took a breath and pushed another button. "Hello."

"Cary here, sir."

"Well?"

"No luck."

Donlevy closed his eyes and allowed a long, slow sigh to escape from deep within. He decided to vent some of his frustration. He spoke quietly, but with an intensity Cary could not mistake. "What did you say?"

"We almost had him, but he was on to us."

"How in hell could he be 'on to you'?" asked Donlevy, mimicking the agent's words and tone.

"Sir, I don't know, but he was. He traded some clothes with a drunk, and—"

"Okay," interrupted Donlevy. "Okay. What are you going to do now?" It really was a simple assignment, Donlevy told himself. "Christ almighty, what was so hard about that? Now you've got us in an even bigger mess!" Again he paused. "I asked you what you're going to do now." He knew exactly what his agent was thinking. He could predict the words. "We're going to do anything we can. We're going to start from scratch."

"We're going to have to start from scratch, sir," the agent said.

Donlevy saw no irony in Cary's words. His silence indicated his disapproval.

"One thing, though," continued the agent. "He had someone meet him."

"How do you know that?" demanded Donlevy.

He's going to love this, thought Cary. "She had him paged."

"Christ!" Donlevy sounded defeated. "And you still didn't…" He stopped, feeling no compulsion to finish what was depressingly obvious. The long silence that followed was worse for the agent than anything Donlevy could have said to him.

When the silence had become too uncomfortable, the agent spoke again. "We got a good description of the girl, though."

"Terrific. Great. Wonderful. Send me a copy." Donlevy slammed down the phone on the cradle. And suddenly he was embarrassed. He did not usually do things like that. Now the embarrassment grew into anger. It grew more and more as each minute passed. But the agent wasn't the proper object of his anger, that he was sure of. At first he thought his anger should have been directed inward. Then, as he searched out its source, he realized the truth. The anger was caused by a phone call he knew would inevitably come. The caller would ask about progress in the matter at hand. Donlevy would report that there was no progress. He would have to listen to a predictable tirade. As he prepared himself for that moment, he knew all too well the object of his simmering fury.

"Hell!" murmured Donlevy as he suddenly straightened up. "Who in hell does he think he is that he can put me—put the whole damn Agency in such a goddamn tenuous position?" Donlevy's indignation was short-lived. His forthright and accurate assessment was tempered by another, one that he assumed to be equally accurate: I *know* who he is, Donlevy thought. And he slumped back into his chair. He was defeated. He listened to himself as he whispered the words aloud. "I know who he is."

But in fact Donlevy did not know who the man was—not really.

12

JASON STOOD AT THE kitchen counter with his back to Jenny. She watched him as he prepared his breakfast. "So tell me," she said, "what's up?"

Jason cracked an egg on the side of the frying pan and dropped it into the bacon fat. It sizzled furiously at first, then quieted. He turned to her. "Someone's trying to kill me."

Jennifer worked to keep her composure. It wasn't the statement that hit her; it was Jason's tone. It carried an awful sense of finality. It was cold, unmoved, unquestionable. The pronouncement had hit Jason, too. Jenny could see that.

The words were like a crystalline wedge, sharp and utterly transparent, but a thing of substance, nonetheless, a thing slicing between the two of them and forcing them apart. Both reflected on these terrible words. For Jenny's part, they were totally alien, lacking any point of reference. For Jason, it was exactly the opposite. Richard Sullivan had provided an undeniable point of reference two nights ago. Jason suddenly felt closer to the dead man than he ever imagined possible.

He was also struck with an uncomfortable irony. For years his work had focused on getting others to make their own statements. The quasi-therapeutic jargon called for "making 'I' statements." He worked hard at stating things in such a way as to elicit dialogue rather than agreement or disagreement. It was an intentional style of ministry that he worked hard to maintain. Now his sudden abruptness surprised him. There was no room for conversation here.

"Well, for God's sake," Jenny interrupted his thoughts. "You don't have to sound so definite."

Jason coughed a hollow laugh, and this, too, reminded him of the man who had been Alpha.

They were silent as he cooked his meal. It allowed each of them to rehearse the next scene. Then, as he ate, sitting across from her, looking into her eyes, he related the events of the entire previous forty-eight hours in detail. He started with the Sunday morning meeting in church with Sullivan.

"You know something?" Jason remarked at one point. Jenny shrugged. "I think I've got it memorized."

"When this crap is over," Jenny responded, "you'll be able to go out on the speaker's circuit. I'll line you up with my boss's agent." She smiled in a way that seemed more like a challenge than anything else. Even so, the thought left Jason with a strangely refreshing sense of assurance. It was the first time he had considered that his life could actually return to the kind of normality he had known two days ago. The fact that someone else saw the possibility strengthened him. That Jenny had said it out loud made things seem suddenly better. But the sense of hope was fragile and in an instant it had shattered into sharp and fearsome fragments, for almost immediately he realized the other possibility.

Yes, the situation could be resolved, but in Omega's favor. Or worse, what if it were *never* resolved? Would he ever reach a point when he wouldn't worry about being tracked down? How long could he live without knowing what might happen? Could he survive as Sullivan survived? For as long? The words of Allen Funt on "Candid Camera" found a sardonic paraphrase echoing in his thoughts. "Somewhere, sometime, when you least expect it...smile. You're in Omega's sights."

He forced himself to concentrate once again on the details of the story. As he talked, Jenny listened attentively. Jason was aware that she was being unusually subdued. It was a state that belied her growing uncertainty. Occasionally she would ask a question. Sometimes he could answer; other times he could simply shrug and gesture helplessly. Her questions were always asked to clarify his own perceptions. They were helpful and he desperately wished he had the answers to all of them. He was glad he was with her. For the past two days he had felt so alone. Now those feelings faded.

When he got to the part about the FBI or whoever they were, she interrupted. "Then neither of them was Omega?"

"No," said Jason tentatively. He did not quite see how she had made that assessment.

She continued. "If this Omega character was really intent on killing you, he would have come alone and done it. Why would he involve anyone else? Then they'd have something on him as well. The circle would be getting bigger. But if he did it himself, the circle would be..."

"Ended," completed Jason. He considered Jenny's thought. It made sense, except for one thing. "Then what are these other guys doing?" Jason asked.

Jennifer shrugged. "Maybe they're just keeping tabs on you."

"Until he's ready to..." Jason stopped.

"To blow you away, waste you," said Jenny, abruptly battling her feelings of heaviness. She smiled, as if issuing a challenge. Jason accepted.

"Yes, that's the phrase I was searching for," said Jason. "Thanks." He rolled his eyes upward.

The questions that had hammered at Jason throughout the past days formed again in his mind. Who was Omega? What was he like? Because there was no way to answer that rationally, Jason's imagination took over. It created a scene from the Old West.

The dusty street of the town suddenly cleared as a clock somewhere struck noon. A glance at his pocket watch told Jason that the hour had arrived. He stepped out into the street. At the far end of town, a figure stood with his back to Jason. So this is Omega, thought Jason. The figure started to turn. At last I'll see who he is. In the brilliant noonday sun, the man's face remained hidden in the heavy shadows of the hat he was wearing. Where Omega's face should have been, there was simply blackness.

"Jason." The sound startled him. He turned to Jenny. "You left us. Gonzo. Space cadet." She followed this with an eerie whistling humming sound. "O-o-o-whew-o-o-o." She smiled. Again, she was poking fun at his preoccupation with the enormity of the situation. And again, it was okay.

"Sorry," Jason said sheepishly. He continued telling her his story, ending finally with his experiences with the drunk at Union Station. When he had finished, they sat in silence for a long time. Jenny watched him working to make sense of things. She could see him thinking the way one can see others struggling to lift stacks of wood. But just exactly *what* is he thinking? she wondered. She frowned. She didn't have a clue. After several minutes had passed, he looked up at her. When he spoke, his words sounded different. The hard edges had been smoothed. He was gentler.

"Jenny, I've got to say this to someone," Jason began. "I hope you understand." He took a breath. "It's not the threat...or the uncertainty...I think I can live with that. But I'm not sure I can live with what it's doing to me." The look of desperate helplessness flowed back into his being. He continued. "It's changing me. I'm being forced away from everything that I've cared about for the past ten years.

Everything. Peace, and justice, and truth...and in their place, I'm living with lies, and violence, and...using people." Peace, truth, justice—it sounded like the Boy Scout oath or something. He shrugged. Now that he had actually said the words, he felt even more uncomfortable. It all sounded so naive.

Using people. Jenny thought she saw a wave of nausea course through him as he said it. She had to look away for a moment. His morality was embarrassing. Even in the midst of this, he was responding with a sense of almost childlike innocence. She thought of all the people she knew who used people the way she used a paper towel. In fact, she was aware—at the moment, painfully aware—of those times in her own life when she had been guilty of the same thing. But Jason was different; he always had been. She had always sensed a unique quality in the man who sat across from her. In some ways he was naive, perhaps even unrealistic, and yet, at the same time, he presented an overpowering attraction.

She found herself responding to his words, but not really saying what she was truly thinking. "It will be okay, Jason. I know it will." That's a lie, she thought. She knew the empty comment did nothing to ease her vague discomfort. She doubted it had any effect on Jason, either. She paused, then added hastily, "And you're welcome to stay here as long as you need to." She said it as if the idea had just then burst into her consciousness. She knew, of course, it had not. From the moment he had stepped into her apartment, she had hoped he would be staying. Her anticipation and hope overpowered the guilt she was now feeling. At this moment, she was glad he was here—regardless of the reason. Was there anything wrong in that?

Jason had come to the end of his story. Now both he and Jennifer sat quietly, not speaking, as if each was unaware of the other's presence. Though unspoken, they shared similar thoughts, thoughts about life and how quickly it can change.

When she could no longer bear the silence, Jenny spoke in a burst of energy. "Kee-rist, what a stench!"

"It's not me, it's..." Jason began a quick reply.

"What's this? A little defensive, are we? Maybe it *is* you!"

"It's the pants!" He sniffed the air, then looked at Jenny quizzically and frowned. "Maybe it is me," he added. "Mind if I use your shower?"

"Anything to clear the air," Jenny answered. She led him to the bathroom, and pointed out a towel and facecloth.

"Jenny..." Jason continued reluctantly, "ah, I had to leave my luggage in my car."

Jenny sized up the situation immediately. "No clothes."

"No clothes," confirmed Jason, with a somewhat pained expression. "And I'd like to get rid of these pants as soon as I can."

"Promises, promises," said Jenny, smiling lewdly as she turned away from him. "Tell you what. I'll see if I can get some from Walter. He's about your size. Looks a little like you, in fact."

Again Jason seemed tentative. Cautiously he asked, "Your boyfriend?"

"My what! Boyfriend!" Jenny's laughter was unchecked. "Hell, no. He's...just a guy. Lives upstairs."

Now Jason shrugged sheepishly and reddened slightly. Mind your own business, he thought. He smiled self-consciously, stepped into the bathroom and closed the door.

"Leave the clothes outside. I'll throw 'em in the washer," Jenny called.

"Thanks," came the muffled response from the other side of the door. "Dump the pants," continued Jason. "Wouldn't want the machine to have a breakdown!"

Jason slowly removed his clothes. When he heard the apartment door open and close, he dropped the clothes out in the hallway. He realized now just how filthy the pants really were. A shiver of disgust surged through him.

He stepped into the shower and pulled the curtain closed. A combination of hot water and thick lather convinced him that he was really getting clean at last. The steamy shower seemed to cloud his mind. It lulled him, and he was grateful.

Suddenly the bathroom door swung open, jarring him from his relaxed state. He almost lost his balance.

"Take it easy." Jenny sounded as though she were practically whispering in his ear. "It's only me. Here's some clothes." She paused, then added, "I hope you like his taste." This was followed by the distinct sound of snickering. What's she up to now? Jason wondered. "I borrowed a razor, too. I'll be down in the laundry." Again she paused. "Don't drown!" she called as she exited. After a moment, the apartment door again opened and closed.

"God," Jason murmured, "she makes me nervous." As he turned off the water and stood dripping in the tub, he thought about his decision to stay with Jenny. He was glad to be with her. In fact, he felt excited just by being around her. But he was also uneasy. He was aware of a growing feeling that he would be in the way. How could you be anything but? he asked himself. You just show up, and expect God knows what. You could really screw up her life, to say the least. But, he argued, hadn't she said he'd be welcome to stay as long as he wanted? Right, but you know how people are. He'd talk to her. It was simple enough. He reached out and pulled back the shower curtain.

As he stepped out of the shower, he glanced down at the clothes and razor sitting on top of the toilet. He frowned, almost as a reflex. On top of the pile, just under the razor, there was neatly laid out a pair of—what were they called? There were a dozen brand names for them, but they amounted to those bikini underwear briefs for men. He always felt somewhat embarrassed when he saw them displayed in department stores. "Damn," he said, sighing. She did this on purpose. Big joke. She's probably laughing her ass off right now. He chuckled in spite of himself. The shirt was no prize, either. It was just about the gaudiest purple print he'd ever seen. Walter. He ran the name around in his mind. I can't wait to meet the guy, he thought.

He toweled himself off, wrapped the towel around his waist and began to shave. He heard the apartment door open again.

"Jason! Jason!" Jenny was obviously excited. He could hear her footsteps fast approaching. As he bent down to rinse the shaving cream off his face, she again burst into the bathroom.

Jenny knew instantly she had intruded. Jason's eyes narrowed ever so slightly. He probably wasn't even conscious of the change, but she was. She half expected him to say, "Can't you knock?" but she didn't give him the opportunity.

"Jason, what's this?" She held up a card. Not waiting for a response, she continued. "I found it in your shirt pocket."

"Jeez..." he exhaled, with a grimace that more than adequately expressed his feelings of stupidity. He squeezed his eyes closed and frowned. The frown was followed by a long sigh. "I forgot all about that. It's the card those men gave me. Supposed to be the FBI offices here."

Now Jason forgot about the silly discomfort caused by Jenny's intrusion. Instead he was caught up in her unchecked exuberance. He looked from Jenny to the card, and back to Jenny. He grinned.

"Maybe it will be simpler than you thought?" Jenny expressed his thought, his hope, exactly.

Then suddenly, his face darkened. "But it's a fake! Bogus! They must've figured I'd never use it."

"Christ, Winslow! You're supposed to be the optimist in the group. Isn't that what you get paid for?" she needled.

"Only at Christmas and Easter," he responded in kind.

She looked at the card again. "Well, I can tell you this much: the address? The J. Edgar Hoover Building, at Pennsylvania and 10th?"

"Yeah?"

"That's really the address for the FBI's main office."

Jason grew more sober. This was beyond him. All these things were. The feelings relentlessly gnawed at him. Again, he felt things slipping away. Moment by moment, his ability to control his own life grew hazier.

"But," Jennifer went on, now seemingly far away, "the area code's not D.C.'s . . . it's Virginia." Again they glanced at each other.

"Hurry up and get dressed," she urged. "This is getting exciting." She stepped backward into the hallway and closed the door. "He who hesitates is lost," she taunted from the other side of the door.

When he emerged from the bathroom, he found Jenny sitting cross-legged on the sofa. She gazed intently at a page in the D.C. phone book. She looked up.

"Well?" she asked. He looked puzzled. "Everything fit okay?"

He was thrown off guard, and his answer was careless. "Like a glove." Only after he said it, did he realize what he was saying, but it was too late. He reddened obligingly as his mind flashed to the underwear. Damn, he cursed himself.

She had always set him up like this, and he'd always managed to respond to her satisfaction.

Jenny's eyebrows lifted. "Like a glove," she said brightly. "Yes, I'll bet they do." Her eyes flashed deliberately downward to his pants, then back to his eyes. She was delighted by his flustered state.

Damn, he thought. "Subtlety, Jenny. You haven't lost it."

"Never had it to lose," she answered without missing a beat, then, mercifully, she looked back to the phone book. Her smile, however, remained.

"It's not here...the number, I mean. The exchange is for McLean, but there's no FBI office listed for out there." It was disturbing news and their silence confirmed their uneasiness. Abruptly, Jenny reached for the telephone.

Jason's eyes widened. "What are you doing?" he asked.

"I'm going to call." Jenny's tone was just slightly condescending. It had an implicit "What do you think I'm going to do?" attached to it.

"No." Jason spoke with an explosive urgency.

"Why the hell not?"

"Because..." He paused, thinking, then continued. "Okay, we'll call, but from a pay phone."

"Why not from here?"

"So they can't trace the call."

Jenny's face took on an expression of skepticism. "D'you really think..."

"We need to?" Jason completed her thought. He simply nodded.

As they walked to the elevator, both felt a sense of anticipation. Both felt like explorers anxious for the first glimpse of a distant, uncertain goal. There was a sense of hope, but also a lurking feeling of fear, of uncertainty. While they waited for the elevator to arrive, Jason talked about something that had the promise of an easier solution.

"Jenny?"

"Yeah?"

"I've been thinking." He paused. "You don't have to come along with me...." He looked for some sort of reaction. There was none. He continued, "Ah, don't you need to go to work? I mean..."

"You kidding? And miss this!" He rolled his eyes, then she continued. "Listen, Jason, let me try something on you. I've been thinking about this since you started telling your story. Now don't get all hot and bothered, just listen. This'd make a great feature...hell, even a book!" Jennifer glanced at Jason in much the same way he had glanced at her just moments ago, looking for some reading of feelings. He had had trouble reading her feelings; she was having no trouble reading his. "When it's all over," she added quickly. Jason looked down at the floor. "I mean, I won't ever mention it again if you don't want to, but I was thinking, it would be a great way to get some unbeatable help." Jason looked up questioningly.

"How?" he asked.

The elevator arrived and the door opened. Jason turned from it to Jennifer. She took a breath, and began with some intensity.

"I have a friend, well, actually, he's Eleanor's friend—an acquaintance, I guess you'd say—who works for Drury."

"Who?"

"Who's who?"

Jason smiled and shook his head. "Eleanor. Or Drury. Take your pick."

"Eleanor's Eleanor MacMillan. Drury's..." She paused and grimaced as if tasting something sour. "Drury's... you know, LeRoy Drury." Jennifer watched a flash of understanding pass across Jason's face. She moved the plot further. "He's got more power and more contacts than most of the cabinet. My friend—my acquaintance, Eleanor's friend," she corrected herself, "is on his research staff. Christ, it's like a mini-CIA."

"Just what I need—more spies," mumbled Jason.

"Except they'd be working for you...if Drury likes it. If we can get to him." Jennifer thought that little doubt might help to build her case. "Suppose we make the call," she continued. "Suppose there's more to it than simply a fake number."

Jason shrugged. "I don't know. I was thinking about talking with the CIA anyway...just to see if they could tell me anything about Sullivan." Then suddenly he was drifting off somewhere. Jennifer could see it happen. "It's weird," he said reflectively. "You know a man for years. You see him function day in and day out. You think you understand all there is to understand. Then one day, all of a sudden—" Jason shrugged "—you discover he's someone entirely different." Again he paused, and summed up with, "Weird."

Jason intrigued Jennifer. He seemed to function on two totally different levels at the same time. One was the conscious, present level, but the other was faraway, disinterested. Only rarely did the two become entwined. But no, she thought. This is not disinterested, it's dispassionate; he's present but apart, somehow aloof.

She reflected on her memories of him from years past. Even in the moments of highest passion in his life, she thought he had been able to function on this other level, almost as an impartial observer. She had run into these qualities only in a handful of other people. They were all in positions of power, either in government or business. In a way, Jason puzzled her, even troubled her. Why, she asked herself, when he could have done so many other things, did he choose to do what he was doing with his life?

There was something else. Although the thought wasn't fully formed, Jennifer was sensing a contradiction in Jason. He seemed to have enormous control over his life, yet he was so different from others who commanded the same sort of power—Drury, for example. While the others hungered always for more power, Jason acted as if he had no power at all—or desired it.

Jennifer considered his present situation. Surely he must realize he couldn't fight Omega on his own. Surely he knew he would lose. Why, then, was he resisting the offer of help? Did he fear losing control if he were to accept? Jennifer caught herself. Control, she thought. Who was he, that he could have any real control? How could she actually think that he did? He couldn't have, not when compared to someone like Drury. Then what is it, she asked herself, what is it about him?. Power where there shouldn't be power. And more confusing, such vulnerability in the midst of that power. It was a contradiction, one without hope of resolution.

Jennifer returned to the matter at hand. "Drury's people could make one phone call and find out whose phone number that is. Like that," she added, with a snap of her fingers. "They could make another call and get any info the CIA has on Sullivan—any they'd give *you*—and more. And I'll tell you something," she went on. "It would take you weeks, maybe months to get what LeRoy Drury can get in a day."

Jason stared at her for a moment, fingering the fake business card. He reached out and pushed the Down button. As the door opened in front of them he looked back at her. He shrugged. "I dunno. Maybe."

He stepped into the elevator, and she followed. Jennifer shook her head and made a low growling sound. She had presented her case perfectly, and yet somehow, he had disregarded it completely.

Once the elevator started moving, Jason spoke again. "Maybe I ought to find another place to stay."

Jennifer was dumbstruck. Her feelings were fully evident in her response. "Why!" Its intensity surprised Jason—and her.

Jason shrugged and frowned. "If for no other reason, simply because I'm going to be a royal pain. I mean, you've got your own life." His eyes searched hers for any messages. She seemed hurt. And disappointed. For some reason that surprised him. "You're a free spirit, Jenny, you know? Your life-style and mine..." He snickered once and shook his head. "They're just...different," he said softly.

By now the elevator had descended to the lobby. Impulsively, Jenny reached out and punched the red Stop button. Somewhere in the bowels of the apartment building an alarm sounded.

"For Chrissakes, Jenny, what are you doing?"

"I just want to say something. First, yes, I do live my own life. Don't we all? That's one. Two, I think you called this morning and asked for help. I want to help. Simple enough, so far? I think so," she answered her own question. "And three..." She stopped and changed her thought. "Winslow, this has got to be one of the all-time goddamnedest, most bizarre conversations ever. And three, where else would you go?"

He shook his head blankly.

"And another thing," she continued, "four—if you're keeping count—if you *are* going to stay, let me make a suggestion: you watch out for the Reverend Jason T. Winslow, and I'll watch out for Jennifer P. Seidkamp! Deal?"

Jason was amused by her forcefulness. He also realized she was absolutely correct. He *had* been making decisions for her. What he had meant as concern got expressed as condescension.

"I'm sorry, Jenny. I would like to stay, but on one condition." Jennifer folded her arms and frowned. "If it ever," Jason went on, "gets to be a problem—in any way—tell me."

"You'll be the first to know," Jennifer responded.

"Now, can we shut that bell off?" asked Jason.

"Done," said Jennifer, removing her finger from the button.

The door obediently opened. The two occupants stepped out just as the building supervisor stepped into the lobby from the stairway. He looked questioningly.

"I fixed it, I think," Jennifer volunteered.

"Yeah?" the man replied. "What was wrong with it?"

"I don't know," Jennifer called over her shoulder as they walked out the front door. "I think I leaned against the button."

Jennifer led Jason northward, through her neighborhood. It was a pleasant area in the southwest section of Washington. It couldn't be called elegant—like some parts of northwest Washington—but it was comfortable. It suited Jenny. Jason felt that almost immediately. It seemed as though she fit here as he fit into life in Craig's Harbor. But now, right now, being here with Jenny somehow seemed exactly right. He felt unusually contented as they walked together up the street. It was quiet and warm and hopeful.

13

JASON AND JENNIFER WALKED a few blocks north, then crossed M Street. They found a phone booth just outside a People's Drug Store. Jennifer, they decided, would make the call. If there was something unusual about the number, maybe the people on the other end would be thrown off by the fact that a woman was calling, not a man.

Jenny deposited the coins, glanced at Jason, and then dialed. Jason moved closer. The phone rang just once. Then a pleasant-sounding female voice answered.

"Good morning. Federal Bureau of Investigation."

"What," gasped Jennifer. She snapped her head around to catch Jason's reaction and almost smashed her nose into his ear.

"This is the FBI, ma'am," the woman responded.

"The FBI?" Jennifer repeated. "Boy, did I get a wrong number!" She hung up. Jason and Jennifer stood for a moment longer at the phone.

Jenny started to speak, but Jason put his finger to his lips. "Wait," he said softly. They moved away from the store, avoiding some patrons who were coming out of the doorway.

"Sorry," Jenny said after a few steps. "This secrecy shit takes some getting used to."

Jason shrugged. "It grows on you." It was a humorless statement.

They walked along M Street, each thinking about the next step.

For a good part of the walk, they were silent. "Damn," said Jason finally. "They really are the FBI."

"Either that," Jenny replied, "or they're working hard to make it seem that way."

Jason looked sharply at her and sighed. He stuffed his hands into his pockets and after a few more steps spoke again.

"Which is worse?" It was a question not meant to be answered.

When they reached Maine Avenue, Jason shared the thought that had been recurring in his mind for the past few minutes. "Maybe you better go see your friend, Drury's guy."

Jennifer nodded quietly. "If Drury buys it, he'll want to talk to you."

Jason nodded.

In unspoken agreement, they turned and started back toward M Street. As he did so, Jason glanced upward at the street sign. "Maine." It brought a flood of thoughts and images. He realized how much he had missed the place. It not only looked different. There the sounds were different; it smelled different; it felt different. It was, in a word—cleaner.

Life Down East dealt more with the basics. There was an innate suspicion of change. When change did come, there had to be a pretty good reason for it. He missed those people, the natives. They were different; they were true Yankees. Their ways of doing things—their ways of sometimes just surviving—gave meaning to the terms *Yankee ingenuity* and *Yankee frugality*. The people there *were* different. Maybe it was in their blood, maybe it was the rugged environment; whatever the reason, they were a people prone to conservation. They tended not to waste anything: food, water, clothing, money, even talk.

Nobody who went to Maine could fail to experience the uniqueness of the place. Once, when he thought he was lost, Jason stopped to ask an old-timer for some directions. The man, who was weeding his garden, never even looked up as Jason approached.

"Excuse me," he had said. "You know where the Ames live?"

The man never altered his routine. When he spoke, he still worked around his petunias. "A-yuh," he replied. Jason waited for the rest of the information. It did not come.

"Well," said Jason in a slightly irritated tone, "where *do* they live?"

Now the man stopped and, recognizing Jason's dissatisfaction, slowly looked up. "Well, sonny, ya' didn't ask me that. They live ovah they-ah." The man swung his arm out past Jason and indicated the house across the street.

Jason looked again at the street sign on the corner of M and Maine. The old man had been absolutely correct. The difference between "Do you know where they live?" and "Where do they live?" was considerable. He smiled now at the memory, as he and Jennifer started back to her apartment.

Jason's thoughts drifted to Dog. God, he missed him. It amazed him how attached he had become to the animal. Dog was a pet, but defining their relationship as master–pet hardly did justice to the bond between them. He talked to Dog, touched him, and found comfort in his presence. In quiet moments in the parsonage, when he and Dog were alone, he sometimes wondered what his parishioners would think of his attachment to his dog. At times the relationship even bothered him. In many ways, he was closer to Dog than he was to most humans. There was a real understanding between them. When Jason was depressed or uncertain about something, it was as if Dog could sense it. The animal would somehow force Jason to refocus his attention. At times, what Dog seemed to understand was astounding.

"What are you thinking about?" Jennifer's words intruded upon his images of Maine and the golden retriever.

"Home."

"Sidell?"

Jason laughed and shook his head. The town in Illinois where he and Jennifer had grown up seemed a long way from home. "Craig's Harbor. Where my parish is."

"You like it there," she stated.

Jason nodded his head in gentle agreement. "A lot."

By now they had moved back along M Street to the drugstore where they had made the phone call. Jason began to explain how he felt about the Maine coast. "The natives say…" Jason stopped dead. Jenny turned toward him. She was shocked by what she saw. He suddenly seemed consumed by a fiery alertness. His eyes flashed from one side of the street to the other. He searched for cover—and for an avenue of escape. Just a few feet ahead of them was a shelter at a bus stop.

"What's the matter?" demanded Jenny as Jason took her by the arm and ushered her inside the thing. It was one of those cubicles with clear plastic walls…except the once clear plastic was now milky. Graffiti covered much of it. Jason leaned against the back wall and faced her.

"See the drugstore?" Jason asked. Jennifer looked past him and nodded. He continued, "There's a car in front of it."

"Navy-blue. There's a man in the driver's seat," confirmed Jenny.

"Right. Now look around the car, at the phone booth, where we made the call. There should be another guy with blond hair. See him?"

Jenny strained. Jason watched her eyes as they scanned the area first around the car, then the store, then the sidewalks. "No...I don't..." Her eyes moved back toward the car. "Wait! Yes! Inside! He's talking to the cashier!" Now Jenny understood what was happening. "The men from the train station," she announced. Her eyes moved off the men and onto Jason. His reaction was troubling.

"No," Jason corrected her. "The fake FBI from Maine." His answer sent a chill through Jennifer's body. It started in the back of her neck and spread downward throughout her torso, and finally into her legs.

Jason glanced sideways to his left. There was a bus a few blocks away. Theirs would be the next stop.

Across the street, a man who had been walking opposite them came to a shelter similar to the one in which Jennifer and Jason were standing. He entered and sat casually. He slowly lifted his left hand to his mouth.

"Yellow light's on. We've got company," he said into his fist. The man reached up to what appeared to be a hearing aid and gently pressed it farther into his ear. His eyes stayed, unblinking, on Jason and Jennifer. After a moment, he again spoke. "Affirmative."

"Let's get out of here, please." Jennifer's voice sounded suddenly different to Jason. He shifted his gaze to her.

"Wait. If we walk out of here now, they'll have a better chance of seeing us. We're obscured in here. And there's a bus coming along. We'll just get on it. They may never notice."

Jennifer nodded in agreement. "How do you think they found us so fast?"

"Must have traced the call," Jason responded.

"Even though we told them it was a wrong number?"

"Thorough."

"Jason," Jenny whispered breathlessly, "he's coming out."

"Move away from me so we don't look as though we're together. Keep an eye on them, so we know what they're up to." Somehow in the midst of the uncertainty, Jason's tone brought a sense of reassurance. He glanced over at her. "And don't stare." She looked at him and started to speak. "And don't look at me!" he added emphatically.

Jenny was again agitated. Despite that she did look away, muttering, "How the hell am I supposed to watch them if I can't look at them! And have you ever tried to talk to someone without looking at them?" Jason chuckled once.

"Try it sometime, fool," Jenny added.

Jason glanced up. The bus was a block away.

"He's getting into the car. They're moving," Jenny said. Then she added, "Am I being cool?"

Jenny watched the navy-blue car as it backed out of the parking space and headed for the exit at the opposite side of the lot. As it neared the exit it slowed.

"He's looking our way." Jenny's whispered words were full of fear.

"Here comes the bus," Jason announced, seemingly unmindful of Jenny's statement.

"Forget it, Jason. They've seen us. They're coming." One glance confirmed Jenny's assessment of the situation.

"Shit," he muttered. "Come on." He took her by the hand and started across the street. The bus, which was to be their escape, barely stopped in time. The air brakes emitted great moans as the bus rocked to a halt. Jason thought for certain that they would be hit. But they weren't. They stepped past the bus and ran. Cars screeched to a halt. One swerved onto the median divider.

"Christ," breathed the man who sat in the bus shelter across the street, "you should see this circus!"

Of all the drivers in the world to trust to stop in time, thought Jason, it sure as hell wouldn't be D.C. drivers.

In the distance behind them, he heard someone calling his name.

He glanced to his right. Jenny was there. She stared to her right to the traffic that was coming at them from the other direction. Her faced was drained of color. Her usual vital expression was absent, replaced now by the sober, empty look of a corpse.

"We've got to go," Jason mumbled even as they were stepping into the traffic. Cars surrounded them instantly. They sidestepped one car that wouldn't have—couldn't have—stopped in time, paused for another to pass and, finally, stepped up onto the sidewalk.

Once off the street, Jenny let out the breath that she had held since they started across. Jason glanced over his shoulder. Cars continued moving. He was aware of the drivers, who were staring wildly at them. Horns sounded in disapproval. He could feel the drivers' anger.

One of the men, the one who called himself Mac-Dougall, was also dodging traffic. He was approaching the median. His partner was driving the car out of the parking lot.

"Come on, Jenny, down here."

Jason and Jenny ran past the other bus shelter. The man inside watched in apparent amazement. Then they moved into an alley between two buildings. At the other end, they emerged into a side street, a dead end. They looked around desperately.

Diagonally across the street a gray car was pulling out from a basement parking garage. Farther down the street, a woman was walking with a baby carriage. Jason's first impulse was to head toward the end of the street, but the appearance of the navy-blue car convinced him otherwise.

Again he glanced around. What was going to help? His eyes again scanned the gray car as it cleared the top of the apartment driveway. A large metal door started to descend behind it as it drove away.

"Come on," breathed Jason. He pulled on Jenny's hand. He heard a sort of moaning sigh as he pulled her. From the corner of his eye, he could see the blue car approaching. Now he could also hear MacDougall's footsteps as he closed in. The air whistled by his ears as they ran toward the driveway. The door was a quarter way down. As they stepped into the street, they heard the car's engine accelerate.

"We can't make it," Jenny cried.

Jason squeezed her hand and ran faster, pulling her along.

"Winslow! Winslow, stop!" MacDougall shouted. He sounded as though he could reach out and touch them.

"I can't," breathed Jenny, "I can't."

The door was halfway down. They were at the top of the driveway.

They could hear MacDougall breathing behind them. His breath was coming in short, hard strokes.

The door was two-thirds of the way down.

"Duck!" Jason's voice sounded far away. She felt his hand tighten around hers. His rough and brutal tug at her arm felt suddenly slow and ponderous, as if she were living a nightmare. It threw her off balance and she, along with Jason, fell to the pavement. They rolled—or slid—under the door just before it clanged shut.

An instant later they heard MacDougall crashing into the door. For a moment, they were only aware of their breathing. Then Jenny heard herself crying softly. Her knees throbbed with pain.

"Damn it! Damn it!" MacDougall's muffled voice filtered through the door. "Go get the building super. Damn it!"

Jason first shut his eyes, then opened them wide. He saw Jenny's vague outline crumpled nearby. He reached out and touched her. "You all right?"

Jennifer emitted only the most tentative whimper.

"We've got to get out of here; they'll be in any minute. Come on, Jenny."

They moved quickly to the elevators, checking the few cars left in the garage. They were all locked.

On the garage level there was a laundry area, two elevators and a stairway. The elevator required a key to call it down to the garage. The door appeared to be similarly secured. Through the laundry was a door to the boiler room. It was slightly open.

"In here," Jason urged. Jenny needed no prodding. Together they stepped from the fluorescent brightness of the laundry room to the darkness of the boiler room. The walls were cool and damp. They stood on a steel stairway. Their breathing grew quieter.

"Let's see what's down there," Jason said. His tone was calmer now.

As they prepared to move Jennifer grabbed his arm. She said nothing. Outside they heard the elevator bell sound its arrival. There were two voices. One Jason recognized as that of the man called Foley. The other sounded older and unfamiliar. It belonged to the building supervisor.

Jason and Jennifer leaned backward out of any possible view from the area in front of the elevators.

"What's in here?"

"Just the laundry and the boiler. But like I said, there's no way out without the keys. And the boiler room. I'm the only one with a key for that. Nope. They're in here, all right."

Jennifer squeezed Jason's arm tighter. He reached around and held her.

"Tell you what, you stay here," Foley was saying, "and I'll go let my partner in."

"No way, fella. I ain' standin' alone so no couple of murderers can adds me to their list. I'm comin' with you. You're the one who's got the gun! 'Sides," he added, "ain' no way for 'em ta get out; they ain' got no keys." The superintendent seemed particularly proud of his reasoning skills.

Jason listened as the footsteps faded from their hearing.

"What are we going to do now?" Jennifer whispered. Her words carried the hopelessness of a cornered criminal.

"Come on," Jason said, as he moved her gently out into the laundry room. They squinted from the brightness of the lights. Jason looked around, desperate for an escape.

"Jenny, trust me. I want you to get into the dryer." Jenny started to protest then, looking around, realized there was no better solution. She agreed without discussion. Together they moved to the first industrial-size dryer. In the distance they could hear the motorized hum of the garage door opening.

Jason helped Jenny into the dryer. As he started to shut the door, she held up her hand.

"Where will you be?"

"Right next door," replied Jason, indicating the dryer next to hers.

"Like two peas in a pod," Jenny said as she shut the door.

Jason climbed into his dryer. "Damn," he muttered. There were clothes in it. As he started to shut the door, he could hear approaching footsteps. He closed the door and settled in.

"You sure there's no way out of here?" Jason recognized MacDougall's voice.

"Look," said the superintendent, "I told ya—" his tone was patronizing "—the door, the elevator, the garage door, the boiler room. They all take keys." The voices were indistinct and muffled. Jason wished that he had left the door ajar. No you don't, you ass, he told himself. He grimaced. The old man continued. "With them damn vandals in this neighborhood, we need them keys and locks but good." A shadow passed over Jason. One of the men must be standing practically on top of the dryer.

The superintendent was pretty wound up. "Now there's sumpthin' for you boys to do. When you gonna' do sumpthin' 'bout this damn vandalism? It's a disgrace! You know you can't even—"

"Okay. Okay. Unfortunately, that's not in our territory." MacDougall cut the old man off. Jason strained to hear. The men were discussing their search pattern. First they would check the cars. Jason heard their footsteps move away, and then there were only the occasional sounds of car doors opening and closing.

God, thought Jason, how the hell are we going to get out of here? The only way out was with a key. The superintendent's words played over and over in his mind. He sighed, realizing suddenly how cramped he was. He thought for a moment about James Bond. Hell, he'd never hide in a damn clothes dryer. Just pretend it's a pit full of snakes, he told himself. You ass, he responded.

The sounds of the men once again focused his attention. They were apparently coming back to the laundry area.

"There's no way they could get out?" MacDougall repeated the question he had asked only minutes earlier. Jason closed his eyes and grinned. He was certain the superintendent would not take kindly to MacDougall's unyielding doubt.

Instead of answering, the superintendent simply asked his own question. What made it so effective, so cutting and damaging, was its utter innocence. "You sure you got the right buildin'?"

MacDougall's answer was immediate. It was filled with the indignation one would expect. "The FBI doesn't make mistakes, Mr. Johnson."

"That's Johnston...with a *t*," the superintendent replied. His answer was fast and decisive. It was as if he had been waiting for the agent's mistake. Jason grinned again, but almost immediately his senses refocused his attention. There was a new sound...a hum, a rumbling hum. The elevator. There was a small "bing," then more footsteps.

"Who's there?" MacDougall spoke with imposing authority.

"It's only me," came the reply. It was the bright, spirited voice of an older woman. "I've come for my laundry."

Christ, thought Jason, this is it. It's all over.

"And," continued the lady, "who are these gentlemen, Mr. Johnston?"

"These here are G-men, Mrs. Hutton. The genuine articles!" There was obvious pride in the superintendent's voice.

"Oh my! In our building? Whatever for?"

There was a pause, then MacDougall spoke ominously. "We're looking for two murderers."

Murderers! thought Jason, as he listened to Mrs. Hutton drawing in her breath. It was a high-pitched, drawn-out "Ooh!"

"It's all right. They're trapped in the boiler room," Foley interjected.

"We think," said the superintendent emphatically.

Now the footsteps moved away again. Jason took a deep breath and waited. He expected Mrs. Hutton to reach in at any moment, grab his hair instead of her whatever and scream bloody blue murder.

Instead, he heard her footsteps shuffle on along, presumably following the others.

"We'd advise you to get your laundry and get back upstairs, ma'am," said MacDougall, "for your own safety."

"Oh dear, yes, of course," the lady replied.

Now the steps resumed—some cautiously moving down the steel stairs of the boiler room, others shuffling toward the dryer.

Jason hated to do what he knew he must. The door of the dryer opened. He lunged forward, up into her face. "Don't say a word," he hissed.

Poor Mrs. Hutton's eyes widened. Jason realized she was too shocked to emit any sound at all.

"Just be quiet and you'll be all right." He was suddenly worried that he might literally scare her to death. She continued to stare wide-eyed. Her skin was turning a yellow-gray color. Jason spoke again as he climbed out of the dryer. "You're all right, aren't you?"

Mrs. Hutton nodded. Her mouth dropped open even wider. Jason was aware now just how cramped he had been. He hurt as he straightened up. He moved to the other dryer and opened the door. Mrs. Hutton stared in disbelief as Jennifer climbed out.

"Get your key and open the elevator," Jason directed. Mrs. Hutton required no additional prompting. As Jenny moved off with the little old woman, Jason removed her clothes from the dryer and loaded them into her clothes basket. By the time the elevator door had opened, all three were ready to step in.

Once the doors closed, the movement of the elevator was a signal for only the slightest relaxing.

Jennifer was the cordial one. "How do you do, Mrs. Hutton. I hope we haven't ruined your day." Mrs. Hutton stared blankly from one to the other and shook her head—in a bewildered sort of way—indicating that they hadn't.

By now they had reached the first floor, and were stepping off.

"I'm certainly glad of that, ma'am," added Jason, handing her the laundry. He reached around back into the elevator, pushed a button and the doors started to close. He smiled at her as she disappeared from sight.

Together they ran out of the building, down a walk, through some neighboring yards and across the street. They were safer now, they felt, and wound their way back to Jennifer's neighborhood.

They went to Jenny's back door, entered and immediately went to her apartment. They drew the drapes across the windows in the front of her living room. Then they knelt to watch the street below. The curtains of loosely woven fabric allowed them to see almost perfectly.

"Ouch." Jennifer's knees stung as they touched down onto the floor. They were not bleeding, but nearly. She realized how tense she was, even now.

They watched for two, three, then five minutes. They grew more and more uncertain. They had expected to see the men almost immediately. Where were they? Had they somehow found Jennifer's apartment and were just waiting for the proper moment? Were they approaching from the back? Jason rose to check. He moved into Jenny's bedroom. He had barely entered when Jennifer's whispered call brought him quickly back to the living room. He knelt beside her.

First Foley appeared. He looked cautiously from one side of the street to the other. Then he gestured down the street, and turning in the direction he had indicated, they saw

MacDougall approaching from the other end of the street. Then, behind Foley, appeared the building superintendent. Finally, behind him, came Mrs. Hutton, still carrying her laundry.

"Poor Mrs. Hutton," Jason whispered, as he watched the events below.

"Poor Mrs. Hutton," repeated Jennifer with disbelief. "Poor Ms Seidkamp," Jenny taunted.

Foley waited as MacDougall walked toward him. They were visibly disappointed. MacDougall shook his head despondently and gestured helplessly. As they started back, both men were silent, the building superintendent was talking right into Foley's ear, and poor old Mrs. Hutton stood on the corner looking first one way, then the other. Finally, shrugging, she turned to head back with the others.

Now Jenny and Jason both exhaled deeply. They rolled away from each other and lay flat on the floor, just thinking. It was Jenny who finally spoke.

"'Trust me.' The man said, 'trust me.' I did and I ended up in a clothes dryer."

"But we made it." Jason said, turning to her. He leaned on his side, propped up by his elbow. He grinned a wide, free grin. Spontaneously, they both started to laugh. Their shared laughter released the tension of the past thirty minutes.

"We did, didn't we?" Jenny repeated in the midst of the laughing. The moment was not without a strange sense of accomplishment.

"Thanks to Mrs. Hutton," Jason continued.

"Screw Mrs. Hutton," Jenny responded. "*We* did it!"

They laughed once more. Jenny felt safe now. Again she was aware how glad she was to be together with Jason. She thought—hoped—he was feeling the same.

In fact, he was. He was very conscious of his feelings in the moments they were sharing now. As the laughter grew calmer, gentler, Jennifer turned and reached up to Jason's face, drew him toward her and kissed him. The kiss, like the laughter, was uncomplicated. It was spontaneous and honest. He looked at her and smiled. Then he, too, reached out. With the back of his fingers he touched her cheek. His touch seemed like the gentlest thing she had ever felt. Its quietness awakened her senses. He gazed at her, seemingly lost in thought. What are you thinking about, Reverend Jason Winslow? she wondered. What are you thinking? His eyes blinked once, twice.

Still staring into her eyes, Jason allowed his hand to ever so slowly drift downward to her cheekbone. "Jenny," he whispered. "I'm sorry... I'm so sorry." Then carefully, as if wanting to lift his hand from a pool of water without leaving the slightest ripple, he drew his hand from her face. He continued to study her eyes. Again he smiled gently. She knew that signaled the end of that exquisite moment.

Jason studied her. He thought she wanted him just as he wanted her. But he would not allow it to happen. These emotions, so long dormant, troubled him now. Slowly, moving his eyes back to the curtain and focusing down onto the street, he forced all those thoughts from his mind.

"We have to talk to Drury," he said softly.

"Yes," Jenny replied. "We will."

In the apartment building across from Jennifer's, a man moved a pair of binoculars from his eyes. Then, glancing down at the street below, he picked up a walkie-talkie.

"We've got a green light," he murmured.

14

WORLD SYNDICATIONS WAS NOT particularly impressive. Somehow Jason had pictured a grand, black marble skyscraper, complete with gleaming interiors, private elevators and neatly attired attendants at every corner. His image of the place was certainly not of a nondescript office building just off DuPont Circle.

Jason realized that he must have passed the building with tour groups, but it had never been pointed out as the place of business for one of America's true power brokers; in fact, like most other people who passed by the building, he had never really even noticed it.

The interior was as bleak as the outside. A sloppily uniformed guard, probably a student working part-time, listened to rock music on a radio that was held together by scabs of yellowed, curling pieces of Scotch Tape. The entire scene was bathed in a pinkish, flickering light pulsing down from one sole fluorescent tube. The light buzzed almost as loudly as the music played.

"Hi, Jennifer!" said the guard, half standing. From his tone, Jason suspected Jenny's entrance was the most exciting event in his day. As soon as the youth realized Jason was with Jenny, a look of disappointment spread across his face.

"Hi, Todd," Jenny replied. "Mr. Drury in?" she asked as she continued walking toward the elevator.

"Yeah," the guard answered. "Got back from lunch a few minutes ago."

"See ya."

"Yeah."

The elevator doors closed and Jenny pushed the button labeled 6, the top floor.

"He's in love with me," Jenny said flippantly. She turned to Jason and gazed into his eyes. "In love with my bod," she further clarified. She struck a laughably seductive pose. She leaned into Jason to force an even greater reaction from him. He shook his head, laughed slightly and looked self-consciously downward. She was puzzled by his halfhearted reaction. When he finally looked up, he was aware that she was waiting for him to say something.

"Drury?" Jason asked tentatively.

Instantly she changed her pose to one of defeat. "Beg your pardon?"

"You talking about Drury?" Jason asked again.

A look of puzzlement came over Jennifer's face, then suddenly it became clear. "God, no!" She exhaled. "Drury?" she repeated amid rather overblown laughter. "Hell no! The kid in the uniform."

The opening of the elevator door brought a merciful end to Jennifer's taunting. If Jason had expected some impressive change for the better on the top floor, he was mistaken. He and Jenny wound their way through a maze of overstuffed desks in overstuffed cubicles scattered in no apparent pattern throughout the area. A bluish haze of cigarette smoke caused Jason to blink and wonder how people survived in the place.

Drury was in, but wouldn't be free for another ten minutes or so. Jennifer decided to check in on things in her own office. Jason was glad he was following her. If someone had tried to explain how to get from here to there in this maze, he was certain that success would have eluded him.

Jenny shared her space with two other editorial assistants. Her desk was a mire of file folders and envelopes of all kinds. A typewriter was pushed into the corner. Its ribbon spilled over onto the keys. Some kind of dead plant was sitting inside on the type. Jenny caught Jason staring, wondering.

"It's dead," she explained.

"The plant or the typewriter?"

"Uh-huh," she answered. "I use Eleanor's word processor when I need to. She's hardly ever here anyway."

"Can't blame her," said Jason unenthusiastically.

"Too Spartan for you, hmm?"

Jason snickered. "Spartan isn't exactly the word I had in mind."

While Jason and Jenny waited for the call from Drury's secretary, the guard at the entrance was again interrupted from his nonstop dose of rock music. The boy glanced up as a man came into the dreary lobby. Probably a lawyer, or maybe—he reconsidered—some congressional assistant. The man wore a dark three-piece suit. The shine on his shoes was unblemished. He carried a small bouquet of flowers.

"Hi," the man said brightly.

"Hi," responded the guard.

"Say," the man began with unchecked exuberance, "is Jenny in?" Then, realizing that he wasn't being clear, he smiled and added, "I mean Jennifer, Jennifer Seidkamp."

"You just missed her. A minute earlier and you could have gone up in the elevator with her," the guard answered.

A look of momentary disappointment swept across the man's face. He shrugged slightly, then brightened again. "What floor's she work on?"

"Sixth. But I don't think she's going to her office. Sounded like she was heading in to see Mr. Drury." The man seemed surprised at the mention of Drury's name, but the guard knew that was a common reaction. In fact, he often derived a sort of pleasure from just such a reaction, and the realization that he was the one causing it.

"Oh," the man said, nodding. "You think it'd be all right if I just dropped these off in her office?"

The guard shrugged. "Sure, why not?"

The man had already turned and was heading for the elevator. Then, as he approached it, his pace slowed to a stop, as if doubt had paralyzed him. He turned toward the guard again. When he spoke his tone was subdued.

"Say," the man began, "there wasn't anyone with her, was there? A guy about my age, blond hair?"

Now the guard felt a twinge of remorse, as he looked at the man waiting for a response. "Yes," the youth replied soberly, "'fraid so."

The man winced a little, frowned and let his hand and the flowers drop to his side. "Damn," he mumbled, and slowly began walking toward the exit. Just before exiting, he turned to the guard once more. "Do me a favor?" The guard looked up questioningly. The man continued. "If you see her, don't mention I was here . . . okay?"

"You got it," the guard responded.

The man managed a half smile. He held the flowers out to the guard. "You have a girlfriend?" The guard shook his head sadly. The man again lowered the flowers, nodded and exited.

Once outside, he stuffed the flowers into a trash receptacle and moved quickly to a car parked almost next to it. Once inside the vehicle, he reached for a microphone.

"Prime, base," he said.

The radio crackled to life. "Base. Go."

"I've got 'em," the man responded.

"Affirm. Base clear."

The man returned the microphone to its holder. He adjusted the mirror so that the entrance of the World Syndications Building was centered in the reflection. He opened a small notebook and began writing, stopping frequently to check the mirror.

The minister's an interesting character, the man thought. He had seen him operate at the train station and he had been briefed about the antics in the Seidkamp woman's neighborhood. The clergyman had foiled presumably some of the best agents the government had. The man was pleased to know they had the minister right where they wanted him—and that the others didn't, at least, not yet. Jason Winslow, the man thought, you're one resourceful son of a bitch. He looked back down at his notebook, and sighed. "You'll have to be," he murmured, moving his gaze back to the mirror.

Six floors above the street, a buzz drew Jenny's attention from the explanation she was giving Jason about the way World Syndications worked. She picked up the telephone. It was her friend. Drury could see them now.

LeRoy Drury was impressive even if his place of business was not. He and his office were bold exceptions to the rest of the building. They were an assertive testament to success.

Drury was, as the saying goes, bigger than life. Jason felt immediately compelled to watch him. Everything about him—his hands, facial features, voice, thinking capacity, and probably his ego as well, thought Jason—were all exaggerations. He almost seemed like a caricature, except there was nothing comical about him—nothing at all. Jason was also certain that Drury, perhaps more than anyone, was aware of his imposing presence.

Drury was in his late sixties. He was slightly overweight, but solid. His face was round and ruddy. His hair was graying and combed straight back. Despite the man's powerful persona, Jason could see that he was tired. It was not the kind of tired that comes from a late-night party. No, this was a fundamental fatigue. It was deep and lurking, but at any minute capable of erupting into a devastating case of exhaustion. It was most visible in the folds around Drury's mouth and the puffy bags of discolored skin under his eyes. The half-frame glasses that he wore did a fair job of covering the swellings from all casual glances.

"Mr. Drury," Jennifer began, "I'm Jennifer Seidkamp. I work with Eleanor. I know Mike Hoyt."

"Of course, Jennifer, Mike's mentioned you often."

"Oh?" Jennifer spoke with mild surprise. She spoke before thinking. Almost instantly she realized Drury was lying and she wished she had just not reacted at all. Now she knew that Drury knew that she knew he was lying. As gracefully as possible, each let the moment pass.

"This is Jason Winslow," Jennifer said, recovering. "He's really why we're here."

Drury suddenly leaned back, away from Jason. His eyes narrowed. For just a moment, he surveyed the younger man with an artist's intensity. He did not rise from behind his desk, but after a momentary pause, leaned comfortably forward again and thrust out his hand in a deliberate, almost threatening manner. Jason reached across the space between them and grasped the massive hand that waited for his. Like the rest of the man, Drury's handshake was no-nonsense. Drury let Jason's hand go and leaned back into his richly upholstered chair. He studied Jason, who now, though uninvited, also sat. Jennifer occupied a third chair. She sat apart from them and from her vantage point could see the confrontation growing. They were all aware of it.

Jason felt the piercing stare of the man behind the desk. He realized how intimidated he felt. What was it? The room, the man, his appearance, his fame, his eyes? Yes, his eyes. It was his eyes that sent out the message of condescension.

Jason wondered about the man. Was this the way he usually treated people? It was—at least—discomforting. Jason could not recall ever having been quite so intimidated merely by someone's glance.

It was Drury who suddenly broke the spell. He wheeled around in his chair. The back of the chair covered the man. Only his hand was visible as he reached out to a huge multi-tiered rack holding a vast collection of pipes. Drury selected a well-smoked, virgin block meerschaum, obviously one of his favorites.

"Well, well," Drury murmured, tamping his tobacco in the pipe's bowl, "Jason and Jennifer . . . Jack and Jill." He swung around in his chair to face them once again. "Alliteration," he mumbled, igniting the tobacco with his lighter. Between the moments in which he sucked the flame into the pipe, he spoke. When he did, the flame again exploded into its fullness. "Jack fell down." He puffed. "And broke his crown." He puffed again. "And Jill came tumbling after." The flame of the lighter ceased. Drury rotated his chair to face Jennifer.

She smiled pleasantly. "That's Jason and Jennifer," she gently corrected.

Drury's response consisted of a shrug and a smile, and just the slightest bow, in fact, more of a nod. His pipe was anchored firmly between his teeth. The smile remained. It was an odd sort of smile, Jason thought. Not one born of real freedom; instead, it was forced. Rather than set him at ease, it did just the opposite—as, in fact, it was intended to do.

Now Drury turned his attention back to Jason. This time Jason let his own strength flow into his eyes and he met Drury's gaze with equal intensity. He would not let the man make him uncomfortable.

Drury watched as the younger man's resolve strengthened. "So, Jason, what can I do for you?" he finally asked.

"I'm looking for some information."

"Aren't we all?" Drury responded casually. He glanced over at Jennifer. "Information, my friends. It's the most valuable commodity a man can possess." He puffed on his pipe as he continued. "Information," he said reflectively. "The right information can put a man in the White House...." He paused. "Or yank him out." Drury smiled again with a contentedness born of the knowledge that his skillful merchandising of information had caused no small discomfort among several White House occupants.

"Jason is a minister," Jennifer interjected. Drury looked over his glasses, again tightening his gaze on Jason. Jennifer continued. "And the other night, he had a kind of interesting pastoral visit. Interesting enough, Mr. Drury, to provide a dandy exclusive. Right down your alley."

Drury shifted his gaze to Jason. "That so, Pastor?" Drury asked pointedly.

Jason shrugged, but Drury's curiosity had apparently been teased. He held his arms out in a gesture that invited Jason to begin. For the second time that day, Jason related the events of the past forty-eight hours. He reflected on his story—the telling of it, at least. It seemed to him that it kept getting longer. As he talked, he watched Drury settle deeper and deeper into his chair.

This man, who had seemed so remote just moments ago, was now being pulled into Jason's narrative. He drew in easily on his pipe. With that exception, and one other, he made little movement. Occasionally he made a note on a three-by-five-inch note card—one note per card. Jason smiled, thinking: so writers really do that. He remembered in high school when he had to write his first term paper. The teacher made the class take notes just as Drury was doing now. Jason thought the procedure was a pain. Obviously Drury did not. Jason could see no particular rhyme or reason to the information Drury was recording.

When Jason mentioned the phone number, Drury asked to see the business card. Jennifer had the card and quickly handed it to him. Drury frowned once and pushed a button on his phone. Almost instantly, there was a knock on the door.

"Come in, Mike," Drury called. The young man who entered had all the bearing of an aggressive junior partner in a successful law firm.

Drury spoke to him. "Check this number with Les down at Telco." Mike took the card and started to exit, but Drury stopped him. "What do you make of the card?"

Mike held the card close to his face. He angled it to capture the most light. He turned it over a couple of times. He shrugged. "Looks like any other Bureau card to me—except for the phone number."

"Mmm," Drury murmured. Jason and Jennifer glanced at each other. That simple little sound told much—none of it what they were hoping to hear. Drury continued. "Just for the hell of it, do a check on it."

Again Mike shrugged and started to exit.

"Let me know as soon as you've got something," Drury. said. The assistant nodded, stepped outside the sanctum and quietly closed the door.

The three people remaining inside sat in silence for a moment, each thinking about what the outcome of the assistant's work might mean to them. When the silence—and its weight—became obvious, Jason resumed his story. As he finished relating his experiences at the train station, there was a knock on the door.

"Come in, Mike," Drury called. Mike reentered. He carried a sheaf of papers. Jason's thoughts drifted to Drury. I wonder, thought Jason, how he knew it was Mike.

"What did you find out?"

"I'll do the easy part, first," began the assistant, laying the card on Drury's desk. "The card is genuine. Looks like any other." Despite all Jason's work to prepare himself, this news caused a distinct tremor to pass through his body. He wondered if the others saw his reaction. Now the assistant placed a second card on the table. Jason and Jennifer moved in for a closer look. They studied the cards for a long time, feeling them, holding them up to the light, laying one on top of the other. They were not exact duplicates, but the differences could easily be accounted for by simple printing variations. Finally Jason sat back down.

"Well," he said, still focused on the cards, "at least I know *who* I'm dealing with."

Drury shook his head. "Things are not always as predictable as you might think. Some things happen that you'd never think possible—no matter how thoroughly you've planned. Believe me." His face formed the closest thing to a smile Jason had yet seen. Drury continued. "What about the telephone number?"

Mike frowned. "It sure looks like the Bureau. That number is currently in the safe file."

Jason looked puzzled.

"There are several phones assigned to clandestine government operations," Drury began. "Even the most secret ops-off requires a telephone—even if it's just to call out for pizza."

"Ops-off?" interrupted Jason.

Drury smiled. "Operations office," he explained. "Anyway, the phone numbers aren't included in any normal telephone company listing."

Jason stiffened. He sat up straighter in his chair. Questions flooded his mind. Why the FBI? Was Omega related to them? Why the confusion in Maine? Had he acted foolishly? Should he have simply remained in Craig's Harbor? He thought of all the trouble he had created. He could feel his face reddening.

"Now remember, don't go jumping to conclusions," Drury urged, responding to Jason's discomfort. He then turned to his assistant. "Can Les find out who the number was assigned to?"

Mike slowly shook his head. "He doesn't have a lot of hope," the assistant replied, "but he's going to try. He'll call back in fifteen or twenty minutes."

"Let us know."

Mike nodded and was on his way out.

Jason was despondent. He felt foolish and embarrassed—feelings he was not used to, feelings he did not like. "Seems pretty stupid to continue this. It's obvious that I just overreacted." He shrugged. "I panicked." He pressed his hands together, carefully aligning his fingertips. He gently pushed them against each other, performing a sort of isometric exercise.

"Perhaps," said Drury with a strange, almost cryptic smile. "Why don't you hang in a little longer? Just for the hell of it."

Jason shrugged. He knew Drury was gloating over his embarrassment. It's feeding him, Jason thought. Look at him in all his high-and-mighty glory. But, Jason reasoned, I came this far; I might as well see it through—through to its foolish end. As the man says, just for the hell of it.

Occasionally, as he continued telling Drury his story, Jason turned to Jennifer. He could see she felt sorry for him.

In fact, she *was* feeling sorry for him—more than he realized. She remembered the few times in high school when

he had been proved wrong or when he had seemed to have
gone overboard on an issue. It was strange, she thought. In
some matters, ones that would matter dearly to her, Jason
seemed totally unconcerned about people's reactions. Yet in
other matters, often the most trivial, how people viewed him
was of the utmost importance to him. She thought about his
refusal to drink alcohol. In high school that had been the
source of unending taunts, and yet Jason had not seemed to
give one damn what people thought. But then there were the
other times. She remembered one incident in particular.

Once he had worn a sweater, a cardigan, to school. It was
clearly not the "in" style of the day. Now Jennifer shook her
head, still wondering what could ever have possessed him to
wear it. As she reflected on the incident, she realized that it
was simply one more sign of Jason's innocence. In some
ways, he was incredibly naive. Even now, ten years later, she
was aware of this. It surprised her because, in other ways,
Jason seemed as worldly as the most sophisticated corporate types in Washington, LeRoy Drury included.

Anyway, one kid had inevitably made some sort of half-
witted remark about the sweater. The scene was still vivid in
Jenny's memory. Jason had been crushed. His eyes filled
with tears and his breaths came quickly. He hung his head
so that the others would not see his pain. The boy who had
made the comment then made a fateful misjudgment. He
made one more, equally inane remark. But in that moment, Jason had changed. When he looked up an instant
later, Jason's eyes were not filled with tears, but with fire.
His pain had given way to anger, to fury. His look quieted
the group immediately. They were staring at him in just the
way the myths say a cobra's victim stares, transfixed by the
snake. Never taking his eyes from the boy, Jason walked up
to him and breathed a few words. At that point, the others
didn't even know what Jason said. But whatever it was, it

stunned the boy, who became so furious he stopped thinking. Jason turned instantly and started walking away. And then the fool spoke once more and in so doing, destroyed himself. He became the butt of jokes throughout the rest of his high school career.

"I don't screw anyone's pigs!" the boy yelled down the hallway. Jason did not react and the bully realized his error too late. The others laughed without restraint—without mercy. When he tried to explain, they only laughed harder. By that time, Jason was gone.

Jennifer's thoughts moved from the memory to the man who had suddenly reappeared in her life. He was changed. There was still a strange quality of innocence, but that razor-sharp rage seemed to have been buried deeply out of sight. She wondered if it ever surfaced now.

When Jason finished relating the most recent events, those of that morning, he expected Drury to jump up and summarily dismiss them. But that did not happen. Instead, Drury sat unchanged and continued to puff on his pipe.

Drury finally moved. It was as if he thought of himself as a one-man show. When the lights had dimmed and the audience quieted, then—and only then—would he go onstage. He began by raising himself upward. Then he leaned forward. It was as if a camera had zoomed in on him. His face dominated the scene. He calmly looked downward at his assortment of note cards, then up at Jenny. Finally he turned deliberately to Jason.

"This Omega," Drury said soberly, leaning toward the pastor. "You have no clue about who he might be? No clue whatsoever?" The intensity was surprising. There was just a hint of uncertainty in the question.

Again Jason looked surprised. The answer was obvious, and yet Drury acted as though it shouldn't be. Jason gestured helplessly. "No," he answered.

"You're absolutely sure?"

"Yes," returned Jason. His dissatisfaction with the question was obvious by his tone.

Drury sat back in his chair, apparently satisfied. The intensity that had suddenly appeared in the preceding question had disappeared just as suddenly.

"And Sullivan didn't mention any other names?" he asked a moment later.

"No."

"Think about this before you answer," Drury chastised mildly. "You overheard nothing from our FBI agents? They didn't refer to any other people? No other names? No one who might be a supervisor or anything?"

This time Jason waited before he answered. "No."

"Anything from the people at the train station, this morning?"

"No. No..." Now Jason paused. A puzzled look crossed his face. Drury sat forward again.

Jennifer watched as Jason struggled with something. "What is it, Jason?" she asked.

"At the train station. They were outside. They did mention someone's name." Again there was silence. Jason finally shook his head. "Damn," he muttered. "They said something about what were they 'going to tell...'" Again he stopped, shaking his head. He looked at Jennifer, then Drury, and abruptly rose and walked to the window and looked out. He took a deep breath and slowly exhaled. He stared up and out into the pale blue of the sky and ran the tapes of the morning through his mind.

"They were upset with themselves. They had missed me. One of them said..." Jason spoke tentatively. "What are we going to tell... Damn!" He started again, more slowly this time. "What are we going to tell... Dan..." It was starting to come. He returned to his chair, sat down and closed his eyes. He again folded his hands and relaxed. It seemed to Jennifer that he had entered some sort of trance. He continued. "What are we going to tell Daniel..." He shook his head. "Donaldson." His puzzled expression remained. "It was shorter," he mumbled. "Donnelly." An instant later the name exploded into his consciousness.

"Donlevy!"

Drury straightened and quickly removed his pipe. There was no doubt about his reaction. Drury was clearly surprised, perhaps even alarmed.

"You know him?" Jennifer breathed.

Drury had no time to answer. His assistant was entering even as he was knocking on the door. He, too, was clearly in an agitated state.

"'Scuse me. Les just called. Almost lost his job on this one." He took a breath. "That phone number was just being pulled out of service. That's the only way he found it. It was just dumb shit luck." The assistant's infectious excitement spread quickly. Jason felt his heart begin to beat faster. Something terribly significant was about to happen. Maybe he'd even find out who Omega really was.

"It wasn't the Bureau," the assistant began.

"I know," Drury announced, leaning back and drawing again on his pipe. "CIA."

The assistant felt a swell of admiration surge through him. He didn't know how his boss knew, but he did. He was sharp.

Jason sat, appearing almost lost. He glanced at Jenny and scowled. Then he looked past Drury and out the window, to the sky beyond.

The CIA. On one level it was merely a fiction to him. It was spies and make-believe. It was James Bond's American cronies. On another level, it was a vague representation of the international audacity of the United States. Its well-documented examples of indiscretion and outright, blatant arrogance of power in the international arena were anathema to him. Now, to have it entwining itself with his own life suddenly hit him with full force. It was the worst thing he could have imagined.

Jason remembered, at one point, considering the possibility that Omega was involved with the CIA, but he had quickly dismissed it. After all, hadn't Sullivan said Omega was hired from the outside? But beyond that, to consider the CIA was just too big. It was beyond his ability to cope. He wouldn't have a chance.

Drury spoke again, short-circuiting Jason's racing thoughts.

"Christopher Donlevy is a second-level executive over in Langley—"

"CIA headquarters," Jennifer interjected for Jason's benefit.

"—in charge of clandestine operations, Central America," Drury concluded, glancing in his assistant's direction for confirmation. Mike nodded dutifully.

Jason was trying desperately to sort through this new data. He sat, numbed. His heart pulsed in a slow throbbing rhythm. He drew in a breath and exhaled slowly and deeply.

"But I thought the CIA only worked outside the country," Jason said.

"You're right...generally," explained Drury. "But there are exceptions every now and then."

"But," interrupted Jennifer, "harassing U.S. citizens isn't one of them."

Drury smiled, then turned to his assistant. "Good work, Mike. Ask Betty to come in in a few minutes, would you?"

Mike came to a sort of attention, bowed and exited.

"But why would CIA people use FBI IDs?" Jason asked. He felt as if a perfectly logical explanation was for some reason just beyond his grasp.

"Maybe you're trying to make it too complicated. Maybe they just didn't want you to know who they were," Jennifer suggested.

"Or," Drury added, "they didn't want you to go calling on the FBI. They thought they could head you off." Drury shook his head much as a parent might when informed of a child's indiscretion. "A stupid, risky bit of business, if you ask me," he added.

Jason's heart was suddenly working harder now. He could feel the blood surging through his arteries. It pulsed through his body into his brain. He was aware of the slightest stimulus: movements, sounds, feelings. Those primal senses that found their use in hunting were taking over. The question to be asked was obvious.

"Is Donlevy, Omega?"

In response to the question, Drury merely smiled his now familiar but impenetrable smile. "Donlevy is a career man. Always seemed like a decent sort. I can't imagine him getting involved in something like this." Drury drew again on his pipe, then allowed the exhaled smoke to mingle with his words. "Besides, I think he's a little too young. Omega would be more my age." He paused, mulling over what he had just said, then added, "But you never know."

Again a knock on the door interrupted their conversation.

"Come in," Drury called. This time a woman in her late forties entered. "Betty," Drury said, "this is Reverend Jason Winslow. I want you to draw up a standard contract for exclusive rights. I want him to have the papers by tomorrow morning."

"Yes sir, Mr. Drury," Betty said, scribbling in short-hand all the while.

"You need any information from him?"

"Just your middle initial," Betty said, smiling at Jason.

"T," replied Jason.

"And that's W-I-N-S-L-O-W, for the last name?"

"Yes, but—"

"That'll be all, Betty," Drury interrupted. "Thanks." The secretary exited.

Jason looked at Jennifer. She was clearly satisfied with what was happening. She smiled reassuringly at him. Then he shifted his glance across the desk to Drury.

"I'm not sure I understand," Jason said.

"All principals in my stories—unless they're public officials, of course—get contracts," explained Drury. "In exchange for a sum of money, you agree to give me exclusive rights to your story." He smiled. "It's all spelled out in the contract."

"I...I don't know, Mr. Drury..." Jason paused. "I'm just not sure—"

"I'm a businessman, Reverend Winslow," Drury interrupted. "As I said earlier, I market information. I'm willing to pay for the raw materials, so to speak." He smiled again. "A simple business arrangement."

"Well, I'd like to think about it," Jason persisted.

Drury waved off the comment with his hand. The motion formed small whirlpools of tobacco smoke that swirled across the desk. "Of course, of course. Now then," he said, rising, "see Betty on your way out." Jenny and Jason also rose. "She'll have a $1,000 advance for you." Jason started to protest, but Drury would have none of it. "No strings attached, Reverend Winslow. No strings. Besides," he added cryptically, "you have already provided me with a grand's worth of... raw materials." The smile returned to his face.

Now Drury gestured toward the door. Jason gladly turned away from the columnist, for in that instant he had glimpsed something that surprised him, and he did not want the man to see his reaction. As Drury had begun to step forward, he had had to reach out to the desk to support himself. The columnist walked with a pronounced limp. This infirmity was the only bit of weakness Jason had detected in Drury during the entire meeting. He was irritated by his reaction. Why shouldn't a man like Drury be disabled? he asked himself. Still, it did surprise him, and he hoped Drury hadn't noticed.

"Just stay near the phone and relax," Drury said as they exited, then added dryly, "Jennifer, you take care of him now. We'll be in touch tomorrow."

The door closed. Even before he sat down, Drury was on the telephone. "Mike, get me anything you can from Langley on Morrison, Samuel, aka Sullivan, Richard. By the way," he added, shifting his attention to another matter, "did Betty add that stuff to the Delacourte file?"

"The stuff last week? I suppose so."

"Bring that in, would you? I'd like to check something," Drury said and then hung up.

He moved to the window and gazed downward at a blur of inconsequential people. It was pure luck, he thought. Incredible luck. Unimaginable. The minister was too much an innocent to get in the way, but he could be invaluable. Drury drew on his pipe.

Out in the reception area, Jason watched Betty as she wrote out a check for one thousand dollars. He was somewhat dazed by the casualness of the entire affair. He didn't know quite what to make of Drury. He was certain he did not like him, but beyond that, well, he just didn't know.

Mike stepped into the reception area and spoke with some intensity. "Betty, do you have the Delacourte file?" The secretary looked up, obviously somewhat unhappy at the interruption. "No, Mike, I finished the memo addendum and put the file back in the archives."

Mike grimaced. "Christ," he breathed. "Drury wants it now."

Betty looked at him unkindly. "It's only down one flight of stairs."

"I know," said the assistant, "but I hate going into that hole down there...." He started to walk toward a door marked For Emergency Use Only. He opened it, mumbling as he went, "It's like being in the damn catacombs."

The secretary looked from the closing door to Jason and frowned, shook her head, then smiled pleasantly once more.

"Here's your check, Reverend Winslow. You can cash it at the bank across the street. Jennifer knows where. And you'll be in tomorrow to sign the contract?"

Jason nodded.

"Fine, then. Anything else?"

"This is enough!" Jason said pleasantly. He looked up from the check and smiled. "Thank you."

As Jason stepped out of the office building, the brightness of the late-afternoon sun made him squint. He was glad to be outside again. Now, standing on the street, he made his confession to Jenny. "I really don't like that guy."

"Drury? No one does," Jenny replied without hesitation. "In fact, some people *really* don't like him. I mean, most of the time when he's out in public, he's got a bodyguard with him. He's always getting some sort of threat." She paused, then spoke again. "Hey, listen, the man's got lots of power. That bothers a lot of people." She shrugged. "But you know what they say."

Jason shook his head. "No, what do *they* say?"

"Better with you than against you." She smiled.

"I guess so," Jason concurred, then changing the subject, added, "Hey, was Mike talking about Delacourte as in National Security Adviser Delacourte?"

Jenny shrugged again. "Could be. Word has it they were once good friends, back after the war. Actually I guess it was more like around the Korean War." She frowned, considering the possible dates. "Anyway," she continued, "Drury worked as an international correspondent and Delacourte was with the Agency."

"CIA?" Jason asked.

Jenny nodded in response. "Actually, for a short time, so was Drury. Being an international correspondent was a great cover—at least back before that became a big moral conflict for members of the fourth estate."

"He was a spy?" Jason asked in a tone of amazement.

"Spy is a funny word," Jenny began. "It conjures up images of movie stars. But actually, most operatives lead pretty quiet lives, from what I can determine. You run into them all the time in D.C. They live in the suburbs, and have kids, and drive station wagons just like everyone else." She paused for a moment. "Anyway, seems Drury and Delacourte were always running into each other. Then something happened. There was some kind of falling-out."

Jenny realized she had been making quite a speech. Jason was clearly caught up in it, yet she was aware that most of what she had been relating was merely the wildest kind of gossip. It was embarrassing for her to have Jason so attentive. "'Course that's just the poop around the office. Who knows what's really true?" she said. She hoped this statement would properly qualify her rambling and wildly speculative commentary. It did not, and she continued to feel uncomfortable.

"Can I trust him?" Jason pressed.

"No," Jenny responded, "no more than anyone in this town." Jason looked at her for a moment. Immediately she realized her error. "Except for me, Jason. You can trust me," she said soberly. He smiled, both because of her sentiment and because it was one of the few occasions when he could remember her being self-conscious. It did not quite fit her, he thought.

"What do you think about the contract?" he asked.

"Sign it," Jenny answered quickly. "What have you got to lose?"

Jason shrugged. "Tell you what. Let's cash this thing, then I'll treat you to dinner."

"Deal," Jenny said. "Afterward we'll get you some clothes."

Jason looked down, suddenly conscious again of the wild purple shirt he was wearing. He looked back at Jenny. "Maybe we ought to do that first," he said, grinning.

In a car nearby, a man watched Jason and Jenny move across the street behind him. He reached for the microphone, and spoke.

"Prime. Base."

"Base. Go," the radio responded.

"They're on the move," the man stated.

"Stay with them."

"Affirmative," the man responded.

15

JASON CASHED HIS CHECK in the bank across the street from World Syndications. As soon as the teller realized the check was drawn on LeRoy Drury's special account, there was no problem getting the money. The bank seemed used to such dealings.

Turning from the teller, Jason began counting the money, but stopped. "I ought to call the bishop's office," he announced.

"Counting money made you think of the bishop?" Jennifer prodded.

Jason smiled and stepped to a row of phone booths in the bank lobby. Using his credit card, he dialed Bishop Merrill's office directly. Jennifer listened and smiled when, after pressing several buttons, Jason offered a mechanical, lifeless "You're welcome." She knew he was mimicking the electronic voice that thanked all credit card users for the proper numbers.

"Hello, Bishop Merrill's office."

"Hello," Jason began, then paused. Could his pursuers be listening in? "This is Reverend Asbury calling."

"Reverend Asbury?"

"Yes, I'm an old classmate of the bishop's. I wonder if I might speak to him."

"Why certainly. Just a moment."

"Asbury," Jennifer demanded.

Jason put his hand over the mouthpiece. "Later." Then, into the phone, "Roy, how are you? Frank Asbury here."

"Frank Asbury?" Jenny whispered, and pressed in on Jason so as to hear the other side of the conversation.

"Frank," the bishop was saying. "Where are you now on your circuit?"

"Oh," replied Jason, "about halfway or so."

"Well," responded the bishop, "how is your—is it revival work you're doing?"

"Yes, yes. It's slow, Roy, it's slow out amongst the heathen."

"I know, I know.... Ahh..." The bishop paused and seemed to be debating how to proceed. "But I've heard a lot about you lately. From some of your followers." He gave an odd sort of emphasis to the last word.

"Really?"

"Yes," responded the bishop, "from your last charge. In fact, I ran into a young couple right here in the office! Terribly interested in your itinerancy. They must have been very close to you. They certainly seemed to know all about you."

"It's nice to know you're remembered."

"You're all they could talk about. In fact, it was clear they'd love to visit you."

"I understand. Well, I'm sure they would, but it wouldn't be the best thing right now. Not until the revival's a little more organized. Say, it's good to talk with you, Roy. It's been so long."

"Seems like two hundred years at least!"

"It does." Jason laughed.

"Well, you take care of yourself out there. Remember, be wary of the eighth plague in the land of Egypt. The plagues still come today."

"I'll remember."

"Godspeed, Frank. Godspeed."

Jenny was asking questions almost as soon as Jason hung up the phone. "You leading a double life? Who the hell is

Frank Asbury? What's he talking about—the eighth plague?''

"I *think* that the eighth plague was mosquitoes or locusts."

"Insects?"

"Bugs," Jason responded. "I think the ol' bishop was trying to tell us the lines were bugged."

"Well, shee-it! That ol' devil. What else did he have to say?"

Jason smiled at Jenny's confusion, and briefly explained the whole conversation. "Frank—Francis—Asbury was a circuit rider. He visited little churches all up and down the East Coast around the time of the American Revolution. Halfway through his circuit would have put him somewhere in Virginia or Maryland. The bishop was telling us that the people following me have made inquiries. Two even came into the office. They wanted to know where I was. The bishop seemed to think they were close to finding me, at least that's what I think he meant."

"A bishop, huh? I've got to meet this guy sometime," Jenny said. There was true admiration in her voice. Jason chuckled at the prospect of a face-to-face meeting between the bishop and Jenny. "What's so funny?" Jenny demanded as they stepped out of the bank into the afternoon light.

"Nothing," Jason responded. "I was just thinking about you and the bishop meeting. It'd be nice."

"Nice!" Jenny echoed, and Jason's eyes sparkled as he formed a broad smile.

From six floors above, LeRoy Drury watched as Jason and Jennifer came back out of the bank. He had been watching ever since they had gone in, and now, as he gazed down on them, they seemed like tiny insects. He reflected on the comparison for a moment and smiled. " 'Will you walk into my parlor?' said the spider to the fly; ''Tis the prettiest little parlor you ever did spy,''' he whispered. He smiled again and watched them as they merged with the dozens of other pedestrians on the street.

As he continued to gaze out the window, he reached for his phone, pressed a button and spoke into the mouthpiece. "Get me Chris Donlevy." Drury paused, reconsidering. "No, wait," he said impulsively. "Never mind." He pressed down on the switch hook, then turned to his Rolodex, thumbed through to the Ds and dialed a number.

"Office of the director," a woman answered.

"Alex Delacourte, please. LeRoy Drury calling."

There was just the slightest pause before the woman responded, "Just a moment, please."

A full minute passed. Drury continued to watch the activity in the street below. He knew exactly what Delacourte was doing: playing the power game, making him wait. But for this one, he would be willing to wait all day.

"Alex Delacourte."

"Hello, Alex, this is LeRoy Drury."

"Long time," said Delacourte.

"Years," confirmed Drury.

"What can I do for you?"

Drury smiled, considering all the ways he might respond to that question. He chose to ask simply, innocently, another.

"Do you remember Sam Morrison?"

There was silence at the other end. Drury tried to read the silence, but it was impossible.

"Who?" Delacourte finally asked.

"Sam Morrison. He left the Agency in the mid-fifties."

"Morrison..." said Delacourte, trying to remember. "Oh Christ, sure. The librarian! Haven't thought about him in years! What about him?"

"He died yesterday."

"Boy, who's left from the old days? Seems like old age is on the warpath." Delacourte paused. "Was he sick?"

"My source doesn't think so."

"Source!" repeated Delacourte. "You make it sound sinister."

"I think it might be," responded Drury.

"You ought to take that to the FBI."

"Right," said Drury, "but I seemed to remember you were on pretty friendly terms with Morrison." He paused. "I thought you might want to know."

Again, there was silence for a moment at the other end of the line. Finally Delacourte responded. "Damn decent of you, Lee." Another pause followed. "You didn't call just to tell me about some old Agency guy kicking off, did you?"

Drury smiled. All right, he thought. "Okay, Alex, I thought you might be able to shed some light on this Alpha/Omega thing?"

"Alpha/Omega?" Delacourte began. "What the hell's Alpha..." He was silent a moment, remembering. "Oh, Christ," he murmured. "What's this—Trivial Pursuit?"

"Sort of," Drury snapped. "Morrison was Alpha."

"Damn," breathed Delacourte. "No wonder the guy disappeared the way he did. How the hell'd you know that?"

"My source," responded Drury. "Actually, I was just trying to do a little checking on his story. To be honest, I can't find too many people left from the old days."

"That's the truth for damn sure," Delacourte affirmed, then added, "What's your interest?"

"Just the story. A guy who knew Morrison is staying with someone one of my people knows."

"Who?"

"It's not important. Someone in Eleanor MacMillan's office. They came to see me today."

"Did they say who Omega was?" Delacourte asked casually.

"I didn't ask, actually. But they're coming back in tomorrow. Maybe I'll find out then. Anyway, back to the question at hand. Do you have anything I could use?"

"On Alpha/Omega?"

"Right."

"Not a clue. Besides, Drury, what the hell makes you think I'd give you anything?"

"Just a long shot. I guess somewhere in the back of my mind, I thought you and the bookman were pretty good friends."

"The bookman?" Delacourte paused. "No, no; it was Bookworm. That's what we called him. Anyway, yeah, I knew him. Liked him—a lot. He did good work." Again Delacourte hesitated. "Too bad he's dead."

Drury frowned. He'd been hoping for more from Delacourte. "Well, you've sure managed to make it sound pretty dull," he responded. "I hope the minister can provide a little spice, after what I've advanced him."

"Minister?" inquired Delacourte.

"The girl's friend. Well, Alex, I tried. You're as tight-lipped as ever."

"Loose lips sink ships."

Drury laughed once. "Depends on your line of work, I guess."

Drury hung up before Delacourte had a chance to even say goodbye. He slumped into his chair and scowled. Had he made a mistake in talking with Delacourte? "What the hell did you expect from him, anyway?" he asked aloud. He glanced down at his pipe. It had gone out.

16

THE REST OF THE DAY was a happy change from the tension Jason had been feeling. Jennifer and he had gone shopping. Her taste was flawless. Following what could only be described as a spree, they headed for a restaurant. The one Jennifer selected was a quiet little Italian place tucked into a building just off Connecticut Avenue.

They didn't talk about Omega or CIA or FBI or much of anything else for that matter. They ate slowly, and mostly just quietly studied each other. At one point, they did talk about high school.

"Remember Piggy McCauley?" Jenny asked.

Jason's face darkened. "Yes."

Jenny leaned over her scampi. "Did he really screw the hogs?"

"Jeez, Jenny," Jason said in whispered tones. He looked quickly around as if he expected Piggy to be listening at the next table. "What made you think of that?"

"I don't know. I was thinking about it this afternoon."

"Not one of my prouder moments."

"Why not? Everybody hated his guts. You just put the bastard in his place."

Jason frowned. He clearly did not want to talk about it. Jenny graciously changed the subject. For the rest of the meal, they spent the time recalling happier moments.

They got home just a little before nine. When they had stepped off the elevator and moved to Jenny's door, the stairway door opened, and a man stepped into the hallway.

Although the initial sound set Jason on guard, the man himself told him all was normal. This, thought Jason, has got to be Walter.

"Hey, Jen," the man called. "You got anything goin' on the tube?"

Jenny turned to Jason. "You want to watch anything on TV?"

"Nope," Jason answered directly.

"It's yours," Jenny said brightly.

As Walter stepped up to them, Jason reflected on what Jenny had said earlier in the day. He had often been told that he looked like someone else. Now he had a chance to decide for himself. He studied the man approaching him. They *were* about the same build, but as far as Jason was concerned, that was about it. Jason also noticed the clothes. How come they look better on him? he wondered.

"Walter, this is Jason," Jennifer began. "Jason, Walter." They exchanged greetings and stepped into the apartment.

"Thanks for the clothes," Jason said. "They really saved the day."

"Must be hell losing your luggage in New Haven."

A momentary look of puzzlement passed across Jason's face. Then he realized that Jenny must have told Walter he had lost his luggage. "Oh, right," he said, recovering. "It really kind of put a crimp in the whole day. Anyway, I'll get your stuff back to you tomorrow."

"No hurry," answered Walter as he turned on the television. He settled into a beanbag chair. "Tuesday night. The one point of order in my life: talk to Mother at eight, then the movie at nine."

"Damn!" Jason muttered.

"What's the matter?" Jenny asked.

"I've got to call my parents. It's their anniversary. Damn."

"No problem. Use my phone."

"I'll keep tabs on the bill," he said, dialing.

"Don't worry."

He took the phone and moved farther away from the television. After a pause, he spoke. "Hi, it's Jason."

"Oh, Jason, I'm so glad you called." The voice on the phone sounded gentle and reassuring, but there was also a strange tenseness to it. Jason noticed it immediately.

"Are you all right, Mother?"

"Well, yes, of course we are...now. Oh, Jason, we've been so worried."

Jennifer glanced over at Jason and immediately knew something was wrong. The relaxed feeling of the evening had suddenly given way to that now familiar tension. He stiffened and turned.

"What's wrong?"

"Well, the FBI called—" his mother replied.

"Mother," Jason interrupted. "I'll call you right back. If anyone else calls, *anyone*, hang up right away." He slammed the phone down. "Those bastards. They've even gotten to them!" He stared angrily at Jennifer. "They've been to my parents! Can you believe it?" As he left the apartment, he called back, "I'm going to a phone booth." Jennifer and Walter looked at each other for just the briefest moment, then she shrugged as if to say, "What's he talking about?"

"I'll come with you," Jennifer called. She grabbed her keys and started to exit, then, leaning back into the apartment, she spoke to Walter. "Make yourself at home. Just lock up if you leave."

The night inexplicably seemed cooler. Jason felt his body brace to fight the cold. Standing in the phone booth, he shoved his free hand into his pocket and pulled his arm close to his body. He shifted his weight from one foot to another, as he waited for the operator to complete the call. He looked at Jenny as she stood outside the booth. The phone rang just once.

"Hello?" Jason's mother sounded more tense this time.

"Hi, Mom," Jason said quietly.

"Dad's on the extension, dear."

"Hi, Dad."

"What the heck's going on, son?"

Hearing both their voices together was reassuring. "Listen, please. I can't tell you much, because I don't know much myself. But I'm all right. You didn't tell them anything about people I know in Washington, did you?"

"You mean, Je—"

"No!" shouted Jason. "No names."

"Well, no, son, we haven't mentioned anyone."

His mother's answer gave Jason a chance to regain some of his composure. "Good, good," he responded. "I know this is all pretty confusing, but please do not mention any names to anyone. No matter what they tell you. Okay?" There was silence on the other end. Jason's fury at Omega, or the CIA, or whomever, was surging to the surface. He desperately fought to keep from having his parents sense his anger—and his fear. "Okay?" he repeated, more intently.

"Yes, Jason," his mother answered.

"Now, they're probably recording all your phone calls, so do not discuss me or our friends or relatives at all. And do this for me...." He paused. "Promise?"

"We will, son," said his mother, sounding even more uncertain.

"Call Sheriff Hall tonight. Ask him to send someone over to stay with you."

"But the FBI said—"

"No, Mom," Jason interrupted. "They just . . . just pretended to be the FBI. They really aren't. Don't tell them anything else."

Then Jason took a deep breath and lied to his parents. "This will all be over in a few days. Then I'll explain the whole thing. I promise." Again he paused, and knew that his mother and father were trying to sort the past few minutes into some sense. "Listen," he continued, "I'm sorry, but I really have to go now. I'm sorry," he repeated more softly. "See ya' later." He started to hang up.

"Jason!" his mother called desperately into the phone.

"Yes?"

"I love you."

"Take care, son," his father added.

Jason could feel the tears welling up in his eyes. He sighed deeply. "Goodbye," he whispered.

For a long time, he stood thinking, worrying, seething.

"Christ, Jason, we better get going or we'll have the Keystone Kops on our tails. Come on."

Jenny was right, of course. Their experience of the morning had confirmed that. They quickly moved to Jenny's car. As she drove toward her apartment, Jason stared unfocusing at the roadway. Finally, quietly, he murmured, "I don't think I'm going to make it." The statement rang with defeat. Jennifer waited, holding back on an impulse to make an immediate response.

"They won't bother your parents, you know. They won't hurt them." Jason looked at her. "There'd be no point. Hell, now that they've been found out, they're probably pulling out right now. Really, Jason. Think about it. There'd be no point."

Her logic was unassailable.

Jason coughed a brittle ironic laugh. "Omega said there didn't have to be a point. He just likes killing. That's what he said."

"Come on, Jason," Jenny said abruptly. "Let's stop for a drink."

"I don't drink."

"Well," she snapped, "maybe you should." She spoke with more force than she intended, but the result was not disagreeable. Jennifer looked at him and grinned.

Jason glanced back at her. He remembered something his uncle used to say. "Might as well laugh," he'd say, "sure as hell can't cry." Jason snickered. He shook his head and smiled in spite of himself.

"Tell you what," he said. "You order a drink; I'll order a root beer."

"But what are the other kids going to think?" Jenny said. She looked at Jason with mock disapproval and continued to drive toward the closest pub. It was a busy spot. Several cars were moving in and out of the parking lot as Jenny drove in. She had to wait for a space. Once she got the car parked, they moved inside, losing themselves in a mass of noise and smoke and people.

Outside, another driver waited for a place to park. When he had finally slid the car into a space, he spoke into a microphone.

"Prime, base."

"Base, go," came the radio's reply.

"They've gone into the Foggy Bottom Pub. Looks like they'll be here for a while. I'm going inside."

"Affirmative. Keep your channel open."

The man sighed, dug into his suit coat pocket, pulled out a small transceiver and checked some adjustments. Then he reached out to turn the car radio's on-off switch but paused momentarily while he listened to a transmission from his colleague, whom he had left in the apartment opposite Jennifer Seidkamp's.

"Sector one, base."

"Base, go."

"Listen, as long as they're going to be away from the apartment for a while, is it all right if I break?"

There was a pause, then, "Affirmative on your request. Commence, 21:45 hours."

"Sector one clear."

"Base clear."

The man in the parking lot chuckled as he turned off his car transceiver and stepped out into the cold night air. His colleague had just returned from a job in Mexico, and was suffering the inevitable intestinal results of such an assignment. He knew all too well why the guy required a break. He smiled once more, shut the car door and headed for the entrance to the Foggy Bottom Pub.

IN A QUIET VIRGINIA SUBURB, Christopher Donlevy hung up the telephone and sat entranced, his hand still on the receiver. He frowned slightly, then lifted it to his ear once more. Perhaps with this call, he thought—he hoped—this business might come to an end. He dialed and waited.

"Sorry to bother you, sir," Donlevy said finally. That's the truth and then some, he thought.

"Well?" The voice was cold and unresponsive.

This was the second time today that Donlevy had updated the Alpha/Omega case. He would omit all the problems he had encountered during the day and keep to the positive.

"We've got a location for Winslow. Just a few blocks from the pay phone they used this morning. My people will move in and pick him up." Donlevy waited for some sort of affirmation. None came. He had thought this was just what the man would want.

Instead Omega coolly posed a question. "Does he know you've made him?"

Donlevy was surprised at the noticeable tone of irritation in the man's voice. "No, I don't think so," he answered.

"Is the location under surveillance?"

"Not yet."

"Look," Omega began, "your men have had a long day. And it sounds as though we've got him, so I wouldn't bother sending out a team tonight. The pressure's off now. Why don't you give your people the night off? What's to lose?"

Donlevy realized that the suggestion was in fact a command—puzzling, but nonetheless a command.

"They'll appreciate that, sir," Donlevy replied.

"Good job, Donlevy." The usual abrupt click followed.

What the hell was that all about? thought Donlevy. First he was crawling all over me for information. Now it seems as though he couldn't care less. It didn't make sense. Donlevy was bothered. His thoughts ranged from his belief in the system of which he was an integral part, to the sudden importance of one country pastor, to his superior's equally sudden lack of interest. The latter occupied most of his thoughts. He simply couldn't figure it out. Why? he asked himself in a dozen different ways. Each time, his logic failed. Something was missing in each hypothesis. And then, slowly, another thought formed.

The idea was, at first, simply an uncomfortable tear in the tapestry that he was carefully weaving. And yet it was the only way Donlevy could logically explain what was happening. The thought was becoming a fearsome, undeniable reality. Sitting in the security of his own home, he felt suddenly alone and abandoned. He knew what he would do next was going to put his very life in jeopardy, but he had no choice, at least not in his mind.

Donlevy stepped out into the hallway, grabbed a jacket and walked into the family room. His wife was watching TV and knitting. He walked over to her, leaned down and kissed her.

"I'm going over to the office for a while," he said quietly. "I'll be back before midnight."

"Take care," his wife said, looking up at him. He smiled back at her and stepped out into the chilly night.

ACROSS THE POTOMAC, a man sat impatiently drumming his fingers on the wheel of his Mercedes coupe. He almost wished he had called for his limo and driver. The traffic clogged the streets and nothing moved. How the hell could things get this jammed this late at night? he mused. "Damn!" he shouted. Again for the fifteenth time he looked down at his watch. This was one appointment LeRoy Drury didn't want to miss.

17

OMEGA STARED into the dimly lit apartment. There was apparently only one person there, the minister. The solitary figure was silhouetted against the television screen. Damn it, thought Omega. Crawling around on a goddamn fire escape is ridiculous. And yet, it was the only place he could get a clean shot without actually entering the building. And going into the building would have been foolhardy.

The man watched his victim and slowly shook his head. There was nothing about the job that he liked. He tightened his body to defend himself against the persistent chill. "Christ!" he breathed. "It's too damn cold." He wore calfskin gloves to warm his hands. Now that he was ready, he removed one glove, reached into his suit coat and withdrew his gun. His body had kept it warm, and now the weapon warmed his hand.

He aimed carefully through the window. That also bothered him. Sometimes glass could do strange things to a bullet. It could alter its trajectory ever so slightly, but enough to create problems. He again checked the window with care. It was pointless to try to open it.

Now his intended victim straightened up, lifting himself part way out of the beanbag chair in which he was sitting. Had the man heard a noise? Omega readied himself to react quickly. But then he realized why the man had moved as he had. He was reacting to the television. As Omega targeted the man in the beanbag chair, the man watched virtually the same scene unfolding on the TV. On the glowing screen, a killer pressed against the wall of an alley, hidden in the shadows. His uplifted hand held a 1940s vintage Luger.

Omega smirked. A Luger P-08, he thought. Totally unrealistic. No one who was serious would use a weapon like that. It looked nice, but it was clumsy and the trigger pull was heavy. And its accuracy was as questionable as its functioning.

On TV the apparent victim approached. The images cut faster and faster between close-ups of the victim, then the assailant.

Omega settled. His eyes moved in a cycle, first on the screen, then on the man in the beanbag, and back again. Omega had already determined the next bit of action in the unfolding scenario. The killer on the TV screen lowered his gun as the victim stepped into range.

Omega smiled and began to squeeze the trigger of his own weapon. Not a quarter second elapsed between the firing of the two guns. There was the familiar "pumpf" of the silencer and just the slightest tinkling sound as the bullet broke through the window. The man's head jerked toward the TV. Simultaneously the screen flashed, then went black.

Omega knew instantly something was wrong. His eyes widened; he could see a vague form standing, wheeling, staggering. Then he lost it. Suddenly the door to the hallway opened. The man was attempting a desperate escape, but instead, all he had really done was to give Omega the light he needed to finish the job. You fool, thought Omega, you've ended it.

"And you said you weren't afraid of death," Omega whispered. His victim staggered into the stream of light, his right hand pressed against the side of his neck. Blood drained between his fingers and down his wrist.

Omega's second shot cut a new hole in the glass and found its mark, slamming the man's head into the door. The third

bullet was unnecessary. It completely shattered the window-
dowpane. The bullet pounded into the man's temple, knocking his face away from Omega. The body slumped downward. A smudged trail of red traced its descent along the
door.

"Damn it," muttered Omega. He was visibly shaken. For
whatever reason—it must be the glass, he told himself—the
job had been sloppy. His feelings were jumbled. He should
have felt a great sense of relief, but there was none. He had
accomplished his goal, and yet he felt no triumph. Instead
he felt uncertainty, almost a brooding, vague fear. Now he
only wanted to get away.

He stumbled down the fire escape. As he stepped off it he
glanced quickly around. Then he moved back into the
nighttime shadows and disappeared. He had made his second mistake of the evening. Later he would realize it. You
were in too much of a hurry, he would tell himself. But at
that moment, he was only interested in disappearing. Had
he taken more time, had he looked more carefully, he might
have noticed the frozen, shocked visage of a man partially
hidden in the shrubs of the apartment building across the
street.

Christopher Donlevy stood motionless. What he had just
witnessed stunned him—no, that wasn't the right word. It
was a gnawing kind of slow panic. It was the kind of panic
that comes when one is suddenly wrenched into the realization that something basic and fundamental is founded on
emptiness, on nothingness. Donlevy sighed deeply, desperately trying to purge his system of the filth that he now felt
filling him. Everything he had built his life upon was now
merely shifting sand. He felt sick and weakened.

"There's nothing to be done here," he whispered to himself. He slowly walked to his car. He thought of the people
who would find whatever was left up there in that room. He

felt sorry for them. But most of all, he felt sorry for himself. He was defeated and there was nothing he could do, not now anyway. For the first time in nearly twenty-five years of service, he felt betrayed. What he had just seen unfolding was immoral, and he had been a part of it; he had allowed the Agency to become part of it. As he drove homeward, he worked to move his thoughts away from that scene, but he could not. It would be with him for a long time. He knew he would not sleep tonight. But—"Goddamn him!" he whispered—he knew Omega would.

IN THE APARTMENT across from Jenny's, the man returned from his break. He spoke into the walkie-talkie.

"Sector one. Base."

"Base. Go," returned the small speaker.

"Returning to service," the man responded casually. He reached for the binoculars and glanced across to Jenny's apartment.

"Affirmative. Time in, 22:08 hours," the radio responded routinely. But in that moment, the man saw something that pumped his system full of adrenaline.

"Red light."

"Go sector one," prompted the radio, with a sudden sense of urgency.

"There's evidence of assault over there. The hallway door's open. Blood." The man lifted his thumb off the Transmit button of his transceiver and muttered, "Jesus Christ."

"Hold position, sector one," the radio responded. Then the man heard a short, sharp tone.

In the Foggy Bottom Pub, another man heard the same tone. Instantly, he tensed, looked around and leaned away from the people nearest him. He reached into his left sleeve and pulled a small wired object into the palm of his hand.

He lifted the object to his mouth and spoke. "Prime to base."

"Your people okay?"

"Affirmative, base," the man responded.

"We've got a red light at sector one."

"Damn," muttered the man, then into his radio, "How?"

"Unknown. Lewis and Tomacelli are meeting you at your location," the reply came.

"Affirmative," the man answered.

"Base, prime, clear. Sector one."

Now the man in the apartment across from Jenny's again spoke. "Sector one. Go."

"Hold position. We'll report to D.C. locals."

"Affirmative," the man responded. He sat back to wait. It would be interesting.

IN A WAY IT WAS simply a reminder. If either Jason or Jennifer had ever thought this was simply some sort of exciting, wild interlude, in otherwise humdrum lives, that it was something that would merely provide a great story for boring parties, this event shattered that notion as surely as Omega's bullets shattered the window and what now lay beyond.

In fact, Jason and Jennifer had never really allowed this possibility to exist. It was too awful. Neither had acknowledged that something like this would—could—actually happen. But now it had. Now, as they stood over Walter's lifeless and violated body, that terrible, hazy possibility seemed to triumph over their willed ignorance. It had become, in an instant, a frightening reality.

Police officers and detectives filled the apartment. Most just seemed to stand in groups of two or three, talking idly in hushed tones. They gathered in the room, on the fire escape, in the hallway.

Jennifer and Jason had heard the sirens as they drove back from the bar, but sirens were common, and they thought nothing of the sounds until they saw the patrol cars and the ambulance in front of Jennifer's building. Even then, they did not connect the police cars with their own worries. Somehow local police involvement had never been a part of the scenarios they had constructed.

Jenny had been the first to sense the danger. It was simply a vague agitation until she saw figures in her apartment. Then she noticed LeRoy Drury standing in the doorway.

"God, you're both all right," Drury said when they came upon him. He looked shaken. The color had drained from his face. Turning to Jenny, he spoke again. "I was afraid..." He let his thought trail off.

Now Jenny experienced a momentary spark deep in her consciousness. She began to understand the reality. "What happened?" she demanded. "It's Walter, isn't it?"

"I don't know," replied Drury. "After dinner, I got to thinking about our meeting this afternoon. There were some details I wanted to follow up on, so I thought I'd come by and go over them with you. I stopped at the office to pick up a few things, and got delayed." Now Drury's anxious tone blended with a sense of irritation. "When I got here, the police were just arriving."

The three of them had studied one another in silence. Jennifer had never experienced anything like the sensation she now felt. She couldn't quite make herself move inside.

"You'll have to go up sooner or later," Jason said with gentle forcefulness. "Let's go." Jenny looked at him in a way that revealed utter vulnerability. He gently took her hand. "Come on," he said simply.

As they started in, Drury had stopped them. He spoke
quietly in whispered tones. "Maybe you shouldn't say anything about...your suspicions." He could see the confusion and resentment forming in Jason's eyes. He continued
quickly. "I just don't think it would help anyone. It would
be better not to mention this Omega thing—just for a day
or so, until we get some answers."

Jason was quick to respond. "But that's..."

"Withholding information?" completed Drury. Jason
nodded. He glanced at Jennifer. Drury continued. "It will
just muddy things up right now. It won't help you, believe
me. In fact, it may well hurt you." Jason's stare was one of
contempt, and it demanded more from Drury. "If you tell
them everything you know—we know," he corrected himself, "what do you think's going to happen?" Drury did not
wait for a reply. "They'll go directly to the people you're
worried about finding you."

"Looks like I've already been found," Jason said soberly.

Drury frowned. "Just try it my way for twenty-four
hours. If there're no results, you can do whatever you
want—whatever you think is proper."

A glaring light had suddenly assaulted their privacy.
Drury glanced out at the TV cameras that were bearing in
toward them.

"And for God's sake," Drury added forcefully, "don't
say a word to those vultures."

Jason looked at Jennifer. He could see she only wanted
to get past the horror of what was happening. He looked
back at Drury.

"Trust him," Jennifer said.

Jason had exhaled slowly. He almost felt guilty for hesi-
tating, but what he was about to agree to seemed wrong. It
was wrong. It was that simple. Anyway, he had agreed.

It seemed as if that had been hours ago. In fact, Jason had lost track of the time. He had no idea how long they'd been there. Now standing above the body, he felt the anger again welling up inside of him. The police were asking questions of both him and Jennifer, and all he could do was shrug and mumble, "I don't know." For a while Jenny had struggled to hold back her emotion, but now pain and fear flooded out. Jason said nothing; rather, he simply held her hand tightly.

The questions from the police were relentless, but even those eventually melted into blurred ramblings. Jason drifted away, his thoughts dulling the confusion of sounds and voices around him. Slowly, one thought emerged. It caused his eyes to glisten with tears of sorrow and regret— and also of burning, blinding anger. The thought was one that he could scarcely bear.

It was because of him—there was a direct, undeniable link—that a totally innocent person now lay dead at his feet. It was as if he had pulled the trigger himself. And mixed with that thought was another. If I hadn't left the apartment with Jenny, I'd be dead now. My God, he thought, and Jenny would be, too. The anger became entwined with guilt. It ate at him.

"God help me."

"Beg your pardon," said one of the police officers.

Jason glanced up quickly at the officer who looked in his direction.

Jason looked down again, and embarrassedly shook his head. "I must have been mumbling to myself," he said. "Sorry."

"It's okay, Reverend," responded a detective. "I guess we have all we need from you, anyway. If you think of anything else that might help, give us a call."

Now another detective spoke. His words, carefully phrased, shattered the promise of escape. "By the way, Reverend Winslow," he began casually, "I can't help but notice a kind of resemblance between you and the deceased." Jason felt his muscles tighten. His face grew hotter. The detective continued. "You don't think the killer was really after you?"

It felt as though a knife had sliced slowly through an artery in the side of his neck, draining the blood from his brain. Now his face cooled. He looked from the detectives to Jenny, to Drury. They seemed suddenly far away. He shook his head, and forced a strange smile to form. He felt panic begin to flow in where his blood had been. When he spoke, he sounded tortured. In fact, he was, tortured by his own lack of conviction, by the lying that he had bought into.

"N-no," he stammered. "I . . . I . . ."

"Don't you think these people have been through enough for tonight?" Drury's voice cut through Jason's cold panic and saved him.

"Yeah, of course, Mr. Drury," said the policeman. "Sorry." The detectives looked at each other. They both wondered what the minister might have said, had Drury not interrupted.

By midnight all the outsiders had gone. Someone from the medical examiner's office wheeled Walter out on a stretcher. He was wrapped in a dark green plastic body bag. The finality of the act was unbearable.

"Take care, you two," Drury said, and left with the last of the police.

Jenny and Jason could hear the shouts of the news media who had held their station below all night. The darkness was shattered by flashes and television lights.

Without conversation, Jenny moved to the kitchen and filled a basin with hot water and soap. First, she washed the door, then the spots on the floor, and finally the beanbag chair. She worked at her task solemnly, her face stern and gaunt. Jason stood there and watched, motionless and silent.

When Jenny stood up, holding the basin in her hands, she stared into Jason's eyes. Between devastating sobs, she confessed her feelings. "My friend's been destroyed tonight... and I'm worried about stains." Jason stepped beside her and held her tightly. He could feel her stiffen and struggle to bring herself under control, and after a moment, she moved away from him, into the kitchen. She disposed of the fouled water and returned to stand with Jason, still in silence.

There was a chill in the room. They both felt it. Jenny slowly rubbed her arms, as if to brush the coldness of death from her. She was the first to speak. "I can't stay here tonight," she said desperately. She glanced at the broken window, as if it somehow explained her need to leave. Jason nodded.

Without speaking, they packed some clothes and left the place.

18

"WHERE ARE WE GOING?" Jason asked. The words were the first either he or Jennifer had spoken since leaving the apartment.

"The Holiday Inn over in Arlington. Just across Key Bridge," answered Jenny.

They asked for two rooms. The clerk seemed mildly surprised. "I can't give you two rooms. I'm sorry. There are a couple of conventions in town," he added.

They settled for one room with double beds. While Jenny changed in the bathroom, Jason took off his shoes and socks, shirt and pants, and slipped into his bed. He switched off the light, turned to face the window and thought about all that had happened to him.

He lay there and began to seethe, as he reviewed the past few days. With each thought, he grew angrier. But central to his anger was his sense of helplessness. There simply was nothing he could do. Thinking only made things worse. He realized how exhausted he was. He forced himself to concentrate on something different. He focused on the kind of crisp clear autumn day it must have been in Maine. He thought about Dog.

The bathroom door opened. A shaft of greenish light flowed across his bed and onto the drapes of the window. Then Jenny flicked the light switch and the darkness brought them the emptiness they both sought. She climbed into her bed.

"Good night, Jason," she said quietly.

"'Night," he murmured.

In the darkness, they listened to each other's breathing, to the bed clothes rustling as they tossed about restlessly, to their own hearts beating, to their own private thoughts that flooded in great swells upon their consciousness.

How much time had passed? An hour? Two? Or perhaps only thirty minutes. Jenny's faltering words shattered the brittle silence. Her voice was that of a frightened child. "Jason? I can't sleep."

He rolled over and looked up. In the dimness he could see her vague outline standing next to his bed.

"Neither can I." He spoke in a whisper. The words caught in his throat. He hitched himself up, and leaned on one elbow. She held out her hand. He took it in his and she sat, almost slumped onto the bed next to him. He pushed himself up and leaned against the headboard. He put his arm around her and drew her close to him, lowering his lips to the top of her head. She rested her cheek against his chest. As his tears mingled with her hair, he felt her tears on his skin. Her body broke into heaving.

"Why, Jason, why?" she sobbed.

"I don't know," he whispered, resting his cheek on her head. "I don't know."

"Doesn't your God have anything to say about that?"

Jason gave a dry, ironic snicker, but no words came to answer her question.

"Can't you say something to make it better?" Jenny pleaded.

"No," he said sharply. "I'm not a magician." He stopped abruptly, alarmed at his coldness. Any other time, when he counseled bereaved people, he did so with the utmost precision. In the business, it was called "grief work," and he was a master at it. His callousness shocked him and in that instant he felt a shame flow into his soul. Jenny was not the object of his fear and uncertainty. No, he told himself, those feelings ought to be directed elsewhere. She needs you, he thought. And you need her. Help her. Do what you do so well.

Now he deliberately channeled his attention to Jennifer and her needs. It was one way to deal with his own pain. Force it out of the way by dealing with someone else's.

He began again, this time softening his tone. "What can I say to you, Jenny? What can I say that won't sound hollow and empty? You deserve more than that," he whispered into her hair. He held her tightly. He knew, of course, what he would say next, but he paused. When the time was right, he spoke.

"Tell me about Walter."

Jenny was silent for several minutes. Her grip on him was almost painful in its intensity. Her breathing was heavy and labored. It seemed to Jason that he could feel her thinking. Finally she began.

"There's not much to tell, really." She paused. When she spoke again, she sounded guilty. "I guess I really didn't know him that well.... I mean, I did, but I never really let him know what a good friend he was."

For the next hour or so, Jenny talked about Walter. At times she cried, occasionally she laughed. She told stories about apartment problems; she told about Walter's former wife—they had been divorced years ago—and his daughter, whom he loved dearly. Here or there Jason would ask a question, but most of the time he simply held her. As she talked, he could feel her relax. Her comments became fewer. The pauses lengthened. Finally, she fell asleep, still holding on to him.

When she was sleeping soundly, Jason gently removed himself from her grasp. Quietly, he slid out of the bed. She was lying on his covers, so he took the blankets from her bed and covered her.

He found a spare blanket, wrapped himself in it and moved toward the window. As he did so, he caught his reflection in the mirror. He looked like some penitent medieval monk in the dim light that filtered through the window. For a while he stood before the window. He held open the drapes and looked out across the Potomac to the glow of nighttime Washington.

"Jesus Christ," he murmured. "What am I going to do?" His anger and guilt returned in a rush of burning emotion. It grew from the knowledge that he had caused the death of at least one person, from the fact that he knew he was awash in hopelessness, from the fact that he had asked that stupid question too many times in the past few days.

Slowly he sank to his knees. You cynical, hypocritical bastard, he thought. When it's all said and done, you're just like everyone else—"calling on the Lord" to make everything all right. Still, he felt compelled. And in that moment, his motivation was genuine. He was not the image of a prideful man, kneeling there. He despised the preachers, the "Christians," who boasted of their humility. It nauseated him—seeing them merchandise this humility on television, hearing them on the radio.

This was a sacred moment, an intensely private moment, one that would forever remain secret. He was the vision of a defeated man, bent over, spent, in desperate need of forgiveness. So much haunted him, and he sought just the glimpse of some strength that could overpower the evil that he felt gnawing away at him.

A few words began to form in his thoughts—vaguely at first, and without substance. They slowly took on form: "Out of the depths..." The words repeated themselves and would not leave him. He was unable to force them from his consciousness. They hypnotized him; he could not move past them. And yet the fullness of the message they carried remained hidden from him. He looked around and saw a Gideon Bible on the table beside him. Paging through to the Psalms, he found the passage that would bring wholeness to his incomplete thought.

"Out of the depths," Jason whispered to the emptiness, "I cry to thee, O Lord.... There is forgiveness with thee...." He turned away from the book and again focused on the glow of the city across the Potomac. He stared at nothing while the words, like dreamed waves, surged across his memory. Finally he looked back down at the page. "I wait for the Lord," he read, "...my soul waits for the Lord more than the watchmen for the morning . . . For with the Lord is steadfast love...."

He crouched motionless for a long time. More than once silent, wrenching sobs shook his body. When he finally stood, he was different. Quietly different. It was nothing miraculous or supernatural. No heavenly fluorescent light shone. He hadn't been "born again," not the way the TV evangelists sold the idea, anyway. He was simply different. He stood straight and breathed in deeply. He was rested and exhausted simultaneously. But more than anything, he was, fundamentally, at peace.

He moved to where Jenny slept. For several minutes he stood above her and gazed down on her covered figure. At one point, he reached out intending to touch her. A perceptible tremor passed through him. Then he stood back, slowly shook his head and moved to the empty bed. Sleep came almost immediately.

19

OMEGA SHUT OFF THE RADIO with a brutal snap. Until this moment, he had been content with the knowledge that he had reached his goal, despite his unexpected feelings of disappointment at the moment of the minister's death. During the hunt, he had willed the final moment to bring exquisite satisfaction, but, strangely, he felt empty. He regretted not being able to confront the man face-to-face, to see close up the fear that flowed into his being. But it was with a certain smugness that he had turned on the radio this morning, expecting to hear a full account of his handiwork. When he discovered his error, he was enraged.

"Damn it!" Omega fumed. His fury was directed toward the minister. Had Omega been honest, it would have been directed inward. He had chosen an action that he had known from the start was rushed and ill-prepared. The death of an "innocent bystander" was of little consequence to him. But his preceding night's work did bother him on two counts. He had been careless. That was almost unforgivable. If it had been anyone else it would have been. And then there was his obsession with the minister. What was there about that man that drove him?

In his more lucid moments, Omega reasoned that the clergyman probably did not know his identity. Or if he did, so did any number of other people by now. But it's not whether the minister knows or not, Omega thought. No, it is the minister himself. It is the man. A gnawing hatred now probed at Omega—at his very sense of security. It had begun during his phone conversation with the minister. And it had possessed him ever since.

Be reasonable, Omega told himself. Forget the minister. Give it up. He snickered. It was precisely this kind of thinking that drove Omega to long for the clergyman's death. It was unreasonable. It was dangerous. It was something that didn't make sense. And yet deep down, Omega understood that there was something about the pastor that made him feel insecure. Perhaps the pastor's quiet superiority was what compelled him. Perhaps that was what was driving Omega. Whatever it was, Omega knew he would not rest until he had found the man and killed him, and killed the feelings that now tore at him. His feelings were irrational—that he knew—but he could not help it. It was as if some long-suppressed hunger had finally emerged. In this moment of turmoil, Omega became convinced this one death would appease that hunger.

SOMETHING WAS MOVING JASON from the emptiness of deep sleep to consciousness. His sleep ended suddenly. He opened his eyes. Jenny stood next to his bed.

"I'm sorry," she said quietly. "Your blanket fell off, and it's cold."

Jason realized now that he was cold. The blanket felt good. He smiled. "Thanks. What time is it?"

"Ten to eight."

He breathed in sharply and sat up.

"Jason." He looked at her. His eyes followed the contours of her body, clearly defined beneath her sheer nightgown. God, you're beautiful, he thought. She sank down on her knees and leaned on his bed. She took his hand in hers. Their gazes drifted upward and met.

"Thank you." He raised his eyebrows questioningly. "For what you did last night," she continued.

"You did the work," he said quietly. "I just listened." He smiled, pleased at her appreciation.

"You did more than that. You know you did." She paused. "At least I've..." She paused and began again. "At least it's bearable."

Jason smiled again. She was more comfortable with her feelings now and that was good. Jennifer smiled back, then slowly stretched upward and kissed him. It was a deep, searching kiss. It awakened him. It removed any inhibition he might have felt. Normally, a debate would rage within him in a moment like this. Do I allow my desire to move me toward fulfillment or do I force myself to subdue the physical urgings and maintain that vague, institutional sense of moral purity? But now the argument itself was lost in a swell of fiery emotion. His response was complete and unchecked.

Jennifer moved with an effortless fluidity. In a moment, he felt her body easily conforming to his. He could feel her hot breath move across his face, onto his neck. She was in constant motion. His hands moved over her body even as her hands coveted his. Her fingertips sparked life wherever they touched.

Now she breathed words of hope into his ear. "Stay with me, Jason."

The effect was sudden and numbing. She felt a cold distance flow between them. It confused her, frightened her. He rolled away from her and exhaled deeply and slowly. After a moment, he swung his legs over the edge of the bed and sat up. He leaned his arms on his knees and looked down at the floor.

"What's wrong?" Jenny asked. There was a quiet desperation in her voice. "I'm sorry," she continued, thinking she had pushed him too far. "I didn't mean—"

"No, Jenny," Jason interrupted. "It's not you." Again he sighed. As she watched him, she began to see clearly that she was not the problem; what bothered him was coming from within. She waited. When he finally spoke, his words were cradled in gentleness. "Jenny," he began. "Last night, I decided to go home."

"Maine?"

He nodded. She looked at him for a long time.

"When?"

He did not respond immediately. Before he did, he turned to face her. She deserved that at least. "Today," he said. The word hung like the sweltering wetness of a summer day. Jenny looked at him quietly. She could see his decision was firm. Her eyes wandered from him, only to return a moment later.

"But why?" She probed him with her gaze.

"Because."

"Because?" she echoed softly. The question was full of pain.

He shook his head. He again saw vulnerability in her eyes. "Jenny." He reached out and gently touched her cheek. "I care about you too much." He paused. She could see him working to shape exactly the right words. "Look what's happened." He spoke with desperate intensity. "Yesterday morning you were just as I always remembered you." He smiled gently, then added, "Only more so. But not now. Now your life is a series of...of...terrible possibilities. That's one reason. Walter is another. If I hadn't been here, he wouldn't have died. It's that simple. He'd still be alive. And who knows who might be..." He did not finish the sentence. "And my parents," he continued. "And how many others? How many lives have I screwed up? Destroyed?" Again he paused, carefully running his next thought over in his mind. Did he really believe what he was thinking?

Jenny could see him working. She saw him change as he thought. She saw the desperation replaced with resolve, the uncertainty with conviction. The power that now suddenly filled his eyes frightened her.

"He's too much for me, this Omega." He spit out the name. It was filled with venom. "Maybe he's not too much for someone like Drury, but for me..." Again he paused, weighing the words carefully. "I'm going back to where I can get back what I've lost."

His calmness was remarkable. She knew he meant exactly what he had said. Jenny stared at this person leaning over her, speaking in quiet, gentle tones. He was staggering in his unpretentiousness, formidable in his simplicity. In this moment, everything felt strangely unreal. He said that she had changed very little, but she felt an eerie awareness that he had changed, he had changed a great deal. In high school, he had simply been different. While most kids seemed almost to revel in their rage, he recoiled from displays of anger. For that he was labeled a wimp. Kids confused his timidity with weakness. Now, the timidness still apparent, but there was no mistaking it for weakness. Now, in his quiet strength, he seemed in ultimate control of his destiny. The word caught her. Ultimate. Yes, she thought, in this moment he is in control. She wondered what it was that had changed him. She looked at him with a sense of envy. She doubted that he was even aware of the power he seemed suddenly to possess. She had seen glimpses of it earlier, but now it seemed to pulse completely, quietly, through him. It was a power that no one could intimidate. He was at peace.

She would accept his intention to return to his home. If he were someone else, she might have tried to talk him out of it, but not Jason, not now. And then she sensed something else. It was only a vague awareness. It felt almost like fear, fear of coming too close to some unknowable power.

"What are you going to do when you get there?"

"Nothing," he said. "Nothing out of the ordinary. If Omega's going to come after me, let him come. If I can stop him, I will."

She looked deeply into his eyes. "And if you can't?" He gazed back at her, his eyes never betraying even the slightest doubt.

"Then it will end." He paused for a time. "It *will* end, Jenny. I'm not going to run anymore. Or hide anymore. Or drag anyone else into this. Or allow Omega to turn me into something I despise even more than him."

As his eyes moved slowly across her body, his mind was filled with painful, conflicting thoughts. At this moment, he wanted more than anything to remain with Jenny; yet if they stayed together, surely she would die. He knew that; the thought was more than he could bear, and he forced it from him.

Again there was a long silence. Finally, Jason spoke again. "I need to call home. Then I'll go see Drury and give him his money back."

"He won't take it back," Jenny responded. "And he'll give you a hard time."

"There's not much of a story left."

"He won't like it."

"It's my life!" Jason blurted out. He had spoken too quickly. His words had just the merest hint of a deep, hidden fury, but this gave way to the empty sound of flippancy. He looked away, brooding. "It's my life," he repeated softly, "at least for the time being."

"How are you getting back?" Jenny asked.

Jason shrugged. Again a period of silence punctuated their conversation. Jenny reached out and touched him gently on his chest. Her hand moved slowly downward. Her eyes focused on his. He leaned toward her and grasped her hand, stopping its movement.

"Jenny..."

"Hey," she began abruptly, "remember that night in the cornfield!"

Jason closed his eyes and smiled, shaking his head. "I'm cursed. I can never forget."

"Right," she interrupted. "You mastered a bra strap?"

Jason reddened at first, then laughed. Jenny joined him.

"I got the damn car stuck in the mud!" Jason continued. "The next morning when I got down to breakfast, my father looked up at me and said, 'Next time you want to go on a date, take the tractor.' That's all he ever said to me, but for days I was convinced he had been out in that field watching our every move!"

"Must have been pretty boring!" Jenny said.

"God, they were good days, you know it?"

Jenny nodded in agreement. Their laughter eased, and she knew the time had come to leave this fantasy of memory.

"Well, we can't stay here all day, I guess." She slipped out from his grasp and moved quickly into the bathroom, picking up her clothes as she went. Jason stood and dressed, then packed up his few things. Then he sat down on the bed and dialed the parsonage number in Craig's Harbor.

"Hello?" the voice said.

"Hi, this is Jason Winslow."

"Oh, hello, Jason, this is Pastor Grant."

Damn! thought Jason. My people have been saddled with him!

"Willard, how's everything going?"

"We've got everything under control here. Your family's doing well, I trust."

Jason took the lie in stride. He assumed that Grant had been told he had a family problem to tend to. "Things are better than they were."

"Praise the Lord."

"Right," said Jason coolly. "In fact, I'm coming back today."

"Really!" Grant sounded surprised. "That's too bad."

What's he mean by that? Jason wondered.

"Oh, I mean," said Grant, reading the silence, "that I really enjoy every chance I get to keep my finger in the stew!" Then he added in a confidential tone, "You know, retirement isn't all it's cracked up to be."

"I guess," responded Jason.

"Yes, yes," replied the older minister in a pastoral way.

"Any news?" inquired Jason casually.

"No, same old quiet place. Oh, some of your parishioners are wondering about a memorial service for Mr. . . . ah . . . ah . . ."

"Sullivan?" Jason interjected.

"Yes, exactly," Grant said. "People are pretty upset, you know. Folks just never quite get used to a person taking his own life."

Jason sighed. The lies continue, he thought.

"When is it?"

"I was planning the service for tomorrow morning."

"Listen, Willard," began Jason, "do you mind if I handle that?" There was a silence at the other end. Jason quickly added, "I know it's not really fair, after all the work you've done in preparation." Jason smiled. Grant probably hadn't put in *any* time for preparation. He didn't even know Sullivan's name. "I'd really like to take care of this one, under the circumstances."

"Yes, of course. I understand," answered Grant, but Jason knew the older man did not understand.

"Thanks, Willard, I really appreciate that. By the way, how's my dog?"

"Oh, him." The older minister cleared his throat, then continued. "We have an uneasy truce. I stay in the porch and the kitchen, and he goes everywhere else." Jason smiled, picturing Dog herding the pastor around the house.

"Well, tell him I'm coming home. That should make him a little easier to get along with. I'll be leaving here soon. See you tonight."

Throughout the conversation, Jason had been mindful of the people who were undoubtedly tracing the call. He smiled, suppressing a desire to scream an obscenity at them. He pictured the good Reverend Mr. Grant's reaction to such an outburst.

"Goodbye, Willard," he said.

"Godspeed, son," came Grant's practiced reply.

Jason waited for Grant to hang up. When he heard the click at the other end, he spoke again. "And you others...you henchmen...be sure to tell Omega where to find me." Then he slowly placed the receiver on the phone.

"Not too smart, big guy."

The words startled him. He looked up at Jenny. "You always sneak up on a person that way?" he asked.

"Not really. You always talk to henchmen that way?"

He shrugged.

"Come on," Jenny urged. "They're probably on their way here right now."

They stepped out of their room, moved down the hallway and waited impatiently for the elevator. They both felt as though they wanted to continue the conversation they had begun earlier, but they were inhibited by the presence of a couple of maintenance workers who tinkered with some sort of electrical box nearby. Jason looked over at them and smiled uncomfortably. One of the men nodded back. "Mornin'," he said, then he looked back into the mass of wires.

The elevator doors finally opened and Jenny and Jason stepped in. The doors closed. No one else was on the elevator. Both were relieved to be alone again.

When the elevator doors had closed, one of the maintenance men removed a small radio from his pocket.

"They're on their way down."

"Affirmative. By the way, looks like we've picked up some Agency folks," came the filtered reply. The two men glanced at each other, shook their heads, and frowned.

Now they heard a new voice on the radio. "McCann, the admiral wants to see you, ASAP."

"Now what?" breathed one of the maintenance men.

20

"He's going back to Maine."

"What!"

That sure got his attention, Donlevy thought, even if the account of Walter's murder hadn't.

Omega pondered this new bit of information. "When did you find that out?"

"It just came in," Donlevy replied. Then, after a pause, he continued. "There's more."

"Well?"

"Winslow said..." Donlevy stopped. "Wait a minute," he began again, "I'll patch in the tape. Listen for yourself." Omega could hear the tape running at high speed. Then there was a click and a few more sounds. "Ready?" asked Donlevy.

As Omega listened to the minister's voice, he could feel the hatred percolating up through his body. "And you others," said the voice on the tape, "you henchmen...tell Omega where to find me." Damn him, thought Omega, damn that audacious son of a bitch. Tell Omega where to find me. That bastard! Omega snickered. It was as close to a laugh as Donlevy had ever heard from the man on the other end of the phone. "He thinks we're this Omega character," Omega said to Donlevy. "Can you believe that guy?"

Donlevy chose not to respond to the last remark. Instead, he drew in a slow, deep breath. What he was about to do was tantamount to committing bureaucratic suicide, but at this point he really didn't care.

"Listen," Donlevy began, "this one's too hot. It's getting much too involved. I have five of my people on it already. It's not simply doing you a favor anymore. People are getting killed. I think it's about time Talbot got into the picture."

"Seems to me," said Omega, "that would only make things messy for you. It'd mean a whole lot of explaining."

"I'm trying to be accommodating," Donlevy countered. If he had listened to himself, he would have realized how desperate he was sounding. "You know I always try to help out. But this one's too risky. If anyone ever gets hold of this, they'll nail my ass to the floorboards."

"Okay, okay, Chris," Omega replied. "If you feel that strongly about it, just forget it. Pull your people back. Today. Now. Forget it."

Sure, thought Donlevy, I can do anything I want, now that you know where the preacher's going to be. Donlevy pulled out his handkerchief and wiped his hands. They had become wet in the past few moments. When he spoke again, he was subdued. "That's fine with me." He waited for a response. When none came, determined to let Omega know he knew the truth, he added, "There's something else." His voice was taut.

"What's that?"

Donlevy started to speak, but stopped. Don't be a fool, he screamed at himself. If he knows you saw him last night, he'll kill you. It's that simple. He'll kill you. Now he realized Omega was waiting.

"Ahh . . ." mumbled Donlevy, his mind racing for something to fill the hole he had created for himself. He glanced down at the dossier he held in his hand. A paper on the top recapped Jason's conversation with the other minister.

"Winslow," he said, recovering, "is going to be doing a funeral service for Sullivan tomorrow."

Again Omega snickered. "That so," he said. Then he hung up.

Christopher Donlevy leaned back in his chair, relieved. You fool, he told himself, you almost dug yourself a grave that time. Whatever happens now, at least you'll be around to enjoy your pension. He sat, thinking quietly for a long time. He did not move. He sat and stared at the telephone as though the thing were a strange source of power, throbbing, alive, drawing him. At one point, he realized that he had no recollection of the past several minutes. They had been simply an emptiness. But even as he realized this, he felt a vague compulsion to continue to stare at the phone.

"Jesus Christ," he murmured once and shook his head, as if to free himself from the unseen force. He reached for the receiver, punched a few numbers, paused, then spoke.

"Patch me through to Randolf." Again he paused. "Randolf, it's Donlevy. You with them yet? Good. Stay with them. But don't—do not—let them know you're on them. Stay on this channel. I'm coming out."

OMEGA PONDERED THE conversation he had just completed with his contact at the Agency. There was something wrong. From the beginning, he had sensed something in Donlevy's voice. Something was not quite right. He played the conversation back in his mind. As he thought, he toyed with a paper clip. When he reviewed Donlevy's final comments, he grew even more uneasy. Everything about that information, except for the actual data itself, indicated it was of great importance: its position in the conversation, Donlevy's buildup, his tone, his obvious nervousness. Slowly Omega realized that what Donlevy had told him was not what he had started out to tell him.

Well, thought Omega, why the hell did he do that? What made him decide to change his story? As he pondered the question, Omega tapped the end of the paper clip against his desk. Suddenly he leaned forward. The paper clip abruptly and sharply banged into the desk top a final time.

"He knows," murmured Omega. Is that possible? No, he told himself. There's no way Donlevy could know. But suppose he does. Omega pursued the thought. He reviewed the past few days. He had talked with Donlevy more in the past forty-eight hours than he had in the previous year.

Omega bent the paper clip back and forth as he thought about the conversations he had had with Donlevy, especially the one of the previous evening. He was certain his tone had been as relaxed and as casual as it ever was. But he had asked specifically for the minister's location. Now he forced himself into the role of an observer. He thought about the situation. He realized how strange it must have seemed for him to request such information. Under ordinary circumstances why would he care so much about the preacher? Suppose, he mused, that Donlevy had also asked himself the same questions? Suppose he noted Omega's unusual request? How would he have responded? How would I have responded? Omega asked himself. I would have been suspicious enough to check it out.

The paper clip seemed as though it would burn his fingers. Then it suddenly snapped in two. "Damn," breathed Omega. "He knows. Damn it." He let the pieces of the paper clip fall into his wastebasket and moved to a filing cabinet. He turned the combination lock a few times, opened the drawer and removed a folder. He slammed the drawer shut and returned to his desk. Picking up the receiver of his private phone line, he dialed.

René Fragonard answered the phone on the third ring. *"Oui, bonjour."* He sounded groggy.

Christ, Omega thought, speak English. "Did I wake you up?" he asked.

Who the hell is this? wondered Fragonard as he squinted at his wristwatch. Then he realized the voice, the vaguely familiar voice, had asked a question. "No," he lied.

"You bastard, don't you lie to me."

Fragonard rose out of the bed, fully alert. He now knew the voice. "Yes, sir," he responded.

"It's about time," sneered Omega.

Fragonard raked his hand through his oily dark hair and stretched to get the blood flowing through his arteries.

"Look, I've got a rush job. Can you take it on?"

"When and how long? I've got a seat on tomorrow's Concorde."

"You're safe. I need you now, for five, maybe six hours maximum."

"What does it involve?"

"Following someone—government type."

"Sensitive?"

"No."

"Following, that's all, *oui*?" Fragonard asked suspiciously.

"That's it."

"How much?"

"How much do you want?"

"Four thousand. A bargain."

"Right," Omega snapped back.

"American, thirty hundreds, the rest fifties and twenties."

"Of course. Your pigeon's Christopher Donlevy. Get the particulars from your regular sources. No, wait...." Omega thought for a moment. "He's CIA," he said finally.

"I thought you said this wasn't sensitive."

"He isn't." Omega spit out the words, then added, "At least not today. Pick him up at Langley." He paused. "What do you have for communications?"

"What do you want?"

"Let's keep this out of the government band."

"Say where."

"49 megahertz."

"Fine," said Fragonard. "Just one thing." He paused. Omega waited. "The price just went up." Again he waited, expecting some outburst from the caller, but there was none. "Twelve thousand," he continued.

"Fine," responded Omega. "In an hour, then."

Fragonard was prepared for the click that announced the end of the call. What he was not prepared for was the caller's acceptance of the increased price. He shrugged, stood up and walked into the bathroom.

Omega called his secretary into his office. "I'm going to have to cancel my appointments for today, tomorrow and most of Friday."

"Yes, sir," she replied.

"Set up urgents for Friday, after 2:00 p.m. Any others on Saturday."

"Yes sir," the secretary replied, bowing slightly.

She noticed something unusual in her boss's demeanor. She sensed a tenseness, an electricity. It should have been something positive, but it was troubling. It bothered her.

"Yes?" Omega asked.

The secretary realized she had been staring. "Oh. Excuse me, sir." She reddened. "I'm sorry. It's just . . . rather sudden. Is everything all right, sir?"

Now her, too, thought Omega. He smiled reassuringly. "Yes, yes. It's just that something has come up. Actually an old friend has just passed away, and I need to pay my last respects." He smiled again. "That's all."

"I'm sorry, sir," the secretary replied. She turned and, closing her steno pad, exited.

21

ADMIRAL PEDERSON SAT quietly behind his desk. His remarks were to the point. "We've got to make something happen."

James McCann sat motionless and studied his superior. He knew what was coming.

"Do you understand me, James?"

"I understand," the younger man replied flatly. He shifted slightly in his seat. "Do you have any ideas?"

"Possibly," the admiral returned. "Where do we stand?"

"We've got the minister any time we want him. But I'm not convinced we do, not now, anyway," McCann replied.

"We do what?" the admiral pressed.

"Want the minister. We've had him on a string since he left Boston. We can pull him in whenever. But I'm not certain we'll get what we're expecting. There're just too many others involved right now. You yank him and the whole town'll know it."

"So?" Pederson asked. McCann frowned.

"I've been asked to conclude this brutish business," the admiral began in a way that indicated more was to come. "I intend to comply." He came as close to rambling as the younger man had ever heard. McCann knew a pep talk when he heard it, and he knew what they were supposed to accomplish. Despite that, McCann had a gut feeling, and after a few years in this business, he had learned to trust his gut as much as anything else.

"Give me twenty-four hours," McCann finally responded. "Let him get up to Maine. Up there, things'll open up a little; we'll have more control." He waited for the admiral's response. When none came, he continued. "Something's happening, Admiral. We know that for sure." He paused for a moment, then resumed. "The minister hasn't much time left. I think even he knows that. When we decide to move, we ought to be sure that will end it. Cleanly. Without compromise."

"Well, I agree with you there." The admiral closed his eyes and leaned back. "All right," he said softly.

IT WAS NINE-FIFTEEN when Jennifer and Jason entered the World Syndications building. A different guard stood watch over the radio, though the uniform certainly looked the same as the one yesterday: rumpled, faded, filthy.

They did not have to wait to see Drury. The secretary ushered them in immediately.

"Well," said Drury, "I hope things have settled down a little." Then without pausing for any sort of response from either Jason or Jennifer, he turned his attention to more pressing matters. Picking up a sheaf of papers, he asked Jason, "You ready to sign your life away?" He looked up at Jason and smiled. It was a forced smile, empty of truth, and Jason wondered why the man even bothered with such a pretense at pleasantness. Drury held the papers out to Jason.

Jason did, in fact, start to reach for the papers, but then he stopped. He looked directly at Drury and spoke forcefully. "Actually, Mr. Drury, I've come to give you your money back."

This was not the kind of "negotiating session" LeRoy Drury was used to. It caught him off balance. His smile faded. "I guess I don't understand, Mr. Winslow," said Drury.

"It's quite simple, really. I've done a lot of thinking in the past few hours, and I've decided to go home."

"Home?"

"Maine. Back to where things are more certain."

"But what can you possibly be thinking about?" Drury interjected. He glanced at Jennifer with a clear look of dissatisfaction. "You know he's not going to give up! You just can't walk out, not now." Drury was showing just the slightest signs of agitation.

"That's exactly what I'm going to do," Jason answered.

His comment caused a fleeting but visible hitch in Drury's rhythm. "You'll end up dead without me." Drury sounded triumphant. He held, he thought, the winning hand.

Jason's response unnerved him. He was unprepared for it. As he probed the minister, he found no weakness, no hint that he was bluffing, or that he did not believe what he was saying.

"Mr. Drury," Jason began, shaking his head slowly, "I do not care what happens." He said it without bitterness or cynicism—or fear. He simply said it. "For three days now, I have lied...lied to..." He abruptly stopped. He considered his thoughts for a moment, then revised what he was going to say. "Mostly...to myself. I have sold out. I will not continue this way." The solemnity with which he spoke caused Drury to sit motionless, almost hypnotized. "I've made a desperate attempt to save my life." Jason said the words with an unmistakable sneer. "But in doing so, I have lost every shred of self-respect I ever possessed. And if I continue, I may indeed save my life, but the irony is, I don't think I'd be able to live with myself." He paused, reflecting on what he had just said. It called up a New Testament passage. "Remember the scriptures, Mr. Drury. 'The man who shall save his life, shall lose it.' The cost is too great."

Jason looked at Jennifer, and she watched him settle into that now familiar attitude not of defeat, but of resolve. She could feel it; it was as real as the muscles that gave tension to Jason's body. Drury, she thought, was also aware of that new power in Jason. He was making Drury uneasy, and that was unusual.

When Jason spoke again, he caused an unmistakable tenseness to pass through the man who sat across from him. The hair on the back of Drury's neck bristled.

"I don't expect you to understand, because I don't understand myself," he began. "For the past three days, I have been a man with a desperate need." He smiled, and riveted his gaze upon LeRoy Drury. "'Are you right with God?' Ever hear that, Mr. Drury? A little evangelical for my blood...but that's really what it boils down to. I sold out— gave up my right to choose how I will live. But I reclaim that choice. A silly thought? Unquestionably. Without logic? Certainly. Suicidal? Perhaps. Except it doesn't make any difference. Because this is what I must do. It's right." Jason was whispering now. His voice was barely audible, but the words were sharp and unmistakable. "What will happen, will happen, Mr. Drury."

The older man had to forcibly shake himself in order to break the spell that Jason had created. He reached up and ran his hand down the back of his head. The warmth of his hand on his neck drove out the chill. He felt his heart, which had pounded with anger and uncertainty, become quiet.

"So, Mr. Drury," Jason was saying, "I appreciate your offer. I appreciate your advance money, but I cannot accept it. Here's what I haven't spent. I'll send you a check for the balance when I get home. Thank you. I'm sorry."

Jason stood. Jennifer, after a moment, stood also. She, like Drury, had been entranced. She had never imagined Drury would react as he had in the past few minutes. All the drive and energy normally attendant in the man had suddenly disappeared. He sat motionless and struggled to shake off the paralysis that had closed in on him.

With effort, Drury stood. He reached out and offered Jason his hand. Jason shook his hand and again looked into Drury's eyes. There was a look there, not of awe or admiration, but another look—a look almost of fear, and Jason felt odd shaking the hand of a man who now seemed as much an enemy as an ally.

"We have to go, Mr. Drury. I'm sorry I've been a bother to you."

The door closed and LeRoy Drury was alone. He sat in silence for several minutes. He breathed heavily, deliberately. Then suddenly in one explosive thrust, he swept up the money Jason had returned. He crumpled it in his massive hand and threw it into the wastebasket. Then he sat back, fighting an emptiness left by the just-ended confrontation. As he slowly exhaled, a single word drifted from his mouth. "Suicidal."

"THEY'VE BEEN IN THERE fifteen minutes or so," the agent said. He nodded in the direction of the World Syndications building.

"Hmm," murmured Donlevy, "they'll probably be in there for a while yet. You want a cup of coffee?" He got out of the car and leaned back down, looking in at the man across from him.

"Sure," the agent replied. "Cream, no sugar." He started to reach into his pocket.

Donlevy frowned, shook his head and waved his hand. "I'll buy."

He started off. Almost immediately, however, he heard the car door open. As he was turning, the agent called to him. "Mr. Donlevy." By now they were staring at each other again, the car separating them. "That's them," the agent said calmly, "across the street."

Donlevy glanced over in the direction the agent had indicated. He smiled slightly. So that's the man, he thought. That's the guy who's been turning half the intelligence community in D.C. on its ear.

"Okay, Randolf," said Donlevy quietly. "Here's a buck. Buy yourself a coffee. I'll take care of this, now."

"You want a backup?" asked the agent.

"No, no need. Thanks." Donlevy handed Randolf a dollar and stepped into the street. In a minute he was almost on top of the subjects. He slowed and gradually moved up to within three feet of them.

"Please don't turn around, Reverend Winslow. My name's Christopher Donlevy. Please keep walking just the way you are."

When Jason and Jenny heard the voice behind them, they hesitated for only an instant. To the casual observer, nothing would have seemed unusual. Jason turned to look at Jennifer, but his eyes continued to strain to see behind him. He could see only the vaguest outline of a man. He nodded. "Okay," he said without commitment.

"I have some information for you. I can help you, but I've got to see you face-to-face."

"Fine. What's wrong with right now?" Jason responded, still walking.

"Too public," Donlevy replied tersely, as if it were painfully evident. "Meet me in the main parking area of the zoo. Miss Seidkamp knows where it is."

"Why should I do that?" Jason demanded. "It seems like I could be stepping right into someone's sights."

Donlevy sighed audibly. "My men have had you in their sights since you left the hotel." He paused. "Reverend Winslow, I want to *help* you. But you'll have to trust me."

Jason thought the man sounded desperate, but he also thought he heard a quality of troubled honesty.

"Okay?" Donlevy pushed.

"Okay," Jason replied. He was aware of a sharp glance from Jennifer's direction.

"I've got a white Ford station wagon. Be there at ten-thirty."

Jason heard a slight change in the footsteps behind him. When he and Jennifer got to the corner, they paused to look back up the street. The man who had been following and talking to them was gone. He must have stepped into one of the shops that lined the sidewalk. Had they looked back at the World Syndications building, they would have seen LeRoy Drury looking down on them. They didn't see him, but he saw them.

Drury also noted another man, a man totally unknown to either Jason or Jennifer. And they were unknown to the man. He had noted their presence, but that was all. Whatever had transpired between his subject and the two younger people had been slick and professional. In fact, to be honest, René Fragonard was not even certain anything had taken place. He had, of course, a professional's sixth sense about these things, but the truth was, he really did not care if anything had happened or not. The young people were not his problem.

Originally Fragonard had positioned himself in front of a shop window on the corner across from where the young couple was now standing. He had watched the business between Donlevy and them in a display mirror in the window. Now, however, he turned and moved across the street, almost bumping into Jennifer as they met in the crosswalk.

Fragonard smiled. He would wait until Donlevy exited from Hansen's shoes. With Donlevy's agent in getting a cup of coffee, he felt totally safe.

CIA, he sneered to himself. He doesn't have the slightest idea he's being watched.

From six stories above the street, LeRoy Drury glanced down for a final time at René Fragonard, Jason and Jennifer and Hansen's Shoes. He noted the time. Okay, he thought. Maybe not all is lost, after all. He reached over to his phone, dialed a number and waited.

"Good morning, National Security Administration," said a warm-sounding voice.

"Mr. Delacourte, please. This is LeRoy Drury calling."

"Just a moment, sir, I'll connect you," the voice on the other end said. Drury snickered under his breath. Those pleasant receptionists with their pleasant voices usually betrayed their political leanings whenever he identified himself. This once-warm, suddenly cold voice at the other end was no exception. He waited.

"Office of the National Security Adviser."

"Alex Delacourte, please. This is LeRoy Drury."

"I'm sorry, Mr. Dru—"

"Look, just tell him I'm on the phone, and I've got something for him." He waited. There was silence on the other end. He knew the secretary was trying to decide what to do. "Tell him it's about Morrison." Again he paused, then continued. "Just tell him that. If he doesn't want to talk to me then, fine." The secretary put him on hold.

A moment later Alex Delacourte picked up the phone. "Hello," Delacourte said flatly.

"Listen," Drury began, "I'm going up to a place called Craig's Harbor—it's in Maine—where Morrison lived. Morrison's funeral is tomorrow. Thought it might make a good story."

"Well?"

"You interested in coming along? I've got Corporate's plane all lined up. We'll go up tomorrow morning and come back in the afternoon."

"I told you yesterday," Delacourte began, "that I didn't even know the guy that well."

"Yeah, I know," responded Drury, "but it's almost like the end of an era. It's sort of like severing your roots. You know what I mean?"

There was a long period of silence on the other end of the phone. Drury wondered what was going on in the man's thoughts. Finally Delacourte spoke. "When's the service?"

"Tomorrow morning."

Again there was a pause. "What's your sudden interest in my nostalgic past?" Delacourte finally asked.

Drury answered immediately. "I told you, it'll make a good story. Especially now, if the British are going to press us on Alpha/Omega."

"If," repeated Delacourte. "We've heard nothing from them on that."

"The British? They haven't said anything?"

"No," Delacourte said without emotion. "Nothing."

"Too bad," Drury responded. "Anyway, it'll make a great story—especially if you're there."

"Let me think about it. I'll call you back this afternoon."

Drury started to respond, but Delacourte had hung up. Drury smiled. He dialed his secretary. "Put a hold on the plane. There'll be two traveling tomorrow morning out of National."

"Yes, sir," she responded.

Drury leaned back and smiled. The end was getting nearer.

22

"YOU'RE CRAZY—straight out, bouncing-your-head-off-the-padded-cell, crazy! You go into that meeting with Donlevy and you're committing suicide. Guaranteed. A sure bet. What do you want the gravestone to say?"

Jason was aware that despite her comedic emphasis, Jennifer was absolutely serious in her concern for his safety. She continued. "I mean, Jesus jump out of the jack-in-the-box, get serious, Winslow! You think this is some kind of movie, you goddamn nitwit, you! Dustin Hoffman you're not!"

"You finished?" Jason asked. She continued to drive furiously down Massachusetts Avenue. She leaned forward stiffly as though that would move the car and herself ahead more rapidly. She did not answer him. "You know where you're going?" he pressed.

"Yes," she snapped, then, "No." She swerved the car to the side of the street and stopped.

"Where are *you* going, Winslow? That's the question. Where are you going? Right down the tubes, that's where. Whatever made you agree to that?" Her question demanded an answer. She was not kidding in any way.

But Jason had no answer, not a satisfying one, anyway. He simply shrugged. He sighed and picked at the louvered air vent in the dashboard. "You know what it's like to be dreaming when you're right on the edge of sleep?" he began. "You wake up and you don't know if you've just dreamed that you're awake or whether you really are?

That's the way it's been for the past three days. I don't know what's real and what isn't. This is a way to find out."

"But you ass, you'll find out you're dead!"

Jason sighed again, deeply this time. He turned and looked out the side window. The action tore at Jenny. It was almost as if he had said, I'm sorry. You can't come with me any farther. You're at the boundary, and I'll go on alone from here.

"Cut the shit, Jason." Her angry tone surprised him. "Go ahead. Explain it. Try, anyway. You make it sound as if I'd just never be able to understand." He turned to her and stared for a moment. "Is that what you really think?" she pushed.

"What will happen, will happen," he repeated. "Here's a chance for all this to end. I'm going to take the chance. It just seems right." He shrugged. "That's all," he added softly.

Jenny studied him carefully. She put the car in gear and moved off. "Christ, Winslow," she said somberly, "you're something goddamn else."

They drove in silence. When they got to Jenny's apartment, she stopped. "Will you come up while I pack?" she asked.

"While you what?"

"Pack. If I'm going to Maine, I've got to get my toothbrush."

Jason stared at her. "You can't..."

"I sure as hell can," she asserted. "I'm just not going to let you walk out of this and leave me here in some sort of limbo!" Again Jason started to protest, and again she cut him off. "You owe me that much."

"It's not even reasonable," Jason countered.

Jenny laughed savagely, despite the burning tears of pain and anger that filled her eyes. "Christ, Winslow—reasonable. You don't even know what the goddamn word means! How were you going to get back, anyway? You probably haven't even thought about that, have you? Why don't you consider using my car? And, just for the record, I want to make something perfectly clear: I'll come anyway, no matter what you do. I wouldn't know Craig's Harbor if it bit me on the hiney, but I'll get there. Read my lips, Winslow: *I want to go.*'' These last words she enunciated slowly and emphatically.

Again Jason sighed, preparing to counter her tirade, but in a stunning, quieter attitude, she murmured something that stopped him cold. "Christ, Winslow," she began, wiping a tear from her face, "don't you know I care what happens to you?''

Jason gazed at Jenny. The fight flowed from him; he changed. She watched as the slightest, gentle smile turned his mouth. Yes, she thought, she could see it. He knew. She resisted an urge to reach out and mother him. Instead, she abruptly turned her attention back to the road.

"Well, then, let's get on with it." She pulled out into the traffic flowing down Massachusetts Avenue.

When they stepped into the apartment, a wave of cold apprehension passed through Jenny's body. She felt Jason's arm around her and that helped. Together they stood and quietly stared at the room before them. Though each of them worked at forcing the memory out of their consciousness, the events of the previous night would not allow themselves to be forgotten. And so, silently, together, they remembered in those first few moments.

After several minutes, Jenny turned to Jason, eased herself out of his grasp and headed for her bedroom.

"I'll just be a few minutes," she said quietly.

While Jenny packed, Jason stood as a lone sentinel. His arms hung limply at his side, he looked about the room, lost in his own thoughts.

"Who are you?"

Jason wheeled at the sound of these unexpected words. The old reality returned in a steaming wave of readiness. His reaction to the intruding question was so quick and sharp that he stunned the man who had asked it. Jason stared at the man, still without speaking. Finally, he realized the man was waiting for a response.

"Who are *you*?" Jason countered.

The man seemed uncertain. He felt something strange in the room, something that he couldn't quite identify. Whatever it was, he wasn't sure he liked it.

"Vince Salerno, from the *Post*."

Jason nodded slowly once. "Reporter."

Salerno nodded in response, suddenly feeling more comfortable. "I'm doing a follow-up to the murder—" again a wave of uncertainty passed across his face "—of...of..." He faltered. He looked down at his notepad. "Of Walter..."

"Borman," Jason completed.

Salerno stood mute. Jason watched as he struggled to gather his thoughts. Finally he was ready to proceed. "Did you know the deceased?"

"Not really."

"Well...um...what was your relationship with him?"

"I am visiting the person who rents this apartment."

"The police don't seem to have any leads. None. They're really stumped." Jason nodded without feeling. Salerno continued. "You have any ideas?"

Now Jason looked down. "No," he murmured, "not really."

"I'm sorry?" Salerno said. Jason looked up. The reporter began again. "I'm…I'm sorry, I couldn't hear you."

"I said, 'No, not really.'" Jason's tone echoed his irritation.

The reporter nodded as if he had just heard some revelation of consequence. "You know what intrigues me," Salerno continued. "You know, someone, somewhere knows why this happened. I mean, people just don't get blown away the way this guy did. There's got to be a reason. Know what I mean?"

The reporter watched Jason grow more uncomfortable. He pressed. "Things like this don't just happen," he repeated.

"You're right," Jason responded quietly.

"You have any ideas how to get a handle on that?" Salerno continued.

"None at all."

The voice startled the reporter. "And who are you?" Salerno asked Jenny with a note of annoyance. He had felt he was about to get something useful and all of a sudden his chance had been shut off.

"I'm the tenant. I live here," she added with extra emphasis. Her stare was unrelenting.

Salerno looked back at Jason. Jason stood quietly composed. He had recovered from his faltering, and the reporter knew he had blown it. He decided on a different tack. He nodded at Jenny's backpack. "You planning a trip?"

"Oh, for Chrissakes," Jenny began, "you've been watching too many bad TV shows. Listen to yourself: 'You planning a trip?' Yeah, up the river in cement shoes! Next time try it with a Bogart accent, schweet-haart. You a cop?"

"No," Salerno responded with diminished enthusiasm, apparently stung by Jenny's attack.

"Oh." Jenny's tone suddenly became sweeter. "You must be a reporter then."

Salerno nodded with a somewhat inappropriate enthusiasm.

"Then my plans are none of your damned business," Jenny said with continuing sweetness. She moved past the man to the door. She turned to him and waited. After a moment, she made her intentions clearer. "Goodbye," she added.

Salerno stepped, defeated, past her.

When the reporter had left, Jenny turned to Jason. "You would have told him."

Jason shrugged.

Jenny simply sighed. "Come on," she said finally. "We've got a date, a very important date." She turned and again headed toward the door. As she exited, she added one more thought. "You decided on your epitaph yet?"

23

CHRISTOPHER DONLEVY glanced around as he approached the rest area just off the Rock Creek Parkway. He had a few minutes to kill and this was a favorite spot. On more than one occasion he had come to the solitude of this place to ponder some troublesome circumstance. He often wondered why more people didn't stop in the area. It had to be one of the great undiscovered spots in D.C.

Except for a park service truck with a couple of men emptying the trash cans, he was alone. He pulled in. He shut off the engine, breathed in slowly, held it a moment, then exhaled, long and deep. It was the meaningless act of a man trying to rid his system of some fundamental impurity. It was an act that only left him with the desire to repeat it once again.

He opened the car door and strolled casually to the stream that trickled along beside the roadway. A few of the yellowing leaves of fall fell into the stream. They were carried along the currents, twisting, turning, sometimes barely moving, at other times racing down the currents, tumbling over themselves. He absently followed the course of one of the leaves, one that he thought was distinct and easy to identify. His intention was to watch it for as long as it was in sight, but a sudden impulse to check his watch distracted him. He still had twenty minutes to wait before he was to meet Winslow. When he looked back for his special leaf, it was gone, or if it was still in sight, it had suddenly blended with all the others. He allowed his eyes to narrow until the leaves blurred with splashes of light. He listened to the constant, reassuring sound of the stream. It was soothing.

In the distance, the truck started up. A sharp backfire cracked into Donlevy's solitude. He jumped, turned and began to crouch. When he realized what had happened, he shook his head gravely. Relax, he told himself. You're doing the right thing. You know you are. He told himself that when the truth was known, the system would be redeemed. It had to be. The system had been his life for the past twenty-five years. If the corruption could not be smothered and removed, what was there to believe in? No, the system could—had to be—redeemed. He would see to it. Even if his own position were somehow jeopardized, it was okay. It would be worth it. His thoughts churned like the miniature whirlpools and rapids before him. He continued to gaze downstream.

Had he turned his head in the other direction and studied the foliage hidden in the shadows of a high, arching bridge, he might have noticed a figure, crouched, motionless, nearly invisible. He did not look in that direction, however, and so had no idea he was being watched. But René Fragonard had taken certain notice of Donlevy.

"He's squatting by the brook," Fragonard whispered over the radio that he held in his hand.

"Just keep an eye on him." Omega's reply crackled over his earphone. "I'll be there in five minutes."

For the first time in several hours, Donlevy began to feel at peace with himself. A struggle had been raging within him, but now, having made a decision, he was beginning to get a new hold on the anchors that rooted his life. The risks were undeniable, but by telling Winslow, he hoped to minimize the potential dangers. In fact, Donlevy viewed the next few minutes as the most critical. Once he got the information to Winslow, he could really begin to relax.

He picked up a twig and flipped it into the stream. He watched it begin its journey to God knows where. How far would it go before it got tangled or wedged among the rocks or waterlogged and sank? After a moment, he rose, glanced at his watch and headed back to his car.

JASON AND JENNIFER drove in silence. As they rounded a bend near the Kennedy Center, an accident up ahead slowed the traffic. Jason glanced at his watch. His expectation—his hope—made him uneasy. He strained to see how long the delay would be. Jenny looked in his direction, then back to the road.

"Don't worry," she said, "I can see the cops up there. It's not bad." She paused. "We won't be late."

Jason frowned. In fact, Jenny was right. By the time they had reached the scene of the accident, some of the police cars were moving away, and traffic was flowing more smoothly.

"THAT WASN'T PART OF THE DEAL." René Fragonard was adamant.

"I'm making it part of it." Omega stood before him, imperious and unyielding. "Name your price. I've got $35,000 in cash, and I'll forward the balance to your account in Bern. Whatever you want."

Fragonard studied the man who stood opposite him. Why? he wondered. What's Donlevy got on him? But "why" was a question someone in his profession never asked of the client. That his services were requested was enough. But things were happening too fast. On the other hand, Fragonard knew the client; he had done work for him before—both officially and unofficially. He was an honorable man; more than that, he was a cautious man. He did not make mistakes. Fragonard admired that part of him.

What he did not admire was his relentless bargaining. And frankly, this was one of the things that bothered him now. This unqualified offer to pay whatever he wanted was totally out of character. But then, the man was obviously in a hurry. Men do strange things when they're under pressure of time.

Fragonard shrugged. What the hell, he thought. "Okay, $68,000."

"I'll wait. You'll get your money when you're finished."

Omega bowed slightly. The Frenchman nodded, then turned abruptly and stepped off the sidewalk to begin his descent down the wooded embankment of Rock Creek.

As he sidestepped his way down the fifty-foot drop, he wondered what there was about Donlevy that demanded this sort of attention. But then, he really didn't care. All in all, he reflected, it really shouldn't be too messy. The area was secluded; he'd have plenty of access to the subject. It would be over almost immediately.

Christopher Donlevy checked his watch, and sighed again. He looked up, straight out over his steering wheel, past the hood of his car, to the inviting rustic scene before him. It is time, he thought, it's off to the zoo. He turned the ignition key and glanced into his mirror.

At that moment René Fragonard leveled his weapon and brought his victim into his sight.

Donlevy turned, looking over his left shoulder, ready to back up the car, his hand on the gearshift. There was no time to react. The first shot found its mark. Donlevy's body shuddered violently. His hand uncontrollably wrenched the gearshift downward. The car lurched forward, up over a low curb, and finally settled, listing to the left, in the brook that only moments before had so soothed the driver. The door on the driver's side of the car had sprung open and Donlevy's body slumped out over the stream. Two more shots rang out, shots that were unnecessary, for Christopher Donlevy's lifeblood flowed from his limp body. The thick bright fluid fell into the churning stream and quickly merged with the water as it was carried on its uncharted journey.

René Fragonard looked nervously around. The car's engine raced, making odd noises. He turned and moved quickly back up the steep incline toward his car. His interest at the moment was to get as far from the area as possible. The climb, though short, was tiring.

One of the police cars that had cleared the way for Jenny and Jason moments earlier now turned into the rest area. Fragonard heard the sound of the new vehicle. When he saw it was the police, he was suddenly aware that his little job had momentarily become more difficult. Not that the local police were a match for him, but they had weapons, and they had communications. In short, they were an irritant. Now, a fast escape was the important matter at hand.

The two policemen in the car knew almost immediately something was terribly wrong. As soon as they had pulled up into the rest area, they saw the disabled car. Then they saw the driver. While one officer radioed the situation to the dispatcher, the other approached the car. Within seconds, he knew this had not been an accident. The officer's heart suddenly pounded, his body became taut and alert. Simultaneously, he became aware of the noise of someone scrambling up the slope above him. He stepped away from the dead man, and shouted to his partner.

"This guy's been shot. There's someone up on the hill!" Immediately he splashed across the stream and began the climb upward. His partner relayed the new information and joined in the chase.

In his struggle, Fragonard was getting careless. Once, losing his footing, he started to slide backward. He grasped wildly at a bramble. It saved him from falling; it also cut into his hand. As he recovered and began moving forward again, he felt the stinging pain caused by the lacerations. "Damn," he said with a huff.

When he was within a few feet of the top of the overgrown embankment, he was vaguely aware of a new sound, but in his hurry, he concentrated more on the sounds of the two men below him. When he slipped, he had lost valuable time. If Fragonard had allowed the awareness of this new sound to move fully into his consciousness, he might have had a chance. When he finally did look, he saw his employer standing ten yards ahead of him, weapon drawn and smiling gently. The man appeared odd, totally relaxed. Fragonard's final thought struggled to find its way to his lips. But when he expected to hear his own whispering voice, he instead heard nothing. The thought faded quickly to nothingness. An honorable man. Bullshit.

Neither officer knew exactly what had happened. They only realized that the noise of the fleeing assailant had suddenly ceased. They instinctively slowed. After moving forward a few more yards, they saw the body of Fragonard.

Omega chuckled to himself. The fools, he thought. They're not even looking where they should be. In quick succession he killed the trailing officer, then the one who had crouched over Fragonard's body. That one had just enough time to turn toward Omega. When he saw him, his face registered momentary shock, for in that instant the police officer recognized a person he knew about from the papers and TV. He started to smile, as if to say, "Boy, I'm glad it's you." But then, as Omega returned the smile, the officer's face grew ashen and unexpressive. A knowledge deep within his consciousness insisted that he lift his gun, but it was too late. Later, others would find his body slumped over Fragonard's, his gun lying, unfired, at his side.

DONLEVY HAD BEEN RIGHT. The National Zoological Park was a quiet place this time of year. The expansive parking lot was less than a quarter full. A few school buses were sitting to the left of the main entrance. In the distance, in addition to the occasional sound of some strange animal, the screams and shouts of children enjoying themselves drifted toward Jason and Jenny.

"Where the hell is he?" Jason demanded.

Jenny tipped her head slightly to one side and gestured her uncertainty. It was not a question that could be answered. It was, instead, a question that reflected Jason's frustration, his suddenly fading hopes and perhaps even his fear.

"He didn't sound like a man who makes it a habit of being late."

"You're right there," Jenny responded.

For the fifteenth time in ten minutes, Jason looked at his watch.

"He's ten minutes late."

"Ten minutes late and counting," Jenny interrupted. Jason looked at her and snickered. "Tell you what," she added, "let's call."

"Who?"

"Donlevy. Or his office, anyway."

As they sat and looked around, a new sound merged with those of the children and beasts. In the distance they could hear sirens—it sounded like dozens of them—converging somewhere not too far away. The sound added to their uneasiness.

"Okay," Jason said finally. "Only let's get out of here. Let's call from somewhere else."

They drove northward on Connecticut Avenue. Not far from the entrance to the Beltway, they stopped at a gas station. Jenny placed the call.

"No," the secretary said, "Mr. Donlevy is not in, but if you leave your number, he'll return your call."

"No, it's not important. We'll call back. Thank you," Jenny replied. Then she turned to Jason. "Nobody's home."

"Damn!" Jason sighed. "What do we do now?" He and Jenny stood by the phone booth in silence. Finally, he looked up at her. When he spoke, it was with an odd combination of despondency and resolve.

"The hell with it. I'm going home."

24

ONCE JASON AND JENNIFER left the Beltway and headed up into Maryland, past Baltimore, they began to relax. Jennifer pushed the car along at a steady sixty-five miles an hour. The sound of the tires humming over the pavement lulled them. The miles passed, often without comment from either of them. They did talk some, but mostly they just listened to Jenny's tapes and considered their own private thoughts.

Jason liked being on the road. In moments such as these, he often did some of his best thinking. On the long stretches of road between Washington and Maine, he planned the funeral service for Mr. Sullivan. He was glad he was going to do the service. He felt, or at least hoped, that the act would somehow resolve the uncertainty of the past few days.

At times his mind also wandered to Donlevy. What had happened to him? What would he have told him? Another thought caused him to shudder. Am I lucky I'm not dead? he wondered. He glanced over at Jennifer. It *was* a stupid thing to do, he thought. Now, however, he felt safe, and he was glad that Jenny was with him.

They stopped at the first rest area on the New Jersey Turnpike. Jason moved into the driver's seat, and again they moved out onto the seemingly endless road. After some time had passed, Jason glanced over at Jenny. She had twisted herself slightly and was facing him. She studied him. He smiled back at her and then, feeling somewhat uncomfortable under her gaze, turned back to the road. He continued to feel the discomfort, but was determined not to look back at her. Even so, he was certain she continued to study him. When she finally broke the increasingly heavy silence, he was—for an instant—relieved.

"After you left for seminary, how come I never heard from you?"

Jason shrugged in the characteristic way that meant something more significant was coming. He was quiet for a long time. The sounds of the automobile became oppressive as Jenny waited for his response. She could see him working the reason around in his own thoughts.

"I heard someone say something once. 'Never,' this person said, 'date a seminary student.' Seminarians don't have a lot of money—most of them.

"And then there's the whole issue of morality, or whatever. Talk about putting a damper on things. It's as if they say, 'he won't play.' And..." He shrugged again. "Most of the time, they're right." He paused. "Loving a person does entail some kind of commitment. I believe that." He paused again. "I guess it doesn't always translate to a lot of fun times."

"So?" Jenny pressed.

"So?" repeated Jason.

"How come you ignored me?" Again Jenny watched the strain come into Jason's face as he thought.

"I guess..." He cocked his head slightly and gazed intently ahead at the highway. "I don't know...I guess I just thought you wouldn't be interested in hearing from me anymore. I mean, let's face it, I always felt you were a little out of my league."

Jenny studied him carefully as he drove along, silently watching the highway stretching out ahead of them. How could a man be so certain about some things and so uncertain about others? It puzzled her. It fascinated her.

"What made you think that?" The words were out before she could check them. They had, in fact, startled her. It was exactly the question she had wanted to ask, but the force with which she asked it surprised her. Now she looked at Jason, wondering how he would react.

"I've always felt that you had too much going for you to be interested in me." He turned deliberately from the road to watch her reaction. She seemed grave. "You were always exciting, free...spirited...always moving. I guess I felt you could choose to be with whomever you wanted. In high school, I just couldn't imagine someone like you wanting to hang around with someone like me. There were so many others who seemed more like the people you'd want to be with."

"You thought you were too good for me."

"No," Jason replied forcefully. "I...I..." He chose his words carefully. "I thought...I wasn't good enough."

"But," Jenny continued, "after those first few dates, you never even tried...never asked me to go out with you again." She paused and realized that she was sounding much more intense than she had intended. "I mean, I thought it might have been my breath or something!"

Jason continued driving without moving his eyes from the road. He shrugged. Then he turned to her again. "Actually, I guess I was a little afraid," he continued. "I thought you expected things I wasn't ready for. I wasn't sure I could keep up."

"Has anything changed?" The question cut through the space between them like a bolt of lightning. "I didn't mean that. I'm sorry, Jason, I didn't mean—"

"No," Jason interrupted. "No, it's okay. I've asked that question a dozen times since I've been with you." Again he looked over at her. "I don't know," he continued. "That's the answer I keep getting. We're two different people, Jenny.

We live in two different worlds. I just don't know." He
paused, thinking. "I want you to know something, Jenny."
Again he paused. "I...I..." He frowned, paused, then
began again. "Thank you. That's what I really want to say.
Thank you."

Jenny looked away now. She knew he meant what he had
said, but she also had the feeling he had really wanted to say
something else. For all the power and freedom she saw in
him, she also sensed something else. Something he had
forced to remain far from his consciousness. What was it,
she wondered, that was so difficult for him to admit? She
wished there was some way to open him up. Then another
thought came to her. She turned back to him now.

"You really believe in God, don't you?" she asked quietly.

Jason looked sharply at Jenny, surprised at her ability to
make incredible leaps from one topic to another. He smiled.
"Yeah, Jen," he said, "I do."

As she studied Jason, she felt almost jealous of this unseen God. She wished Jason could trust her as he must trust
his God. But Jenny would have been surprised had she
known how her question had seared deeply into his being.
He did have faith, there was no question of that, but he also
had doubts. At times they seemed to give extra credence to
his belief; they pushed him toward hard truths—truths that
in turn stretched his faith to the boundary. One of the things
that angered him about TV preachers and the so-called
electronic church was that their faith was all too easy, too
brittle, too blind to the realities of God's creation and what
humankind had done to it. Some of his colleagues made
faith seem too easy, and that was precisely what frightened
him. For him, none of it was easy.

He knew there would be a moment when his belief would
be tested, a moment when he would come face-to-face with

his God, and when his actions would affirm or deny every-thing—everything. He would come face-to-face with the Ultimate Truth. He knew too well his weaknesses, and he was haunted by the possibility that in that moment, when it came, he would fail.

This was something he simply could not share with any other living soul. To admit that he had based his whole life on an uncertainty, on something that, in the final analysis, he simply couldn't know absolutely, was irrational. It didn't make sense. He couldn't expect anyone to understand that. He didn't understand it himself.

His feelings were not rational; he knew that. They were the ghostlike shades of possibility that hovered just above the raw edges of his consciousness.

"Yeah, Jenny, I believe in God."

They drove on in silence.

"WHO DO WE HAVE ON THEM?" Admiral Pederson asked.

"Miller and LaConti," Agent McCann replied.

The admiral nodded his approval. Leaning back in his chair, he folded his hands, moved them to his mouth and pressed one of his knuckles against his teeth. He let his eyes close.

"This is going to be it," McCann said quietly. "We're not going to get another chance."

Pederson opened his eyes just slightly. The slits were black and empty. "We had one chance already. It's just shit luck that we didn't get our ass caught in the trap."

"I know that, sir." McCann paused. Though he couldn't see his superior's eyes, he knew he was studying him. It made him uncomfortable. McCann looked away and added, "We all do."

"There'll only be one more chance. And I want him. When the time is right, I want you there. I want him—once and for all. *I want him!*'' The admiral paused, then eased up a little. ''Then we'll all be able to relax.''

"Yes, sir," McCann replied. "We're already moving our people into position. We'll be ready. He'll never know what hit him." McCann glanced self-consciously back at the admiral. An odd sort of smile formed on the admiral's lips. Slowly his eyes narrowed and closed out all light and vision.

25

IT WAS AFTER ELEVEN-THIRTY when Jenny and Jason finally got to Craig's Harbor. A fog had settled in. A heavy, chilling wind blew off the water into Jenny's face. She could see nothing of the place, but her other senses were active. The wind carried with it unfamiliar smells that seemed to sting as they swirled around her. There were the smells of salt air and spruce trees. She turned to face the wind and hold her head defiantly high and resist its effect. She closed her eyes and braced herself against the biting wetness.

As she stood, feeling the relentless press of the wind, Jennifer became more conscious of the foreign noises it carried with it. It conjured images of romantic tales of the sea. She heard the wind first as it whistled and rippled across the water and around the boats and buildings. In its gusts, it brought waves of pulsating sounds. Once she heard a voice. It startled her for it sounded as if the person should have been next to her. But when she opened her eyes, she saw nothing. The wind also blended the rustling it made as it moved ceaselessly through the trees, and the rhythmic gentle lapping of the ocean over the rocky shoreline of the harbor. In the distance, she heard the steady, strong, somehow reassuring boom of the bell in the outer harbor.

But there was also another sound in the distance: an inconstant, low, pounding sound, one of intensity and, she felt, possible brutality.

"What is that, Jason?"

"What's what?"

"That noise."

He looked puzzled. He had lived with these sounds for so long that he barely noticed them, except in those moments when he forced himself to pause and actively direct his attention to them. He did that periodically, whenever he felt he needed to be reminded of the Creator. These sights and sounds spoke to him powerfully about his relationship to the One whom he worshiped.

"The bell?" he asked tentatively.

"No, that other noise, that pounding noise."

He listened. "Oh," he said quietly, and listened for a while longer before continuing. "There must have been a storm out to sea. That's the sea breaking against the back shore. There are cliffs along the shore down around the corner of the harbor. The seas roll in there from the open Atlantic. It's the first land they hit."

They listened to the muffled, powerful thunder. Jenny felt awed by the sound, which seemed increasingly to dominate all the others she had first heard. It was omnipresent. It excited her, but it also caused a shiver to move across her being. Deep inside she felt a vague, quiet apprehension.

Jenny now focused on another sensation. A raw cold was infesting her body. It was strange to her. In her childhood she had known the cold of the Midwestern farmland. She was also a skier, and knew the cold of the mountains, but this cold was different. The cold she knew was dry, and people could escape it. They could, for a while at least, fight it. When it finally began to affect a person's body, it started nibbling on a hand or a nose or ear. It was sharp and crisp, not like the cold that now moved across her body. This cold was dull and draining. She became conscious of it not in any one part of her body, but all over. It tightened her. She felt as if she should close herself off from everything, to preserve what warmth was now losing the battle with the cold.

As she folded her arms tightly in front of her, she wondered what kinds of people would choose to live in a place like this. Then she felt an arm move around her. It startled her. She had closed herself off and was surprised when another person suddenly entered into her space. Jason's grasp brought with it a sudden surge of warmth. She looked up at him and was glad she was not alone here.

When they got inside the parsonage, Reverend Grant was waiting to meet them. So was Dog.

God, Jason thought, how he had missed that animal. After initial introductions, he sat down on the floor and butted and patted and hugged Dog. The animal responded just as enthusiastically. Jennifer could easily see the love they had for each other. She even felt the slightest jealousy, then shook the feeling off, telling herself how ridiculous that was—jealous of a dog.

Mr. Grant had the kettle boiling and quickly provided Jenny with a cup of tea. It forced the chill from her. Grant had been watching the news when Jason and Jennifer had arrived. Now, as Jason sat in front of the television, he heard something that caused his mood to suddenly change.

"Quiet, Dog. Down." He spoke sharply, and it stunned the others in the room, most of all Dog, who seemed visibly hurt by his master's words. He sat dejectedly in front of Jason and waited. Jennifer noted the dog's apparent pain and was surprised at Jason's sudden outburst, until he turned to her and spoke.

"What did he say?"

The TV announcer was standing somewhere in front of a battered white station wagon making some vague summarizing statement.

"Oh, he's talking about that killing," Grant said casually.

Jason turned to him. "What killing?"

Grant seemed surprised. "That one in Washington, this morning. Some G-man or something."

Jason and Jennifer looked quickly at each other, but before they could say anything, the newscaster confirmed their fears. Christopher Donlevy had been murdered along with two Park Commission police officers and a fourth, as yet unidentified, victim. The murders occurred sometime shortly before 10:30 a.m. At present, CIA, White House and State Department officials were simply making routine statements of condolence to the family. Privately the investigation was centering on several Central American revolutionary groups that may have been victims of CIA operations. It was Donlevy, the announcer reminded the viewers, who headed up the Central American desk at the Agency.

Again Jason and Jenny glanced at each other. In consort, they both sighed. Jason reached out and patted Dog as he continued to watch the report. There wasn't much from Jason's point of view that was useful. The program had reports from various correspondents speculating on the possible implications of the assassination on foreign policy, current and future CIA operations and on the "age-old concern," as the newsman put it, "for the protection of our public officials."

Then, just before the show's end, the announcer was given some information on the fourth victim.

"The fourth man, until now only identified as a male in his early forties, has been positively identified. He is René Fragonard, also known as Jean LeNuage. Our correspondent at the FBI, where this investigation is being based, is ready with this live report."

Now another face appeared on the screen.

"I might say that there is apparently some tension between the FBI and the CIA because of jurisdiction issues in this case. Obviously Agency personnel wanted their people handling this every step of the way... and while there are CIA representatives on the investigating team, the FBI has been given the power to organize and oversee the entire investigation.

"Now then, while details are still a bit sketchy on René Fragonard, the fourth victim, it appears that he is known to both the FBI and CIA. He is identified as a French citizen who functions in the murky world of free-lance espionage. When pressed, our sources suggested Fragonard's job description could include everything from stealing of state secrets, to murder, to things as 'petty'—to use our source's words—as drug dealing. Fragonard would presumably perform any or all of these activities for the highest bidder."

The newsman now interrupted. "John, is there any speculation on what this Fragonard was doing with Donlevy?"

"Well, the CIA people are adamant on this. They're saying that Fragonard murdered Donlevy and was then himself shot by possibly a fifth person. It appears that both the police officers and Fragonard were killed with the same weapon. The FBI, on the other hand, refuses to discuss the case on this point at all."

"I see," added the announcer. "What about the weapons? Is there any information on those yet?"

"No, not at this point, though we're told that the FBI's ballistics laboratory is going to be working through the night on this. We've also been told that the White House has ordered the task force working on this to take whatever steps necessary in order to bring the investigation to a swift and complete conclusion."

"Okay, John," the newsman spoke again, turning to the camera, "thank you for that report. And so," he went on, speaking to his audience, "in this bizarre day of violence and death, most of the important questions remain to be answered...."

The announcer continued to talk, but Jason had heard enough. He reached out and turned off the television. Even that action was filled with a kind of final defeat. For a long moment, they all sat in silence. Jason continued to comb his hands slowly, deeply into Dog's fur. Jennifer sat quietly watching him, dazed at this latest development, wondering what was safe to say in front of the older minister. He was an intruder. She was irritated that he was even with them now. He seemed like a warder whose presence prevented them from speaking of consequential things. Perhaps, she told herself, if we wait long enough, he'll go to bed.

Reverend Grant had not failed to notice the reactions of the two people who now sat before him. It was odd, he thought, and he resented the way they were acting. It was as if they had some deep, dark secret that they were unwilling to share with him. Well, he thought, why don't they just tell me to leave?

Grant did not really know Jason Winslow, although he had heard about some of the "stunts" the young clergyman had pulled. He couldn't say that he approved of the way the younger man was ministering, and thus he didn't have too much interest in him. He'll learn, Grant thought. I pray he does, anyway, for the sake of the people who have to put up with him. He frowned as he studied Jason and he waited to see what would happen next. And beyond all that, who was this *girl* he'd brought back with him? The frown on Grant's face turned downward even more, if that was possible.

"Damn it," muttered Jason. He continued to scratch Dog's neck. Jennifer casually glanced up at Grant in time to see a further note of disapproval registering on his face.

"I think I'd like to get to bed," Jenny said finally. "I think we could both use a good night's sleep."

Jason bent over and rested his head on Dog's. A long deep sigh emanated from his body. It shouted louder than words: I cannot escape.

Dog was content to sit complacently and let Jason pat him. The animal could sense something was not right with the man. For Jason's part, he was glad simply to be back with Dog. There was solace, merely being near him. It was comforting, reassuring.

Jennifer watched this interaction between pet and master. It was odd, she thought. She had never really thought much of pets. They had always made her uncomfortable. This was one of the rare instances in which she felt at all drawn to an animal. She studied Dog carefully. There seemed to be something almost human about his eyes. He's thinking, she thought. He knows that Jason is upset and he's simply sitting there to comfort him.

The line from a country and western song came floating into her mind and she worked to suppress a smile. She imagined the twangy music backing up the words as she viewed the real support that the dog was offering to his master. "Stand by your man..." The words—she could only remember the one line—became an endless refrain in her thinking.

"Before I go to bed, I think I'll take Dog for a walk." Jason's words forced the tune out Jenny's mind. She also noted the dramatic effect the words had on Dog. Instantly he was standing, tail wagging. He stretched up and, with his mouth, grabbed Jason's hand and pulled at him. "All right. All right, Dog, just give me a minute," said Jason as he got up off the floor. He walked to the doorway and turned. "Let me get you some sheets and towels," he said as he turned.

"Or would you like to come with us? We'll only be a few minutes," he added.

Jenny weighed the possibilities and shrugged. "I don't know—" she started to say.

"Oh, come on," Jason interrupted. "Go on, Dog, bring her along, too." Dog trotted over to Jenny and before she had a chance to pull away, took her hand and pulled her firmly toward his master.

Jenny had been surprised when Dog took Jason's hand in his mouth. She was certain the animal's massive teeth must have hurt as they clamped down on Jason, but now that her hand was in Dog's mouth, she was even more surprised. The animal held her hand with a gentleness, with almost a delicacy, that was uncanny. She stood, hardly believing that she was allowing this to happen.

"Not too tight, Dog," Jason said softly. Instantly, Jenny felt Dog's jaws loosen, but he still held her firmly. When Jenny and Dog had moved to Jason's side, the animal dropped her hand, sat and looked up, waiting.

"Well," said Jenny, wiping her hand on Jason's shirt, "I'm glad you don't have a pet tiger."

Everyone laughed politely. Grant announced that it was past his bedtime, and he would see them in the morning. They said good-night. Jason gave Jenny one of his heavy wool sweaters and an oilskin jacket. He put on a parka. Then the three of them stepped out into the foggy air. Jenny carried her tea with her, sipping it occasionally. Dog walked on ahead of them. Jason called to him, "Let's go down to the landing, Dog." The animal woofed quietly once, as if in acknowledgment, and continued on.

"He really seems to understand," Jenny said with a note of mild amazement.

"He does understand," Jason responded.

"You must have worked pretty hard training him," Jenny said.

"Someone else really trained him. I got him when he was about a year old. I was student pastor in a small church Down East, and the family who owned him decided to move. They couldn't take him, so they asked if I'd like to have him. I used to smuggle him into the seminary dorm during the week." Jason smiled. "We had one or two close calls, as a matter of fact."

They walked on without speaking, following the road down toward the water. As they approached, Jennifer could hear the gentler sounds of the water in the protected harbor. From a distance, she had only been able to hear that all-pervasive thundering, muffled roar of the wild Atlantic hitting up against the shore, but now that heaviness was tempered by the light, almost tinkling sounds of the inner harbor water. It lapped quietly against the boats and the wharf. At one point, Jenny turned around. She could see nothing of the places they had just been. Jason noticed her reaction.

"A-yuh," he breathed in, imitating the Down-East twang, "thick 'a fog. Won't do much ta go too fa' t'night."

"It's really kind of peaceful," Jenny said slowly, "when you get used to it." Jason nodded.

Then they reached the wharf. Jason leaned casually against a wooden piling at the edge of the structure. Jenny faced him. Though she had finished her tea, the mug was still warm and she wrapped her hands around it, warming them. She was glad she had the sweater and the rain gear on. It kept the biting wind away from her, except for her face. In a way, that limited exposure felt good. It brought a sort of sharp consciousness to her.

"I've got to tell them," Jason began.

"About Donlevy?" Jennifer responded.

Jason nodded. "About everything. Tomorrow, I'll call the FBI." Jennifer was silent. "If I had known about Donlevy, I would have gone to them this morning." Jason's tone was heavy. It carried with it a glimpse into the guilt that had haunted him throughout the entanglement of the past seventy-two hours.

"I know," Jennifer said quietly.

"No protest?" Jason asked.

Jennifer had nothing to protest. She had finally accepted the fact that he would do what he felt he needed to, regardless of what she said. And, beyond that, she had decided that he was probably right, that he had probably always been right. She wondered if he was aware that she, too, was feeling pangs of guilt.

They stood quietly facing each other for a moment. Then Jennifer reached out and embraced Jason. He wrapped his arms around her and they held each other tightly.

The wind whistled through the spars and lines of boats hidden in the fog and darkness. The boats creaked as they rolled and swung on their moorings. The few streetlights in the area illuminated the waves of fog as it blew in off the water. It painted a layer of moisture on their faces. Jenny leaned into Jason and held fast. Jason lowered his face to her long, thick hair. Into it he breathed a lament that seemed to well up from the depths of his soul.

"Oh, God, why? Why did it all have to happen?"

Neither spoke for a long time. Together there, in that moment, in that place, they felt totally alone. The elements surged around them, and they knew that they were but one small part of all that was happening in the world. Their problems suddenly seemed lost in the whiteness that surrounded them. The realization of their insignificance made things strangely bearable. In this moment of swirling sounds and water and wind, they needed to be together. They were, and they were safe. It was a moment in which Jenny began to understand why Jason seemed so possessed by the place.

Dog's barking finally brought them to a different consciousness.

"Your master's calling," Jenny said quietly, releasing herself from Jason's hold.

"Jason!" she said suddenly.

Jason looked at her, then in the direction of her gaze. Not twenty feet away, two shadowy figures stood, apparently watching them. Now Jason and Jennifer realized Dog was in fact barking at the strangers.

Almost immediately, one of the men called out. "'Lo, Rev'rend Winslow."

Jason recognized the voice of his neighbor, Calvin Hawkins.

"It's okay, Dog," Jason said. "That you, Calvin?"

"A-yuh. Just checkin' up on things, ya' know," he answered uneasily. "Well good night, Reverend."

Both figures waved and then moved on, disappearing almost immediately in the fog.

"Weird," Jennifer whispered. "I looked up and they were just standing there. Scared the be-jesus out of me."

"Wonder who was with him?" murmured Jason. He put his arm around her. Together they walked back through the fog, to the warmth and light of the house.

THE MAN WHO WAS OMEGA sat, staring at his modified Colt handgun. He turned it slowly, studying its every angle. It was alive; from it, the man could feel a power surging into his hands, through his arms and into his very being. It brought him life. It was a friend, trusted and too long absent.

The man turned the gun once again and a dull sheen of reflected light glinted off the barrel. It was a slow-moving blue-gray light. It spread from the barrel up toward the cylinder. It flowed evenly across that part of the weapon, except for the sharp relief of the furrows that were machined at precise locations around the cylinder. It made a stark rhythmic pattern of light and dark. The man flipped the gun and a catch snapped open with a crisp, metallic sound that shattered the silence around him. It sounded louder than if he had fired the weapon. He held the gun to the light and checked the cylinder. It had been cleaned and well oiled. Each chamber was loaded with a fresh round. He smiled momentarily, then snapped the weapon once again, and once again that awful sound echoed across the room. Reverently, the man who was Omega reached out, laid the gun in its case and placed the case in his suitcase.

The smile faded from his lips. He sat in silence. Wasn't there a better way, a safer way to do this? Why had he made this choice? Why was he driven? He would not allow the answers to intrude upon him. Tomorrow, he told himself, he would be at home with the man who had haunted him for the past three days. Yet, surely, he was safe. No one—the minister, least of all—could have even the slightest inkling who he was. But the nagging feeling remained. It would not let him be at ease. The minister had unwittingly foiled him at virtually every step of his plan. Now, even in his absence, the minister presented a formidable obstacle.

Omega was a man of instinct. He had survived as long as he had, in a world where today's friend may be tomorrow's enemy, precisely because he allowed his instincts to reign. And so, he would overpower this insidious doubt that had been creeping into his thoughts. He worked slowly and methodically. It required a physical effort, but he felt the doubt being overcome. "Damn it to hell...*I* am Omega." The barely audible words formed tortured shapes on Omega's lips. Then, as he had willed, a reassuring thought broke jubilantly into his consciousness. *I will triumph!*

26

JENNIFER AWOKE SLOWLY, as if her waking were itself a dream. Consciousness came upon her in gentle waves. For several minutes she lay quietly in the bed where she had slept. It was an old, overstuffed, sagging bed. Its one redeeming quality were the layers of quilts that had kept her warm and secure. They were heavy, and at first Jenny had thought their weight would make it impossible to sleep.

There were other things that had prevented her from losing herself in sleep. The strangeness of the place did not exactly frighten her, but it was new and unsettling. The sights, the sounds, the feelings: not frightening, but sources of discomfort. As she lay there in the stillness, working at emptying her mind of the thoughts that pushed away the sleep, the elemental forces of nature again surged upon her awareness.

The sounds were dampened by the walls around her, but they were still evident. That distant, deep rumbling ocean, the wind and all the sounds that carried with it, they all gathered into a presence that became a strange alien being. It had a form, a shape, a physical reality. She could feel it moving in on her. Once, she had moved abruptly, as if to say to the invisible presence, "There. See. I am still alive." But then she thought how childish her feelings were. She breathed in deeply and sighed. Relax, she told herself.

She had thought sleep would never come. Beyond the strangeness of the environment, there were the insidious thoughts of the day's events, which kept flooding in upon her. She worked to drive them out, and for a while she was able to succeed, but then, as she began to relax, they, like the surf she was hearing in the distance, flooded back in upon her.

At one point, she had thought, I've been awake half the night, but when she'd turned on the light and checked her watch, it was only 12:45. She switched off the light and sighed. The coldness of the bed was gone by then, and she had felt her body easing. Almost immediately, then, she had fallen into a deep and restful slumber.

In fact, now, as she lay there reflecting on the previous night, she realized that she had slept better than she had in a long time.

The daylight, which filtered through the sheer white curtains, was a dull gray. It must, she reasoned, still be foggy. Slowly she slipped out from under the bed clothes and padded across to the window. The panes of glass were old and imperfect. As she came closer to them, tiny blemishes in the glass made what lay beyond appear to move in odd ways.

When her gaze moved off the windows, to what was outside, she was startled. What she saw was nothing. It was a heavy gray-white nothingness. She felt a discomfort growing from within. She looked straight down to the ground, two floors beneath her. It was but a vague, pastel image of what she expected to see. Her eyes moved outward, searching for some object that would lend reality to the unreality that, at that moment, seemed to surround her.

As she slowly lifted her eyes, the grayness became lighter, and slowly the emptiness became filled with the possibility of substance. After gazing for several moments out past the window, she slowly came to realize that there was a form before her. The presence caused her to pull abruptly backward. When she realized the effect that it had on her, she frowned. "Christ," she murmured aloud, "it's the damn church!"

Now, as her eyes traveled upward, she could make out a steeple. How far away was the building? She had no idea. The fog had the unexpected and quietly irritating effect of rendering distance meaningless. The church could have been fifteen feet from the parsonage or a hundred. Then, as her eyes grew more accustomed to the layered gauze that veiled her vision, she could identify other shapes: a stand of spruce trees, a large boulder and a smaller building, a shed, to the side of the church. And farther on behind the building, the fog lifted for a moment, just enough for Jenny to catch sight of rows of stone—the cemetery. Just as quickly the fog again crept forward. It again shrouded the dead, and moved them once more beyond her sight.

Jennifer now became aware of the cold, damp floor. She lifted one of her bare feet and rested it on top of the other. The chill caused her to shiver. As she pulled her nightgown up around her neck, she realized how cold she had become. She started to turn away from the window, but another eerie vision delayed her course. Above the church, a brightness grew in the midst of the fog. In the center of this brightness was another, the only really distinct thing she had seen in the few minutes she had been looking outside. It was a pure white, sharply defined disk. It disappeared as quickly as it had revealed itself. And again, the fog rendered distance meaningless. If she had not known that she had in fact been looking at the sun, it could have passed for a strange unearthly object that had somehow come to rest on the roof of the church.

Now she turned away, moving toward the bathroom to dress. On the way, she stopped at Jason's room. The door was ajar and the room was empty. It was a place of extreme simplicity. There were a few pieces of rough furniture, a telephone and some books scattered on the bureau and the floor around it. In addition, there were books, magazines and papers stacked in a high pile on an old milk crate next to the bed.

The only truly interesting thing about the room was an impressive-looking telescope. Jennifer entered the room and examined the telescope. It was mounted on a pedestal rather than a tripod, and a stool was placed behind it. Apparently Jason would sit there and peer through his telescope—at what? Jennifer wondered. The steeple? She looked past the instrument to the window. The glass was different from the other windows. Instead of being composed of small panes of glass, as her window was, this was one large heavy pane, exceptionally clear, with none of the distracting ripples of her windows. Jason must be heavy into watching, she thought. But what?

She was uneasy about being in Jason's room. She knew he would not mind her being there, but still she felt as though in his room, she was seeing something of him that was personal and perhaps intended to be beyond her reach. She was careful not to disturb anything and left quietly.

The warmth of the bathroom felt good. She was glad to be finally in a warm place. As she dressed, she thought about D.C. and how different life suddenly seemed. It was in every way unfamiliar. Alien. For all she was experiencing, she could be in another universe, a universe with a different reality, with a different set of rules. Despite this strangeness, she was aware of the deep sense of peace she had felt the night before. But Jason's here, she told herself. You have a guide in this "twilight zone." You're not alone. Again she felt a tremor pass through her, though this time it was not caused by the cold.

Downstairs, Mr. Grant was puttering around in the kitchen. When Jenny finally appeared, he glanced up, said good-morning and checked his watch. Not too subtle, Jenny told herself. She was tempted to ask him if she had broken some rule against sleeping late. Late. It's only eight o'clock! The minister made Jenny ill at ease. He displayed a sort of sublime unpleasantness. She simply did not know how to deal with him. God, she thought as she smiled pleasantly back at him, he gives me the creeps.

"Where's Jason?"

"Over at the church preparing for the service with Mrs. Watson."

Jennifer raised her eyebrows questioningly. "The organist," Grant explained.

Jenny nodded understandingly. "Where's Dog?" she asked next.

Grant frowned in a mechanical sort of way. Jenny thought he had tried to check the reaction, but failed. "The dog's with him."

Jenny decided to try a more neutral subject. "What about this fog?" She paused, expecting some response to the open-ended statement. One came but it was hardly definitive.

"Yes."

"I mean," she recovered, "is this bad? Or is it always like this?"

"Always is a long time," said Grant in his pleasant, condescending way. He smiled a smile that betrayed his own inflated sense of self-worth or at least his one-upmanship. "Actually," he continued, "it's probably just out on the point, here. Go ten miles, even five, up the road, and you'll like as not see bright, blue sky. This'll probably burn off by midmorning, 'less o' course the wind comes 'round to th' easta'd."

Jenny listened to the man, first for the information, and secondly to the fascinating Down-East accent. She hadn't really noticed it before, but she realized that he hadn't said much before, either.

"In fact," Grant continued, "if you were ta climb up to the top of the steeple, you might well find yourself surrounded by clear sky."

"Really?"

"A-yuh, I've seen th' time when th' fog's laid down across the land like a blanket of cotton. Just a matter of feet. Here you're in it...five feet higher, you can look down on it. The Good Lord sees fit to do some mighty strange and marvelous things." Grant looked to Jenny for agreement.

She smiled and, out of desperation, caught herself nodding stiffly, much to the minister's satisfaction. Her obvious discomfort did not seem to matter; in fact, the clergyman did not even seem to be aware of the awkwardness Jenny was feeling.

Christ, she thought, I'm agreeing with this fool. Get me out of here!

Almost immediately, the back door opened, and Jason and Dog came into the room. My prayer has been heard, Jenny thought cynically. She heard herself mumbling something about "Strange and marvelous."

"What?" Jason asked.

"Huh? Oh, nothing," said Jenny, looking up embarrassedly.

"Well, is the great coast of Maine everything you hoped it would be?" Jason stepped between Jenny and Grant and peered down at her. As he asked the question, he crossed his eyes and grimaced.

"Why, Jason," Jenny began pleasantly, in a tone that mocked the older man's speech, "you didn't even half prepare me for what I'd find here." She smiled and rolled her eyes upward.

In their shared peevish thoughts, they wondered if the older clergyman had caught on to the fact that he was the object of their conversation.

Dog moved over toward her and wagged his tail in a friendly greeting. He sat calmly at her side and flopped his head in Jenny's lap. She looked up at Jason.

"I'd say he wants you to pat him." Jason interpreted Dog's action. With that, Dog picked up his head, woofed, picked up his paw and placed it on her arm. It was obvious that he wanted exactly what Jason had suggested. As Jenny patted him, he stretched his head upward and closed his eyes.

"It's nice to know I'm good for something," Jennifer said. Dog casually opened one eye and looked at her as if to agree, then let his lid close over the eye once again.

"He likes you," Jason said.

"I'm not a great pet person," Jenny admitted, "but he seems more like a friend than a pet."

"Friend and confidant. He hears everything that's on my mind. I've often thought he'd be the perfect example of good pastoral counseling technique."

"Humph," interjected Grant.

"Well," said Jason, shrugging, "it was just a thought." He glanced back at Jenny and smiled. "By the way, I called about the Bureau."

"Bureau?" Jenny began uncertainly, then realizing, "Oh, the Bureau. Oh." She nodded. "What did they say?"

Jason glanced quickly at Grant. "They're sending someone down to talk with me."

"When?" Jenny looked down at Dog and added quietly, "Okay, Dog, that's enough." Dog looked resigned and flopped casually at the foot of her chair.

"Quote—soon as possible—unquote." He snickered cynically.

Jenny nodded. "Of course."

Then Jason turned abruptly to Grant. "Have you heard a weather forecast?"

"Well," the minister began, "I ran into Mr...." He paused, trying to remember the name. He waved his hand to provide the proper punctuation. "Oh, you know who I mean...that retired seaman, down at the store.... What's his name?"

"Waters. Salty Waters."

In the midst of Jason's sentence, Grant exploded with a physical response that indicated success. "That's it," he sputtered.

"Salty Waters?" Jenny repeated incredulously.

"I bet there are a hundred Salty Waters living all up and down this coast," Jason asserted. "It's a natural."

Jenny shrugged, unconvinced.

"Anyway," Grant interrupted, "he says the fog will burn off 'round ten or eleven, the wind'll come 'round, and we'll get a taste of Indian summer. Temperatures up in the sixties."

"That will be welcome." He glanced at Jenny and smiled, then looked back to Grant. "Salty have any other news?"

"Yes. He said Avery somebody said a big power yacht's come into the harbor this morning. Seems this Avery even rowed out to take a look. Early. Waters was quite surprised and said whoever was pilotin' had a bit o' luck 'cuz he hadn't ended up on the ledges."

When Jason heard Grant mention the somewhat unusual appearance of the boat, he felt himself stiffen. He was aware how he had grown to see potential dangers in anything even a little out of the ordinary. And if ol' Avery had seen fit to go out into the harbor, poking around a pleasure boat, that was something more than a little bit out of the ordinary. Jason covered his concern, however, and smiled, recalling the dozen or so times some "leisure craft" had ended up on the shoals that rimmed the entranceway to the harbor.

"Wouldn't be the first time," he said softly. "Hey," he added, turning to Jenny, "you interested in seeing the church?"

"Oh," Jenny responded, "sure." It was at best a response that lacked conviction. As soon as she had spoken, she realized she had sounded less than enthusiastic.

Stepping outside was painful. A sudden brilliance had spread throughout the fog. It seemed as though the fog was just barely shielding a thousand blinding lights. Jenny wished she had sunglasses. As she turned toward Jason, she squinted until her eyes were barely open.

"I thought you might like to get out of there for a while."

"Is that guy a friend of yours?"

"Hell, no," Jason said forcefully.

"Kee-rist, is he an ass!" Jenny was glad to have a chance to say that out loud.

Jason smiled gently, then turned to things that mattered more. "I'm glad I called."

"I can tell."

He paused and looked at her for a moment. "They didn't believe me . . ." he began. "Or . . . let's say they were skeptical. I told them if they didn't believe, to check the bullets that killed Donlevy and the assassin with the bullet that killed Walter."

At the sound of Walter's name, Jenny glanced up quickly. She knew immediately that Jason was correct. No one had apparently linked the murders, and the FBI should be aware of that.

"Then they got a little more interested. They said they would check into it and they'd send someone down to talk to me as soon as possible."

"What are you going to say at the funeral? You going to tell them that Mr. Sullivan was murdered? Not a suicide, the way they're saying?"

Jason showed a momentary pang of remorse, of dissatisfaction. "The people at the FBI asked me not to say anything until they've had a chance to talk with me." He shrugged and grimaced.

"So what's new?" Jenny intoned.

They walked toward the church door in silence. The wind had died down, but the sound of the seas pounding against the shore still rumbled in the distance. Added to that was a new sound, one alien to the environment. It started as a quiet rush, but quickly grew to a thunderous roar. As it approached, Jason and Jenny stopped talking, and peered upward through squinted eyes.

"I know," shouted Jenny, "we're really on an aircraft carrier!"

Her words were barely audible at the height of the roar. "Jesus, jumping jiminy!" she added as the jet passed overhead.

Jason chuckled at her unchecked passion.

Despite their probing of the shrouded sky, they saw nothing. The jet sounded as if it were right on top of them. It was as frightening as anything Jenny had experienced recently. Though the noise built slowly, and its screaming seemed to hang upon them longer than expected, when it finally passed overhead, it diminished quickly. With the sound dying, Jason spoke.

"There's an airport ten miles or so north of here." He looked heavenward once again. "But that one was low!" He listened for a moment to the relative silence, then added quietly, "It's a little unusual for something like that to come in this time of year." Again he looked upward, as if checking for something that might yet linger. Jennifer followed his gaze. Neither saw a thing.

"I thought it was nice of them to leave your steeple," Jenny added as they stepped into the sanctuary.

"Well, how do you like it?"

Jenny shrugged. "It's…um…" She looked around. "I'll tell you what. The last time I was in a church was two years ago, and that was St. Paul's in New York."

"Oh," Jason said flatly.

"Churches really aren't my thing," Jenny added quickly. Jason nodded.

"I mean, it's…it's quaint."

"Quaint," Jason repeated.

"Um…nice…it's nice."

"Nice," Jason repeated, intentionally not letting her off the hook.

"Really nice," Jenny added. Damn, she thought, it's getting worse. "Christ, Winslow, what the hell d'you want me to say?"

Suddenly an outrageously cacophonous sound burst from the front of the church. It lasted only an instant, but it frightened Jennifer enough to cause her to jump. That noise was followed, almost immediately, by a voice, equally rasping. "Which hymn did you want me to play first, Reverend Winslow?"

Jennifer was stunned. God! she thought. There's someone else in here. She's going to think I'm a heathen!

Jason was moving toward the front of the church now, and he took Jennifer by the hand and pulled her along. He smiled at her.

"Christ," Jenny breathed, "why didn't you tell me someone else was in here?"

Jason turned and again smiled pleasantly.

"You bastard!" Jenny hissed. "You're loving this, aren't you?"

Another smile from Jason confirmed this. Now Jenny could see a little, shriveled old lady peering out from behind an electric organ off to the side of the chancel area.

"Play number 28 first," Jason said loudly.

"28. Good. Thank you," the woman replied.

"Oh, Mrs. Watson, I'd like you to meet a friend of mine, Jennifer Seidkamp."

Now the little lady stood, and again that terrible sound struck out from the instrument. This time Mrs. Watson jumped, almost losing her balance.

"Oh, those pedals." She sighed. "What's your name, dear?" she asked as she held out her hand.

"Jennifer, Jennifer Seidkamp."

Mrs. Watson took Jennifer's hand, but instead of shaking it, she simply held it in a limp grasp and patted it with her other hand.

"Why, it's nice to meet a friend of Reverend Grant."

Jennifer smiled pleasantly and turned to Jason. Her smile broadened.

Mrs. Watson was flustered, suddenly realizing her error. "Oh, I mean, Reverend Winslow." She grew a bit graver now, and gazed up into Jenny's face. "You're not from around here, are you dear." It was not phrased as a question.

"No, Mrs. Watson, I'm not." Jennifer was not sure she liked to be called "dear" by anyone.

"Jennifer's from Washington, D.C."

Mrs. Watson drew in her breath slowly. "Why, you don't say. Washington, D.C. My, my. Aren't you lucky you're here instead of there?"

Jennifer looked slightly puzzled and uncertain as to her proper response to the old lady's statement, but she smiled and replied, "Well, I'm not sure. The fog's been so thick I haven't been able to see what *here* is really like!"

Now Mrs. Watson's face reflected a certain confusion. She turned her head toward Jason expectantly.

Oh God, I've done it now, thought Jennifer. I've offended her.

"I don't think Jennifer's a great fan of the fog, Mrs. Watson," Jason said loudly. Slowly Jennifer came to realize that the woman was hard of hearing. She was suddenly relieved to know that Mrs. Watson probably had not heard her early comment from the rear of the sanctuary. Then, however, her relief changed to irritation, as she realized Jason had known that all along and had done nothing to put her at ease. She turned to him now and his expression told her that he knew exactly what she was thinking. After a few more inconsequential pleasantries, they ended their conversation with the organist and again walked outside.

"Well, I'm glad you two had a chance to meet, dear." Jason patted Jenny on the hand.

"Bastard!" Jenny smiled at him.

"Actually, she's really quite the trooper, once you get to know her."

"Right," replied Jenny. "I figure that'll take about four years."

Jason shrugged. "More or less." He paused, then changed the subject. "You hungry?"

"Sure."

"Let me introduce you to the local gourmet's hideaway. The fishermen will all be there this morning. It should be a real treat—if you don't mind a little leering."

Jennifer frowned slightly.

27

JUST A LITTLE BEFORE ten o'clock, Jennifer again stepped into the sanctuary of the little white church. She was met at the back of the church by an usher.

"Wh-ayuh would you like t'sit, miss?" the man asked.

"Toward the back, please." Jenny had no desire to be up front. In fact she really didn't want to be there at all. The church made her uncomfortable. She followed the usher, who led her halfway down the aisle. She almost balked at sitting there, for she would have preferred farther back, but she sat anyway. Don't do anything, she told herself, to make a scene.

She was there out of obligation—to Jason. She owed him that much. As she sat there, she realized there was another reason. She was curious: about how many people would attend, about their reactions. But most of all, she wanted to see Jason at work. She wanted to know what he would say, how he would say it. It would be interesting, despite her discomfort.

She sat in the midst of people she didn't know and stared at a closed coffin that had been placed at the head of the sanctuary. She hated funeral services and if she hadn't been thinking about so many things, she would have had a hard time sitting there.

Mrs. Watson was at the organ. A young woman, perhaps still in high school, sat quietly beside the organ. She wore a simple dark blue robe with a white collar. Her hair was long and blond. She wore it in braids. Her face had been scrubbed so that it was shiny. She wore no trace of make-up. There was something pure and innocent about the girl, something inviting. Jennifer vaguely wondered if the girl, as she grew older, would grow more stolid, more like the distant people who now surrounded her.

Mrs. Watson was playing some tired old songs that sparked a vague and not altogether pleasant memory of a similar occasion in Jennifer's childhood. A great-aunt had died suddenly and her parents had decided it was time for their children to understand what funerals were all about. It had been a frightening experience for her and she wondered now how many of her feelings about funerals and about religion in general had been affected by the trauma of that moment.

She stared as if mesmerized at the simple, dark wooden box. It held her attention until she forced herself to focus on something else. She looked around at the congregation. Although there were only a few people sitting in front of her, she knew more were behind her. She guessed twenty or so people were in attendance. She wondered what that meant. Was that a big or a small crowd? Was the man liked or disliked? Was he even acknowledged by the community? At least no one's weeping uncontrollably, she thought. Then she slowly came to realize something, something that seemed odd, very odd.

She looked around again. No one was showing any emotion whatsoever. None. Every funeral had at least one sniffler or one tissue dauber, but not this one. Were these people simply attending out of some sense of duty or propriety?

That thought led her to another, more sinister one. Again she scanned the rows of motionless people. Could one of them be a killer? She shifted a little in the pew. It creaked slightly, then snapped loudly. No wonder nobody's moving, she thought. It was ridiculous, she told herself, even to pretend one of these people might be Omega. Omega, here, now? She shook her head imperceptibly, finding fault with her overactive imagination. It was a melodramatic touch, and she quickly thought about other, more immediate things.

What, she wondered, is Jason doing? She glanced at her watch. It was time to begin. She wondered how he prepared himself for an event like this. Only moments earlier, he had been his usual self, pleasant and full of good humor. When she saw him next, would he be different somehow? He would have to be. It would be time for him to do his "religious" thing. He would wear those black robes and all that. He would be imposing, the way clergy types were. Again she shifted in her seat, more carefully than before, however. She was not sure she wanted to see Jason in this role.

She had little choice in the matter. As she sat there in the solitude of Mrs. Watson's droning, Jason and Grant stepped into the chancel area from a small doorway off to the side. The organist abruptly ended the tune she was playing. Had it actually come to an end, or had she simply stopped playing? Jennifer smiled, reflecting on the "rough edges" of the experience.

Grant was the first to speak. He mumbled something vague about Mr. Sullivan, he labored overdramatically as he read some lines from a book. They must have been scripture, she decided. God, how he made her uncomfortable. For one thing, he directed most of his words downward to the book from which he read. As he continued to speak, her thoughts drifted from the words Grant was mouthing to Jason.

She thought about their relationship. In just hours, really, it had grown strong. She loved being near him, near enough to touch him and to share her thoughts and feelings with him.

Jason stood and she surveyed him from the distance. For three days, she had been with him almost constantly. Now, sitting here in the quiet of this place and time, sharing him with all these people, what new information would she learn about him? He was wearing one of those awful black robes, but somehow, it didn't seem quite as awful as she had expected. It seemed to fit him. She was surprised. She had thought she would suddenly experience a new Jason—a sort of stranger. But that was not what she was feeling now. No, she thought, I know this person in the black robe. She was aware of the same qualities Jason had shown in Drury's office. He seemed filled with . . . with what? It was an unidentifiable . . . something. What the hell is that? she asked herself. It was a confusing mixture of sublime confidence and humility. It was a quality that said, "I'm in ultimate control," but at the same time also said, "I am powerless." Whatever the hell it is, she thought, it is compelling.

At one point she told herself that it was simply her feelings toward the man that made her read these unsettling powers into his personality, but as she looked around the room and gauged the reaction of the others, she wasn't sure.

Her thoughts turned once again to her own relationship with Jason. She recalled the moments she had lain in bed with him earlier in the week. Those moments, as short-lived as they had been, were unexpectedly fulfilling. She sat there now watching and half listening to him and remembering the closeness they had shared in the hotel room. The vividness of the memory caught her and she suddenly felt her face growing warm. She glanced casually around the church wondering if anyone had noticed this irreverent person. Christ, she told herself, relax, no one even knows you're here. She wondered, in fact, if Jason was even aware. Despite the fact that she was almost constantly watching him, he had, to the best of her knowledge, not even glanced in her direction.

In contrast to Reverend Grant, Jason rarely seemed to look even at a note. What he said—even the parts that apparently came from the Bible—seemed to come from within. Where Grant bellowed in imitation of some pseudo-majestic Cecil B. De Mille character, Jason spoke with a quiet, riveting authority. He spoke with such casualness that she felt she had to listen, much as she would if she were in conversation with someone. She wondered if the other people there were drawn in the same way.

Now he was asking the congregation to stand and sing hymn number 28, ''O God our help in ages past, Our hope for years to come.'' Jennifer watched as Jason deliberately turned away from the congregation and closed his eyes. What's he doing? she wondered. Weird. He seemed at the moment to be in a totally different place. Then suddenly, it struck her. He must be praying, she thought. It's a prayer! For himself as much as for the guy in the box! And strangely, surprisingly, she found herself quietly singing the words of the hymn along with the others. She wasn't sure why, but she knew she wanted to. So she did. She didn't remember the last time she had participated in a church service. The few times she had been in a church, it had merely been as an awkward spectator, usually watching someone equally awkward going through the mechanics of a wedding.

Now it was different. In fact, as she read the words of the hymn, she felt a pressure, an emotion, building inside. It was a new feeling, and, she told herself, not necessarily comforting. It made her uneasy, on guard. As they neared the final verse, she realized the words in the hymnbook were out of focus. Then she realized it was because of a wetness in her eyes. She reached up and wiped a tear away. Well, she told herself, at least there's one snuffler at this funeral. The final verse almost made her angry. It surprised her and she found herself turning from the hymnbook to study once more the man who bowed in prayer before her.

O God, our help in ages past,
Our hope for years to come;
Be thou our guide while life shall last,
And our eternal home.

"While life shall last," she repeated. Suddenly the horror of the possibilities came surging in upon her. The sounds drifted into a hollow distance and death confronted her. What if he is killed, she thought desperately. And this led to another, even more troubling awareness. It became a dull, thundering reality: he won't stop it. "Whatever's going to happen, will happen." He's resolved. He's preparing himself right now!

She was glad to hear the "Amen," and the rumbling, creaking rustle of the congregation as they sat down. She felt weak and disoriented.

Jason now stepped to the pulpit. He took a breath and began to speak, but suddenly stopped. Behind her, she heard the door open and someone, maybe more than one person, come in. She felt mildly irritated, she felt an urge to turn around and stare, as a woman who sat a few rows ahead of her was doing. The woman turned only for an instant, then suddenly back again. Jennifer looked at Jason.

What she saw brought her to sharp awareness. Something had happened. It must have been whoever came in. She wished now to turn in earnest, to see who had caused this disruption, but she continued to stare at Jason. Clearly the mood, if there had been a mood, was broken. Even old Grant seemed somewhat disoriented.

Jason worked at settling himself. He did it quickly. Just before he began again, he glanced downward. For seemingly a full ten seconds, he gazed fully and directly at Jennifer. It was as if they were the only people in the room. Was he trying to tell her something? Perhaps, though the message that kept repeating itself was "I care about you. I care about you." She resisted an urge to move to him. And then, without knowing why, she knew implicitly it was all right. Jason continued to gaze at her, then smiled an almost imperceptible smile and immediately allowed that impenetrable aura to flow in and about him once more. The words he then spoke were as compelling as any she had ever heard.

"First Corinthians, chapter 15, verses 35..." Again he stopped. He reached for a Bible and began again. "Verses 51 to 55."

"Behold." The word was like an electric arc, sparking out across the congregation. It was said with almost a whispered anger. Jennifer thought she saw a sudden movement among the parishioners at the word. Then Jason continued: "'I shew you a mystery! We shall not all sleep, we shall all be changed. In a moment, in the twinkling of an eye...at the last trump: for the trumpet shall sound, and the dead shall be raised incorruptible, and we shall...be...changed... Then shall be brought to pass the saying that is written, Death is swallowed up in victory. O death, where is thy sting? O grave, where is thy victory?'"

The fact that Jennifer was not a believer did not change the power of the words. She was caught up in them as if they had been an incredible web woven of golden threads. In the moments that she was able to step away from what was happening, she knew that much of the impact resulted from her knowledge that the words Jason spoke had grave implications for him. They would—she could not let herself think that—they *might* possibly be the words he would recite when he came face-to-face with Omega.

She listened, she reacted, she hurt. She wanted to shout, "No! Stop!" but she could not; she was helpless.

"We are here today to celebrate a life...to celebrate Richard Sullivan..." Jason took a breath and continued. "...to celebrate Samuel Morrison, for Richard was also Samuel before he came to live in the community of Craig's Harbor." He could see the confusion on some of the people's faces. "For Richard Sullivan, there is less mystery in death, than in life. One day...soon perhaps...we all can know more about the man, but until then, let me share with you a few things he told me just before he was...before he...died Sunday night."

Jennifer listened while Jason created the image of a man strangely tormented. The congregation, she realized, would be hearing things one way—Jason was careful not to reveal any details of the Alpha/Omega operation—but she was hearing them in an entirely different way, in a way, she told herself, that no one else in the room would be hearing them. But she was wrong.

The man who was Omega sat quietly, uncomfortably, listening to the words. The audacity of the man, he thought. His anger fumed, and yet it was critical that he appear as casual as any other person there.

Omega seethed. It was a mistake, he told himself, to have come here. The clergyman was having an unexpected and disquieting effect on him. He had felt it on the telephone that first day, and he had felt it at other times since, but now it was more than a feeling; it had become a presence. It had become a reality in the man standing before him. But I can fight it, he argued silently, I must fight it. "'Death, where is thy sting?'" he mouthed. The sting is still there, my friend. It is another presence. It is undeniable and it is stronger. I have seen death. I know its victory. I witnessed it. I have created it!

At the same time, Omega knew that the person standing before him would not be like the others. It should be easier to kill him, but... He is unskilled, uncertain, and claims not to fear death, Omega told himself. Easy prey.

Once more, the man who was Omega drifted from the place where he sat to the distant hills of India and relived the ritual of the tiger. He closed his eyes for deeper concentration. He worked to force the words of the minister out of his consciousness. He struggled to recall the details of the stalking. His breathing grew more rapid in the effort. At one point, he almost stopped, but he would not allow the minister to thwart him. He had to prove he could achieve his goal. He settled down. The tiger sprang.

Omega started to turn, but caught himself. Out of the corner of his eye, he had seen the man sitting next to him jump. He wondered what caused him to do so. Maybe he had just dozed. Maybe, but he did not believe it. Now, slowly he glanced toward the other man. Whatever had caused him to jump had left him flushed and troubled. He stared straight ahead, straight at the minister.

The man who was Omega smiled, and wondered about the man next to him, about the minister and about the next few hours.

Jason had finished his remembrance. It had been short and compassionate. It spoke of human things, which anyone in the sanctuary could understand. Now he sat, and the young woman sitting next to the organ stood. She sang without accompaniment. Her voice was untrained, but it was pure and clear. She sang with uncomplicated emotion.

Amazing grace! How sweet the sound
That saved a wretch like me!

I once was lost, but now am found,
Was blind, but now I see.

Again, Jenny was caught in emotions of frustration, anger and pain.

She studied Jason, she probed him with her eyes. She wanted him to turn to her and tell her it was all right. But he did not. He simply sat, resting one arm on his knee, leaning over, looking downward to the floor.

The hymn's phrases crept into her consciousness and punctuated her emotions. "Through many dangers, toils, and snares . . . grace will lead me home . . . as long as life endures . . . yea, when this flesh and heart shall fail . . ." Now, for the first time, Jason looked up. He turned toward the congregation and sat with the quiet resolve that Jenny had come to recognize with fear and awe. "And mortal life shall cease, I shall possess . . ." She gazed upon him. She loved him, but somehow the words, when she formed them in her mind, seemed too casual, somehow unimportant. I love you, she thought. ". . . Within the veil, a life of joy and peace." I love you, Jason Winslow. I love you, and there's nothing I can do to stop this thing that is happening to us. There's nothing I can do. The words pounded in her thoughts. God, I've got to get out of here. She wanted desperately to move, to get up, to run, to run to Jason, to run away from him, to be with him, to get as far away as possible, to forget what she felt was inevitably going to happen.

She didn't hear, was not even conscious of Reverend Grant standing before them offering another meaningless assemblage of words. What she was aware of, was the congregation rising and moving toward the front of the sanctuary. They passed around the coffin, some of them pausing beside it, then out through a door at the side of the church. Jennifer followed.

When she stepped outside, she was stunned. If she had been less involved in her own realities, the sudden vision of a clear day might well have caused her to stop abruptly and stare in awe at the beauty before her. As it was, she looked dully from the cemetery to the spruce stand behind it, to the crystal-clear blue sky, to the sparkling blue sea. She turned slightly away from the sun; its brightness hurt her eyes. She blinked and again wiped a tear. She glanced around and realized that people were gathering next to an open pit. Jason stood there, as did Grant. Jennifer glanced now at some of the others. The faces were all stern. The pallbearers moved the casket to the appropriate spot and Jason again spoke.

"For as much as the spirit of the departed hath returned to God who gave it, we therefore commit Richard's body to the ground, earth to earth, ashes to ashes..." Jason faltered. Jennifer looked up. He appeared momentarily troubled. It was only for an instant, but she noticed it. She looked in the direction he glanced. "Ashes to ashes," he repeated, "dust to dust."

There by the corner of the church she saw a man. He simply stood, watching, like a sentinel. But now she realized she was virtually staring through two other men who were already part of the mourners. Jennifer felt an uneasiness growing in her. These two must have been the ones who had interrupted the service earlier. Was one of them Omega? The question drummed in her mind. None of these men seemed to be from Craig's Harbor. They all appeared to be FBI types. She had seen enough of them in Washington to recognize that there was a type, but who they were, she couldn't guess.

Now the casket was being lowered into the ground. Jennifer looked around and noticed that some of the people across from her were studying her. They did not stare, and if they made eye contact with her, they would quickly look away, but they were watching her. They're trying to figure out just who I am, no doubt. Well, good luck, she thought.

Jason knelt in the soft ground beside the hole and took a handful of gravel. He said a short prayer and let the earth slowly sift from his hand. He stood. Now Mr. Grant opened a book and prepared to speak, but Jason stopped him. Jennifer noted the older man's dissatisfaction. She wondered what Jason had on his mind. The silence grew awkward.

Jason slowly scanned the entire crowd. Then, after he had looked at each person assembled, he opened his Bible. He turned to the very end, thumbed through a few pages, then stopped and once more looked at the gathered people. He spoke slowly with his familiar forcefulness. Jenny felt it, and she judged from the expressions on the faces of others, they felt it, too.

"From the Book of Revelation, where the author speaks of things that are to come. 'This, too, he said to me, "Do not keep the prophecies of this book a secret, because the Time is close. Meanwhile, let the sinner go on sinning, and the unclean continue to be unclean; let those who do good go on doing good, and those who are holy continue to be holy. Very soon now I shall be with you again, bringing the reward to every one according what he or she deserves."'" Jason again stopped and again began looking across the faces of those who stood before him. As his eyes traveled from one to the next, he spoke more words from the scripture. Words that sent a chill through more than one person who heard them.

"'I am the Alpha . . . and the Omega . . . The first and the last . . . the beginning . . . and the end . . .'"

The words faded. In the distance, the sea continued to rumble, proof of some omnipotence. Jennifer moved her hands up and down her arms, to rub away a numbness. She knew only too well what Jason had done. It was as if he had intentionally placed himself at the call of Omega—if Omega were within hearing. The thought—the potential outcome—was too great and Jennifer actively forced herself to focus on other things.

She was totally unprepared for the scene that the disappearing fog had revealed. The harbor was beautiful. It was typical of those quiet scenes on the calendars from *Down East* magazine. The clarity of the air created a crisp separation of colors and shapes. The buildings, most of them white, spaced along the shore; the trees—predominantly tall, solid pine or spruce, but a few maple and oak—the fields of yellow-brown hay, a colorful array of boats still at their moorings, and farther out, closer to an island at the mouth of the harbor, there was the boat Grant had spoken of earlier. It was a massive thing—big enough, Jenny thought, to be called a ship—sleek and solid, seeming as substantial as the island behind it.

But the thing that dominated everything, even that gleaming white boat, was the overwhelming power of the blues. The water and the sky, both deep, saturated blues, each of slightly different hues. The color seemed to blanket everything with a mystical, powerful sense of calm—of order. It was soothing. She gazed out at the blue of the water and sky and marveled at it. Despite all her imaginings while the fog had hidden this from her view, it had been impossible to picture this magnificent serenity.

People were now moving quietly away. Some came up to Jason and spoke in whispered tones. Jenny listened to those who approached Jason, and waited for an opportunity to move closer to him, herself.

"Good morning, Jason," a man said.

"Hello, Calvin. I'm glad you could make it," Jason responded.

Jenny watched as the conversation unfolded between Jason and two other men. These people—or at least this one man in particular—seemed to lack confidence. They seemed to carry about them an ingrained sense of uncertainty. It was odd.

"I'd . . . I'd like you to meet my cousin Alvin's boy, William . . . William Hawkins."

"I was with Uncle Calvin last night," the younger man said.

"He's down for a visit . . . and I told him he owed it to himself to come hear you preach . . . ah . . . um . . . even if it was for a funeral, ya' know," Mr. Hawkins explained.

"Well," said Jason pleasantly, "nice to meet you. You going to be here for a while?"

"Not nearly long enough—now that the fog's gone!"

Jason smiled and nodded. "Enjoy yourself while you're here, fog or no fog," he responded. Jenny watched with no little admiration. Jason seemed totally at ease and totally interested even in Cousin Alvin's boy, William. It was beyond her how he could focus his attention in this way. Jenny watched the two men walk away from Jason. As they left, they, like many of the others, turned in her direction and stared. Not a real friendly bunch, Jenny thought. Not even the out-of-towners.

"Good morning, Jenny." The words—and the voice—startled her. She turned. Immediately, the FBI types were explained. She realized that all the stares she thought had been directed to her had in fact been directed to the two men who had been standing behind her. Now she faced them, LeRoy Drury and Alex Delacourte.

"Good morning," she heard herself saying.

"Do you know Alex Delacourte?" Drury was asking.

"No," Jenny replied. "We've never met."

"Alex Delacourte, Jennifer Seidkamp," Drury said mechanically.

"Nice to meet you," Delacourte responded, equally mechanically.

Jennifer smiled, then felt someone approaching. As she turned, Jason stepped beside her.

"Ah, Jason," Drury said before either Jason or Jennifer could speak, "I can certainly tell you're back in your element."

Jason smiled. "It's home." He had been very aware of Delacourte's stare. He had felt it during the service and then out here. The man continued to stare at him. "Mr. Delacourte," he said as he deliberately stuck out his hand, "it's not often someone of your stature visits Craig's Harbor. I hope you enjoy your stay."

The two men studied each other, sizing each other up.

"I'll let you know when it's over," Delacourte said, smiling back pleasantly.

"Mr. Delacourte knew Richard Sullivan." Jason turned abruptly from Delacourte and glanced at Drury, who had offered the explanation, then back to Delacourte.

"You did?" Jason asked.

Delacourte nodded. "Back in the early fifties..."

Jason was on guard. A tightening pulsed through his body. Of course. God, he thought, I'm staring at Omega. This is the man. He debated about blurting it right out. "You're Omega," he'd say casually. What would the man across from him do? How would he react? Jason never had a chance to find out. Delacourte's next statement short-circuited Jason's fanciful inquisition.

"When I was with the Agency," Delacourte completed.

Jason did not need to ask which agency. He also knew that Sullivan had said specifically that Omega was only connected to the Agency through him. Delacourte did not qualify.

Delacourte and the others had noticed Jason's momentary reaction to Drury's statement. They could all pretty well guess it was because Jason suspected that Delacourte was Omega. None was prepared for what Delacourte said next. It caused each to stiffen and await the next pronouncement.

Delacourte smiled pleasantly. "I'm Omega." The listeners stood motionless, numbed, hearts pounding. "That's what you're wondering, aren't you?" Now Delacourte laughed. "Damn," he continued, turning to Drury, "now that *would* make a hell of a story, wouldn't it?"

Drury stood motionless and drawn. He had been unprepared for this. As his mind raced across the possible reasons for Delacourte's comments, he realized the man was waiting for a response.

"Well," Drury responded coolly, "I can write up a headline if you like."

"Don't bother. I know how you squirm when you're forced to print a retraction," Delacourte responded. Then, turning his attention to Jason, he continued, "If you know anything about the Omega operation, you know that the Agency stipulated that Omega would be an outsider. He'd come from the outside...."

"Like René Fragonard," interrupted Jennifer. Delacourte directed his attention to her now. He was irritated by the boldness of her pointed interruption, but he reacted with characteristic coolness.

"Like Fragonard," Delacourte replied, "only better." He smiled. "Well," he said, abruptly signaling the end of the conversation, "sorry to disappoint you about Omega." He shrugged, then continued. "I appreciated what you said today, Reverend Winslow." He smiled again. "By the way, when I found out that I would be here today, I arranged to have my yacht meet me here. Perhaps you'd care to be my guests for dinner?" He looked around. Drury seemed somewhat perplexed by this development. "You don't need to fly back right away, do you, Lee?"

Drury shook his head.

"And you, Reverend? Miss Seidkamp, you will join us?"

Jason and Jennifer exchanged glances. Jennifer turned to Delacourte. "Yes. Yes, we'd be pleased."

"Fine, it's settled. Seven-thirty then. One of my men will meet you at the dock. Now, you'll excuse us."

Delacourte and Drury turned and walked away. The man who had been standing at the corner of the church fell into step about twenty feet behind them. The other two men, the two Jenny had noticed earlier, watched as the three men left the cemetery grounds, then moved toward Jason and Jennifer. A few of the local people, including Calvin Hawkins and his cousin William, had remained to watch the celebrities in their midst, but now with their departure, they left also, apparently satisfied they had seen all that they needed to see.

"Now what?" murmured Jason, indicating the approaching men.

"FBI," Jenny responded, "I predict."

Jenny was right. After identifying themselves, they asked if they could talk privately. Jason glanced at Jenny, then spoke. "This is Jennifer Seidkamp. She has been involved in some of this as well. She may be able to provide you with some details that I'd overlook." The men shrugged.

As they walked toward the house, the men made casual conversation, though later as Jason reflected on it, he wondered just how casual it really was.

"You have a rather interesting congregation, Reverend."

Jason looked at the man who had spoken. "You mean Delacourte and Drury?" The man looked back and nodded. "I didn't know they were coming." He paused and again probed his questioner. "Neither did you, apparently." The FBI agent felt mildly uncomfortable under the minister's penetrating gaze.

"Drury's here because we've talked to him about this," Jennifer broke in. "And he must have pulled Delacourte along because he says he knew Sullivan way back when."

"I didn't know anyone pulled the national security adviser anywhere," the second agent said. There was an unmistakable cynicism in his voice.

Jennifer smiled in acknowledgment of the truth.

"At least it's turned out to be a nice day, hasn't it?" the first agent said. As they moved past the side of the church, they could again see the entire harbor. Delacourte's huge power yacht gently rode the low swells that found their way past the protection of the island at the mouth of the harbor.

"See that," Jason said cynically. The agents turned and stared out at the vessel. "If you'd come a little sooner, maybe you'd have gotten an invitation to dinner tonight as well." He turned and frowned at Jennifer. She realized now that perhaps he did not want to eat with Delacourte tonight. She'd discuss it with him later.

As they walked into the living room of the parsonage, Dog met them and positioned himself in front of the agents. Jennifer noticed that he now seemed less friendly than he had been this morning. She was surprised. As she looked down at him crouching before the two men, she was not so certain he was the lovable, cuddly animal she had first thought him to be.

Before they had a chance to get started, Reverend Grant came down from upstairs. He had his bag with him and was preparing to leave.

"I'll be going now," Grant said. He looked disapprovingly at Jason's guests and even more so at Jason. "You could have told me," he continued, "that this was going to be a command performance."

"Didn't know myself," Jason responded. "Thank you, Willard, for filling in for me. I know the congregation appreciated having you here." He stopped, then added as an afterthought, "And so did I. Thank you."

"Oh," said Grant soberly, "it was nothing. Got to keep your finger in the stew, I always say."

Grant and Jason shook hands, and Grant prepared to leave. At the doorway, he leaned back in and spoke to Jennifer. "Nice to meet you, miss."

Jennifer's smile in response was as purposefully uninspired as his sentiment. When he had finally left, Jennifer murmured, "Up yours, too, fella." The agents turned quickly toward her and then looked uncomfortably downward to their feet.

"Jennifer," Jason said with mock concern, "that's not very nice."

"Mmm," she replied. Then she glanced over at the agents. They continued to stare at the floor. "They still there?" she asked pleasantly. Finally one of the agents looked up, realizing she was talking to them.

"Ma'am?"

"Your feet."

The agent smiled uncomfortably.

"Excuse me," Jason interrupted to the relief of all. "Can I see your IDs again?"

The agents looked at each other, then reached into their pockets and displayed their cards.

Jason took them, moved to the phone and dialed. After a moment, he spoke, occasionally glancing over to the agents. They were puzzled by what was happening.

"Who's on the duty desk, now?" Jason asked. The agents again exchanged glances. "Okay," Jason continued, "let me speak to him." He paused. "It *is* important, and if you do not let me speak to him, I'll want to be speaking to your superior, Mr. . . ." He paused and looked down at a piece of paper next to the phone. "Polanski," he continued. Again the agents reacted. "Thank you," Jason said after a pause, and then after a longer pause spoke again, "Yes, hello, this is Jason Winslow calling. You were sending an agent out to talk with me. I'd like you to identify him or her." Again he paused, looking over at the agents. "Oh," he said, "there are two. Good. Names, please? Okay, and can you describe them?" A long pause followed. "Thank you, very much. I'm sorry to have bothered you. I appreciate your help. Goodbye."

Jason moved to the agents and handed their cards back to them. They looked relieved. "I've learned," Jason explained, "not to take too much for granted." The men nodded, but Jason knew they still disapproved of him. Hell, he thought, I don't give a damn what they think.

"We almost put you down as a crank," the first agent said.

"Really," replied Jason coolly.

"Yes."

"What changed your mind? You get the results of the ballistics tests?" Jason probed.

"Actually, headquarters has told us that report won't be ready for several more hours."

"Actually," began the second agent, "it was you, Reverend Winslow. For the past hour or so we've been watching you, and we've done some checking around. You're what we'd call a 'credible source.'"

Jason thought that sounded like a compliment, though he was not sure. He glanced at Jennifer and she smiled gently at him.

"So," continued the agent, "why don't you just begin?"

They did. Jason and Jennifer reviewed the story in detail. The agents spent close to three hours with them.

"Who else knew you were to meet with Donlevy?" one of the agents asked finally.

"We told no one," Jason answered.

The other agent picked up an envelope and removed a photograph. "Do you know this man?" he asked, handing a picture to Jason. Jason studied the picture, shrugged and handed it to Jenny. They both shook their heads.

"You've never seen this man?" the agent pressed.

"No," Jason replied.

"No," Jennifer echoed.

The agent sighed, took the picture back and slipped it into its envelope. He looked at his counterpart.

"René Fragonard," the agent explained. "Anyone unusual in town, Reverend? Aside from celebrities?"

"A few visitors," Jason responded.

"Cousin's Alvin's boy," Jenny volunteered.

One of the agents nodded dutifully and made a note. The other agent placed his hands on his knees and pushed himself up. "Okay, Reverend Winslow. Miss Seidkamp. Thank you very much. We'll be in touch if there's anything else we need from you."

"What about the other way around?" Jenny asked.

"Excuse me?"

"What if we want some assistance from you?" The two agents exchanged glances. Jennifer continued. "I mean, we're sort of under the gun, so to speak. What about protection of some kind until this thing is settled?"

"We've rented a cottage down on the shore. A phone's being installed this morning. I will be staying there for a few days. I'll either be there or be here."

"Thanks," Jason said, "Agent McCann, wasn't it?"

"Yes," the man replied. "James McCann." He smiled pleasantly at Jason and Jennifer. The two men walked toward the door. Then McCann turned and smiled a curious kind of smile. "Frankly, if you're spending the evening with Delacourte and Drury, I think you'd be about as safe as anyone could hope to be. Delacourte has his own secret service people with him all the time." He smiled again and both agents stepped outside into the warm fall sun.

"Hope it's going to stay warm, for a while," Jason said as the agents moved down the walk.

McCann smiled broadly in agreement. "You've read my thoughts," he called back. Perhaps that was partially true; but it was not totally true. Agent McCann's thoughts were not focused on the weather. At the moment, they had more to do with getting back to the admiral as fast as possible. There was a lot of planning to be done.

28

TWO HOURS HAD PASSED since the FBI people left Jason and Jennifer. Jason was restless. That was unusual, and he was making Jennifer restless as well.

"Come on," Jason said finally. He turned to Jennifer, took her hand and together they moved out the door toward the car.

"Where are we going?"

"I want you to see something."

"The ever mysterious Reverend Winslow," Jenny said melodramatically.

They rode in silence along a paved road, then on a dirt road and finally arrived at nothing more than a rutted trail. There Jason stopped. He shut off the engine and opened the door. He turned to Jennifer.

"Listen."

The deep, thundering crashes came in rhythmic waves. How close were they? Jennifer tried to imagine what they might look like. In the sound alone, she was able to sense the fierce power of the sea as it met the land.

Jason moved around to her side of the car, and took her hand. As he walked along the path, he pulled her along, frequently turning to urge her on. His enthusiasm was infectious. He was like a child, impatient with his parents as they neared a carnival.

"Okay, okay," Jenny responded. "I'm coming!"

A stand of spruce trees shrouded her view. A carpet of needles that had fallen over the years cushioned their movement. The contrast of the soft rustle of the wind that surrounded them as they walked, and the crashing surf was hard for Jenny to reconcile. As they moved nearer, Jenny could see the distant ocean. The closer sight, the one she was trying to picture, was kept from them by the scraggy brush that clung determinedly to the granite coast.

Then as the trees thinned, she felt a mist, almost a rain falling across her face. For a moment she was puzzled. There were no clouds in the sky. Her tongue moved across her lips. It was saltwater! Even at this distance, the spray from the surf provided an inkling of the place they were approaching. Then walking around a bend, down a small gully and around a jutting ledge, they came face-to-face with creation.

Jennifer stopped suddenly, frozen in the steps she was about to take. Never in any picture, never in any description had she met anything like it. For a full mile, the ocean assaulted the cliffs. It rolled in from miles out. Jenny could see the waves forming long before they struck the land. They built as they neared, gathering in strength and stature, as if mindful of the impending battle. The ocean seemed to increase not only its strength but its speed as well. Then suddenly, inevitably, it struck with all its summoned might, pounding at the earth that presumed to break its course.

The rolling, angry, black-green sea poured over the rocks and ledges that lay hidden farther out, but when, in the final moment, the water struck the constant land, it burst explosively into a fury of raging white water. Every second, tons of it foamed furiously across the cliffs below them.

Jennifer's heart pounded. When she had stepped into the clearing that opened on the brink of the awesome sight, she had stopped. Her legs would move no farther. But she was unable to move back. The presence of this mighty force had paralyzed her. She could not look away but for the slightest moment.

When she did, she realized that Jason, who stood only a few feet in front of her, was shouting at her. He gestured downward, and then started to move toward the edge of the abyss, but she reached out to stop him.

Jason turned to her, stepped back, wrapped his arms around her and guided her slowly downward. Then she realized there was a path of sorts that he was following. For part of the way, they were hidden from the open sea and the sound took on a muffled quality, but then suddenly they stepped out in plain view of the water as it made its final run at the shore. Jenny held Jason tightly. She hadn't felt this way since her first ride on a roller coaster as a small child. It was at once frightening and exhilarating. When the waves finally struck, the concussion they created caused the earth to tremble under her feet. Simultaneously a cold, damp, salt wind beat upward, almost lifting her and pressing her backward.

The wind came whenever a wave struck, and Jenny finally realized that it was caused by the water suddenly displacing vast amounts of air. She stepped back and watched as Jason crouched down, drawn to the water. He seemed to lean out toward the sea. Occasionally he would turn back toward her and smile. He seemed to have no fear of the power before him. It was more like a friend to him. She watched him as minutes, first ten, then fifteen, then thirty minutes passed. The seas swirled around them. Her ears rang.

She reflected on the nature of the battle between land and sea. Despite all its force, the sea seemed to be the loser. The land was, after all, immovable. But her assumption caused her to wonder again, and she looked around at the torn and pitted ledges that formed the boundary between ocean and land. How many thousands—no, millions—of years had this same water pounded at this land? How much ground had inevitably been lost to the relentless battering of the water? Who could possibly know the answer to that, and yet, it was clear that the land had lost, that slowly, in time measured by centuries, the sea was the victor.

Despite a sort of rhythm, the water was never the same. It more precisely reflected an Indian raga, constantly changing and ultimately unknowable, except to its creator. As she watched, she too felt herself begin, unbelievably, to relax, to be drawn to the surging, thunderous force they faced.

It was a power that had overcome her. She had to simply stand there and let it do whatever it wished. She was dazed, and yet alert. She was lulled, yet on guard. She tingled with a keen sense of vitality, aliveness.

Suddenly, Jason stood and turned. His face had changed and Jenny could see clearly that he was concerned. He came toward her, and without speaking took her and moved her back up the path, back to the place where she had first stood.

"What's wrong?" she shouted.

He pointed seaward, and Jenny's eyes traced the course he had set out. At first, she saw nothing, then, in the rapidly diminishing distance, she saw what he was seeing. It was a wave, a massive wall of water dwarfing the others that had preceded it. She knew what was about to happen. She knew that this one wave would produce an immeasurable effect. It would be, she thought, like watching an erupting volcano. As they stood there, Jason again wrapped his arms around her. It was only then that she realized she was shaking uncontrollably. It was the cold she was feeling, and the excitement—and the fear of what was about to happen.

The wave, unlike the others, seemed to slow, rather than speed up. It moved with an assumed independence—with an imperious quality. A king. Was it her imagination, or had all the sounds of the other waves actually died? A sudden quiet—a commanding stillness—settled around them.

"Get ready." She heard Jason's whispered words.

And then it struck. The sound grew from below them and roared upward. It thundered so that Jenny covered her ears with her hands. It carried with it strange scraping, jarring noises. The ground shook. And suddenly a massive white wall of boiling water rose up, up above the rocks, up above them, towering up above their heads. For an instant, it seemed just to hang there, then just as suddenly, it fell, tons of it, back earthward. The foaming whiteness ran at them. Jason covered Jenny and himself with his jacket. They heard the water, the edges of it, falling upon them, and then it was quiet again. They turned back in time to see the last remains of the wave draining back into the sea.

Together the two people stood in silence and watched for another five minutes. Jenny was no longer sure she wanted to stay; she was not sure she wanted to leave.

When the five minutes had passed both of them turned as if on some unspoken command and walked away from the ledges back into the woods. Neither of them turned to look behind. The experience was over.

Stepping into the stand of spruce, they were again startled. Now, as the night before, Mr. Hawkins and his cousin's boy stood unmoving before them. Stepping out of the shadows of the spruce, the younger man spoke. "Cousin Cal wanted to show me this spot."

"It's something else," Jennifer replied.

She and Jason smiled and kept moving.

"They give me the willies," Jennifer whispered as they walked along the path. Jason nodded, but their thoughts about the two men were overwhelmed by the still raging emotions of what they had just experienced.

When they reached the car, Jason and Jenny let go of each other. They remained, standing still, facing each other, saying silently that they were different people now.

"You're soaked..." Jennifer had tried to say once, but the words caught in her throat and only the whispered ghosts of the thought were formed. Jason simply nodded. He moved slowly toward her now and took her once more in his arms. She looked up at him and he kissed her. It was a deep, hard, almost violent kiss, one that caught, in its power, the intensity of the experience they had just shared. He pressed her body to his and moved his hands across her arms and back. Jenny's emotion began to swell within her. She fought it. She knew that this time, like the previous ones, would only end in disappointment if she were expecting fulfillment. But for the moment, this was enough. It would have to be. Slowly, then, she eased herself away from him. Their gazes burned their emotion into the other's eyes, and without words, both spoke of their longings. They remained facing each other, wanting each other, but knowing it could not be—not now, not with the horrible possibilities that pressed in on them.

Coming to this place had been part of Jason's preparation for whatever was to be. Jennifer knew that, and she felt pleased that Jason had wanted her to share in it. She had been conscious of all this even as they were approaching the abyss. What was it he had said yesterday? It provided him with a context. Things took on perspective. That was what he was about. Her gaze followed him relentlessly as he moved around the car to the driver's side.

He was more in touch with who he was and where he was, than anyone she had ever known. And yet, he was prepared to give it all up. In a flash. To give in to death. Even in the midst of life. She knew what he had said, but it didn't make sense. It made no sense at all. His intention moved into the unknown; it moved ruthlessly beyond reason. It was frightening.

She had been to the brink of creation. She understood Jason better now than even he might have imagined. The past incredible minutes overpowered any fears or confusion that had once filled her thoughts. Instead she simply allowed the memories of the moments they had just spent together to dominate her. She felt exhausted, but strangely satisfied. She suspected, despite her hopes, that these feelings would not last, but for now, it was all right. It was okay.

A bond had been formed between them that was stronger than any physical one, stronger than any emotion. There were elements of both in what they now shared, but it was more. It was somehow spiritual. Each of them knew this; each one's silence was confirmation for the other.

When he heard the car begin to move back toward the harbor, Cousin Alvin's boy pulled a small device from his pocket.

"They're heading back, now," he said simply.

"Affirmative. Base clear," came the electronic response. It was barely audible over the pounding surf.

The younger man smiled reassuringly at the older man.

29

NEITHER JENNIFER NOR JASON spoke on the way home. There was so much to say. But trying to voice these thoughts would have destroyed this shared communion. Both of them knew that; and so, for now, at least, their covenant would remain pure, undefiled by imperfect speech.

When the two stepped out onto Jason's driveway, the brown sun, laced with a long narrow cloud, stretched infinite shadows out from their bodies. The coldness that the sun had subdued earlier now stealthily moved from the earth.

"Look," Jason said, pointing out past Delacourte's yacht, past the island, out to the open sea. There, in the distance, was some vast object with sharply defined edges. It stretched unbroken across the far edge of the ocean.

"Fog?" Jenny asked.

Jason nodded. "It's coming back. Sometimes, during the day it backs off away from the land, as if it knows it cannot survive, but then, when darkness comes, or when the wind turns 'round, it steals back in like the coward it really is."

The sight surprised Jenny. It seemed as if some vast, unseen barrier were holding the smoky substance from the land as long as possible.

"Has it been out there all day?" Jenny asked.

Jason nodded.

"I never saw it."

"It was there. Just a band, a line, at the horizon."

"It gives me the creeps. Will it be like last night?"

Jason shrugged. "I don't know. Sometimes it seems as if you could shovel it like snow; other times it just evaporates. Like your breath on a cold night."

Dog met them at the door. He was, as usual, glad to see Jason.

"Why, Dog," Jason said, "I'm surprised you're not mad at me. You would be if you knew where we went."

The animal stopped wagging his tail and looked from one of them to the other.

"Come on, Jason. You don't expect me to believe..." Jenny stopped and realized that she should not question anything about Dog.

"I think he thinks the cliffs are his own special territory."

A sudden dull thump sounded from the front door. Jennifer jumped and Dog immediately tensed and barked.

"Dog, it's only Jimmy," Jason said as he stood and moved toward the door. As he walked, he twisted around and said to Jennifer, "The paperboy." He retrieved the paper, came back to Jenny and handed it to her. "How about a fire? To take the dampness off."

"I think I'll take a shower first. Gotta be at my best for Alex."

Jason's expression darkened. "Right," he responded coolly.

"He's a powerful man," Jenny continued.

Jason grimaced. "You know something? When he said he was Omega, I wanted to believe it. I could picture him doing the kinds of things that man has done. I could see him hunting, enjoying the kill."

Jenny watched Jason grow more and more intense. It made her uncomfortable. She agreed with him, and yet like so much else of the past days, she was helpless to do anything to change things—they both were. After a moment she excused herself and went upstairs to shower.

When Jennifer came back down the stairs the room was bathed in an undulating yellow light. The sounds and smell of the fire drew her. Jason sat on the floor, in front of the fire. Dog lay beside him with his head in Jason's lap. As Jason stared at the crackling fire, he absentmindedly scratched Dog under his ear, unaware that Jenny was watching him. He leaned back against the sofa, apparently deep in thought. She watched him a moment longer before she began to feel like an intruder. Finally, she cleared her throat. "Your turn."

He slowly turned to face her and held out his hand to her. She moved beside him and crouched. Once again she was aware of his vulnerability. As the reality began to crystallize, she felt a hot, choking ball of panic growing in her breast. She struggled to subdue it, to force it from her, but it would not leave. She forced a smile, and then slowly, hot tears welled up in her eyes and rolled down her face. Lowering her face to his head, she encircled him with her arms. She wanted to say something, but couldn't, and so she simply continued to hold him tightly—to keep him from slipping away. They sat quietly facing the fire. It had a calming effect.

"Today I have everything I have ever wanted," Jason said slowly. "I am where I want to be. You're a part of that, Jenny." They continued to gaze at the fire, almost afraid to look at each other. "I move from happiness to absolute fury, because you've been drawn into this...because *I've* drawn you into this."

He looked back at the fire. "I shouldn't have done this to you."

"It's okay," Jenny said gently.

"But I can't..."

"Don't say anything," she whispered. She did not want or need to hear the words he was about to speak. She was afraid they were the same ones she was thinking.

"I love—"

Jenny moved her hand to his lips and prevented him from finishing. He looked over at her and his dark, liquid eyes reflected the flames that grew opposite them.

They sat in the stillness for an hour or more, each of them afraid to move, for fear that the moment might shatter into a million irrecoverable fragments. It was enough just to be together.

Finally Dog's movement brought them to consciousness. He lifted his head and woofed a barely audible bark. Then Jason heard the phone. How long had it been ringing? He had no idea. He turned to Jenny and shrugged, then slowly raised himself up and answered it.

"Reverend Winslow?"

Jason tensed. He did not recognize the caller. "Yes?" he asked warily.

"This is Agent McCann . . . down at the cottage?"

"Oh, yes."

"Is everything all right up there?"

"Yes, yes, we're fine."

"I just thought I'd check. I also want you to have my phone number here."

"Oh, thanks."

The agent gave the number to Jason and asked him to repeat it. Jason did.

"Good," replied McCann. "Have a good night, now."

"Thank you," Jason answered. "Good night." He hung up the phone.

"Hey, it's getting late," Jenny called.

Jason checked his watch. "Damn," he muttered. "It's after seven."

Jenny smiled. "You can't put it off any longer. Go take that shower."

"Yes, Mother."

30

JUST AS ALEX DELACOURTE had said, a crewman in a dinghy was at the public landing waiting for them. The fog had settled in over the harbor, but there was still enough visibility to navigate.

When they reached the yacht, another crew member helped them out of the boat and up the stairway that had been rigged over the side.

Delacourte was waiting for them on deck. Jason was surprised by the man. Somehow he had expected him to be wearing a white yachtsman's hat and an ascot, but he was, in fact, dressed much as Jason was.

"Welcome aboard, Miss Seidkamp, Reverend Winslow. Come in."

"In" was like stepping into someone's lavish living room. Elegant brass fixtures reflected a warm light. An Oriental rug covered the floor. Finely upholstered furniture was arranged tastefully throughout the room. "Care for a drink?" Delacourte asked.

"None for me, thank you," Jason replied.

Delacourte looked at him for just an instant longer than one might expect. Then he smiled. "A soft drink, perhaps? Juice, apple cider?"

"Cider sounds good," Jason said.

"And you, Miss Seidkamp?"

"Could I just have a glass of wine, please? White?"

"Of course." Delacourte responded, moving to the bar.

"This is magnificent, Mr. Delacourte," Jason began.

Jennifer watched Jason as he interacted with Delacourte. He's trying, anyway, she thought.

Delacourte nodded. "136 feet. My pride and joy." He returned with a glass of wine and a crystal goblet of hot mulled cider. "There you are. Careful . . . Jason, right?" Jason nodded and Delacourte smiled and continued. "It might be a bit hot."

Jason put the goblet to his lips. "It's fine, thank you."

"Where's Mr. Drury?" Jennifer asked.

"Oh, he'll be right along. He went ashore to call in a story or something." He waved his hand expressively. "Newspaper stuff."

"I didn't think you and LeRoy had all that great a relationship." Jenny's statement was more like a question.

Jason turned abruptly toward Jennifer. He almost swallowed a steaming mouthful of cider. Jennifer's question had also engaged Delacourte's full attention. He smiled.

"My, you do get right to the point, don't you?" Delacourte replied. "Actually, Miss Seidkamp, I'd say we don't have any relationship at all. And to answer your question," he continued, "I came along because I wanted to—" he turned to Jason and shrugged "—pay my respects to a former colleague. *And*, I wanted to get out of the office for a day or two." He smiled pleasantly. "But let's not talk about that. How about you, Jason? How do you like it here on the rugged Maine coast?"

Jason tried to read the man. He was finding it disappointingly difficult. In all he had ever seen of Delacourte or read about him, he appeared to be simplistic and crass. The man who now entertained Jenny and him seemed far from the boorish man on TV and in the papers. And yet, there was a quality about him that was hard to get a firm grasp on. Jason was uncertain about the best way to respond to him.

"Well, Mr. Delacourte, I . . ."

"Alex, please. Call me Alex."

Jason smiled and continued, "I like it here very much." He thought about what he would say next. He chose his words carefully, calculating a way to draw Delacourte out. "It offers a serenity and dependability in a world torn apart—uncertain from one moment to the next whether there will be a nuclear annihilation or not." Jason watched. Now he's gone and done it, Jennifer thought. People are hanged for less than that.

Delacourte listened carefully to Jason's words. He seemed to ponder each one, reacting thoughtfully. At the end of the sentence, he actually seemed sympathetic to Jason's sentiment. He looked at Jason for a moment, then nodded easily.

"It sounds like a nice place to live." Delacourte turned to Jennifer and smiled, then back to Jason. In that instant Jason caught a glimpse, just a hint of the man he had expected to see. Delacourte's face hardened slightly, then, in the midst of his response, it softened to the pleasant demeanor it had shown earlier. "We won't agree on much, I suspect," he said to Jenny, "but we'll agree on that . . . if nothing else." Again he smiled at Jason.

The conversation continued like this for another twenty minutes. It was cordial, seeming potentially important, but ultimately inconsequential. It was as if everyone were waiting for LeRoy Drury to appear to "make it official."

"Sorry, folks, I hope I haven't upset things too much," Drury began when he finally entered the main cabin. He turned to Delacourte. "How come, Alex, the government can run okay without you, but my little syndicate falls apart forty-five minutes after I leave?"

"Government has a life of its own," Delacourte responded. "There isn't much that can stop it. That's the good, the bad and the ugly, all wrapped up in one big bureaucracy." He paused and peered into his wineglass. "But I imagine," he continued easily, "that somebody's missed me somewhere along the line today; I just hope it wasn't the President." He smiled. "That makes for a little unhappiness, let me tell you." He still peered into the wine that he gently swirled, then looked up at his guests and smiled. "Let's move into the dining room, shall we?"

If the main cabin was lavish, the dining room was elegant. It was filled with light. A large crystal chandelier swayed gently over the Louis XIV furnishings. Pale blues and eggshell white predominated. A deep, plush white carpet cushioned the party's footsteps. Jason realized the effect the exquisite decor was having on him and on Jenny. It heightened the stature of their host, adding yet another dimension to his bigger-than-life personality. Awesome, as the kids liked to say, often inappropriately. Jason recalled the few times he tried to put "awesome" into the proper perspective for them. Now he wished they were here. The entire experience hinted at "awesome." He glanced at Jennifer. She was so taken in by what she was seeing, she was almost giddy. If the room had been in a house, it would have been stunning, but the ever-present gentle movement of the yacht only added to the effect.

Jason struggled to keep the proper distance from his host. He remembered all the times he had yelled at the television or radio in disgust because of this man—this very man who now seemed so cordial. A regular Jekyll and Hyde, Jason told himself. Nevertheless, he realized, it was interesting to see the man "up close and personal," as television sports announcers used to say. The close view forced him to deal with this other apparent reality. He enjoyed the intellectual stimulation it created. It sharpened his senses.

A uniformed crewman seated them around the table, and the first of several courses were brought out.

"Something the matter?" Delacourte asked casually. Jason looked up and Delacourte's gaze led him to Jenny. She held her hands just slightly above the table. She seemed to be trying to keep her balance without calling attention to her action. She looked up with an embarrassed smile.

"Oh, no, not at all. I've just never sat at a table on a boat before. I'm not quite used to the movement, I guess."

"It does take a little getting used to, but in a snug little harbor like this one, you might as well be in a bathtub."

The dinner was sumptuous, with baked stuffed lobster as the main course. It was a dining experience out of a movie. From the custom-designed bone china and silver service to the food itself, everything evidenced careful planning and consummate taste.

Jason could see that Delacourte was enjoying the experience as much as anyone. He appeared to take great delight in letting a couple of bumpkins into a fairyland world. As Jenny and Jason savored their food and the ambience, Delacourte savored their reactions. It was fascinating, thought Jason, especially because they both knew they were being studied by the other. Fascinating.

With Drury there as a sort of moderator or guide, the conversation became more substantive. After the first course of shrimp cocktail, Drury leaned back in his seat. He breathed in slowly.

"So, tell us, Alex, how you knew Sullivan."

"Ah," Delacourte said, lifting the corner of his linen napkin to his mouth. "I knew him only as Morrison, of course." He leaned and bowed slightly toward Jason. "You're not surprised, certainly." Jason shook his head. "We actually first met in the old days of the OSS." He looked past the others, as if focusing on a place long ago. "Those were the days. We knew who the enemy was and we could do what was necessary."

Jason glanced up at Delacourte abruptly. The man's tone was surprising. He and Jenny glanced for an instant toward each other as if cued. They looked away just as quickly. What shocked Jason was the unbelievable mix of warm nostalgic tones and the cold, ruthless sentiment all in the same breath.

Delacourte had picked up on the reactions of the two younger people. "What I say surprises you." Delacourte paused, then shrugged. "Well," he continued. "Look at it from my perspective. You know what it is? Today you don't have that luxury. You rarely know who the real enemy is." He leaned forward slightly in his chair. "Oh, hell, occasionally you know, you know for damn certain, but most of the time—" he relaxed again "—most of the time, it's all shadows and ghosts of the good, the bad. And no one acts on their own anymore. It's all got to be checked, then rechecked, then checked again. And then, damn it, it's usually too late." He summed up. "It's...it's just a hell of a lot tougher to do your job." The distant longing note returned, and then he abruptly focused on his dinner guests once again.

"Well, that's a long way from Sam Morrison." He shrugged. "Thinking about the old days and the old ways triggers the old struggles. Sam Morrison. You know, he never left the office. At one point, he was one of the most valuable members of the team, but he never left his damn desk. You know what he did?" Delacourte turned to Jennifer.

"Not really, something like a librarian?"

"Right!" Delacourte replied. "Exactly! In fact we used to call him Bookworm. At first it was just one of those flippant nicknames, but then it became his code name. Bookworm! That's what he was called. We raucous hoods in the field used to get into a jam and we'd hurry off a message to the home office: 'Bookworm, help. Info on subject of history lesson needed to complete class project.' And there it was, in the next mail drop, everything you'd ever need. Complete, in order...and accurate! That was Bookworm.'' Delacourte allowed a smile to grow and he relaxed. ''Every once in a while, we'd try to get him to come out to play—to run an errand for us in Europe or someplace—but he never would. The strange thing was, he loved to travel. You may not have realized it, Jason, but he did. Every spare moment, every vacation, he'd go somewhere—to places I've never been, places I'd never want to go to! He did, though, but never with a cover. He always went as an out-and-out tourist. The really uncanny thing was he'd come back from these little jaunts with as much information as some of the boys would gather in months out there.''

Jason reflected on the things Delacourte was saying about Sullivan. He had never pictured Sullivan as a traveler; in fact he had never known Sullivan to go much farther than Portland, and he'd never be gone overnight. God, thought Jason, the man's entire life must have been turned upside down. How could he have stood it? Then a chill flowed through Jason's body. Maybe that was why life could end for him with such ease. Maybe it had really ended a long time ago.

Delacourte continued. ''The man had an incredible mind. I'd stop by his desk—you can just picture it, neatly organized stacks and stacks of information—and ask him a question. 'Some Ruskie bigwig's going into the Urals next week. How come?' I'd ask. Morrison would take off his glasses, lean back and close his eyes. We boys used to think he was falling asleep, but he'd be *thinking*! And surer than hell, after a few seconds, or maybe minutes, he'd all of a sudden open his eyes wide, like some bell had just gone off, reach here or there, under this pile or into that folder, pull some snippet of paper out of a file and announce, 'That's where bigwig's mother lives. It's her birthday next week.' He was the best at what he did! And that was before all this computerized diddly-doo. Christ—'scuse me, Pastor—it takes a day now just to get the damn computer debugged or some damn thing, before you can even get a question asked!''

"Did he ever talk about Omega?" Jason asked innocently. Drury reacted with mild surprise. He slowly leaned into the conversation, as if he did not want any morsel to miss his hearing. Delacourte seemed to grow physically smaller.

"Now, Reverend," Delacourte began, "I could tell you that that's classified information. Especially now. But, truth is, I didn't know Morrison had anything to do with it. Oh, hell, we knew there was an Omega. Everybody did. He kept us all guessing. You never quite knew where he'd hit next. It was weird. Everyone, their side, our side, *everyone* got spooked. Omega was doing the impossible. One day you'd hear about an Omega job in some little town in England, and the next day, he was supposed to have done a job in South America. Just no way back then he could have gotten from the one place to the next in twenty-four hours. No way. But people insisted. Just some of the mythology, I guess." Delacourte chuckled gently and turned to Drury.

"The spooks got spooked," he murmured. "I'll say one thing, though." He shrugged. "The operation was good. It kept everyone tuned up. Our people haven't worked harder before or since. No one wanted to come up with a bloody nose. And their people . . ." Delacourte laughed at a just remembered joke. "Their people were stretched out so tight, they'd forget the little stuff. Because nobody knew where the orders were coming from. The West, right, everyone knew that. Only the Reds—on both sides—were getting it, but no one knew why or when. It was Lone Ranger time. We had a field day.

"I'll tell you one thing. Right in the middle of it, our embassy in Berlin gets a message from the East. They want to have a meeting. We send our Mr. Big, they send theirs. 'This can't go on,' they say. 'We agree,' we say. 'Not good for morale. To say the least,' they say. 'But,' we say, 'we don't know where it's coming from. Not from our house. Not from the Limeys.' The biggest laugh came when their guy says—the only thing he said in English in the whole meeting— 'Well, it's sure as hell not coming from our house!'"

Delacourte leaned back and roared. He imitated a Russian accent and repeated, "'W-wh-ell, eet ess shoor ass hhell nut comink from oour hus.'" He looked around the table and, seeing that his companions were not sharing his jubilation, slowly settled down.

"I guess," Delacourte said, calming himself, "you had to be there. But anyway, that was it, for Omega. It stopped as suddenly as it started. And as far as Alpha went, we never had a clue. When LeRoy told me it was ol' Bookworm, you could have knocked me over with a feather." He sat, cooling off, breathing easier, gently shaking his head. "Ol' Bookworm," he murmured again.

For the remainder of the meal, Delacourte was the one asking questions. What had Sullivan done in the years since he left the Agency? Had he got along okay in the community? Had he had many visitors? What had he told Jason about Omega?

Jason told him a lot of what Sullivan had told him, but he also omitted a lot. In most instances, Delacourte was content to let the empty places pass without note. Occasionally, he would press on a point, but to Jason's thinking, it was usually an unimportant point. In fact, it seemed at times as if Delacourte were simply making conversation. It puzzled Jason, when he had a chance to think about it. Often, he would be in the middle of something and all of a sudden realize he was saying things that he really hadn't intended to say at all. Delacourte had an uncanny ability to put him at ease, to draw him out. Maybe, he thought, that's what spies are really like. Maybe they're just good listeners.

Following dessert, they moved back into the main cabin. After a short time there, Drury announced he was tired, needed to do some writing and thought he'd excuse himself. He was staying on board for the night. Then tomorrow morning he would fly back to Washington. Delacourte thought he might go back to D.C. on the boat, but he'd have to wait until tomorrow and check on a few things before he knew for certain.

"Well, Mr. Delacourte," Jason said warmly, "I certainly appreciate your hospitality. It's been a memorable evening." Jason smiled pleasantly.

Delacourte responded in kind. "The pleasure is mine, believe me," he said. "You've been something of a breath of fresh air. Usually the people I get to spend my evenings with are more concerned about echoing my thoughts, than enjoying themselves. Thank you." He shook Jason's hand warmly and firmly. He turned to Jennifer and did the same. She half expected the obligatory political kiss, and when it did not come, she was appreciative.

Delacourte walked with them to the gangway. He leaned on the rail as he spoke, bending his right leg slightly then straightening it out again. He pressed his fingers into his knee. "Damp weather," he said with a tone of disapproval. "Maybe it will rain tomorrow. I hope you're not planning anything outside."

"Well, actually, I'd like Jenny to see the island out there." Jason gestured eastward. "It's one of my favorite spots. Early in the morning, if the fog lifts, we'll go out, probably . . . if," he said, turning to Jenny, "that's all right with you."

"I'll pack a picnic lunch." She turned to Delacourte and smiled. "If it doesn't rain."

Delacourte responded, "Sounds romantic—even if it does. If we're still here, stop in. Good night now." He turned and moved stiffly away. When he had gone a few steps he turned again and waved. "Take care," he added and then he stepped, silhouetted, into the brightness of the main cabin. The door closed, darkness spread across the deck and they boarded the dinghy.

The fog had become thicker, but it could not compare with the previous evening's. From halfway in to the dock, they could see the lights along the shore. When they got to the dock, they began to walk toward the parsonage.

"Well," said Jenny, "what do you think?"

"About what?"

"About who! Delacourte."

Jason shrugged.

"Winslow! He's probably the one person in the world you can't dismiss with a shrug. You either love the guy or you hate his guts."

Jason stopped, looked at her, striking a thoughtful pose. After a moment, he spoke with his usual matter-of-factness. "I hate his guts."

"I knew it. Come on, weren't you impressed?"

"Yes, I was impressed. Doesn't mean I have to like him. I don't like what he stands for, I don't like how he gloats over the power he holds, I don't like his values. I don't like him."

"But you did like his boat?"

"His boat? Yes, I like his boat." He grinned. "You?"

Jennifer frowned. "I wasn't crazy about the white carpeting." She paused. "Jason, does the ground feel like it's rocking to you?"

Jason smiled, and put his arm around her. "Landlubber." He glanced along the shore as they started walking again.

"Hey," he said, after they had gone a few steps, "you interested in stopping at the FBI guy's house for a minute? Just to see if he needs anything?"

"If he needs anything?"

"You know, he's probably got nothing to do but sit around and watch television."

"And polish his gun," Jennifer added cynically. Then she sighed overdramatically. "Sure, Pastor Winslow. Feed your flock."

As they neared the house, they could in fact hear the TV. Jason knocked on the door, and almost instantly the sound of the TV ceased. The shade, which had been pulled, lifted slightly out from the sash, and then the door opened.

"Yes?"

"Hi," Jason said, "it's just us." He felt a little foolish now. Somehow his desire to be friendly seemed inappropriate.

"Is everything okay?" The agent's tone was sober and intense.

"Yes, we're fine," Jason responded. "We were just on our way back from Delacourte's boat, and we thought we'd stop in to see if you needed anything."

"Oh," responded the agent. He seemed relieved, then he did something that surprised Jason. He stepped away from the door. "Would you like to come in?"

Jason looked at Jennifer, and she, in turn, offered him one of those "Why are you asking me—you're the one who wanted to come here" looks.

"Why not?" she replied simply.

They stepped inside. The first thing the agent did was to place his suit coat over his gun and holster, which lay on an end table beside the sofa. He did this casually, and seemed self-conscious about someone seeing the "tools of his trade."

"I walked by your house a little while ago," the agent said. "All was quiet." He thought for a moment, then added, "I did run into a . . . Mr. Hawkins. You know, the cousin's boy. From down the street?"

"Oh, right." Jason sighed. "Cousin William. Picked a great time to visit quiet little Craig's Harbor, didn't he?"

McCann smiled.

"Have you heard anything yet from Washington?" Jennifer asked.

The agent shook his head. "Not a thing. But that's not unusual," he added quickly. "It takes a while. Things go up the pipeline a lot faster than they come down." He shook his head, marveling at the idiosyncrasies of the system, and then looked up.

"How's our national security adviser?" The door from the other room had abruptly opened and an older man stepped into the doorway and spoke. His sudden appearance seemed to startle everyone in the room, including McCann.

"Ah," said McCann uneasily, "this is my boss, Mr. Pederson."

Pederson smiled pleasantly and nodded slightly. It was hardly what could be called a warm greeting.

"How was his boat, is the question!" Jennifer asserted.

"I can imagine," McCann replied.

Pederson merely smiled, then he looked a bit more serious. Jason noticed the change. The tone of his voice was still bright and casual, but his eyes belied a particular intensity. "Doesn't it seem odd," he began, "that the head of the NSA would be away from his desk at a time when all hell could break loose over at the CIA?"

A chill passed down Jason's spine. He arched his back slightly to rid himself of it. Yes, Jason thought, it was strange. His reaction came because he had himself wondered the same thing hours ago when Delacourte walked into the funeral service. Why the hell was he here? he'd thought. Jason had had no answer to the question. Later, the fact that Delacourte had worked closely with Sullivan seemed to provide a plausible answer, but now that the same question was being asked again, Jason wondered just how plausible that answer really was. Then he realized Pederson was waiting for him to respond.

"He said he knew Sullivan and simply wanted to pay his respects. Something about the end of an era," Jason said.

"But there was something else, too," Jenny added. "Remember? He said he wanted to get away from his office for a while."

"He did say that," Jason confirmed. "In fact, it sort of stuck out; it didn't quite fit with the rest of the thought."

"Seems strange to me," Pederson said, thinking out loud. "Maybe when you're on the top, you don't have to stick around to take all the flak." He dismissed the thought with a shrug, and turned and left the room.

The conversation then moved on to things more mundane. McCann wanted to know about food. Was there anywhere else in town to go for food other than the little shop up on the main road? Was there any place to get a couple of postcards for his kids? They talked for another twenty minutes or so, then Jennifer and Jason stepped back into the cool October air and headed for home.

31

WHEN THEY CAME through the front door, Jason and Jennifer were met by a dead chill. The fire in the fireplace had burned out quite a while ago. Jason reached out, snapped on the light.

"Want a cup of tea?" he asked, and then with a burst of inspiration, "How about some cocoa?"

"Sounds great," Jennifer said, smiling. "Just let me change my clothes." She started up the stairs.

"I'll be in the kitchen," Jason called over his shoulder. As he walked through the living room, he called out, "Dog. Hey, Dog, where are you?"

He stepped into the kitchen and turned on the light.

"Hey come on, Dog, wake…" On the floor, just in front of the door, Dog lay on his side. He was not asleep. Dark red blood had spread across the floor. Jason felt himself losing focus on things. His head felt unattached to his body and there seemed to be no sound within his hearing at all.

Dog, please, he thought as he moved to the animal. He knelt beside him and gently lifted his head. The animal's lifeless eyes had lost their brightness and his tongue hung loosely from his mouth.

"Oh, Dog, Dog," Jason sobbed. He bent over and laid his head on the animal's tawny fur. "Dog." He knelt there in the quiet, alone, now totally alone. He felt…what? His emotions were so jumbled that it really did not make any difference what he was feeling. He only knew he hurt. It was unbearable. He hugged the animal tightly, and wanted the impossible. He wanted Dog to be alive again.

"So where's the hot..." Jennifer stopped the moment she entered the kitchen. Jason twisted around to face her. His face was a ghostly chalk color. His eyes burned deeply in under his brow. They were, in sharp contrast to the rest of his face, fearsome. Jenny found it hard to look at them, but neither could she turn away. The frightening reality of those eyes along with the tears that flowed from them tore at her. On Jason's left cheek was a blotch of redness—blood, she realized. It sickened her. He knelt there, oddly contorted, weeping. When he spoke, his tone physically wrenched her.

"He killed him. He killed Dog." It was a pathetic wail more than a cry. It lacked all emotion save possibly utter, abject hopelessness.

Jason struggled to pick up Dog's lifeless body. The animal was big and the body, lacking the tension of life, was awkward to hold. When Jason finally got him in his arms and was standing upright, he looked around as if dazed and started toward Jenny.

"Jason," Jenny said firmly. "What are you going to do?"

Suddenly he stopped and again that terrifying, lost, dazed look flowed into his face. He did not know what he was going to do. At first, he had thought about taking Dog upstairs and laying him on a bed. But that's foolish, he told himself, he's only a dog. The words throbbed into his brain. He is more than that. He gazed at her for a moment longer, then slowly crumpled into one of the kitchen chairs. And again, he buried his face in Dog's fur. He sat there making slow, small rocking motions, like a mother rocking a sick child, Jenny thought.

Jenny looked away out of respect and her eyes came to a scrap of paper on the table. She moved to it and tentatively reached out and picked it up. On it were but four scrawled words. Her skin tightened, a coldness swept down her neck. An involuntary contraction contorted her body. She glanced down at Jason. She wished she could help him. The note drew her attention once more. "You were lucky, tonight," it said.

"What's that?" The unexpected words startled Jenny. She looked up. Jason was staring at the note. She felt defeated. I don't want you to see this, she thought as she handed it to him.

Still clutching Dog, he tilted his head to read the scrawl. As he stared, motionless, at the note, Jenny saw him change. It grew from his eyes, and it was more terrifying than those awful words. She realized now that she hadn't seen that look since their high school days. It was a fearsome, all-consuming look of hate and rage, mingled together. He breathed slowly and deeply, like an animal crouching in the underbrush, waiting to spring at the prey. It frightened her, because suddenly he was not Jason Winslow. He was someone alien. He was, in that instant, an entity completely impenetrable.

"Jason!" Her voice filled with desperation. It startled him. She saw the awful strangeness leave him as quickly as it had come. They remained where they were, unmoving, for a long time.

When Jason finally spoke, the words caught and he had to start again. "He was all I had to love." He looked slowly into Jenny's eyes.

Jenny reached out and touched the body in Jason's lap. She looked from it into Jason's hollow eyes. "I know," she said quietly.

Tears—searing, painful tears—again filled Jason's eyes. "What am I going to do?" It was not a question meant to be answered. It asked too much for a simple response. Jenny slowly shook her head. She felt helpless, totally inadequate to offer the kind of support she wanted to give.

"Jason, I'm going to call McCann." Jason looked up, blankly. "The FBI agent. I'm going to tell him what happened. I'm going to tell him to get up here."

Jason looked as though he might protest, but Jenny stopped him.

"I am, Jason. It's the right thing to do." She stepped into the living room. Jason watched as she left, then stood and carried Dog outside to the far end of his yard. He gently placed him on the ground, then crossed to the church's shed, got a shovel and came back.

When Jenny had completed the call, she returned to the kitchen and cleaned the blood off the floor. It was difficult for her. More than once, she had to force the memory of her friend, Walter, from her mind. When she finished that, she watched from the window. Jason dug slowly and deliberately. At one point she left to answer the door when Agent McCann arrived. They both went to the kitchen and watched reverently.

Jason worked with the utmost care for a long time. Finally he stooped, picked up the dead animal and gently placed him in the pit. He stood for several minutes and simply stared, motionless, into the hole. Then, slowly, he knelt and filled in the hole with his hands. He continued to kneel when his task was completed. His form, vaguely visible in the night fog, was an eerie vision.

The two people in the kitchen both felt they understood the pain of the man they watched. Occasionally in the silence, they would glance toward each other. There was nothing for them to do but watch. Anything would seem to be an intrusion into this private—indeed, sacred—moment.

"I'm sorry, Reverend," the agent said softly when Jason finally stepped into the house. Jason looked at him and nodded, and moved to the kitchen sink where he washed his hands. He glanced through the window and stared out again to where Dog now lay. He breathed out a long, deep sigh. His eyes focused onto the window and he saw his reflection, and for the first time, he was aware of the blood on his face. He took a towel and wiped it off, and turned.

"Thanks . . . for waiting."

"We're asking for some additional people," McCann began. "Frankly, unless you feel differently, I propose you go to bed, and I'll stay up and keep an eye on things down here and outside. By morning we'll have some more people, and we'll try to give you some kind of answer on this." He paused then, and a twinge of guilt showed on his face. "I'm sorry. I know it doesn't sound like we're doing anything, but at the moment, that's all I can tell you."

Jason showed McCann where the coffee was kept.

"I think I'll go outside for a while," the agent said. He started to go out the door, then stopped.

"If anything should happen to me, call the house. Someone will be here immediately." He headed for the door and paused again. "They know you might be calling. They're waiting." Then he stepped out into the night air and closed the door.

Jennifer and Jason climbed the stairs together. When they reached the top, Jason turned to Jenny and kissed her. "Thank you," he said quietly. She offered a slight smile and they went into their cold dark bedrooms.

Jenny changed quickly. But instead of getting immediately into bed, she moved to the door and waited. She wanted to go to Jason, to be with him, but she was afraid she would intrude. There were some things he just would not share. His relationship with Dog was one of those things.

She stood for a long time, thinking about a whole range of confused and often conflicting images. A soft knocking startled her and the images dissolved.

"Jenny?"

Jenny opened the door and found Jason standing before her. He looked surprised.

"I was standing by the door," she murmured. It was a pointless explanation.

"I . . . I . . ." Jason faltered, then seemed to give up all resistance. He reached out to hold Jenny—and to be held.

She put her arms around him.

"You're cold," Jason whispered in her ear.

"Freezing," Jenny confirmed.

Together they walked to Jason's room. He led her to his bed. He held the covers open while she slipped underneath them, then he too got into bed. She did not turn to him, but she longed to, to know how he was reacting to her presence. For several moments, she lay still, waiting for him to move to her. But he remained motionless. Slowly, she rolled to face him. She reached out to him. Only then did he respond, taking her hand in his. It was a firm grasp. Its force surprised her. She drew him to her. At first, they simply lay there in the stillness. Then, with a quiet delicacy, Jenny reached out and touched his face. It was a sign, and Jason, as if suddenly given permission, slowly stretched out his arms and embraced her.

Jason's hands moved across her, always drawing her closer and closer. There was a firmness in his grasp that Jennifer did not expect. It was almost painful, but she said nothing. Instead, she searched for his mouth with hers. And her hands moved constantly, slowly, deliberately. Where she expected resistance, now there was none. She moved easily, conforming her body to his. He responded, still holding her tightly. Her fingertips moved fluidly across the hardness of his body. She felt her touches awakening the building, surging need of the man who clung to her. Together they formed a common, yielding shape. His warmth flowed into her body; her openness and love enveloped his. And when each had filled the other's emptiness, they moved apart, now more whole than they had been. Still, he held her.

That night, theirs was not a sound and endless sleep, but the times when one of them awoke, the other seemed to know and was awake also. They said little; instead, they simply lay together, remembering—remembering. In the distance, they heard the sea pounding and swelling against the land. It created a rhythm of power and movement. More than once as she lay there, Jennifer recalled the turbulent surf she had gazed upon earlier in the day. The memory caused her emotions to well up over her, and she reached out again to Jason, sharing the moment with him once more.

Hours passed before they at last settled into a deep, lasting sleep. It could not have come sooner, but when it did, both of them were able to give in to it and allow it to replenish them.

32

JENNIFER ROLLED OVER and squinted. Bright sun flooded the room. She turned to Jason, but he was gone. He must have gotten up awfully quietly, she thought. She got up and dressed, then moved to the window and looked out at the harbor.

The contrast to the previous morning was stunning. The water seemed a vast velvet blackness, covered by countless sparkling gems. Smaller objects, hundreds of lobster buoys, gulls and black ducks, even small boats were silhouetted against the million random specks of reflected sunlight. The sea farther out was a mass of glowing buffed silver. Out there, beyond the bell buoy, even the larger lobster boats were but black specks on that sea of sun. She started to turn and nearly bumped into Jason's telescope. She moved behind it and sat on the stool.

It was simply idle curiosity that caused her to sit behind the instrument. Peering through it was a dizzying experience. Even her slightest movement caused the blurred reflections to swirl into a brilliant disk at the end of the lens. As she moved it, she slowly turned the focusing knob. After a few seconds, she found an object that startled her. The image filled the lens and looked like some kind of massive steel structure.

"What the heck is that?" she murmured. She looked out the window, squinting, trying to locate what she had seen magnified. When she finally realized what it was she was again startled. "God," she murmured, "the bell buoy!" The telescope was more powerful than she had imagined.

Now she tested her skill, training the instrument on lobster boats far out to sea. Once she was able to count the number of lobsters the fisherman saved and the ones he had to throw back. Still farther out, she discovered a broad band stretching the length of the horizon. It seemed like a sort of belt that held the sea against the continent. "Fog," she murmured. As she watched, a fishing boat headed directly into it. Within seconds, the boat had disappeared, totally enveloped by the wall of mist. She watched for a moment longer, wondering if it would reappear. It was eerie. The boat had been there one moment, then in the next, it was gone. It had simply disappeared. The fog created a discomforting effect. What was real? Had the boat actually passed into the bank? Or had it been simply an illusion that evaporated as she watched? "Spooky," she whispered. Then she swung the instrument downward, bringing objects within the harbor into her view.

"Let's see what's happening with Alex this morning," she said aloud. A large blur of whiteness filled the viewfinder and Jennifer cranked the focus knob, first one way then the other. When the boat came into focus, she saw that she had trained the instrument on the bow. Slowly she began moving along the lines of the boat. It was more difficult than she'd imagined. The telescope was really too powerful. She couldn't see as much as she wanted. She moved to the topmost part of the bridge. Methodically she moved across, then down, then repeated her action. All was quiet.

Jenny moved the telescope off the Delacourte boat and was about to stop her spying when she inadvertently swept past a lone figure. The person was in a small wooden skiff, motoring out toward the mouth of the harbor. Something drew Jennifer back to the figure. At first she felt merely a vague alarm. She moved back and focused critically, then watched, her concern growing. The boat was clearly more than a mile from shore, but Jennifer knew immediately the figure in the boat was Jason. Then, as she watched with her full attention, she saw him turn and look back. There was no doubt; it was Jason.

"Where are you going?" she asked. Jenny moved the telescope around slightly. For a moment she took her eye from it. It was clear Jason was heading for the island at the mouth of the harbor. She grimaced. Moving the telescope across the island, she found several small fieldstone buildings—all apparently abandoned. None had windows and the roofs were intact on only a few. There seemed to be two groupings of the buildings. One was down near the water, the other toward the center of the island, on the higher part. The scene reminded her of a small village in Ireland. There, as on the island, construction was almost entirely of stone. There, as here, low stone walls lined the paths and roads. Even the barren terrain of sparsely covered fields and scrub trees seemed the same. The only difference was that the island seemed to be more tired. Its pathways were overgrown, the stone walls had tumbled in places; the island's remains, like crumbling skeletons, merely hinted at what they once had been.

She again trained the telescope on Jason. He had reached the island now, and was pulling the boat up over the pebbles and stones that formed a sort of beach. As he worked, he straightened up, looking back in toward the harbor.

"What the hell is he looking at?" Jenny murmured. She moved the telescope in the direction of Jason's gaze.

Nothing. Nothing. Then suddenly, the stern of Delacourte's boat came into view. And suddenly her anxiety flooded back on her. He was going out there to wait . . . or to hide. She shivered. "No," she shouted. She looked out at the island without the telescope and realized that, in the few minutes that she had been sitting there, the wind had shifted and the fog had begun to cast a haze across the harbor. She saw nothing on the island except for the small, indistinct white spot that she knew to be the boat. She looked back through the telescope.

"I can't find the damn island," she said aloud. In her rush, she first made movements that rendered objects mere blurs of faded color. Finally, she realized her problem. "Slow down," she breathed. She located the island and then Jason. He was moving quickly, sometimes almost running, up toward the buildings on the higher ground.

She had seen enough. She stepped away from the telescope toward the bedroom door. Then for the first time she saw a note taped to the doorknob. It read:

> Jenny, I'm giving him what he wants. Please, get McCann to take you somewhere safe. Leave this place, Jenny, go where you'll be safe. Jason.

She crumpled the paper in her hands and ran down the stairs.

"Mr. McCann! Mr. McCann!" she shouted.

Silence.

She hurried into the kitchen and looked out the back window. Her eyes focused on the fresh grave of Dog, and she felt unable to move for just an instant. She shook her head and walked quickly through the living room and out the front door.

"Mr. McCann." She paused, then called his name again.

This time he appeared, hurrying around the corner.

"I'm here," he said. His tone expressed the alarm he had sensed in Jenny's shout.

"He's gone!"

The agent was quiet for a moment, then spoke with a note of desperation. "Reverend Winslow?" Jenny nodded and he frowned disapprovingly. "Christ," he hissed under his breath. His whole body slumped, in apparent frustration. His eyes slowly closed and opened again.

"He's on the island. I saw him in the telescope," Jenny added quickly.

"What telescope?" McCann asked as he pulled Jenny toward the car. As they drove to the dock, she explained what she had seen.

"And he kept looking at the Delacourte boat?" the agent pressed.

"Yes. Like he was expecting to see someone there."

The agent made no response, except for a stiffened jaw-line and a sigh.

They walked quickly down the dock and onto a float. McCann glanced around, then approached a fourteen- or fifteen-foot skiff that a teenaged boy was bailing. It had a large motor on it.

"I need your boat, son," McCann said.

The boy looked up, puzzled.

McCann pulled out a bill and glanced down at it. "Here's twenty bucks," he said, handing the money to the boy.

"I don't know, sir," the boy said tentatively. "My dad's gonna'—"

"Look—" the agent began.

"What's goin' on, fella?"

McCann and Jennifer glanced back up at the dock to the source of this interruption. A crusty old man was looking down at them from the edge of the dock. His teeth firmly gripped a pipe.

"He want's my dad's boat," the boy said.

"Look," McCann began again. This time he pulled out his identification. "I am an agent of the FBI. I'm taking the boy's boat. This is a matter of national security." He glanced somewhat uneasily at Jennifer. The boy, who had been staring at the ID, now climbed out of the boat.

McCann stepped into the skiff and moved to the stern.

"Untie the boat," he said to Jennifer, as he cranked on the motor's cord. It did not start and he cranked again. Something fell out of his coat pocket into the water. He made a grab at it, but it was too late. "My radio," he said. He looked into the water, as if hoping the radio might somehow be floating back to the surface. Then he glanced up toward the wharf, then back to Jennifer.

"Here," he said, handing her a card. "Go to the house across from the parsonage—"

Jennifer interrupted. "I'm coming with you."

McCann looked up. "You can't come."

"I sure as hell can. I'm coming," Jenny replied.

McCann stared at her for just an instant, then apparently decided the argument would take too long. He frowned and turned to the boy, and handed the youngster the card. "Here," he began again. "Go up to the Hawkinses' house. Do you know where that is?" The boy nodded. "Do *nothing* else, first." The boy stood, heart pounding, entranced by the intensity of the agent. McCann's eyes flared. "Don't go home, don't do anything—ask for Mr. Pederson or Mr. Martin. Tell them that McCann has dropped the hook."

"Y-y-yes, sir," the boy replied. He started to turn and run up the stairs.

"Wait," shouted the agent.

The boy turned.

"Repeat what I just said," McCann demanded.

The boy shifted uncomfortably like a student making an oral report. Finally he began nervously. "McCann has...has dropped the..."

"The hook!" McCann repeated. "Say it again."

"McCann has dropped the hook."

"Good. You might just save someone's life."

The boy's eyes widened. He looked for just a moment longer then raced up the gangway. The man above them had straightened up and taken the pipe out of his mouth. He stood, amazed at the scene below.

Jennifer, too, looked amazed. "Cousin Alvin's boy..."

McCann's nod confirmed her notion before she could finish. "One of ours," he said simply.

He turned again to the motor, yanked at the starter once more. This time the engine sputtered to life. McCann carefully backed the skiff out away from the other boats, then slammed the gearshift to forward, opened the throttle all the way. The boat headed toward the island. In the time it had taken Jenny and McCann to get from the house to the dock, the fog had insidiously moved closer to the land. It obscured the distance. The island was but a vague form. The sun was disappearing. Wetness collected on Jenny's hair and face. I should have brought a coat, she thought as she huddled, crouching low into the shallow skiff.

33

THERE WAS A SMALL SEA running, and as the boat headed eastward, it repeatedly rose slightly, then quickly thumped down, slapping the water. Spray lifted up around the bow and blew into Jenny's face. She pushed her hair away from her eyes, only to have it blow back immediately.

In the time it took them to run out to the island, Jennifer reviewed McCann's conversation at the dock. He had been businesslike, even frightening. She had seen fear in the boy's face. She wondered if that had been really necessary. "A matter of national security." She had never thought of these events in such terms. They were terrible, but could something that happened as long ago as the Alpha/Omega operations possibly be so dangerous to the country today? Still, it mattered little what McCann had said, as long as they got to Jason in time.

As their skiff rushed past Delacourte's yacht, it struck her again just how strange it was that the national security adviser was in Craig's Harbor. Was Jason convinced that Delacourte was Omega? But he couldn't be, she thought. Omega was supposed to have been someone recruited from outside the ranks of the CIA. But who else could it be? It can't be Delacourte, Jenny argued silently. Hell, it might as well be the President.

When they got to the island, the fog had become thick enough to shield the sun's rays, which only minutes earlier had blazed across the sky. Jenny looked up and surveyed the scene. A chill again passed through her body.

The sounds of the place now drifted in on her. The ever-present rumble of the surf down along the back shore; the bell, now much closer; the wind, whistling shrilly through the scrub of the island. They were cold sounds, carrying with them that presence that steals a body's warmth. Apart from those sounds, only a small outboard could be heard. She folded her arms around her and started up the path with McCann.

The place seemed different now that she was actually there. What had looked close together through the telescope was in reality spread out across much larger sections of land than she had expected. The stone-lined path was not as straight as it had seemed, and the climb up the steep rock-strewn trail, coupled with the gnawing cold, was draining.

When they approached one of the larger buildings at the center of the island, Jenny called out to Jason, and a moment later he stepped slowly out in front of them. Jenny ran to him and wrapped her arms around him.

"Why did you come?" he asked.

She looked at him for a long time. "I care." She spoke simply, and her tone carried a quality of disbelief. Hasn't that sunk in yet? she wanted to shout. I care.

Then Jennifer turned and looked back at the FBI agent. His gun was drawn and he faced them. She clung to Jason more tightly than before. We will never know who Omega really is. But we know who he is; he is here before us. Jenny's thoughts grew confused and shrouded. He's hired an assassin. Who is he? She was amazed at how unmoved she seemed. She waited. McCann stepped closer to them.

He looked tense and winded—more winded than the climb to the buildings would have explained.

"Reverend Winslow." McCann studied the pastor closely. "Do you know who Omega is?"

Jason stared at him. "Do *I* know who Omega is?" He
paused, then slowly shook his head. "Hasn't anyone listened to me! No, I don't know who he is! All I know is that
he's here. He knows what we've been doing and where we've
been since we got here. And there are only a certain number of people from out of town." He slowly stepped away
from Jennifer. "How about you, Mr. McCann? Do you
know who Omega is?"

McCann stiffened. "I..." He paused and sighed, slipping his gun back into his shoulder holster. He looked at the
two people in front of him. The woman was pale and tense,
but the minister was different. It surprised him. The minister was cool, he was in control. McCann's admiration for
the minister had grown steadily from the first time he had
seen him in Union Station three days ago.

What he was about to do was absolutely in violation of
the directive issued by his superior. I'm going to do it anyway, he thought. He deserves to know—at least part of it.
He breathed in again and spoke slowly.

"There has been a special group working on the Omega
situation for the past two weeks."

"Two weeks!" Jason repeated. He glanced at Jenny and
saw the confusion on her face, a reflection, no doubt, of the
look on his.

"The President was notified—quietly—a month ago by
the British that this might be coming," McCann offered.

"Then how come the FBI..."

McCann's slow shaking of his head stopped Jason in
midsentence. "It's not the Bureau."

"CIA then," said Jason.

Again the agent simply shook his head.

"You're one of Delacourte's security men?"

McCann smiled oddly. "No, there's a pool of special 're-
source people' working at the highest level of the federal

government." McCann turned to Jennifer. "When I told the boy back there that it was a matter of national security, Miss Seidkamp, I was aware of your skepticism. But believe me; what is unfolding here could affect our country's ability to function in the international forum for years to come." Then he addressed Jason. "It is unfortunate, Reverend Winslow, that you got involved.

"When we found out that you were leaving D.C., we alerted the Bureau people up here, and—" he shrugged "—here we are. There are more strangers in town than you realize. Some of them—most of them, we hope—are from our operation. But there are others here, too. And we're running checks on all of them."

"But why?" Jennifer protested.

"Because we *think* we know who Omega is, but we have no proof. We have to be sure." He lowered his head, looking down self-consciously at the ground.

Jason started to speak, but then turned abruptly away and gazed out into the fog, which moved in gentle waves across the fields. Why? he was about to ask, but he knew the answer.

The agent looked up, first at Jennifer, then at Jason. He suddenly looked tired and worn. He was a tormented man. "We're using you, Reverend Winslow. You are the bait." He slumped, defeated. "I'm sorry," he murmured.

Jenny began to protest, but Jason's glance quieted her. She looked at Jason. He was an enigma. What was he thinking? What was he feeling? She studied him. He seemed moved by the agent's obvious discomfort. Jenny seethed. How could he simply not react?

Jason looked over at McCann. He waited until the agent raised his head. "It's okay," Jason said quietly.

"We'd better get back," McCann said. They started to turn, but then he suddenly seemed to lurch forward, losing his balance. He twisted toward Jason again.

"Get down," he mumbled and began to sink downward. Jason and Jennifer crouched beside him. His eyes seemed to burst from their sockets. His mouth contorted.

A few tiny explosions seemed to burst from the stones around them. McCann reached into his coat, pulled out his gun and, with effort, pressed it into Jason's hand.

"Get away from here," he whispered. Jason started to protest, but the agent again summoned his strength and spoke. "Get away. Get back to town." Jason stared at him for a moment, trying to decide what to do. "Go!" the agent urged. "Maybe that'll give me a chance, too...and Jenny." He smiled a pained smile and his glazed eyes stared into Jason's. "Take my gun. Go. Both of you."

Dazed, Jason looked blankly at the gun he now held. Then he grasped Jenny firmly, and together they ran along the path in a direction away from the boats. A bullet struck the corner of one of the buildings as they raced around it. They ran across a field and came to another path. They still had not seen their pursuer. When they were halfway back to the boats, they came to another little settlement of empty buildings.

"Jenny," Jason said breathlessly, "I want you to stay here." She looked puzzled. "If we're together we'll both die...if he gets us. But he's after me. He'll think we're together, he'll follow me. At least you'll be safe."

"No..." Jenny started to say.

"I'm going, Jenny. Please, this is where it will stop. Please."

He led her over the wall and pushed her down, then bent and gently kissed her. After he gazed at her for a moment longer, without speaking, he stood and ran off. She almost tarted after him, but then changed her mind. She stretched out flat against the wall, and wept silently.

How much time had passed? It couldn't have been more than a few minutes, when she became aware of someone approaching along the path that she and Jason had been on moments earlier. The sound stopped. My God! she suddenly thought. What had they been thinking? Did they think Omega would merely stroll along the path between these buildings? He'll come around the outskirts of the settlement. She closed her eyes. Should she just stand and give up? Goddamn him, she thought. I'm not ready to give in placidly to death. Goddamn him.

Suddenly, from the distance, from everywhere, she heard a bizarre, frightening sound. It had the quality of the wail of some animal calling back to its dimly remembered ancestors. It echoed back and forth across the harbor. It drowned out the other sounds, even the thundering ocean. It was Jason's voice, screaming out a long and tortured cry. It started as a low wail and grew into a monstrous, twisted lament: "Omega!"

It seemed as if it would hang in the heavy air forever. But then, the echoed word began to die in slow stages. Suddenly, almost beside her, on the other side of the wall, she heard a man's rasping whisper. "Fool," he said simply. Then she heard labored footsteps moving quickly off in the direction of the boats.

When the steps could no longer be heard, she stood and started after them. She saw nothing in the fog. After a few steps, she stopped and looked back in the direction of the other buildings. What had happened to McCann? She looked again in the direction of the boats, then defeatedly closed her eyes and sighed. She turned and ran back toward the place where they had left McCann.

As she ran, she heard an outboard starting up. Well, it's beginning, she thought. After a few more minutes, she was back at the higher buildings. McCann lay in about the same place he had fallen. Jenny approached cautiously at first, then ran to him.

"Mr. McCann," she said, turning him. "Mr...." Oh, God! she thought. "Another one," she murmured. She knelt there, unable to move. She felt the wind die. A strange silence suddenly forced its way into her consciousness, and she realized she could no longer hear the outboard motor. Another moment passed and slowly the wind came to life again, but now from another direction. With it came a gentle warmth.

Jennifer stood up slowly, listening, listening for something other than the surf. The air was no longer cold, and once more the sun seemed to be battling with the fog to win back the surface of the earth.

Jenny looked out into the brightening unknown. Something was happening, but she was afraid even to let herself think about it.

How far would the breeze carry the words she whispered so quietly? "Oh, God," she said, "he's yours. Take care of him."

34

JASON SAT QUIETLY in the skiff. For the past several minutes, he had been studying the gun McCann had given him. This was the first time he had held a pistol. It felt heavy and cold. He slid back a lever and pulled back the cylinder. Each chamber held a bullet. He stared at them. Each was shiny and perfectly formed. The symmetry was strangely inviting. He slammed the cylinder closed and looked out through the fog. He felt the gun's firmness in his hand and, despite the warming breeze, a chill pulsed through his body.

When he had traveled about a half mile south of the island, he had abruptly shut off the motor and waited. Swells, about three feet high, rhythmically raised and lowered him as he sat. Behind him he could hear the sound of Omega's boat, though it was hardly audible over the roar of the surf breaking against the shore. The boat was approaching fast and it seemed to be uncannily heading directly for him. He sat, waiting, wondering whom he was about to greet.

Omega's boat must by now be within fifty feet of him, he thought. He did not see it, but its wake hit him. After a moment, he heard it turning slowly, then it came back. This went on for two minutes longer, then the motor died.

"Omega," Jason called. There was no response. "You want to kill me, Omega?" Jason said, not shouting this time. He spoke quietly, because he thought the man was close enough to hear. "I'm sitting here, waiting."

He heard the sounds the water was making under his skiff. They were soothing. He looked up at the thinning fog, the brightening sky. Jason Winslow smiled. "Thank God," he murmured, "it's ending." He was at peace with himself. He had decided back in D.C. that if this was what it were to come down to, then he would submit. The resolve felt assuring; it felt good. He was determined not to let Omega intimidate him. Not now. Not this time. The covenant he had made with his God would remain untouched by Omega.

Omega was on the edge of panic. This was not the way he had planned it. He had not counted on the fog. And yet he was so close. "I had him," he whispered, "he was within my grasp, and now he's taunting me." He snickered. We'll see how collected he really is. Suddenly he twisted around, thrusting his gun out into the mist. He had thought he heard something just behind him.

"Omega," a voice said calmly between the thundering sound of the breakers. Omega spun around again, pointing his weapon in a new direction. No one.

Now Jason put his oars in the oarlocks and rowed quietly. He moved in a circle. "Omega," he called. "I'm waiting."

Omega's heart pounded. He raised his arm to his forehead and wiped a cold sweat from it. He concentrated on his breathing, trying to restore its normal rhythm. The minister was getting to him. Again he twisted around abruptly, thinking he had heard someone behind him, and again there was nothing.

Jason took one more stroke. Finally he saw what he had been waiting for. A dim form appeared slowly in the fog just ahead of him.

He pulled in his oars. The water ran down their blades and into the boat. Jason picked up the gun and held it

traight out. He stood and aimed directly at the man in front
of him. He watched for several seconds.

"Damn him," Omega murmured. "Damn that bastard."

"Good morning..." Jason spoke softly, as he would to
a child who needed to be awakened.

Omega spun around, expecting to see more emptiness.

"...Mr. Delacourte," Jason finished, calmly. Jason was
immediately aware of the man's outward signs of uncertainty. This unanticipated fact impressed Jason. He continued to face Delacourte calmly.

Jason's calmness, plus the gun in his hand, plus his own
desperate sense of being lost in the fog, made Delacourte
nervous. The moment he had turned, he had intended to
fire, to kill Jason. The minister had tormented him so. But
now he waited. He needed this time.

"Ah," Omega said, training his weapon on Jason's head.
"So now we get to discuss things of greater consequence, do
we not, Reverend?"

"We can discuss whatever's on your mind."

"You are on my mind." Delacourte paused. "You and
your damned self-righteousness."

Jason shrugged. The gesture irritated Omega.

"You can't shrug at death."

Jason shrugged again. He summoned all his faith and all
his strength and felt a power flow into the very depths of his
being.

"I believe death is only another beginning. You know
that. I watched you yesterday in the back pew. I watched
you taking in what was happening. I know exactly what you
thought about the entire service. I saw you *squirm*."

You brazen fool, thought Omega. "You also know," he
said aloud, "that your God has abandoned you. I control
your life, now! With a twitch of my finger! You live or die!"

Jason nodded. "It doesn't make any difference what you say—what I say. In a few minutes you'll pull that trigger— maybe now, even—and I'll be your sixth victim."

"Eighth."

Jason tensed. McCann and who else. Jenny? Oh my God, he thought, please, God, not Jenny.

Omega continued. "McCann and my friend who did the Sullivan job." Instantly, he knew he had made an error. It annoyed him. The minister had thought the eighth person was Jennifer Seidkamp. Damn it, he thought. I should have shut my mouth. "You thought Jennifer was included."

Jason relaxed again. "And one more . . ." Bitterness now welled up from within. Jason's hatred returned in a flash of memory. "My dog."

Omega looked momentarily concerned, almost confused, then he smiled.

"When did you know it was me?" Omega asked. It was a question that had preyed on him since the first time he realized Jason might possibly know.

Jason smiled. "When you turned around just now."

Delacourte's face showed just a flicker of disapproval.

"I'll tell you something, Mr. Delacourte: there's a group of agents. I don't know who they are, but they're on to you. McCann was one of them. He said they're all over this place."

"The CIA and the Bureau will never touch me."

"It's not them."

Omega grew even more tense. "Who then?"

"He wouldn't say. Just that they were from the highest level of government."

"You're lying!" Delacourte burst out.

Jason merely smiled gently, conscious of the man's desperate uncertainty. He calmly shook his head in disagreement.

Omega glanced away from Jason for just a moment. He tried to look past the thinning fog to see what was beyond. The massive cliffs of the shore loomed, half hidden in the drifting waves of mist. In the distance, there were the growing sounds of outboard motors, but neither man seemed aware of them. Omega turned back to Jason. He became conscious now of the movement of the two boats. He sought the knowledge that he would triumph.

Jason sensed the change in the man. He knew the time was imminent. He was prepared.

"So," Omega began, "you going to use that thing?" He gestured to the gun Jason was holding.

"I thought once maybe, but then, no, I will not. I cannot."

"Against your religion?" Omega sneered.

Jason smiled and nodded. He breathed easily.

The minister was frightening to Delacourte; he was showing no fear whatsoever. Omega had anticipated Jason's fear, but none came. None. Could the pastor really believe what he was saying? Omega regarded Jason carefully. He watched his every move. He was ready.

"I'll tell you what, Reverend. I won't fire until you do. Go ahead. Shoot."

Jason shook his head.

"Shoot," Omega said more intensely. Something was eating away at Omega's certainty. "Shoot," Omega suddenly screamed wildly.

Jason watched the man lose whatever composure he had mustered. Delacourte was a tortured man, working on raw nerve.

"I feel sorry for you, Delacourte."

Omega seethed. His fury had driven the roaring breakers from his consciousness. All the time they had been talking, the boats had been drifting closer to the ledges. But it did

not matter now. The sounds of the water left him. H
squeezed his eyes shut and fired directly at Jason's head.

Jason saw the man prepare himself. He saw Omega move
his hand slightly, then the finger he had wrapped around
the trigger tightened. Jason continued to gaze gently at hi
killer.

The gun fired. Jason expected to hear a ringing explo
sion; instead, he heard something whistle past his left ear
He sighed.

Delacourte opened his eyes. The man standing in the
other boat should have been dead. For an instant he
thought, he *is* supernatural. No, he screamed silently. Ge
hold of things. You just missed. Shoot him. But instead
Omega screamed aloud at Jason once again. "Shoot me!"

There was a wild look in Omega's eyes now. Jason looked
into the water. At that moment, he saw the reflection of the
sun above him, and the fog cleared around them. Dela
courte was aware of it as well.

Jason looked directly at Omega, lowered his gun, pointed
it at the water and squeezed the trigger. The discharge
caused his hand to jerk upward. The report echoed back and
forth across the harbor. It rang in Jason's ears. Again, Jason
watched the furious Delacourte prepare to fire. His finge
again slowly closed over the trigger. This time his eyes did
not close.

In the midst of this drama, something else was happen
ing, something that, until now, neither man had noticed. I
began as the small swells seemed to diminish. And then
slowly, the two boats began to rise. First Jason's, then
twenty feet away, Omega's. Jason's boat angled higher and
higher. He slipped and toppled back into the boat. The gun
flew from his hand into the sea. Omega's eyes stared past
Jason. Then, as the echoes of Jason's gun were dying, there

was another explosion. Jason lifted himself upward to try to see what was happening.

In that instant, as he was preparing to fire, Omega, like the minister, heard the other weapon fire. Almost instantly he felt a burning, searing explosion ripping through his lungs. His eyes rolled slightly sideways. He fired his own weapon. He saw nothing and forced his eyes back toward the minister, who remained staring down from the boat, now on the crest of the wave. He saw the clergyman begin to move toward him, paddling with his hands. He tried to lift his weapon to fire again, but it was too heavy. The roar of the ocean crashing against the shore again filled his consciousness.

The minister had disappeared on the other side of the mammoth wave. Delacourte struggled to see the top of the wall of water that rolled toward him. He could feel its presence. It chilled the air and filled it with dampness. Its immense, silent presence seemed to darken the sky.

Delacourte's eyes were moving back and forth through a range of focus. He turned again as he began to slump into the boat. Then, for the first time, he looked off to the side. A larger vessel—one of the local lobster boats—rode at a bizarre angle up the same massive wall of water. The pilot of that boat struggled to keep the bow pointed into the wave. Behind the man at the wheel stood another man, calmly grasping a large brass handle with one hand. In his other hand, LeRoy Drury held a revolver much like Delacourte's.

At least Delacourte knew the source of this death that now filled his being. It was only a momentary glimpse, but it was enough. Now the wave that hid the minister from his view crested, and surged over his boat. Though he knew his body was being pounded by tons of raging sea, he felt neither the wetness nor the cold.

Jason worked to keep the skiff on the crest of the wave. He had seen Delacourte's craft blanketed with the angry blue-green water. And then, for just an instant, he caught a glimpse of Omega—of the man's blank stare as his head slipped, unresisting, under the waves.

Jason tried desperately to move the skiff toward Delacourte, but he was gone. The sea would carry the body where it willed. There was a good chance that in the next few hours or even days, it would be found—a mere battered pulp—in the rocks that now seemed to draw Jason and his craft toward them. It was also possible the body would never be found. But it was over. Omega was gone—forever.

Jason glanced, as Omega had done, to the side, in time to see Tom Bailey's lobster boat, with Drury aboard, as it rocked precariously over the crest of the wave. Then they were gone. Drury, Jason thought. So that's what happened. How odd! The thought was a fleeting one, and Jason slowly, dazedly focused on the cliffs, which seemed to draw him. As he did so, a new urgency cut into his consciousness.

Sprawled there, in that fragile vessel, he realized there was suddenly every reason for him to live. But if he were to survive, he must work quickly to pull himself out of the tides that moved him toward the awesome destruction of the pounding surf.

Jason pulled at the oars. Blisters formed and broke and bled on his hands. The back of his shirt ripped as he leaned into the oars and pulled against the current.

I can't, he told himself. I can't make it. "But damn it, you're alive!" he screamed aloud. "You're alive!" The words slowly found his consciousness, and with a new clarity he looked at the ocean around him. The roar of the breakers was deafening now, and the constant spray soaked through his clothes. He had watched this water for hours from the cliffs that towered above him. What chance did he have?

A memory began to form, vaguely at first, then sharpened into an idea for escape. To the north, to his right somewhere, there was a strange quiet spot in this turmoil of sea. At that place, beneath the surface, there was something—probably ledges—that soothed the raging water. If he could find that spot, if he could slide into its protection, he might be able to ride in to the rocks to safety.

To the people watching on the lobster boat, it seemed as if the minister was committing suicide. Tom Bailey wished he could help his pastor, but he was just too close to the ledges. They'd all end up dead. He watched the minister suddenly turn the tiny boat around and head directly for the rocks, which surely would shatter the craft as if it were delicate crystal.

Jason labored to get enough air in his lungs. More than once he breathed in a salty mist and retched at the pain the coughing brought. He looked away from the distant lobster boat, and glanced over his shoulder. There it was! Just ten feet from him. Every muscle in his body felt as if it were being ripped from its anchor. One stroke of the oars. He moved a little closer. He *must* do it now or he would be past the spot. Another stroke. He pulled so hard that the oars slipped from the oarlocks and he fell backward. He was only dimly aware of the burning sensation across his back where he had struck the forward seat. Quickly he reshipped the oars and heaved again. This time, he felt the skiff suddenly slip from the force that, for the past five minutes, had held it, unrelenting, in its grasp. He was even able to rest for a moment. Then, with only yards to go, he took a deep breath, turned the boat around and headed stern first toward the cliffs. As the water carried the boat faster toward the rocks, he slashed at the water with his oars, slowing his movement. Then, with one final pull against the oars, he slowed the skiff just a few feet from the rocks.

A wave now lifted the boat higher, and at that moment Jason jumped. His fingers grasped wildly at the rocks. Barnacles cut into his palms. His feet scrambled to find some support. Finally, he managed to find a toehold, and then, slowly, slowly, he worked himself upward and sideways, and . . . finally to safety. Once—just once—he looked back down over the side of the cliffs. The remains of two boats spread and smashed into even smaller shards. Farther out, he could see Tom raising his arms in victory. Drury stood motionless at the lobsterman's side. Then Jason rolled over on his side, his face pressing into the wet earth. He closed his eyes and shut out the raging storm of surf beneath him and listened only to his breathing.

The lobsterman was now heading back into the harbor, but LeRoy Drury stood out on the deck and stared up at the cliffs for as long as he could. He wondered at the man he had just seen do the impossible. He thought about the minister for a long time, then, abruptly, he shrugged, turned away and gazed out into the disappearing mists.

35

HE FELT HIMSELF BEING PICKED UP, and he opened his eyes to a dizzying swirl of bright blue sky and earth and spruce. He closed his eyes again. A voice was telling him he would be all right. When he thought he had better control, he opened his eyes again. This time, looking to his side, he saw Cousin Alvin's boy, William. The warm breeze blew at the man's jacket, and Jason caught a glimpse of a holstered gun strapped under his arm.

"You're going to be okay," William was saying. He felt himself nodding, and yet his attempt to hold himself up indicated otherwise. As they moved along the path, Jason gazed down stupidly at his bloody hands. He became aware of a pain that ripped in a narrow line across his back. But he was alive. He had survived. It was over.

A few hours later, he longed for the oblivion he had been lifted out of there on the cliffs. As soon as he had been treated for his abrasions, he was taken to a series of tedious and grueling interviews.

The procedures were thorough—and relentless. They began with a paper being placed in front of each person being questioned.

"What's this?" Jason asked.

"An Inadvertent Disclosure form," someone answered. The explanation did not help. The man said more. "By signing this, you're stating that secret information vital to national security has inadvertently come into your possession. Further, you agree to relate this information in no manner to no person, except those present, and further, to report any attempts that might be made to secure such data from you.'' It was all very mechanical sounding, but basically clear—all too clear. Jason signed the paper, only later realizing he never was given a choice in the matter. What, he wondered, would have happened if he had refused to sign?

Next, Mr. Pederson was introduced. He was, in fact, Admiral Pederson. He was clearly in charge. At times, FBI and CIA people were also present. At other times the admiral asked them to leave, and his people alone asked the questions.

Every detail of Jason's story was examined. Everything—from the moment he had first talked to Sullivan, to what he remembered before William carried him back from the cliffs. The people involved—he and Jenny, and Drury—were questioned separately, questioned together, then separately again.

The process was exhausting for Jason. He longed to see Jenny alone; he had only been able to speak to her for a few minutes and they had not been able to talk about the things they really wanted to.

By late afternoon, the population of Craig's Harbor had doubled. Media people were coming in from all over the world. The networks were setting up satellite transmitters for live feeds for the evening news and special shows later on.

When Jason and Jennifer left the fire station where the temporary investigation offices had been set up, they were assaulted by a hundred reporters. They had been asked not to make any comment, and when they saw the hungry crowd waiting for them, neither wanted to, anyway. Two FBI agents—they really were FBI—were assigned to protect them.

The four of them were driven to the parsonage. Food was brought in and a special phone line was installed. Jason's regular phone was finally unplugged, because from the time they stepped through the door, it had been ringing. The agents were helpful in every way. They kept people from the door, they answered the phone, they sorted out a lot of the confusion. As soon as he could, Jason called his parents. He explained as much to them as possible, and told them he loved them. Jennifer also called home.

They ate and watched some television. For all the clamor on the part of the various news services, none of them had an inkling of the full nature of the situation. It was not until a *Washington Post* reporter linked Jason and Jennifer to Walter's murder that the television people began to get a clue as to the true dimensions of the story. All the attention and inaccuracy was irritating to the participants, and not long after dinner, Jason turned off the television. The four of them sat around and played hearts, and finally, not long after nine o'clock, they went to bed. At the top of the stairs, Jenny and Jason held each other tightly.

When Jennifer had first grasped Jason, he winced. "Easy," he murmured. He smiled at her for the first time since they had been on the island. They stood there quietly for a long time. Outside they could hear television crews setting up to do their broadcasts. And in the distance, they heard the relentless pounding surf. Its presence had by now become reassuring. They sighed and leaned on each other.

"It's over," Jenny murmured.

"He was pathetic, Jenny. He really was. If you could have seen him."

Jenny sighed deeply. "Jason," she whispered his name in his ear.

They stood still for a long time.

Finally, they parted, and went to their own rooms, each longing to be with the other.

THE NEXT MORNING there was more questioning. Jason, Jennifer and Drury were asked to repeat some of their previous statements. Whenever there was a discrepancy, other inquisitors would take over. Their approach to their task could best be described as bullying. They yelled at Jason, or Jennifer, or Drury, pressed them, pushed to the breaking point, searching for some weakness. The weaknesses that did crop up from time to time were easily explained away. It was evident that the investigators had been busy long into the night. They had checked with people in Washington: restaurants where Jenny and Jason had eaten, the little old lady at the apartment building where Jason and Jennifer hid in the laundry, the garage where Jenny had called Donlevy's office. The resources available to these people must be incredible, Jason thought.

By midmorning, the information officer assigned to the investigation team had let it be known that the rest of the inquiry would center in Washington, that none of the principals would be available for questions until they arrived in Washington, and that things would substantially wind down from then on.

By afternoon, things were quieter. The principals in the events were brought together one last time—Jason and Jennifer and LeRoy Drury and members of the investigation team.

Drury seemed to be in his glory. He had said he had come for a story, and he had gotten one. He had firsthand information and had already provided most of the "scoops" about the events that had occurred in the past days.

The admiral sat across from the people assembled in the room behind the fire department. In the hours Jason had spent with the man, he had developed a grudging respect for him. How old was he? Jason wondered. He could easily be seventy or seventy-five, and yet he held himself with a certain stiffness, with an aloofness that defined a spirit within him. Age didn't seem to matter. He was strong, forceful, determined.

"There is a lot you'll never know about this...situation," the admiral began. "I will tell you that the President has been aware of the situation from the beginning. To you, Mr. Winslow, Miss Seidkamp, he has asked me to offer his sincere regret that you were involved. As for me personally, I want to add that you have made my task much easier than any of you will ever know. I appreciate that more than I can tell you.

"It's been a terribly costly trail of pain and blood, but I believe our nation will be able to avoid any embarrassments as long as the information all of us jointly possess remains secure." He paused then and gazed first at Jason, then at Jenny and finally at Drury. "Mr. Drury, I know this may be particularly hard on you. I simply ask that you clear all stories on this with the White House."

Drury frowned, but did, reluctantly, agree. The admiral's fiery eyes spoke of secrets and danger and loyalty and a dozen other less obvious elements that would guarantee a successful conclusion to his assignment. Then he smiled, for the first time since Jason had been with him. "Is there anything else you want to say or ask?" The question had been asked dozens of times. And now it was being asked again.

"No," sighed Jason.

"I suspect it seems like a lifetime since you first talked with Mr. Sullivan. I hope as soon as we get out of your life, you can get back to normal." Pederson smiled again. This time everyone in the room did, too. Jenny, Jason, even Drury. There was a strange and welcome sense of peace.

Jason thought of Sullivan and his music and the peace he had spoken of. He prayed that Sullivan was finding that peace now. He thought a moment, then spoke again, impulsively. "What's going to happen to Sullivan's house?"

Pederson shrugged. "We're finished with it." He looked at a subordinate. "The state handles this?" The subordinate nodded.

"He told me about a record he listened to," Jason began. "I'd like to have it. Is that possible?"

Again Pederson looked to the subordinate, who, after a shrug, nodded his approval.

Jason and Jennifer slipped out the back of the fire station and headed for Sullivan's home, while the information officer was holding a final "on-site briefing." The wind had changed again. Once more the fog had begun to sneak back toward the land.

Sullivan's house was just a short distance away, and Jason and Jennifer were there in a few minutes. Once inside, they stood amazed at the sight before them.

"Look what they've done!" Jason lamented.

The house had been checked over thoroughly, but hardly with care. Every book, every file, every drawer, every possible place that some scrap, some bit of evidence could have been hidden had been examined.

They looked around at the scene of sorry confusion. It was painful to Jason as he recalled the obvious devotion and organization with which Sullivan had gone about his daily routine. They moved slowly around the living room, each going in a different direction.

Jennifer came finally to a record player that had been checked and thoughtlessly dumped in a chair. Based on what she knew of Sullivan, she conjured up an image of a ritual. She pictured him there in this once most orderly of places, carefully, secretly, placing this record on the turntable. Then she saw him sitting quietly lost in another world, for as long as the music played.

Now in the total chaos of the house, this upset record player seemed to signal the utter violation of the man—even in his death. With the utmost care and solemnity then, she leveled the machine, plugged it into an outlet and placed the tonearm onto the record.

The recording was haunting. When he first heard it, Jason quickly looked up from the papers he was reading. The sounds provided an eerie, vaguely unnerving counterpoint to the scene of which they were now a part. This was the recording he had first heard an eternity ago. Somehow it seemed to offer a kind of completion to these terrible days. Jason and Jennifer stood immobile. Then, slowly, Jason moved to Jennifer's side.

"Strange tastes...your Mr. Sullivan," Jennifer said softly.

Jason nodded slowly, adding, "He said it brought him peace...that and his garden." His voice trailed off. "Here," he began again, "let me show you." They left the music playing and moved to a window that opened onto the backyard.

"Looks more like a cemetery," Jenny observed. "Look at that grave marker." Jenny pointed to an oddly shaped cement structure.

"He *was* a strange one," Jason said soberly. "That was his incinerator. They said he built it himself." He laughed now. "We've had an ordinance against burning our own trash for three years now, but he still kept it in perfect repair. Used to be the talk of the town."

"Ashes to ashes," Jennifer murmured cynically.

Jason smiled, then straightened up, the smile quickly draining from his face.

"What is it, Jason?" Jennifer said.

"Ashes to ashes," he repeated.

He moved abruptly to the back door. Jennifer chased after him. He had suddenly become a person possessed. It was as if the incinerator had in that instant become a religious monument, deserving of his homage. Then, at the base of the thing, he grabbed her and pointed upward.

"Look!"

At the top of the chimney were some letters shaped in the cement. They were Greek letters.

"The beginning and the end of the Greek alphabet, Jenny. *Alpha and Omega!* Remember? Sullivan told me that Alpha and Omega were dead!"

Jason's mind raced back to five days ago, to Sullivan's words as he was leaving the parsonage. Jason circled the incinerator, probing its every joint. Then he fell to his knees and started scraping at the base. He found a stick and dug with it. As he worked, he quoted Sullivan.

"'I've buried Morrison,' he said. 'I've buried Alpha and Omega and everything about them—'" Jason loosened the central stone under the monument "'—in an airtight casket,' he said, 'so nothing will ever escape. I've buried them under the ashes of time,' he said!" Jason used the stick to pry up the stone just enough to get his fingers under it and then he carefully lifted it out.

He peered into the hole. After a moment, his eyes adjusted to the dimness and he saw what looked like a tiny crypt. He reached in and lifted a rusted piece of plate steel. It was small, but thick. Finally, leaning in again, he could see a box set on the smooth bottom of the crypt. He slowly lifted it out—a box roughly twelve inches by ten inches by six inches. His heart pounded. He glanced at Jenny. Color had drained from her face. In the midst of the waves of fog that insulated them from the rest of the world, they worked quietly. The haunting choir music seemed somehow to have become a part of the mists.

Jason held the object while Jenny carefully removed a layer of plastic, then a layer of aluminum foil that had been coated with wax, finally the box itself, made of oak, also with several layers of wax all around it.

"It must have taken him a while to do this," Jenny breathed.

Jason nodded. They scraped away at the wax around the lid. Slowly they opened it. It was hinged on the back and a small chain prevented the lid from dropping all the way back.

Inside they found several passports. Some, they could tell, were for a much younger Delacourte. None of the passports used his real name. There were also some for another man. Neither the names nor the face of this second man were known to either Jason or Jenny, and yet there was something vaguely familiar about him. The box also contained a gun. For all Jason could tell, it was identical to the one McCann had given him a day earlier. Jennifer held the box as Jason examined the chambers of the revolver.

"It's loaded," Jason said.

What they were most interested in, however, was the sheaf of papers that filled the bottom of the box. Jenny lifted them out and Jason took the box and placed the weapon back in it.

"Operation Alpha/Omega," the cover read. "1953-1955. Operations coordinator: Samuel Morrison." The Central Intelligence Agency seal was located directly below his name.

Jason and Jennifer looked up from the papers to each other. Had they been archaeologists uncovering Tutankhamen, they would not have felt more uncertain, more in awe, more filled with anticipation. They were at a crossroads in time; in the next instant, they would step some thirty years into the past. In the silence, they understood these mystical feelings of discovery, for in this moment, they were about to uncover an astounding, possibly terrible, treasure. In this moment, they seemed totally alone on the earth. A truth, known fully by only one person was about to become a secret shared.

The music of the boy's choir drifted in and out of their consciousness.

Jenny opened the document to the first page. It was a table of contents. First, there were pages containing the general plan and purpose of the operation, then the operatives involved, then a listing of specific assignments.

Jennifer quickly turned the pages, then she read.

I've been duped. I have realized this too late. If anything should go wrong with this operation, I am the one who will take the blame. I will be 'exposed' as a renegade and dismissed, imprisoned or possibly worse.

In order to minimize potential ill-effects of this misadventure, I have revised my initial approach to the operation. This report is the first significant departure from the procedures as directed by my superiors. Since the operation file on Alpha/Omega is significantly different from the actual intent, this record will be available—and verifiable—to substantiate any points in my defense that I may be required to make.

The second departure from the initial directive involves the actual operatives who fulfill the Omega assignments. I have selected two operatives rather than the one ordered in the directive.

Jason and Jennifer looked away from the page to each other. A sudden rush of anxiety now flowed, burning hot, into their beings. Their lives had been different since Delacourte had died. It was over. That gnawing, overwhelming uncertainty had left them the moment each had seen that the other was safe. It was a physical change. They had both felt it, and it was not until it had happened that they were clearly aware of how great a drain those long days had really been. Now, all that anxiety returned in a rush. It was a fear that came with the knowledge that it was not over—that in fact, it had never really ended.

They read on.

"The third change will guarantee me at least a measure of leverage. I have chosen an employee of the Agency to be one of the operatives. This is in direct violation of the operational directive. The recruit is, however, eminently suited for this kind of operation. He is, one might say, my 'ace in the hole.' "

Jennifer turned the page.

"Operative 1. Alex H. Delacourte. Employee of the Central Intelligence Agency. Age 32." The report continued and Jenny and Jason scanned the page quickly.

The music from the phonograph was suddenly interrupted by a loud and jarring scratch. This was immediately followed by a voice, cursing.

"Damn it to hell!" The voice was easily recognizable.

After a moment, the music began once again. The plain, clear voices of the children brought a deceptive calm to a moment that was about to explode into fury and pain. Jason tensed as a shadow stepped out of the house into the mist.

"I'm glad I found you before I had to leave." The ghost, now a man, was smiling. He continued to smile, though as he shed the layers of clouds that had enwrapped him, he became aware of the intense concern on the faces of both his young associates. He was also aware of the papers Jenny held and the box Jason held, and the wrappings at their feet. He knew what these things meant, and though he held his smile, inside it saddened him. He too, like Jason and Jenny, had hoped it had ended.

The man who was Omega slipped his hands into the pockets of his coat. His right hand fingered the weapon that, even now, he knew he would be using before leaving this place. Continuing to smile, he walked a few steps closer, and spoke to Jenny.

"You look like you've seen a ghost." Then he turned his attention to Jason. "Found something interesting?" he asked pleasantly.

"Very interesting," responded Jason. There was something odd about his tone. It caused Jenny to turn toward him and wonder why he was acting the way he was. "I'm certain you'd find it fascinating. In fact, we're just getting to the good part. You see, we're about to find out who the second Omega was—is," Jason corrected himself. He stared at the man. "But it probably won't surprise you much."

Both Jenny and Jason noted the sudden change in the man who stood across from them. As they watched, he seemed to grow visibly older. Neither had expected the man could have looked so old. He slumped, looking tired and pained and defeated.

Jenny turned to Jason. Her body trembled. Why was he acting this way? What was he thinking? Jason could see the puzzlement in her expression. "Turn the page, Jenny," he said softly.

"'Operative 2,'" she read. "'Le...'" She looked up, startled. Her voice fell to a whisper. "'LeRoy...Drury.'"

Drury forced the smile to return. It was an empty grin, which told more about sorrow than joy.

"Why didn't you just forget it? Why didn't you just let it go?" Drury pleaded. "We all had what we wanted. It was over. Everyone believed that Omega was dead." He laughed once. "Even Delacourte." He whispered an echo. "Even Delacourte..." A momentary rejuvenation brought a tired strength to his words once more. "He was so vain. He never could accept the fact that there was another Omega opera-tive. He thought he had become a legend. He dismissed the other reports as imaginings of people who simply jumped to the wrong conclusions.

"I knew, of course, almost from the beginning. Morri-son and I created Omega. We came up with the code names—always thought they were a little melodramatic, myself—but I couldn't have been the only one. It was ob-vious. It took me three years of...research. Three years before I was convinced I knew who the other one was.

"Delacourte: an arrogant egocentric. But effective." Drury hardened for a moment, but just for a moment, and then the edges that defined him softened once again. "Alex never understood people. Morrison, for example. Morri-son was an honorable man. I knew he'd never have told anyone. He must have grown to hate the system, but he'd never have betrayed it. Donlevy, too...same mold." He paused now and looked away at the mist-shrouded colors of autumn reds and yellows and browns. "It was over," he murmured to the trees. He looked back at Jason and Jen-nifer and shook his head sadly.

"It...it was an accident," Jennifer said quietly. The strains of the boy's choir drifted around them, coming in faint waves whenever the wind saw fit to carry the sounds away from the house. The unfolding scene took on an air of sanctity, as if they were participating in some ancient ritual.

"An accident," sighed Drury. He closed his eyes for a moment, and whispered, "It's all an accident.

"It was an accident that your lives and mine entwined. It was an accident you ever got out of D.C." Again Drury laughed that hoarse, empty laugh. "It was an accident that I ever got involved with Delacourte and Morrison in the first place." He frowned at the papers Jennifer held in her hand.

"It was an accident," Drury repeated. "Who can ever predict?"

"But Sullivan's death wasn't an accident," Jason began. "The other deaths weren't accidents. Delacourte's death wasn't an accident."

"Yes," Drury said, frowning. "That much is true. In a way, I'd planned it years ago. Years," he repeated softly. He stared into Jason's eyes now. "You were so hot and bothered about what was happening, you didn't even think about the basic question . . . nobody did." Then a note of pride crept into his voice. "Basics. Where'd the pressure come from? The British reporter. Who was he? Where'd he get the information? Nobody dug.

"I knew the British couldn't let that kind of dirt sit for long. Even if there'd been nothing hard, they'd have made a fuss. So the President begins to feel the pressure. Discreet, quiet. Among friends, and all. All as I predicted. The plan is set in motion. With Delacourte taking the lead. Oh, I didn't know there'd be a special presidential investigation team, but it's made no difference, not really."

"It's kept me alive," Jason pressed.

Drury shrugged and continued his soliloquy. "The good admiral must be slipping. No one looked for the source of the information. No, they were just glad they got it.

"Only Chris Donlevy began to ask the question. But he didn't ask the right person." Drury looked away again and continued. "One cannot predict, and succeed, but one must be prepared." He paused now and changed his stance, settling down for something of more substance.

"It's simply a series of steps, small steps. Eventually, someone would track Morrison down—Delacourte found him easily enough—and then there'd be fewer steps. Under normal circumstances, Morrison would never have talked. But someone was talking. He knew that. He had to assume it was someone in the Agency. And suddenly circumstances are anything but normal." Drury sighed. "Perhaps he would have talked. Why not?"

These were virtually the same words Sullivan had spoken that cold, secret night seemingly so long ago. This memory momentarily distracted Jason, but Drury didn't notice and didn't pause.

"Years ago, I decided to set the trap and remove Delacourte and Morrison. They were the only two that could possibly link me in any way. I got everything ready, but then, I backed off. Morrison would never have talked. And Delacourte was convinced he was Omega. I was safe without any risk.

"But then last winter, a young British reporter pays me a visit. 'You were with the Agency back then,' he says. 'I've heard about an operation called Alpha/Omega. Know anything about it?' he asks. At first, I thought I'd squelch it. But then..." Drury's mouth formed a terrible smile. "What if the kid did somehow stumble onto Morrison? The risk was too big. I realized this was the perfect opportunity. I'd set Morrison up with Delacourte. He'd have to silence him. After that, it really didn't matter what happened. With Morrison's death, I'd be safe.

"So I give the English kid some names of people from the old days; tell him to check them out and keep me informed. He comes up with nothing, as I suspected, and goes home. So then I let a few months go by, and then send him a few bits of information. All carefully sanitized. He has no idea who sent it. I don't send everything, just enough to entice. Like any good reporter, he does a story even with the little material he has. And predictably the British 'cousins' get a little hot under the collar. Now they come to the U.S. And we deny everything, of course. But I send the reporter a little more—including the address and phone number of this very house. And the kid does another story, discreetly omitting the name. But their people get it, and bring it to our people. And guess who finds out?''

"Delacourte," Jason responded and Drury smiled.

"Exactly. And he's already on the warpath. So I just sit back and wait. Except for one more thing. I send one last bit of information. This time not to the reporter, but to our ambassador in London, a man who, incidentally, happens to have low regard for Delacourte. It identifies Delacourte as Omega, and suggests this information might also be available to the British.

"Omega's secret should have gone with Morrison to his grave. And just in case someone began probing too deeply into ancient history, Delacourte, egomaniac that he was, would assure everyone that he and he alone was Omega. And it would have ended—absolutely.

"They could have traced out the trail. *I* would have, had I been on the other side, but I counted on their mediocrity. No one does the job the way we used to. No one digs.

"The roles were set. It would be a masterful improvisation. And they played it perfectly." His expression darkened now. "Except, as sometimes happens in the theater of improvisation, an unexpected character arrived onstage." Drury glanced purposefully toward Jason.

He looked down at the dying flowers that surrounded him. "It should have been over," he murmured, "but it isn't. Never predict...it's always dangerous." He looked up at the two people opposite him. "But soon it will be over. It's what we all want." Drury straightened somewhat and pulled the gun from his coat pocket.

"You don't need to do that," Jennifer said weakly.

"No?" Drury asked. "I'm sorry, Jennifer. I'll be ruined. You know what no one can know, and live. You'll know, then someone else'll know. *People* will know." He sneered and continued, "People have more sympathy for common murderers than for an agent in the service of his country. I'll be ruined." He gazed at her. "You understand, don't you?"

"It won't work, Mr. Drury," Jason began. "What you want to do won't end anything." He paused, studying the man across from him. Though Drury trained the weapon steadily on his prey, Jason felt no fear or panic. In fact, he only felt sorrow. For he knew death was inevitable here. After a moment, he began again. "This will embarrass everyone," Jason said quietly. "Nobody will want this to get out."

Drury allowed his eyes to close. He breathed in deeply before opening them again. When he spoke it was like an academic making an all-too-obvious point one more time. "But *it will* get out. It's inevitable. Morrison knew the importance of the secret. It had been safe with him." Drury paused momentarily. He seemed distracted by the thoughts that pressed in on him. When he spoke again, his voice had a pleading quality.

"Don't you see? That's the one thing Delacourte and I had in common. That's what made us so good. We didn't trust anybody, anything. It kept us on the edge. It's how we survived.

"You—" Drury waved the gun at Jason "—you're a lot like us. You really don't trust anyone either—except you *want* to. It eats away at you, I can see it. You even want to trust me. Here. Now. But, you can't, can you? Don't worry, though, Reverend. You're only human."

Drury smiled cynically. "Yes, you are that. You know..." He paused for a moment. Indecision overpowered his expression, but only for an instant. "My father was a minister. Did I ever tell you that?" Drury looked slightly confused and disappointed by his sudden memory. "What is it with you pastors? Idealistic. Unrealistic. Pathetic. Despite his years of trying to convince me, despite the guilt he poured into me, I never believed. I still don't." As Drury spoke, a terrible searing assurance filled him. "I don't need to," he finished.

Then, for the first time, in a vague gnawing awareness, Drury had an inkling of why Jason had dominated him so. In these moments, he saw a twisted, knotted chain, linking his father and the man who stood before him. "You know something, Pastor?"

Jason shook his head slowly.

"He tried like hell to get me to believe, but I think he tried so hard because deep down, he wasn't sure he was any different than I was."

"You killed my dog, didn't you?" Jason asked abruptly.

Drury faced him squarely. The minister looked pathetic to him. Vulnerable. The pastor stood there, still holding that stupid box in his hands in front of him, as if preparing to offer it to him as a gift. Drury shrugged and looked downward. "It was necessary. I had to force you to do something rash. I needed to push you right to the edge. I had to be sure you'd strike out when the moment came. You'd start it, and if necessary, I'd finish it. I was hoping you'd pull the trigger yesterday. I wanted you to kill him. But then I watched you and I knew you couldn't. It's a weakness that has never troubled me." Again, he paused, then turned to Jennifer. "I'm sorry, Jenny. I'm sorry to have to do this."

Jason watched as Drury settled and struggled to remember something, something far different than the memory of his father. He sank slightly, into almost a crouch.

"Did Sullivan tell you about the tiger?" Drury asked. Jason nodded. The man who was Omega smiled. He moved his gun away from Jason and onto Jenny. She stood quietly, her face the pallid gray color of death.

"I once told Delacourte about that. He liked the story.... Used to tell people it happened to him." Drury's tone changed abruptly. It became cold and hard. "But it was me. It was me the tiger stalked."

Drury's finger began to twist around the trigger of his weapon. It remained pointed at Jennifer.

"Don't. Please, dear God, don't . . ." The words caught in Jason's throat.

"God has nothing to do with it." Drury responded coldly. He felt a momentary relief that the minister was actually beginning to panic at the prospect of his death. It was re-assuring. But it flowed from him as quickly as it had come. He had glanced at the minister, expecting to savor Jason's agony, but was, instead, stunned. Jason's eyes burned with the unyielding fury of a laser beam. His gaze cut into Drury's being. The pastor's face was contorted with a rage which had been allowed to flare from long-smoldering embers. And all of this momentarily froze the man who was Omega.

"God forgive me," Jason whispered as he watched the man across from him. The minister seemed to be in some sort of trance. He, like Drury, had settled himself into a half crouch. His eyes moved downward to Drury's finger on the trigger.

Drury forced his attention back to Jenny. As he did so, a tortured, outraged cry cut through the gentle lyric of the boys' choir. It filled Drury's consciousness and slowed his reactions for just an instant.

"No!" The word tore through Jason's throat.

At the same time, a shot exploded. A bullet ripped through the lid of the box that Jason held in his hand. Drury lurched sideways, then turned, looking terribly confused. "You can never predict," he murmured. His left hand moved to his right shoulder. He twisted his gun toward

Jason. But it was too late. Jason had let the box drop from his hand and, holding the weapon with both hands now, he fired at Drury again, this time hitting him in the chest.

Drury doubled over. The gun fired into the ground, then dropped from his hand. He lifted his head. His eyes widened. His face took on an expression of disbelief. He slumped to his knees.

Jason stepped closer and prepared to shoot again.

"No, Jason." Jenny's words stopped him. His heart pounded. His breathing came in short desperate gasps. He looked down at the dying man.

"Who is the...victor?" Drury labored over the whispered words. He looked up at Jason, forced a smile and, slowly, quietly bent over until his head rested on the ground. So this is what it's like, he thought. Death. And his body twisted sideways and slumped slowly into a torturous, unnatural posture. He did not move again.

The trees rustled in the gentle breeze that carried the echoes of shots from Jason's ears. In hushed tones, the choirboys sang a plainsong of chanted "amens." Jason sank to his knees, still training, as if paralyzed, that ancient weapon of death on the lifeless body across from him. Tears of steaming acid flowed from his eyes.

"Forgive me," he murmured. "God, forgive me." Jenny moved to his side and knelt with him. She held him tightly and rocked him.

"It's over," she whispered. "This time, it *is* over."

EPILOGUE

INDIAN SUMMER HAD COME in earnest these past few days. The bright, clear days allowed the last strong rays of the year's sun to warm the coastal lands. The fog had gone.

Jason awoke and reached down over the side of the bed to pat the animal that was no longer with him. He grimaced when he realized what he had done. He sighed, lifted the blankets and swung his legs over the edge of the bed. He dressed and as he did, he moved to the window to study the harbor.

It was mostly empty now. The workboats had already moved out to the sea to do their work and the pleasure craft had been mostly pulled out for winter storage. It was quiet. He leaned against the jamb of the window and rested his head against the cool glass. His warm breath fogged the glass immediately in front of his mouth. He inhaled deeply, held the air in his lungs, then slowly pushed the air out.

He became conscious of the tenseness that engulfed his body. His jaw ached because of his clenched teeth. His hands were doubled into fists. His legs were locked into position.

A hand gently moved over his shoulder.

"It's all right, Jason," Jenny said gently. She knew he was hurting. Since that awful moment of destruction, he had closed himself off even more than usual. Everything about these past days, he was pulling more and more tightly round him.

He breathed out again and watched the fog appear on the window once again.

"Jason," Jennifer said softly. He did not move. "I know it's eating away at you," she continued. "I know that."

He slowly shook his head.

"And I know that you don't think I understand." She paused. "Maybe I don't—maybe not completely, any way—but I'm trying, if you'll only let me." She looked at him a while longer. "I also know that you wouldn't have done it if I hadn't been there."

Now Jason's rhythmic breathing eased. He lifted his head and turned around.

"No, that's . . ."

"Jason," Jenny interrupted quietly, "you know it's true. If it had been only you and him, you wouldn't have ever thought about it. You would have carried through on the decision you made. But I messed that all up. I wasn't part of the plan. I wasn't part of the bargain you had made with your God."

Again Jason started to protest. Again Jennifer pressed.

"It's the truth, Jason. I know it is. And so do you." She paused now and opened herself to what might come next. "Do you hate me for it?"

What she said stunned him. He opened his mouth to start to protest, but he could say nothing. Jenny felt the silence cut into her. Tears formed in her eyes.

"Jason, you are like no one else I have ever known." She stood, silently watching the man across from her. She reached out and gently stroked his arms and shoulders. She felt the tautness of his body. All the while, she gazed into his eyes. She saw a heaviness there, a sadness, and yet she did not look away. "Sometimes I am in awe when I'm near you. But I also know that you're different—so differ-

nt—from me, that I can never measure up. You. Sitting on
the left hand of God. I just can't come close.''

He watched her as a hot tear streamed downward from
her eye. He knew how badly she was hurting. He knew it!
But he couldn't make it right. But you're supposed to!
You're supposed to make things right! The words screamed
silently in his head. It's your job. Bullshit. He couldn't help
anybody. Not now. Especially not Jenny. It required too
much of him. It was too risky. He knew what she was leading up to. He felt the panic beginning to build. His heart
beat ponderously, and he seemed starved for oxygen.

"I can't stay here, Jason. I can't stay with you. I can't,''
she whispered, in short, hot breaths. "I can't." She slowly
turned and walked toward the door.

"I'm not!" Jason cried. His words were filled with tor-
ment.

Jenny turned and looked at him. There was puzzlement
in her face.

"You're wrong, Jenny. I'm *not* that . . . that perfect thing
you just described." He stopped and dropped his head.
"I'm not," he whispered. A bitterness now seemed to fill
him. Jenny had not seen this before and she sensed something fierce was about to be unleashed. He seemed suddenly powerless, defeated. "I don't know about God. Oh,
God, I like to think I do. I know all the stories, the theol-
ogy, the arguments. I know all that. But Drury was right. I
am like his father. I'm not *certain* there's a God. I don't
know. I can't know.''

Jenny looked at him as he stood there lost in hopelessness. What she was hearing amazed her. That he could say
those things about himself.

"Don't you see?" he continued. "In that moment, I was
finally going to know. Finally. That was my hope.'' He
looked back up at her. His gaze cut through her. He stared

at her for a long time, then slowly bent his head downward and closed his eyes. "I don't know any more about God than anyone else...but I'm supposed to know. It's my job." The bitter words hung between them.

Jenny stepped back and wrapped her arms around him. He held her and gently lowered himself to his knees. He rested his head against her. "God help me, Jenny, I'm only... Only..."

Jenny felt his body suddenly stiffen violently. It was like a seizure. "Human," she whispered softly.

"I'm only human..." Jason repeated weakly. As she held him, she could feel the rigidness flowing away from him; his body softened and opened, as if he had suddenly been freed of some unseen burden. Slowly, she knelt in front of him. His embrace grew stronger. He held her tightly, painfully, and Jenny closed her eyes and wept joyfully. She held his head gently against her breast.

"I know. I know, Jason," she whispered softly. He looked up at her. "I couldn't live with a god. I can with a human."

They knelt together as if at an altar. They said nothing for a long time. Finally Jason spoke again.

"Why couldn't I ever admit that to anyone?" he asked quietly.

"I don't know," said Jenny.

"I didn't think anyone could understand."

Jenny smiled gently through her tears. She did understand. At least she thought she did. Jenny nodded in silence. She felt the sun's rays flowing through the window.

In the distance the surf pounded the shore and the bell buoy sounded with a reassuring rhythm and Jason continued to hold her. Now, here in this place, in this moment, all was right in God's creation.

SURVIVORS IN A WORLD GONE HIDEOUSLY WRONG

JAMES AXLER

DEATH LANDS

Homeward Bound

Adventure and suspense
in the midst of the new reality

This fifth novel in the Deathlands saga introduces vivid new dimensions to the aftermath of global nuclear destruction. Ryan Cawdor's intrepid odyssey across a devastated America is about to come full circle. He can now return home – to the place he was forced to leave by his power-mad brother.

But even the horrors he has faced on his journey have not prepared him for his next confrontation – war against the brutal survivors of his own family.

Widely available from Boots, Martins, John Menzies, W.H. Smith, Woolworths and other paperback stockists.

Pub. January 1989.

£2.50

GOLD EAGLE

"Extra special . . . an unexpected find."
—James A. Cox, *The Midwest Book Review*

A U.S. Army Special Forces team risks capture and
death when it parachutes into North Vietnam

VIETNAM: GROUND ZERO
GUIDELINES

GOLD EAGLE $2.75 62198 ADVENTURE

ERIC HELM

The very latest in this riveting
[seri]es.

[I]t is rumoured that the North
[Vie]tnamese are using a new
[So]viet missile guidance
[sys]tem.

[I]f true, then the air-war over
[Viet]nam would be adversely
[affe]cted. These rumours
[mu]st be checked out.
[C]aptain Gerber and his
[Sp]ecial Forces squad are
[ord]ered to investigate. But

stealth requires a night-time jump
at 33,000 feet from a B-52, using
oxygen, in subzero temperatures.
The mission, suicidal as it
is, initially must come
second to just surviving the
jump!
*Widely available from
Boots, Martins, John
Menzies, W. H. Smith,
Woolworths and other
paperback stockists. Pub.
December 1988.* **£1.95**

GOLD
EAGLE

A High-Stakes Kremlin Conspiracy

A High-Stakes American Nightmare

The bestselling author of AIR GLOW RED

IAN SLATER

STORM

A HIGH-STAKES KREMLIN CONSPIRACY.
A HIGH-STAKES AMERICAN NIGHTMARE.

In the eye of a raging storm, a distress call 80 miles off the coast of Oregon leads American oceanographer Frank Hall to a desolate island.

In the nightmare that follows he uncovers a terrifying Soviet plot to bring the U.S. to its knees – and the realisation that the fate of 2 na ions lies in his hands, in this hig voltage novel of espionage an action. *Widely available fro Boots, Martins, John Menzie W.H. Smith, Woolworths a other paperback stockis Pub. January 198*

£2.

GOLD EAGLE